Hoodwinked
Ashlynn Carter

Copyright © 2024 by Ashlynn Carter

All rights reserved.

No part of this publication may be reproduced, distributed, or transmitted in any form or by any means, including photocopying, recording, or other electronic or mechanical methods, without the prior written permission of the publisher, except as permitted by U.S. copyright law. For permission requests, contact Ashlynn Carter at carter.ashlynn@proton.me.

The story, all names, characters, and incidents portrayed in this production are fictitious. No identification with actual persons (living or deceased), places, buildings, and products is intended or should be inferred.

Book Cover by Ashlynn Carter

First edition 2024

Chapter 1

Everyone has a moment in their lives when they realize they have made the biggest mistake they possibly could have. Millie Larson thought she had that moment eight weeks ago when she woke up in an empty hotel room with no husband. That moment was nothing compared to what she felt now.

She finally went to see her doctor because she had a flu bug that she could not seem to shake. She asked Dr. Spaulding to test for everything. She had midterms next week and needed to be feeling better before then. Millie never expected the doctor to test for this. It had never crossed her mind.

Millie exited the doctor's office with more than one booklet about her many different options and information on what to expect from her body at this point. She was in shock and not sure what she wanted to do. Dr. Spaulding told her to go home and think over everything before making a final decision.

She knew she really only had two choices: keep the baby or give it up for adoption. Her first reaction was adoption. She wanted nothing to do with Lawrence Hansen.

He asked her to marry him after dating for nine months, convinced her to elope, then left before she woke up the next morning. On the nightstand where her diamond ring had been the night before, was a note and their unsigned marriage license.

Millie tried calling Lawrence, but the line had been disconnected, as were all of his social media accounts. It was like he never existed. Millie had been so naive and stupid.

Millie walked slowly through the parking lot to her car. She was just about to get in when she noticed her tire was flat. She threw her bag in the backseat before going to the trunk to get the spare, only to find it was flat too. Her emotions were already close to the surface and tears of frustration spilled onto her cheeks.

Millie slammed the trunk closed before walking back around the car and glaring at the useless tire. "Give me a break!" She yelled before she kicked the flat. She cursed as pain shot through her foot. She lowered herself to the ground, leaning back against her car.

She pulled her knees to her chest as she ran her hand into her long thick hair. Millie fisted her hand at the back of her head as she curled into a ball and started to cry. She had thought she cried all of her tears in the exam room after Dr. Spaulding told her she ran a pregnancy test, and it came back positive. Apparently not.

Her tears were finally starting to slow when she heard loose rocks grinding into the pavement. "Excuse me ma'am, are you okay?" A male voice asked softly.

Millie looked over to see a man crouching down to her level a few feet away. The man watched her closely. She stared at him without speaking. Was she okay? No, she was most definitely not okay.

"Are you alright?" He asked again. Millie felt completely numb and she couldn't seem to get her mouth to form words. "Is this your car? Can we help you change the tire?"

"It's flat." Millie's voice was so soft she wasn't sure if the man heard her.

The corner of his lips twitched a little. "That's why we want to help change it."

Millie shook her head as she leaned her head back against the car. "The spare is flat." she whispered.

"Is the tire behind you flat too?" The man asked.

A second man stepped around the back of her car. "Even if she had a working spare, if that one is flat, she has two flat tires." He said coming to a stop next to his friend.

Millie squeezed her eyes shut as more warm tears slipped from them. Why couldn't something work out today? Her world was already crumbling around her, now she was stranded.

"How long have you been out here, ma'am? Do you have someone you can call for a ride?" The first guy asked. Millie shook her head.

"No, you don't know how long you have been out here? Or no, you don't have anyone to call?" The second man asked.

"I don't have anyone to call." Millie said quietly. "Does it matter how long I have been here?"

"I guess not." The second man said with a shrug.

"Can we take you home?" The first man asked as he stood. Millie furrowed her brows. Did he mean to take her home to their house? No thank you. "That came out creepy. Can we offer you a ride back to your house?"

Millie closed her eyes again. She was so tired. She couldn't bring herself to care about her stupid car anymore. She was emotionally drained, and she was starting to feel nauseous again.

"Ma'am?" The first man asked, sounding concerned.

Millie opened her eyes again and looked at the two men. "Sure." Her voice was still quiet. She couldn't seem to muster any sort of volume.

The first man assisted her to her feet. "Is there anything you need from your car?"

"My backpack." Millie looked at the backseat.

She watched as the second guy pulled her backpack out. "Did you want us to lock it up?" Millie nodded and he did.

The first man walked to the other side of her vehicle and opened the front passenger door of the car parked next to hers. Millie felt like a robot as she slowly followed him and sat down. When she didn't reach for her seat belt, the man buckled her in. She didn't miss the concerned looks the two men shared, but she couldn't bring herself to care.

"Ma'am, were you in an accident? Did you fall or hit your head on anything?" The first man asked.

Millie shook her head again and closed her eyes. She just wanted to get home. "Applegate Apartments across the street from the university. Building C. Unit 312." Millie whispered as another tear leaked onto her cheek. How did she still have tears? She had been crying for what felt like hours.

There was a moment of silence before the car door closed, then two more doors closed before the car started. Millie kept her eyes shut as she tried to block all thoughts of her appointment. She felt nothing but couldn't stop crying at the same time.

"Ma'am, we are at your apartment." A male voice said softly as someone shook her shoulder gently.

Millie opened her eyes and looked around. They were parked in her designated parking spot. She turned her head slowly to look at the man crouched next to the car. She made no move to get up. Millie felt like she was watching herself from outside of her body. The man released the seat belt, and she didn't even flinch as he leaned over her to reach the button. Millie usually liked her space especially when it came to strangers but she was far too exhausted to care.

He stood and offered her his hand. All she could do was stare at it. He firmly, but gently grabbed her hand from her lap and pulled her from the car. The second man was standing a few feet away with her backpack.

The first man didn't release her hand as he led her towards the stairs that led up to her unit. He walked slowly and she numbly followed him. Once they got to the landing, he pulled her close to him to allow the second guy to get to the door. They must have seen her keys clipped to her bag.

The door to the other unit on the landing opened and Millie closed her eyes, praying that her neighbors wouldn't try to pull her into a conversation. She leaned her head forward, resting it against the wall. The wall was warmer and softer than she thought a brick wall would be.

"Oh, good. I'm glad we caught you." Cindy said triumphantly. Millie inwardly groaned. Her luck was holding.

Millie opened her eyes. She blinked in surprise when she realized she was leaning against the man holding her hand. Millie turned slowly to face her neighbor as she tried to force a smile.

"Hey." Her voice came out barely more than a whisper.

"The girls and I were talking about possibly going to Mexico this summer, but we wanted to make sure we were here for your wedding. Have you set a date yet?" Cindy bounced with excitement.

Millie's stomach clenched and her heart felt like someone had stabbed it. "Oh, um. Don't worry about trying to cater to me. I promise your travel plans won't conflict with mine."

"You two have been engaged for almost six months, you kept telling us that you were waiting for the summer. Have you changed your mind about a summer wedding?"

"I...Uh..." Millie couldn't do this right now. Emotionally she was a mess, and she couldn't seem to think straight. "It won't be an issue."

"Why not?" Cindy pressed as she put her hand on her hip. Millie eyed the platinum blonde barbie in front of her. Cindy would never stop asking. Better to rip the band aid off.

"Because he left two months ago." Millie sighed. The man next to her squeeze her hand.

"When will he be back? I'm sure you can still have your wedding this summer?"

"Not with him." Millie said firmly. She heard her keys jingle as her apartment door swung open. "It was good talking with you. I need to study."

Millie moved as quickly as she could into her apartment. As soon as the two good Samaritans were inside, she slammed her door. She didn't look at them as she took a seat on her couch and buried her face in her hands.

Yes, it still hurt to think about Lawrence. She had given him over a year of her life, and she had loved him. She gave him a piece of herself that she could never get back. Millie had thought they were married. They got the license and had a ceremony. But Lawrence never signed it. She had even gone to a lawyer a few days afterwards to look into the legality of the marriage.

He played her and left when he got what he wanted. Now she was carrying his child, even though they used protection. And she was terrified.

"Ma'am, can we go into your kitchen to get a drink." The first man asked.

"There is water in the fridge. Help yourself." To her amazement, more tears welled up in her eyes and quickly spilled onto her cheeks.

"Here." A cold bottle of water was pressed into her hands. The cap had been removed. The first guy sat beside her on the couch. Millie stared at the bottle, unable to do anything. "It would help you better if you drank it instead of watching it." The man commented after several minutes.

Millie slowly raised the bottle to her lips. The icy water pulled her a little from her numbed state. "Thank you." She whispered after taking a small sip. "For the water and the ride." She finally looked at the man's face.

He was handsome with eyes that were the color of milk chocolate. His dark brown hair was just long enough for the front to get in his eyes, and it curled slightly over his ears. It looked like he ran his hand through it often to keep it out of his face, giving him an almost boyish appearance, which was in contrast with the rest of him. He had a strong jaw and a little scruff. His shoulders were broad, and by the way his shirt hung on him, he worked out. He was definitely not a boy, but a man.

He was watching her closely with concern pulling at his features. "Is there anyone we can call for you?" he asked softly.

Millie shook her head before taking another small sip. Exhaustion was settling in, and she handed the bottle back to the man. She lay down on the couch and closed her eyes again. Her head was beginning to pound, thanks to the hours of crying she had done. Now she was starting to pay the price for it. A blanket was draped over her, but she didn't open her eyes.

*   *   *

Millie woke with a pounding headache. The moment she sat up, she regretted it. A wave of nausea hit so fast and so hard that she barely made it to the bathroom before throwing up. It had been like this for nearly two weeks. She was tired of feeling sick all the time.

She jumped in the shower, hoping it would help her feel more human. She put on her robe and was towel drying her hair when she heard a knock on her door. The only person it could be was Cindy. The girl was nosey and was no doubt coming to demand details about Lawrence.

Millie walked to the door and pulled it open, determined to tell Cindy to mind her own business. She froze when she saw the two guys from yesterday standing there. Their eyes widened when they saw her in her robe. Millie tightened it around her as her cheeks felt like they caught fire.

She was glad her robe reached her knees and was thick. "Uh." Millie tried to find her voice, but another wave of nausea had her throwing her hand over her mouth and running for the kitchen sink.

She rinsed her mouth and splashed water on her face after several minutes. When she turned around, her door was still open, and the guys were still standing at the threshold. Embarrassment filled her.

"Why don't you come in and have a seat? I am going to get dressed. It shouldn't take me long." Millie called over her shoulder as she hurried down the hall.

Millie dressed in a pair of jeans and a T-shirt as quickly as possible. Before leaving her room, she glanced in the mirror. Her face was pale, her eyes were dull and slightly red rimmed from all the crying she had done yesterday, and she had lost weight.

Sighing, Millie made her way back to her living room. Her two rescuers were sitting on the couch looking awkward. Millie sat in the rocking chair by the window.

"I can't thank you both enough for helping me yesterday. I don't know what I would have done if you hadn't shown up." Millie said quickly, looking down at her hands.

"Glad we could help." the first guy said with a small smile.

"Glad you got your tongue back." The second guy commented with a light laugh. He looked very similar to the first guy. He had brown eyes, and brown hair. It was a little darker and shorter than the other guy's hair. He was muscular too. If she had to guess, she would think they were brothers.

Millie couldn't help smiling either. "Yeah, I wasn't quite myself yesterday." She normally didn't allow guys into her apartment, but she felt completely safe and comfortable with these two. The shorter haired one seemed to be more of a jokester, while the other one was more chill.

"And today?" The second guy asked as his eyes flicked to the kitchen.

Millie's smile faded as she shrugged. "I'm better than yesterday."

Both men looked at each other briefly before turning back to her. "If you don't mind us asking, what happened yesterday?" The first man asked.

Millie stood and walked into the adjoining kitchen. She pulled bread out of the pantry and popped two slices into the toaster. She moved to the fridge and grabbed the butter. Mustering courage, she turned around and leaned against the counter. She didn't have to tell them everything, but they deserved to know a little of what was going on after helping her.

"I got life changing news yesterday." Millie said quietly as she stared at the floor. "I think I went into shock or something. I couldn't seem to function."

"Is there anything we can do to help?" The first guy asked.

Millie laughed as she turned around to butter her toast that just popped up. "Do you have a time machine?"

"She's got jokes now too." The second man chuckled.

Millie returned to the rocking chair and slowly nibbled on her toast, not wanting to push her stomach too far by eating fast and throwing up again. "So, no TARDIS or DeLorean?"

"No, sorry. But we do have a working car you can borrow until yours gets fixed." the second guy said.

Millie stared at them with wide eyes. "You don't even know me." She breathed out. "Why would you loan me a car?" She was planning on calling and getting a rental until she could get hers fixed.

"We have more than enough vehicles at our disposal. We only drive this one when we drive home once a month." The second guy said as he shrugged.

"Look, I know we don't know each other but Josh is right, we rarely use this truck. We carpool most of the time to save on gas." The first man said, leaning forward, his brown eyes locking with hers. "If you want, we can take the keys to your car and get the tires fixed this next week for you."

"And in the meantime, you can drive Aiden's truck. If we don't return your car, you can keep it. You would be coming out on top, trust me." Josh smiled.

Millie shook her head in disbelief. These guys were the kindest men she had ever met. They had already helped her get home and now they were here checking up on her. They were even offering her a car until she got hers fixed. Lawrence would have never been so generous.

The two men watched her expectantly, but the urge to throw up came over her again. She tried to will her stomach to settle but it was no use. Millie got to her feet and ran down the hall, slamming the bathroom door behind her. She lost every last bit of the meager amount of toast she had eaten. No wonder she was losing weight, she couldn't even hold down toast.

She brushed her teeth and splashed cool water on her face. Resting both hands on the counter, she stared at herself in the mirror. How was she going to get through this? Millie hung her head and prayed for help. She couldn't do this alone. And she had no idea what to do.

A soft knock on the bathroom door reminded Millie she wasn't alone in her apartment. She dried her face before opening the door. Aiden stood awkwardly with his hands in the front pockets of his jeans.

"Were you the one that drew the short straw?" Millie asked as she stepped out into the hall.

"Is she okay?" Josh called from the front room.

"I'm fine." Millie said as she walked to the front door and pulled on her shoes. She didn't want them asking about her throwing up, so she asked the first thing she could think of. "Why don't you two show me this loaner car?"

Millie led the way down to the parking lot. She was surprised when they stopped at the vehicle parked in her designated spot. Her breath caught in her lungs as she stared at the truck. It was a Ford F-150 that was such a dark green color that it looked almost black. You could see the green when the sunlight hit just right. It was her dream car.

"Millie! Are you going to explain what happened?" Cindy's irritated voice broke into Millie's moment of awe.

"I'm a little busy right now." Millie didn't even look at her neighbor as she stepped up to the truck. She ran her hand along the smooth metal as she walked along the side of it, admiring every inch.

"This is serious!" Cindy practically yelled.

Millie glanced over at Cindy. "Cindy, I am in the middle of something." she said as she opened the driver's door to get a look at the interior.

"You really need to get over your fear of commitment, Millie." Cindy put her hands on her hips. "You are showing more interest in this truck than you are in finding a husband. You should be focusing on Lawrence. A truck isn't going to keep you warm at night like a man can."

"You obviously haven't looked inside this thing. The seats are heated and large enough that I could sleep comfortably in them." Millie argued.

Cindy growled as she spun on her four-inch heel and stormed up to her apartment. Millie shrugged and closed the door before making her way to the truck bed. She noted it had a trailer hitch.

"This is the loaner car?" Millie asked as she made her way back around to the front of the truck. This is better than any rental she would have gotten.

"I can't help but get the feeling you like my truck." Aiden chuckled.

Millie could not pull her eyes from it. She had always wanted one just like this but couldn't bring herself to purchase one yet. She had no need for it at the moment. She could not believe these two strangers were loaning her this truck. "I'm in love." Millie whispered.

"You just pointed out that we just met and now you are saying you are in love with Aiden?" Josh laughed.

Millie smiled as she turned to them. "Oh heavens no. No offense." She said quickly and Aiden shrugged. "Your truck." Millie turned her attention back to the vehicle. "I hope you do steal my car so I can keep this."

Aiden and Josh laughed. Millie glanced over at them as she smiled. She noticed that Aiden had dimples and she thought again about how cute he was. She gave herself a mental shake. She was not remotely ready to let a man back into her life. Millie's phone rang and she pulled it from her pocket. It was the doctor's office. Millie walked a few feet away before answering.

"Hello." Millie said quietly.

"Hello, is this Millie Larson?" Dr. Spaulding asked.

"It is." Millie's stomach knotted with anxiety.

"This is Dr. Spaulding. I just wanted to check on you." Dr. Spaulding said kindly. "I know yesterday was quite a bit of a shock. How are you doing?"

"It was. I still don't really know…" Millie's voice thickened with emotion.

"I know this was completely out of left field. And I know you are trying to come to terms with the results. How are you feeling physically? Have you thrown up much? That was your original reason for coming in, wasn't it?" Dr. Spaulding asked.

Millie glanced over at Aiden and Josh to make sure they couldn't hear her. She ran her hand through her hair as she stepped off the curb and walked around the truck again. "I can't seem to hold anything down. I've thrown up three times this morning."

"I know that this isn't what you want to hear but morning sickness is common at this stage of pregnancy. However, you have lost some weight from your last appointment a few months ago, so I am sending in a prescription to the pharmacy for an anti-nausea medication. Hang in there, morning sickness should start lightening up around twelve weeks, and remember to keep hydrated."

"Thank you." Millie said as she climbed into the bed of the truck and sat down with her back against the cab. "Do you have any idea when the medicine will be ready?"

"You should be able to pick it up later today. Don't be afraid to call my office or my personal line if you have any concerns. I put my cell phone number in the packet we gave you."

"Okay. Thank you." Millie said quietly before hanging up.

She closed her eyes and knocked her head gently against the cab a few times. Several more weeks of throwing up constantly. At least her doctor was prescribing something to help. Millie took several slow breaths to try to calm herself. The reality of being pregnant was becoming more and more real.

"You still with us?" Josh asked.

Millie opened her eyes to see Aiden and Josh looking at her with their forearms resting on the side of the bed. Both men looked concerned. She shrugged as she tried to smile. Josh's teasing eased some of her tension, and Millie had the desire to tell them everything, but stopped herself. She didn't know these guys. The only people she had talked to about Lawrence's betrayal were her lawyer, bishop, and Dr. Spaulding.

"Not quite the radiant smile that you had when you saw my truck, but I guess we can take it." Aiden smiled at her, but it looked a little forced.

Millie still laughed as she glanced around her. She really did like the truck. Her notification ringtone went off. She looked down at her phone. The pharmacy had received her prescription, and it would be ready by two that afternoon.

Millie needed to get away from everything for a few days. She needed to eliminate all distractions and come to terms with her new reality. To think through her options and start making decisions. She couldn't live in limbo. She needed a plan.

"So, let me get this straight. You are loaning me this truck to get around for a few days? I can use it to go wherever I need to go?" Millie asked, watching the two men carefully. If they didn't want her driving the truck a lot, she would get a rental.

"Yes," Aiden said slowly as his eyes narrowed slightly. "I have two conditions though."

"Which are?" Millie narrowed her eyes at him too. Maybe she was wrong about these guys. Maybe they weren't as generous as she had first thought.

"The truck comes back in one piece, and I need your number."

"Why would you need my number?"

"That way if I have any questions or updates on your car, I can call you." Aiden answered.

Millie bit her lip as she eyed them. Aiden's request was reasonable. They seemed like decent guys so far. Not once did they take advantage of the situation, and they were going above and beyond in helping her. They knew where she lived, so what harm would giving them her number do?

"Okay. I can agree to those conditions." Millie stuck her hand out for Aiden to shake. After a brief hesitation on his part, they shook hands. "But I do have to warn you," Millie said as she climbed over the tailgate. "I may be out of cell service until Sunday night."

"Why's that?" Josh asked.

"I have some things I have to do." Millie shrugged. "And cell service isn't the best."

"Just be careful." Aiden said as he handed her a piece of paper and set of keys. There were two phone numbers written on it: one for Aiden, the other for Josh. "If you need anything just give us a call."

Millie programmed her number into Aiden's phone. They didn't stay long, since they needed to head to work. Millie immediately went about packing and gathering supplies. It was Thursday afternoon, and she didn't have classes until Monday.

Going on a camping trip for the weekend would give her time to figure things out and to study. Millie packed the truck with tons of blankets and a small bag of clothes before heading to the store. She bought a cooler, tons of food and water, picked up her prescription, and firewood before heading out of town.

Millie drove for hours before finding a campground that was mostly empty. She picked a campsite that was away from everyone. She set up her hammock, camp chair, and pulled out some snacks before grabbing her backpack and settling into the hammock.

She pulled out the packet Dr. Spaulding had given her and laid it in her lap. Millie closed her eyes and offered up a prayer asking for a clear head and understanding of His plan. After closing her prayer, Millie began going through the information.

Chapter 2

Millie lay in her hammock with her book on pregnancy and watched the young family that set up camp a few spots away from her. They had a toddler and a tiny baby. The mother looked tired but happy. The father spent a lot of time with the little boy, playing and having his son help him with various things. The laughter that floated on the wind to her was infectious. Millie found herself smiling and laughing softly as she watched them.

She had wanted that. A family. She was raised by her grandmother who passed away when Millie was nineteen. During her time of grief, two young men had found her and told her about a church that believed in eternal families. Millie had instantly gravitated to the Church.

She had met Lawrence not long before she started to take the discussions. She had been eager to learn everything about the Church, but Lawrence hadn't understood why she wanted to be part of a religion with so many rules. She was baptized, even though Lawrence tried to convince her not to. He backed off from belittling the Church as they continued to date. At times he was irritated with her resistance to become physical, but he never forced things.

Over the next several months, Millie could see herself with Lawrence, building a life together and raising a family. He doted on her, spent all his free time with her, and he made her promises.

After they were engaged, Lawrence kept pushing to move in together, but Millie refused. She told him she wanted an eternal family, and she would not do anything that would jeopardize that. Three months into their engagement, Lawrence suggested eloping.

At first, Millie resisted the idea. But when she thought about it, he was right, she didn't have anyone she truly wanted at the wedding. He said they could hold a party or something with their friends when they got back. Lawrence planned the whole thing and they left for the weekend.

Millie sighed. The ceremony had been beautiful. A few of Lawrence's friends were there as witnesses. He had her sign the marriage license first. Then they went to the hotel. She had been both nervous and excited.

Millie felt hot tears rolling down her cheeks. She banished thoughts of Lawrence as she wiped the tears away. He was no longer a part of her life and would never be. She was fine with that.

After returning home from her false marriage, Millie spoke with her bishop. She had told him everything. He reassured her that she didn't knowingly sin and that she had been manipulated and lied to. Heavenly Father knew of her situation and loved her. They prayed together and Millie felt peace and her Savior's love.

Millie shook her head. It was Saturday evening, and she was unsure of what to do. She had gone through the information from her doctor at least three times. Whenever she read through the info on adoption, she would become anxious. And when she thought of keeping the baby, she became overwhelmed. She would be a single mom and she didn't think she could handle that.

Millie desperately wished she had a friend she could call and confide in. She felt so alone right now. She pulled out her cell phone and looked through her contacts. The problem with being shy was that it was hard to make friends. She talked to people at church and at school, but she hadn't developed a friendship with anyone.

Lawrence was who she had spent all her time with. Millie squeezed her eyes closed as she gripped the book hard. Why did she end up pregnant when she was on birth control? How could he leave her? Millie stifled the urge to scream in frustration. She was so angry with him. She took a deep breath and let it out slowly. The poor family would probably be traumatized by her outburst.

Millie came across Josh's number and paused. She started a group text with Aiden and Josh. She hoped they would answer because she really needed a distraction, and they had a knack for making her smile.

Millie: Hey!
Aiden: Hey, Millie. What's up?
Millie: Nothing much
Josh: Why am I not buying that?

Millie smiled as she laid back. The baby at the other campsite began to cry and Millie glanced over at the family. The mother was walking and bouncing the infant and in seconds the crying stopped.

Millie: It's true. There is not much going on around here.

Josh: So, you are bored and decided what better way to kill time, then to chat with the two of us?

Millie: I needed someone to talk to and I don't really have anyone.

Aiden: We're listening.

Millie took a deep breath. This was so hard. She didn't know where to start or what to say. She didn't know either of these guys. Millie stared at the sky, trying to gather her thoughts.

Josh: You can't drop a bomb like that and leave us hanging!!

Millie wiped tears off her cheeks. She put her phone away and closed her eyes. Why did she even say anything? She pulled the hood of her hoodie more over her head and snuggled deeper into the hammock.

"Are you just going to ignore us or are you going to at least say hi?" A woman yelled at Millie causing her to jump and fall from the hammock. "Oh my gosh! I'm so sorry. I thought you were someone else." The woman hurried over.

Millie looked up at the woman and noticed she was the young mother from the other campsite. Millie glanced around. The adoption booklets and her pregnancy book were on the ground. The woman started picking them up with one hand while she held her baby in the other. Millie hurried to help her.

The woman paused and looked at the booklet in her hand, then to the pregnancy book in Millie's. She looked at Millie with a kind smile. "I really am sorry. You aren't hurt, are you?"

"I'm okay." Millie bent down and grabbed her phone.

There was a text message waiting for her, but she swiped it away. Her lock screen was a picture of her standing with the elders in front of the church building the day of her baptism. Millie felt a wave of peace as she looked at the picture.

"Are you a member of the Church of Jesus Christ of Latter-Day Saints?" The woman asked as she handed Millie the booklets.

"I am." Millie smiled.

"We are too." The woman's smile grew. "My name is Elizabeth Benedict. But everyone calls me Beth."

"Millie Larson. Nice to meet you." Millie stuck the booklets into her pregnancy book.

"I don't mean to be overbearing or nosey, but I couldn't help noticing you are here alone." Beth said, glancing around Millie's camp.

Millie glanced around as well. "I needed to get away from life for a few days. Nature helps me think." Millie shrugged.

"Us too. I needed to get away from everything. My in-laws are the best but since Melody was born, I feel like they are always around trying to help." Beth laughed as she bounced the infant in her arms. "Do you mind if I sit and chat for a while? It's been so long since I talked with someone my age, who isn't my husband, or with someone who wasn't trying to draw on the walls."

Millie laughed. "Sure. I'd like that."

Beth sat in Millie's camping chair with a sigh. "So, tell me about yourself, Millie. Are you from this area or visiting?"

"I'm a student at the University." Millie said as she sat on a log near the fire pit. She was surprised that Beth hadn't asked about the pregnancy stuff. "My life was pretty calm growing up. I lived with my grandma, was homeschooled, graduated high school, met some missionaries, took the discussions, and was baptized eighteen months ago." Millie set the book down on the ground at her feet and looked at Beth. "What about you?"

"I was born and raised in the Church. I fell for my twin brother's best friend, and we were high school sweethearts. Derek and I have been married for six years. We have one son, Bentley, who is five. This is Melody, she is 3 weeks old." Beth placed a kiss on the baby's face.

"Babe, where are the band aids?" Derek yelled from their campsite. "Bentley fell again, and I can't find them!" Beth rolled her eyes and Millie laughed.

"Could you hold Melody for me? It will be faster if I go grab them myself." Beth stood and offered the baby to Millie.

Millie nodded and little Melody was placed in her arms. She watched Beth walk away before she turned her attention back to the baby, and her eyes began to burn. Was she ready for a baby? Whether she was or not, Millie was having one. She gently touched the little girl's chubby cheeks and her heart ached.

"Are you okay?" Beth asked softly as she slowly sat down next to Millie. "Derek, come get Mel and put her in her bassinet please." Beth called.

Millie tried her best to rein in her emotions while Beth lifted the baby from her arms and handed Melody over to Derek, before returning to Millie's side. The tears wouldn't stop. The feeling of having the baby taken from her, even if the child wasn't hers, felt wrong and that terrified her.

Beth remained silent but wrapped an arm around Millie's shoulders, causing Millie's tears to come faster. Beth pulled Millie into a tight embrace and held her as she cried. When Millie's tears dried, she sat up slowly.

"I'm sorry. I am a mess right now and probably the worst person to have a conversation with." Millie wiped her cheeks, keeping her gaze on the ground.

"I think you are the best person to have a conversation with right now. Even if that means you talking and me listening." Beth said softly. "Does this have to do with that book and pamphlets?"

Millie glanced at the pregnancy book and nodded her head as she let out a slow breath. She didn't know this woman, but Millie needed to talk to someone and there was something about Beth that made Millie want to confide in her.

"I met Lawrence not long before I was baptized. We dated for nine months. He was everything I wanted in a spouse. We supported each other, made sure we went on weekly dates, even if life got busy. I thought we were in love. So, when he proposed, I didn't hesitate to say yes." Millie sniffled. "We had been engaged for three months when he suggested eloping."

"Elope? Why?" Beth asked in surprise.

Millie shrugged. "At first, I thought he was joking around, but he wasn't. After we discussed it, I didn't see a reason not to. I have no family or close friends I felt I had to have at the wedding, and neither did he. He decided that we would have a party to celebrate when we got back. Lawrence planned everything for the next weekend."

"What happened?" Beth whispered.

"The ceremony was simple but beautiful. Lawrence even insisted on me wearing my wedding dress. I signed the license first and then was pulled into a conversation with one of Lawrence's friends who was one of the witnesses. Not long after the ceremony, we went to our hotel room. I'm sure you know what happened that night." Millie's face burned with embarrassment.

"So, you and Lawrence are married. Where is he now?" Beth asked, confused. "Is he working?"

Millie shook her head. "When I woke up, I was alone. On the nightstand where I had put my ring the night before was a note that thanked me for the fun night and the ring was gone."

"What?" Beth gasped.

"It gets better." Millie glanced at Beth. "Under the note was our marriage license. Mine and the officiator's signatures were the only ones on it. I tried calling him, but his phone was disconnected, as were his social media accounts. I talked with a lawyer. The man who married us was not even licensed to do so. The marriage is invalid because of that, and not all the signatures were on the license."

"No." Beth breathed out. "So, what did you do?"

"I talked with my bishop and tried to move on with my life. But it's hard. I gave Lawrence over a year of my life. I had trusted him, and he betrayed me." Millie wiped her cheeks angrily.

Beth was quiet for several minutes before she spoke again. "Millie, is he…?" her voice trailed off and Millie nodded.

"I found out a few days ago. I'm eight weeks." Millie said softly. It was still hard to admit that she was pregnant. Beth hugged Millie again. Millie closed her eyes and leaned against Beth. "I was just making progress in moving on from Lawrence's betrayal, and now this. I'm so scared and I don't know what to do."

"I can't even imagine." Beth said softly. "I'm sure it's hard to think about having that link to such a jerk."

Millie nodded. "Whenever I go over the adoption stuff, I feel like I would be abandoning the baby. I always wanted a family, but that's not what I could give this child. I'm just a single college student that was taken for a fool. I don't know if I could give the baby what it deserves." Millie fought the tears that wanted to fall.

"I know I said I would just listen, but can I offer some advice?" Beth asked. Millie sat up, looked at her and nodded. "You seem to be an incredibly strong woman. Families come in all sorts of shapes and sizes. You are young and beautiful. I have no doubt that you will eventually find someone who will accept you and your child. I know this is overwhelming. Honestly, I would probably be hiding in my house crying buckets of tears if it were me, but you and this baby could be a family."

"You think I should keep the baby." Millie stated.

"I think you should pray about it and allow Heavenly Father to help you make this decision." Beth corrected. "But if you do choose to keep the baby, you won't be alone. Derek and I live thirty minutes from the University, and I would be more than willing to help out anyway I can."

Millie stared at the woman. "We just met." She said, confused as to why Beth would be willing to help someone she didn't know.

"Every great friendship had to start somewhere." Beth smiled. "Now, how are you feeling? Any morning sickness?"

Millie sighed. "My doctor gave me an anti-nausea medication to help. I'm so tired, I have to pee all the time, and I can hardly hold anything down."

"Lemonhead candy helped me with my nausea. Having crackers or something to munch on before getting up in the morning helped me as well. As for having to pee and being tired, I don't have any good tips." Beth smiled at her.

"Thank you. I will have to get some Lemonheads when I get back." Millie smiled as well. She was feeling so much better after talking with Beth.

"When do you head back?" Beth asked.

"My ward starts at nine. I should head back early tomorrow morning if I want to make it to church on time." Millie sighed. She didn't know if she wanted to go back to the single's ward. She was trying to avoid her nosey neighbor, and for some reason, attending that ward while pregnant seemed weird.

"You could head back with us and go to our ward if you want." Beth offered. "It starts at two, so we will be leaving here at nine."

Millie thought about it for a moment. Just the fact that Cindy wouldn't be there was enough to have Millie accepting her new friend's offer. Maybe if she liked it enough, she would see if she could move her records into that ward instead.

Chapter 3

Millie stood in Beth's bedroom shaking her head. "I can just go in jeans and a T-shirt."

"There is no reason you can't borrow a dress. Then you can come home with us and have dinner before going back to your place." Beth handed Millie a navy-blue maxi dress.

Millie sighed and headed for the bathroom. In just the twelve hours she had known Beth Benedict, Millie already knew it was pointless to argue with her, especially when it came to things that really didn't matter. Derek had whispered that advice to her when Millie tried to spend the rest of the day at her own campsite instead of joining the Benedicts. She threw the dress on and walked out of the bathroom.

"You look beautiful, Millie. Are you ready? Derek said he has the kids already in the car." Beth asked as she put on a necklace.

"I'm ready." Millie said, and they headed outside. "I'll follow you."

The ward was friendly, and Millie found that she liked not feeling so alone. Beth introduced her around and Millie enjoyed sitting with the Benedicts. Beth had to feed Melody during class, so Millie sat with Derek. She thought it would be weird sitting with him, but it wasn't. No one thought twice about them sitting together. At her ward, rumors would have started spreading like wildfire.

"Hey, Mils, I don't know if Beth told you, but we have a couple of friends coming over for dinner tonight. It's kind of a tradition. The second Sunday of every month they come over for dinner and games." Derek smiled at her as they walked down the hall to get Bentley from Primary after church ended. He had taken to calling her Mils from the beginning. Millie had been surprised that her instant friendship with Beth had extended to Derek as well.

"She didn't mention them." Millie said as she bit her lip. She wasn't sure if she was up to a party. Parties were draining for her, and she was already emotionally wrung out.

"Don't let her pressure you into staying." Derek glanced at her. "We can park your truck down the street and if you want to leave at any point, you won't be blocked in."

Millie nodded. "Thank you. I think that would be best."

After Millie changed out of Beth's dress, she parked the truck around the corner before the Benedict's guests showed up. It was a beast and took up a lot of space. By the time she returned to Beth's house, there were two extra cars parked in the driveway. Millie hesitated on the sidewalk.

She glanced back the way she had come before shaking her head. She promised Beth she would stay for dinner, so she would. Derek seemed like a decent guy, and she couldn't see him hanging around with jerks. Not that Beth would put up with that kind of behavior anyway. Taking a deep breath, Millie forced herself to keep walking.

Millie slipped in silently, trying to go unnoticed as much as possible. Gatherings were not her thing. Being around people was hard for her. Growing up, she did online high school and her only companion was her grandmother, who spent all day watching game shows. Millie never learned how to be around large groups of people.

"Mil!" Bentley squealed as he ran for her. So much for going unnoticed. "Pick me up." the little boy demanded.

Bentley had become her best friend while they were camping and during church. Millie laughed and picked him up. At five years old, Bentley shouldn't need to be carried and Beth often told the boy that he had two good legs. Millie didn't mind though; she loved kids and was enjoying spending time with Bentley. She stepped into the living room that was off the entryway. No one was there, so she continued to the kitchen. Beth looked up from making a salad and smiled.

"Everyone is out back setting up horseshoes if you want to join them." Beth said as she waved her hand towards the sliding door off the dining room.

"Oh, um…" Millie moved Bentley to her other hip. "I thought maybe I could help you prepare dinner or if Bentley wants, I can read him a story."

"Story!" Bentley screamed and wiggled to get down.

Millie laughed and shrugged when Beth gave her a questioning look. Millie followed Bentley upstairs to his room. She settled into the rocking chair and Bentley brought her a book before climbing up on her lap. Millie began reading using different voices for each of the characters and adding sound effects.

Bentley was laughing so hard that Millie stopped reading. "Ben, if you want me to finish, you need to stop laughing." Millie laughed.

"You're good with kids." Derek stepped into the room with a big smile on his face. "Beth sent me up to let you know dinner is about ready."

"We are almost done." Millie tickled Bentley's tummy, causing him to giggle. Derek took a seat on the bed and Millie continued reading.

Derek and Bentley were still laughing by the time the three of them walked into the kitchen. There were two men already sitting at the table and Beth was placing a basket of rolls in the center. Millie kept her focus on the floor, avoiding having to interact with the strangers for a few more minutes.

"Beth, we need to employ Mils to do story time every night for the kids." Derek said with a laugh.

"Whatever." Millie playfully shoved his shoulder with a laugh. "You just need to practice."

"Millie?" Two male voices said in unison from the table.

Millie looked over. "Aiden? Josh?" Her eyes went wide in surprise.

"What are you doing here?" Josh asked, coming to his feet.

"I invited her." Beth looked between the three of them. "How do you two know Millie?"

"We helped her when her car broke down and Aiden loaned her his truck." Josh looked from Millie to Beth. "How do you know her?"

"So, I did recognize the truck. I was a little surprised that someone else could own such a monstrosity." Beth shook her head.

"That truck is not a monstrosity." Millie glared at Beth. "It is God's greatest gift to mankind."

Beth laughed as she threw her arm over Millie's shoulders. "You, my dear friend, are delusional."

Millie smiled at Beth. "Dinner's done!" A man called as the sliding door opened and the smell of grilled fish hit Millie like a brick wall and her smile fell.

Beth grabbed her arm and pulled her quickly from the room and down a small hallway. Millie found herself in a bathroom in the nick of time. Beth held her hair for her as she threw up.

"I'm so sorry." Millie whispered after rinsing her mouth.

"No, I'm sorry." Beth shook her head. "Are you doing okay?"

"I think so. It just hit so suddenly." Millie dried her hands and mouth.

They walked back out to the kitchen. Millie took slow breaths to try to calm her embarrassment and rolling stomach. When they entered, Derek was nowhere to be seen, the fish was gone, and Aiden walked up to them.

"Are you okay, Millie?" He whispered as he searched her face.

"She will be. Where did Derek go?" Beth asked as she looked around.

"The food was bad." Bentley said before shoving a mouthful of mac and cheese into his mouth.

Millie felt awful. She hadn't meant to ruin dinner. Derek stepped back in. When he saw them, he walked over. "Better?"

"You didn't have to do that." Millie whispered.

"Mils, can I have a word with you?" Derek asked. Millie glanced at Beth who nodded encouragingly to her.

Millie followed Derek out into the backyard. He stopped when they were out of earshot of the house. He looked at her kindly and spoke softly. "I don't know your situation and I don't know why you were at that campground by yourself, but I do know one thing; you are pregnant."

Millie wrapped her arms around herself and looked down at the ground. Her eyes burned and she was so embarrassed.

"Mils look at me." Derek said kindly. Millie slowly looked up as she blinked back her tears, refusing to let them fall. "Does Beth know?"

Millie nodded her head. "We talked about it yesterday." She whispered. Derek nodded in understanding.

"Is the father in the picture?" Derek's brows drew down in concern.

Millie laughed humorlessly as she shook her head. "I will let Beth know she can tell you everything." She bit her lip again as she thought about the others realizing that she was pregnant too. Embarrassment colored her cheeks as she dropped her gaze to the grass.

Derek ran his hand through his hair. "Alright, let's get some food in you. I wouldn't worry about the guys, the only reason I figured it out was because Beth reacted the same way with spaghetti sauce when she was pregnant with Melody."

"Okay." Millie whispered, unconvinced.

She silently followed Derek back inside where he whispered something to Beth as he sat down. Millie took the open seat next to Aiden, who gave her a questioning look but said nothing. Derek offered up a prayer and dinner was dished up. Millie had no idea where the fish went to, but there was now grilled chicken sitting on the table.

"Before dinner gets too far underway, we should probably introduce everyone." Beth smiled. "This is my friend, Millie."

"You seem to already know Aiden and Josh." Derek pointed around the table. "And these are my friends, Mark and Jonas."

Millie glanced around at each man as he was introduced. They gave her smiles before they started eating. Conversation flowed around her. Millie did her best to eat, but she was incredibly nauseous ever since the fish.

"Are you okay?" Aiden whispered.

Millie looked at him and his eyes shifted to her mostly untouched plate. "I need my prescription. I forgot it in the truck." she whispered back.

"Where is the truck? I didn't see it when we arrived."

"I parked around the corner so I could leave if I needed to." Millie pushed her mashed potatoes around. "I'll go get it when dinner is done."

"I'll go get it for you while you try to eat something." Aiden excused himself and left before she could say anything. He returned in a matter of minutes and discreetly handed her the pill bottle.

"Thank you." She whispered and he nodded. He studied her for a long minute before turning back to his plate. Instead of the worried expression he had worn several minutes ago, he seemed thoughtful. Almost like he was trying to figure something out.

Millie stayed quiet and only answered the few questions directed to her. Once everyone was done eating, they all moved into the front room for games. She was sitting next to Aiden on the couch as the group played Pictionary. The night wore on and she watched quietly as everyone joked and laughed. It didn't take long for her to start dozing. She woke up several times when the guys yelled or laughed really hard.

She tried to participate but couldn't keep her eyes open. Without drawing attention to herself, Millie attempted to wake up enough to function. She still needed to drive home. Once the round ended, Millie stood.

"I need to get going. Thank you so much for dinner and it was nice to meet you all." Millie said and both Derek and Beth gave her a hug goodbye.

"I'll walk you out." Aiden said as he followed her to the door. They walked in silence until they reached the corner of the street. "I promise I wasn't snooping, but I saw your book on the seat."

Millie stopped walking and looked at him sharply. She had forgotten it was there. She covered her face with her hands in embarrassment. Could this night get any better? First throwing up and ruining dinner, now this.

"It's okay, Millie." Aiden's hand touched her arm gently. "I just wanted you to know that I knew."

"It's not okay!" Millie dropped her hands as tears blurred her vision. "He tricked me and left! Now I'm carrying his child and I'm scared out of my freaking mind! So, no, Aiden, it's not okay!" she yelled and then started crying.

Aiden pulled her into a hug, and she started to cry even harder. Millie couldn't seem to get control of herself. She didn't know how long she cried, but Aiden continued to hold her until her tears stopped.

"I'm sorry." Millie whispered as she stepped back and wiped her cheeks. "I'm a complete mess right now, but I guess you already know that, since you have seen me have two mental breakdowns."

"I wouldn't say a mess." Aiden gave her a small smile. "Understandably upset and overwhelmed, maybe. But not a mess."

Millie returned his smile with a tentative one. "Thank you. But I really do need to get going. I'm exhausted."

"Hey, there you two are." Josh came jogging up. Millie wiped her cheeks again hoping that the darkness of the night would hide the fact that she had been crying.

"I was just walking Millie to the truck." Aiden said, glancing at her.

"You look completely done in, Millie. Are you okay to drive?" Josh eyed her. "I think you also fell asleep during the game a few times."

Millie sighed and rubbed her forehead. She was so tired. Maybe she should ask Beth if they had an extra room, and drive back in the morning. Millie lowered herself down on the curb and covered her face. She couldn't ask more from Beth and Derek. She could always sleep in the truck for a few hours before trying to drive.

"Come on Millie, I'll drive you home. Josh can meet us at your apartment." Aiden grabbed her hands and pulled her to her feet. "You good to leave soon, Josh?"

"Yeah, I was coming out to let you know we needed to head back soon anyway. I forgot about an assignment that is due in the morning." Josh said. "I'll just let Derek and Beth know we are leaving now." Josh turned and jogged back down the road.

"You guys really don't have to. I can just sleep in the truck again." Millie said as she continued towards it.

"You've been sleeping in the truck?" Aiden asked in disbelief.

Millie laughed. "I went camping, Aiden. I needed to figure some things out."

Aiden opened the side door and waited for her. Millie picked the book up off the seat before climbing in. She was staring down at it when Aiden sat behind the wheel. When he saw her looking at the book, he grabbed her hand and gave it a squeeze. Millie looked over at him.

"It will be okay, Millie." Millie started to shake her head, but Aiden continued. "I know this was a shock for you, if your response to the news was anything to go by, but I truly believe everything will work out for you."

Millie took a deep breath and slowly let it out as Aiden started the truck and pulled onto the road. She turned her attention back to the book in her lap. The adoption booklets were sticking out a little and she fiddled with them.

"Can I ask you something?" Aiden asked after several minutes.

"I thought we were married." Millie said as she stared out the window. "Then when I woke up, he was gone and left the unsigned marriage license on the table for me, making the marriage invalid." Millie just wanted this conversation to be over. "He disconnected his phone and pretty much vanished into thin air. Now I'm here."

It was quiet for a while. "Thank you for telling me, but you really didn't need to explain yourself, Millie." Aiden said quietly. Millie glanced over at him at the same time he glanced at her. "I was going to ask what you were majoring in."

Millie laughed as she looked out the window again so Aiden wouldn't see the tear that ran down her cheek. "Early Childhood Development. But I don't know if that will pan out."

"Why's that?"

"Because I'm pregnant. I have been so sick I don't know if I can finish this semester. Then what happens next? I have no family that can help me, and Lawrence is never going to be in the picture. And I have to figure out if I am going to keep the baby, because if I do, I will be a single mother." Millie folded her arms over her chest as she glared into the darkness.

"You're not alone, Millie. Beth has adopted you. You will never escape her now." Millie looked over at Aiden. "Derek seems to be just as attached to you as he is with his sisters." He glanced at her quickly before returning his attention to the road. "Josh and I live close. If you need anything, all you have to do is call."

"You are telling me that if I kept this baby and needed help with it so I could get some late-night studying in, you and Josh would come over and help?" Millie asked, unable to believe Aiden or Josh would actually show up.

"One or both of us would come over." Aiden said seriously. "And if you don't believe we can handle babies, ask Beth. She forced us all to learn how to change diapers and make bottles."

Millie sat in stunned silence until they pulled into her parking spot. Aiden opened the door for her, and she got out. "Thanks for driving me home."

"Anytime." Aiden gave her a smile. "Did you need help taking your camping gear up to your apartment?"

"That would be amazing. Thank you." Millie sighed in relief. She didn't think she would have the energy to do it herself.

Millie helped bring up the first load, but Aiden insisted on getting the rest himself. On the third trip up, Josh was with him. Millie was snuggled under a blanket on the couch. Her eyes fluttered open when they entered.

"Hey, sleeping beauty, did you fall asleep in the car, or did you make it all the way home?" Josh asked with a grin on his face. He dropped several blankets on the floor with the rest of her camping stuff.

"I made it home." Millie got to her feet and followed them to the door.

"Oh, before I forget, Beth said to remind you about lemonheads, crackers in bed and to tell you good luck." Josh said as he shrugged. "Don't ask me to explain, because I have no idea what she is talking about."

"Thanks, Josh. I do." Millie yawned. "Thank you both for your help."

Josh nodded and headed outside, but Aiden hesitated. He looked back at her with a conflicted expression. "You might as well tell Josh, since you signed him up to babysit, if it comes to that." Millie kept her voice low so Cindy wouldn't hear her.

"You sure?" Aiden asked as he studied her face.

"You, Beth, and Derek know, so Josh might as well be informed. If you want a more in-depth story, Beth has all the details. I'm sure she is bringing Derek up to speed as we speak." Millie shrugged.

After talking to Beth, Derek, and then Aiden, it was getting a little easier to talk about the pregnancy. Aiden nodded his head before saying good-bye and leaving. Millie put the contents of the cooler away before heading to bed. In her bedtime prayer, she thanked her Father in Heaven for the friends He had put into her life when she needed them the most and she asked for help knowing what to do about her baby.

Chapter 4

Millie was watching a movie and eating popcorn to celebrate the end of midterms. Her phone rang and she checked to see who it was. Cindy had been trying to talk with Millie all week, but she kept brushing her nosey neighbor off. Seeing it was Aiden, she paused the movie and answered.

"Hello."

"Hey. How are you doing?" Aiden asked.

"I'm doing better now that midterms are over." Millie smiled.

"I hear you. I just finished my last one about an hour ago."

"So, what's up?" Millie asked as she popped a piece of popcorn into her mouth.

"Josh just called to let me know that your car is done. The mechanic apologized again for taking so long."

"Well, that's…good." Millie was glad her car was fixed, but at the same time she was bummed she would have to give the truck back.

"You don't sound too excited." Aiden chuckled.

"I am truly happy that my car is fixed."

"But it's not my truck."

"Yeah." Millie sighed dreamily.

Aiden laughed. "I'll tell you what, you can keep the truck until we meet at Derek's for dinner next month."

"I can't keep your truck, Aiden." Millie sighed. "No matter how much I want to." she muttered.

"We are picking up your car from the garage tomorrow. Will you be home tomorrow evening so we can drop it off?"

"I think so." Millie said slowly. "Oh wait, no I won't be. I have to work, and I promised the kids something." Millie began to pace. She wanted to return Aiden's truck to him, so she didn't feel indebted to him anymore. "If I sent you the address, could we exchange cars there? After like...seven o'clock?"

"That should work. We will see you then." Aiden said and Millie hung up the phone.

Millie was just turning on the movie when someone knocked on her door. Sighing, she paused the movie again and answered the door. Cindy stood there with a determined look on her face.

"What can I do for you, Cindy?"

"You have been avoiding me for months." Cindy accused.

"I got sick and then midterms kept me busy. Plus, I have been dealing with a breakup. I haven't wanted to talk to anyone." Millie shrugged.

"You seem to be getting over Lawrence pretty quickly. Who are those two guys I have seen around? You do realize that dating two guys at once is a horrible thing to do. And where were you on Sunday?" Cindy put her hands on her hips.

"I know this is a foreign concept for you, but a woman can have male friends without it being romantic." Millie glared.

"I saw you holding hands with one of them the other day. I am not an idiot." Cindy snapped.

Millie stared at Cindy in disbelief. "You are not my keeper, Cindy. We are neighbors. My personal relationships are mine and not yours."

"I am your ministering sister." Cindy pointed out. "I'm supposed to be keeping an eye on you."

"That doesn't mean you get to be a part of my personal relationships." Millie fired back. "I am trying to have a relaxing afternoon now that midterms are over, so excuse me." Millie slammed the door.

She was livid. She stomped down the hall to her room and grabbed her laptop before returning to the front room. Millie turned the movie back on as she booted up the computer. She was not staying here anymore. She had had it with Cindy and her constantly demanding to know every little detail about her life. Her rental contract was up in three months, which meant she only had three months to find a new place to live.

Millie spent the rest of the night looking at new apartments that were close to the University. After the first hour, she changed her search to two bedrooms instead of one. If she was going to be keeping the baby, she would need the space. And if she gave the baby up for adoption, she could pull her instruments out of storage and play more. She found several rentals that were great options. She created a list so she could go look at them after class on Monday. It was well after midnight by the time Millie finally went to bed.

The next day Millie ran to the store to gather supplies to pack. She didn't want Cindy to know she was moving yet. She remembered hearing Cindy mention that she would be out of town for the weekend, so Millie did her best to get as much packed away as possible before she had to go to work. Aiden's truck was a huge blessing when it came to loading up the boxes and moving them into her storage unit.

Millie pulled into the parking lot of the children's special needs facility where she worked, a little after five. There were only three kids there at this time of day. Moses was nine and struggled with his speech. He had a severe stutter. Maria was eight and was so painfully shy that she never spoke. Talon was five. He had a lisp.

All three kids cheered when they saw Millie walk into the building. "Who's ready for a party?" Millie asked with a smile.

They changed into their swimsuits, put sunscreen on and headed outside. Millie unfolded the giant tarp she had purchased and her two coworkers, Kevin and Dallen, helped her lay it in the bed of the truck. There were several feet on all sides spilling over the top.

"How ith thith going to be a pool?" Talon asked excitedly. His lisp always got worse when he was excited.

"Moses and Dallen will go get the hose and we will fill up the tarp with water. It will be like a bathtub in the back of the truck." Millie explained.

They had to get special permission from all the parents but that hadn't been hard. All the parents thought it would be fun for the kids to have a redneck pool party during the heat wave.

The kids helped put the clamps on to hold the edges of the tarp as the trunk started filling up. While they waited, Millie helped Maria with her daily goals and the boys did theirs. She planned to only fill it about two thirds of the way full, so the water wasn't too deep.

"Millie, can we get in?" Maria's whisper was so quiet, Millie barely heard her.

"I think it is filled enough we can start enjoying it." Millie smiled at the little girl.

Dallen helped Millie lift Maria into the back of the truck. The girl squealed in delight. Millie climbed in next. The water was a bit cold, but also refreshing compared to the heat of the day. The boys quickly climbed in followed by Dallen and Kevin.

"S-s-s-so, w-w-where d-d-did you g-g-get this id-d-d-dea?" Moses asked.

Millie laughed. "Are you telling me that you never wished to sit in the bed of a truck while it was filled with water?"

"I like thith." Talon giggled and then splashed Kevin.

Kevin laughed before softly splashing back. Talon screamed and hid behind Dallen. Millie laughed as she watched them. Maria smiled shyly as she leaned up against Millie.

"This isn't your truck, is it? I could have sworn you had a little white car." Dallen asked after the boys settled down a bit.

"This truck belongs to a friend of mine. He was nice enough to let me borrow it while my car is getting fixed." Millie explained.

"Is he handsome?" Maria's voice was soft enough that no one else heard her.

Millie thought about Aiden, and she had to admit he was handsome. "Very." Millie whispered back as she tapped her finger on Maria's nose.

A few hours later, the sun was starting to set, and the kids didn't want to get out. She knew they should probably get the kids dry before their parents came to pick them up, but they were having so much fun and Millie hated to have to end such a fun day.

"So, this is why you wanted the truck a little longer." Aiden's laughing voice came from behind her.

She whirled around to face him. "Aiden! I must have lost track of time." Her cheeks flushed.

Millie stood and started to climb out of the truck but slipped. One moment she was falling face first towards the ground, the next she was in Aiden's arms. Millie's hands were on his chest while his arms were around her waist, their faces inches apart.

"Are you okay?" Aiden asked as he stepped back a little and looked her up and down. He kept his arms around her.

"I-I think so." Millie stammered out as she looked down at herself. Her heart was racing, and she was a little shaky, but she didn't think she was physically harmed. Her eyes stopped on her stomach. Her lower belly was sticking out a little more than it usually did.

Millie's head snapped up and she glanced over at the truck. Everyone was watching her. Could they tell her belly was slightly bigger? She should have worn a t-shirt over her swimsuit instead of just the swim shorts.

"Who's t-t-t-that M-m-m-millie?" Moses asked, pulling her out of her panicked thoughts.

Millie put on a smile for the kids and turned to face them. The change to her belly was so small she hardly noticed it, she doubted anyone else would. Aiden put his hand on her lower back as they stepped up to the truck. She was still a bit shaky from her fall and Aiden's presence was comforting.

"This is my friend, Aiden and this is his truck." Millie put her hands on the top of the truck before looking up at Aiden. "Aiden these are the kids I work with: Moses, Maria, and Talon. And those two are Dallen and Kevin, my coworkers."

"It's nice to meet you all." Aiden smiled at everyone.

Millie tried not to smile as Maria watched Aiden closely for a few minutes while the guys pulled Aiden into conversation about different vehicles. His arm was still on her back and Millie found herself wanting to lean into him, but she resisted the urge.

Maria motioned for Millie to move closer, so Millie grudgingly stepped away from Aiden and closer to the girl before standing on her tiptoes.

Maria leaned over to whisper into Millie's ear. "He is handsome."

Millie had to bite her lip to keep from laughing as the little eight-year-old blushed. "I would never lie to you." Millie winked.

"Millie, you are supposed to be encouraging Maria to speak out loud." Kevin teased.

"This is totally in the rules for whispered conversations." Millie stuck her tongue out at him before turning back to Maria and lowering her voice again. "Kevin is such a buzz kill. Girls need their girl talk, don't they? We should put salt on his sandwich on Monday, so he learns not to butt in." Maria giggled and Millie laughed.

A car pulled into the parking lot and Maria's smile widened. When a woman got out of the driver's seat, Maria stood. "Mommy, look at what Mr. Aiden and Ms. Millie did for us!" she yelled.

Maria's mom stopped dead in her tracks as she stared wide-eyed at her daughter. Her surprise quickly gave way to pure joy, and she hurried over with a huge smile on her face. Maria never yelled, and Millie was just as shocked as the girl's mother.

Dallen passed Maria down to Millie. "Why don't you go get your towel and bag?" Millie suggested to Maria and the girl ran inside.

"Thank you so much, Millie. When you asked if you could do this, I never imagined Maria would..." the woman teared up and Millie gave her a hug.

"I'm glad it helped her." Millie said as she stepped back.

"She seems to come out of her shell around you. You are good for her." Maria's mom smiled.

"Maria is a sweetheart." Millie smiled as Maria came running back over. "She and I aren't much different." Millie touched Maria's nose. "Have a good night you two."

"Night, Millie." Maria waved before following her mom back to their car.

"Wait!" Kevin called out before Maria got into the car. "What did Millie tell you?"

Maria's smile reached her ears before she climbed in and closed the door. They all waved as Maria and her mom drove away. Millie turned to tell the boys it was time to get out. As she turned, she noticed Aiden had stepped off to the side just before she got a wave of water in the face.

She gasped and froze. She was drenched from head to toe. Slowly, Millie raised her head to look at those in the back of the truck. All were laughing hysterically, including Aiden as he stood near the bumper.

"You didn't just do that." Millie said in disbelief. When that only caused them to laugh harder, Millie shook her head and walked away. "After all I do for you. After all the work I put into this." she muttered loudly for them to hear, but doubted they could over their laughter.

Millie grabbed the hose and turned back to the group. Dallen grabbed Talon and ran inside just as Millie turned the faucet on. The others were laughing so hard, they hadn't noticed what she was doing.

Aiden was doubled over as he gasped for air. Millie quickly, but quietly, walked up behind him with the hose kinked. When he finally stood up straight and looked at her with his dimpled smile, Millie unkinked the hose and sprayed him straight in the face. He took off running for the far side of the truck.

Millie changed targets and sprayed Kevin and Moses. Aiden helped Kevin get Moses down and they hid behind the truck. Millie smiled. "Kevin, you know better than to try to best me in pranks."

"I don't have a white flag, Millie." Kevin called.

"I don't think I would accept it even if you had one." Millie called back.

Out the corner of her eye, Millie caught Dallen and Talon at the doors, Dallen had her phone and was pointing to it. She kinked the hose and ran over. Dallen had answered it, but she didn't recognize the number.

"Can you take over for me?" Millie whispered as she pointed to the hose. Dallen laughed and nodded his head before heading outside. "Hello?" she said, wrapping a towel around herself before sitting on a chair.

"Hey Millie, I've missed you." Millie's stomach tightened in dread.

"Lawrence?" she breathed out.

"Yeah, baby. It's me. I want to see you." Lawrence's voice was as smooth as ever. However, this time she wasn't buying it.

"No." Millie said firmly.

"No? Since when do you not want to see me?" He sounded surprised, which only made Millie even more mad.

"I can't believe you just asked me that. The answer is not now, not ever." She hung up her phone and silenced it.

Millie sent Talon outside when she saw his parents arrive. The guys were still having a water fight, so Millie changed into dry clothes. The phone call from Lawrence rattled her. Why was he trying to reach out to her now? He left two and a half months ago without a trace.

She pulled out her phone and saw five missed calls from the same number. She was tempted to block it, but something told her not to. Monday morning, she was going to call her lawyer. She would know what to do about Lawrence's sudden reappearance.

Millie also wanted to make sure that Lawrence couldn't take her baby from her. She didn't want anything to do with him. No child support, no joint custody, no contact whatsoever. There was no way she wanted him anywhere near her baby.

Millie drank a glass of cool water to calm herself before grabbing her towel and stepping outside. She turned off the hose without being seen. There was a moment of confusion before three men and a boy turned to look at her.

"Time to get dried off, Moses. Your parents should be here any minute." Millie walked over.

Aiden's smile slipped from his lips when he saw her face. She handed him her towel before following Moses inside. Ten minutes later, Moses was picked up and they were closing up the building.

"Who was on the phone?" Dallen glanced over at her as they walked to the truck. "He was kind of a jerk."

"Someone who's not important." Millie bent down and rolled up her jeans to her knees. "And please don't answer my phone."

"The number called like six times before Talon answered it." Dallen looked at her in concern.

Millie turned her back on the men and used the back tire to climb into the truck bed. She clenched her jaw to keep from yelling. She was so angry with Lawrence at the moment, and she didn't want to take it out on Dallen, Kevin, or Aiden.

Millie sat on the side and dangled her legs on the outside of the water before leaning over and unlatching the tailgate. Water gushed out and Millie stood, balancing on the side of the truck. She carefully walked along it to the front, as the guys protested. She undid the clamp that held the tarp before shimmying along the tiny ridge by the cab rear window. She undid the other clamp.

Now that most of the water was out, Millie jumped down into the bed and lifted the edge of the tarp. She dragged it to the tailgate and pushed it off. Hopping down to the ground she slammed the tailgate closed.

"I don't think I have ever seen you mad before." Kevin said slowly.

Millie pulled out her phone. There were twenty-three missed calls. She swiped them away and opened the app that had her work schedule, choosing to ignore Kevin's comment. "I work on Monday, but I need to do a few things, can either of you cover for me?" She asked. The guys looked at each other before turning their attention back to her.

"I guess I can, but you have to tell us who was on the phone." Kevin folded his arms over his chest. The guy tried to look intimidating, but he was far from it. He was as skinny as a scarecrow with red hair and freckles. He was in his thirties and was already showing signs of balding.

Millie glared at him for a long moment, and he began to shift uncomfortably. She really needed him to cover her shift so she could speak to her lawyer.

"My ex, Kevin. My ex-fiancé was on the phone." Aiden tensed when she said that Lawrence was the caller. Thanks for covering for me. Now good night gentlemen." Millie turned and walked to her car parked several spots away.

She tried to open the driver's door, but it was locked. Sighing, she turned to find Aiden standing a few feet away. "You might want these." He held up her keys.

"Thanks." she said quietly as she took them.

Aiden watched her get into her car, but before she could close the door, he stopped her. "I know you are going to say you are okay, but if you need anything you have mine and Josh's numbers. Don't hesitate to call or text us, okay?"

Millie got back out of the car and wrapped her arms around Aiden's neck, and he returned her hug. "Thank you, Aiden." She whispered. After a long moment, Millie got back in her car. "Goodnight." She closed her door, started her car, and drove back to her apartment.

Her list of To-Dos for Monday was growing by the minute, along with her stress level. The thought of going to church the next day and seeing Cindy was already bad enough. Millie quickly called Beth and asked if she could go to church with them again. Beth was excited about the prospect and Millie was glad she could still go to church without Cindy being there.

Chapter 5

Millie had a restless couple of weeks. Lawrence's phone call had upset her delicate equilibrium. Derek had insisted she change the locks on her door after he overheard her telling Beth that Lawrence had a spare key. He even went with her to make sure Lawrence wasn't in the apartment.

Her meeting with Mrs. White, her lawyer, had gone well. Just over that first weekend, Millie had fifty-three missed calls and almost a hundred texts. Lawrence seemed to go from apologetic to angry to begging for forgiveness to blaming her. Mrs. White assured Millie that no matter what Lawrence said, their marriage was never real and that she would start building a case against Lawrence, so if he ever tried anything, they would have everything already in order.

Millie was told to send a text to Lawrence telling him that she didn't want any contact with him and to leave her alone. She sent it, and then went out and changed her number. Only a handful of numbers transferred but the rest were lost. Thankfully she still had Beth's. They chatted every day and Millie found that she really liked having a good friend she could talk to about everything.

School was going better now that Millie was able to manage her nausea a little. Beth constantly pushed her to go to classes even though she was exhausted and not feeling well. Her workload had increased and if she wasn't doing homework, she was finishing up her packing. She was rarely at her apartment anymore. She was either studying in the library or finalizing things with her new place.

Millie was nearly moved out of her old apartment as well. She had been doing it slowly since her lease wasn't up for another month. Instead of another apartment, Millie found a cute four-bedroom house ten minutes from campus that she purchased. She still wasn't sure she was going to keep the baby yet, but the extra space would be nice.

Millie was on her way to her doctor's appointment. She was so nervous. She had no idea what to expect. She pulled into a parking spot and got out slowly. She stared at the doctor's office for a moment before walking towards it.

"Millie!" Josh's voice called and she turned around to see him and Aiden jogging towards her. "Where have you been?" Josh asked when they finally reached her.

"What are you talking about? I haven't gone anywhere." Millie furrowed her eyebrows.

"You haven't been answering our texts and you haven't been at your apartment." Josh crossed his arms over his chest as he glared at her.

Understanding dawned. Millie laughed before giving Josh a quick hug. "I had no idea you would miss me so much."

"We were worried about you." Josh returned her hug. "Aiden said you got a call a few weeks ago. We didn't know if you skipped town or if he kidnapped you."

Millie's cheeks heated as she stepped away from Josh. "I changed my number because he wouldn't stop calling." Millie shrugged. "Most of my numbers were lost." Millie gave Aiden a hug as well.

When his arms went around her, Millie's heart rate accelerated. "I'm glad you are doing okay." Aiden said softly.

Millie stepped a little away from him. She reminded herself that even though Aiden was attractive, she didn't want to get involved with anyone right now. "I'm doing pretty good. Beth's been keeping me motivated to attend my classes. The exhaustion is ridiculous, no matter how much sleep I get." As if she planned it, she yawned.

"What brings you back here?" Aiden asked with a small smile on his lips.

"I have an appointment." Millie glanced at the doctor's office nervously. "I should probably head in." she said grudgingly.

"You don't sound like you want to." Josh said without his normal joking tone.

Millie shrugged, crossed her arms over her chest, and rubbed her arms nervously. She looked back at the office and her stomach fluttered uncomfortably. Why was she anxious? It's not like Dr. Spaulding was going to deliver earth-shattering news again.

"We were just about to head home, but if you want, we can go in with you." Josh offered.

Millie turned back to them as she bit her lip. She really didn't want to go in alone, but she couldn't impose on Josh and Aiden. She glanced between them and the doctor's office, unable to tell them she was fine.

"Come on, let's go inside." Aiden grabbed her hand and began walking.

"I can't ask you guys to come with me. I will be okay." Millie didn't sound convincing, even to her own ears.

"Good thing you aren't asking." Josh shrugged as he fell into step beside them. "We offered."

Millie gripped Aiden's hand tighter as they stepped inside. Her anxiety climbed another notch as they approached the front desk. Aiden squeezed her hand back.

"Can I help you?" the receptionist asked, glancing between the three of them.

"Appointment for Millie Larson." Millie said softly.

"Only family is allowed in the back." The receptionist commented.

"I'm her brother." Josh said with a smile as he leaned against the counter. "And Aiden is her fiancé."

Millie stared at Josh in disbelief. Did he really just tell this woman she was engaged to Aiden. Aiden looked down at her as she glanced up at him. He gave her a wink before smiling at the receptionist. What was happening?

"You can have a seat. A nurse will call you back in a few minutes."

"Thank you." Aiden said before pulling her to a group of empty chairs. When she sat, he put his arm over her shoulders and pulled her close enough he could whisper in her ear. "If you are uncomfortable with this charade of Josh's, just say the word and we will wait for you outside."

Millie glanced at Josh who was grinning proudly. She wasn't happy with him for making up how they were connected, but she really didn't want to be alone. She laid her head on Aiden's shoulder and waited quietly.

"Millie Larson." A nurse called and Millie tensed. Aiden stood and retook her hand in his. Josh followed behind them as they were led to an exam room. "Ms. Larson, we need you to leave a urine sample. The bathroom is across the hall."

When Millie was done in the bathroom, the nurse pulled her aside to get her weight before she returned to the exam room. Josh was fiddling with a few tongue depressors while Aiden shook his head at him. Millie stifled a giggle at how childlike Josh was acting. She grabbed a large exam glove, blew it up, and tied it off.

"Here you go." She said as she handed it to Josh. "Play with this."

Josh laughed as he took the glove turned balloon. "Thanks. How did you think to do this?"

"I spent a lot of time at doctor offices while growing up." Millie said as she took a seat on the bed.

"Is that why you are anxious to be here?" Aiden asked.

"No, I'm anxious because four weeks ago I came in to see why I couldn't get over a flu bug, only to find out I was pregnant." Millie looked down at her hands. "I'm still trying to come to terms with it."

A light rap on the door sounded before it opened. Dr. Spaulding stepped into the room and smiled. "I see you brought some friends." She paused when she saw Josh with the glove. "And keeping yourselves entertained."

"Dr. Spaulding, this is my mentally handicapped brother, Josh. And my friend Aiden." Millie bit the inside of her cheek to keep from smiling.

Aiden burst out laughing while Josh gasped in mock horror. "I can't believe you called me that." Josh put a hand to his chest.

Dr. Spaulding laughed. "I can believe that young man is your friend, but I have known you since you were five and know you don't have a brother."

Millie smiled. "Josh and Aiden are friends."

"I'm glad you have a support system but are you comfortable having them in here during the exam." Dr. Spaulding asked.

Millie glanced over at Aiden and Josh, unsure of what all the appointment was going to entail. She looked back at Dr. Spaulding. The older woman seemed to understand Millie's uncertainty.

"We will see if we can hear the baby's heartbeat using a doppler and talk about any of your concerns. If you are comfortable with them seeing your stomach and hearing about your current health, they can stay." Dr. Spaulding said as she pulled a handheld computer with a wand attached to it out of her coat pocket. "Have you made a decision yet?"

"I haven't." Millie rubbed her arm, suddenly feeling chilled. "They can stay. Josh would push for details afterwards if they left now."

"We can talk a little more about your options later, right now I need you to lay back on the bed and lift your shirt so I can put this on your belly." Dr. Spaulding helped Millie lie down.

Millie's anxiety flared and it was suddenly hard to breathe. "Millie, are you doing okay?" Dr. Spaulding asked. Millie shook her head. "Everything is going to be okay. Just take a deep breath for me." Millie started to shake as her anxiety continued to rise.

Aiden moved to her side. He gently turned her face to look at him. "Everything is okay, Millie. Just breathe." Aiden's voice was soft and calming.

Millie grabbed his other hand and squeezed her eyes closed. She didn't feel okay. She just wanted to go home and curl up for a good cry. Hearing the baby's heart beating would only make this more real and she didn't know if she was ready for that.

"Millie, look at me." Aiden whispered as he gently stroked her cheek. Millie opened her eyes and met his gaze. He gave her a small smile. "Why did you spray me in the face with the hose? Kevin was the ringleader, and I wasn't even in the truck."

Millie laughed, completely taken off guard. That had been the last thing she thought he would say to her right now, but she could roll with it. "You stepped away and didn't even warn me." Aiden's smile grew and Millie began to relax.

"How are you doing, Millie?" Dr. Spaulding asked. "Are you ready? It is completely painless. I will put a little bit of warm jelly on your stomach and then I will use this to find the heartbeat."

Millie took a deep breath and nodded. Dr. Spaulding lifted Millie's shirt a little before tucking a hand towel into the front waistband of her yoga pants. Just before the doppler was placed on her stomach, Millie tightened her grip on Aiden's hand. He gently smoothed her hair back from her face.

The doppler touched Millie's stomach and she tensed. Her breathing increased as Dr. Spaulding spread the gel around until a fast-whooshing sound came from the handheld computer. Millie looked away from Aiden and over to Dr. Spaulding.

"That's your baby's heartrate." She gave Millie a smile. Millie's breath caught in her lungs, and she closed her eyes. She listened until the doctor removed the doppler from her stomach. "A good strong heartbeat. You can sit up and wipe the jelly off."

Millie held tight to Aiden's hand while using her other to clean off her stomach. She kept her face down so no one would see the tears rolling down her cheeks. A nurse poked her head in, and Dr. Spaulding ducked out for a few minutes.

"Millie?" Aiden asked softly.

That did it, she burst into tears. Aiden pulled her into his arms. She buried her face in his chest when she felt a hand touch her shoulder. She knew what she needed to do about the baby, and she was terrified. For the past week or two, she found herself leaning more towards this decision but hearing the heartbeat was the clencher.

Her sobs turned to sniffles and she leaned heavier against Aiden. She glanced over at Josh. He was still rubbing her back slowly. "Thank you, guys, for being here." She whispered.

"No problem, Millie." Josh gave her an encouraging smile. "How are you feeling?"

"I think I'm okay." She breathed in slowly and let it out.

The door opened and Dr. Spaulding reentered. "Sorry for the interruption. Oh, Millie. Are you okay?"

Millie nodded but didn't pull away from Aiden. Josh returned to his chair to give Dr. Spaulding room to get to Millie. The doctor patted Millie's knee after she took a seat on the wheely chair.

"How have you been feeling? I know the last time we spoke you were quite sick." Dr. Spaulding asked.

Millie sagged a little more and Aiden's arm tightened around her. "Mostly the same. The medication you gave me has made it so I can at least keep toast, crackers, and Gatorade down for the most part."

"You have lost quite a bit of weight in the last four weeks. Now that you are twelve weeks, your morning sickness should start going away. But until then, we need to get some food and fluids in you."

"How? I throw up everything I try to eat. And I am so tired all the time. I feel like if I'm not throwing up, I'm sleeping." Millie sat up a little and Aiden let her go.

"What have you been able to eat and drink today? And how many times have you thrown up?" Dr. Spaulding started typing on her computer.

"Three saltines and a sip or two of Gatorade. Threw them up. A few hours later I tried toast, but only managed a few small bites before I threw up. I threw up again during class and then again on my way here." Millie rubbed her forehead. "I tried to suck on lemonheads to help with the nausea, but they only seemed to make it worse."

She was so tired of throwing up. Aiden put a hand on her back, and she glanced at him; he was looking at the doctor. "That can't be good, right? I mean, she is getting rid of more than she is taking in." Aiden asked in concern.

"No, it's not." Dr. Spaulding sighed as she turned her attention to Millie. "And you have said you are extremely tired." Millie nodded. "Tiredness is normal at this stage of pregnancy, but I think you might be experiencing it more because you are dehydrated, and you aren't getting any nourishment."

Millie rubbed her arm nervously. "So, what now?"

"I am going to have a nurse come in and give you a bag of fluids while I call in another prescription for you. I want you to take both around the clock. And hopefully your morning sickness goes away." Dr. Spaulding gave Millie an encouraging smile before explaining about how the baby was developing at this point and some of the symptoms she might have in the coming weeks.

"Now that we have that out of the way, have you thought more about your options. Knowing you, you have narrowed it down to adoption or keeping the baby." Dr. Spaulding asked.

Millie closed her eyes. Her mother had given her up to be raised by her grandmother. She still had no idea where her mother was or if she was even alive. How could Millie do the same with her baby? Her child wouldn't even be raised by a relative. Then she had heard the heartbeat, and her heart had skipped a beat. Millie felt a wave of peace wash over her. This baby needed her.

Millie opened her eyes and met Dr. Spaulding's gaze. She wiped a tear from her cheek. "I'm not giving up my child." Her voice was soft but firm.

Dr. Spaulding smiled at her before going to get the nurse to start the I.V. line. Aiden returned to sit by Josh as Millie was stabbed and hooked up. The nurse returned with a blanket before leaving again.

"You don't have to stay. Who knows how long this is going to take." Millie yawned as she rolled onto her side to look at Josh and Aiden. "I really appreciate you coming though. These hormones are crazy, and I just panicked."

Josh smiled at her. "Glad we saw you when we left the gym. But I don't think Aiden or I want to leave you alone right now. You seemed relatively fine earlier and then you had a panic attack."

"I don't have anywhere to be. Plus, you still need to tell us where you have been hiding." Aiden sat back in his chair to get comfortable.

Millie gave them a half smile. "I wasn't hiding from you guys, I promise. Cindy is just all up in my business all the time. So I have been studying in my room with headphones on or at the library."

"I didn't realize you had such a tough workload." Josh commented. "Childhood Development doesn't sound like a super hard degree."

Millie laughed lightly. She wasn't just taking child development courses. She had a plan for her career and was doing her best to fulfill it. "I am taking twenty credits this semester."

"Dang girl. That is crazy. I am taking thirteen and it's kicking my butt." Josh whistled as he scooted his chair closer to the bed. Aiden followed suit.

"You look tired, Millie. Why don't you try to get some sleep while we are here?" Aiden smiled at her.

Millie nodded and closed her eyes. It didn't take long before she could feel herself growing heavy and her breathing began to slow. She curled into a ball as best she could and snuggled under the blanket. There was a murmur of voices in the distance and then all was quiet.

Chapter 6

Millie stepped outside and filled her lungs with the fresh air. Josh and Aiden had stayed with her for the whole hour. Dr. Spaulding had given her an anti-nausea medication in her I.V. and for the first time in a long time, she felt hungry. The wind blew carrying the smell of Mexican food on the breeze.

Millie turned her head in the direction the smell was coming from. Her stomach growled softly, and her mouth watered. She began walking across the parking lot, away from her car. She knew that Josh and Aiden were following her, but she didn't pay them any attention. Her full focus was on the little Mexican grill down the road.

"Where are you going?" Josh asked, confused.

"Do you smell that?" Millie inhaled the delicious aroma as she quickened her steps.

"Uh, no." Josh said slowly.

"I don't smell anything either." Aiden commented.

Millie was practically drooling when she stepped into the restaurant. The hostess looked up and smiled as Millie approached. "Table for three?"

"Yes, please." Aiden said, putting his hand on the small of Millie's back.

They were led to a table near the rear of the building. Millie sat on one of the benches expecting Josh and Aiden to sit on the other, but Aiden sat next to her. He didn't look over at her as he asked for three waters.

The place wasn't crowded, and their waters were brought quickly. Their waiter was about her age with blonde hair, blue eyes, and muscles that caused his shirt to look tight. He smiled brightly at Millie and winked when he placed a water in front of her.

Josh laughed at Millie's shocked expression when the waiter walked away. She shook her head and turned her attention to the menu. Everything looked and sounded so good, Millie had a hard time deciding. Aiden and Josh remained quiet as they looked at their own menus. After several minutes, their waiter returned.

"Have you decided what you want, or do you need more time?" he asked. His voice was smooth and rich.

"I know what I want." Millie smiled at him, excited to finally be getting some food.

"And what is that, sweetheart?" The waiter's smile grew.

Millie realized the man thought she was flirting with him. "First off, not you." The smile slipped from the waiter's face. "Secondly, I want a carne asada burrito, chicken quesadilla, and a taco salad with carne asada." She turned to Aiden. "What do you guys want?"

"Anything else?" The waiter asked after Josh and Aiden ordered. He kept looking between the three of them as if trying to puzzle something out. They shook their heads, and he left.

Millie drank half her water before Josh broke the silence. "I can't believe you ordered three meals for yourself."

"You try being sick for nearly eight weeks and then finally finding a medicine that calmed the nausea. I am so stinking hungry. Whatever Dr. Spaulding put in that I.V. is magical."

"Glad you are feeling a little better." Aiden smiled at her.

Millie smiled back then groaned. "I have to pee." She said shoving at Aiden's shoulder.

She didn't stop shoving until he stood and stepped out of the way. Millie got to her feet and walked quickly to the bathroom. She could hear Aiden and Josh laughing as she walked away.

Millie washed her hands and dried them before exiting the bathroom. "So, are one of those guys your boyfriend or something?" Their waiter said from behind Millie as she took a step down the hall, heading for her table.

She spun around quickly in surprise. She hadn't noticed anyone there when she exited the bathroom. "That is none of your business." Millie said firmly and turned, hurrying back to her table.

Millie retook her seat and Aiden sat back down. She was glad he was on the outside. Their server gave her the creeps. She began to relax as she listened to Aiden and Josh talk about an assignment they needed to do for their ethics class.

The server arrived and Millie tensed. His eyes raked over her as he placed her salad in front of her slowly. "The rest of your order will be out shortly, still waiting on a few things." He said as he winked at her.

Millie scooted a little closer to Aiden. "Look, man, I appreciate you bringing her salad out a little early but stop winking at her." Aiden said as he glared at their waiter.

"You can't fault a guy for trying his luck with a pretty woman." The waiter laughed. "Plus, she is old enough to make up her own mind."

"We all agree she is more than capable of making her own choices." Josh commented.

Millie shifted a little closer to Aiden and grabbed his arm. She was so glad that Aiden and Josh were with her. She only wanted food, not to be hit on. Aiden lifted his arm and put it around her shoulders as she slid even closer to him. Millie put her hand on his chest, resisting the urge to cry. Why was she even crying?

"Then agree to go on a date with me." The server's smiled at Millie, ignoring the fact that she was leaning against Aiden.

"I'm sorry but the answer is no." Millie tried to sound firm, but her voice squeaked.

The waiter chuckled but left when someone called to him from the back. Millie tried to keep her breathing normal, but this guy reminded her of Lawrence when they first met. He was relentless in getting her to agree to a date.

Their hostess seated a table not far from them and Millie got her attention. Millie sat up but stayed close to Aiden. "I'm sorry but can we get our order to go, please." Millie asked.

"Sure thing. Is anything wrong?"

"Yeah, our waiter won't stop hitting on Millie, even when she told him no." Josh said angrily.

The hostess gasped in surprise. She looked back over at Millie and started to apologize profusely. Aiden asked again for the food to be boxed up. The hostess hurried off and returned a few minutes later with bags of Styrofoam boxes.

Aiden stood and grabbed Millie's hand while Josh grabbed the bags. Aiden handed over several bills, told the hostess to keep the change and pulled Millie out of the restaurant.

They were halfway back to the strip mall where their cars were parked, and Millie couldn't stand it anymore. "All I wanted was food." She huffed.

"Don't look so cute, and you won't have guys falling all over you." Josh suggested.

Millie stopped walking and rounded on Josh. "I am pale with dark circles under my eyes, I don't think I have showered in three days, and I am dressed in a baggy t-shirt and yoga pants because I can't button my jeans. I am not cute."

Aiden chuckled as he pulled her into an embrace. Millie was still fuming. She was hungry and wanted to eat before her nausea came back. She tried to push away from Aiden, but he tightened his hold on her.

"You can take out your anger on Josh after we get some food in you." Aiden chuckled and Millie sighed.

When she relaxed, Aiden released her. She followed him the rest of the way to the parking lot. Aiden led them to a grassy spot in the shade and Millie plopped down with a huff. Josh was trying not to laugh, and Millie shot him a glare.

Aiden passed the quesadilla over to her and Millie quickly started to devour it. She only had a few bites left when the wind shifted, and the smell of fish hit her. Her stomach clenched as her head snapped up to see Josh taking a bite of a taco. The wind blew again, and Millie was scrambling to her feet.

"Josh!" she yelled as she made it to the tree that was a few feet away and thew up. Her stomach didn't stop forcing up her lunch until everything was out of it.

"Josh, take the tacos to the car and bring me my extra water bottle." Aiden said as a hand landed on Millie's shoulder.

She sagged against the tree as she clenched her stomach. Josh came running and handed a water bottle to Aiden. He unscrewed the lid and passed it to Millie. She took a mouthful of water, swished it around, and spit it out before taking a sip.

She moved back to where their lunch was and sat down. Josh and Aiden sat slowly while they studied her. "I hate you so much right now, Josh." Millie laid back on the grass. "That was the best quesadilla I have had in forever, and you ruined it." Millie rolled on her side and closed her eyes.

"I'm so sorry, Millie. I didn't realize that fish affected you when I ordered, and you didn't say anything." Josh said quickly.

"I didn't hear what you ordered." Millie whispered. "And I didn't know how much my body hated fish."

Millie was curled into a ball with her hand on her stomach. All she wanted was something to eat and she got hit on by some random guy and she threw up her food.

"How are you feeling now?" Aiden asked quietly after a few minutes.

"Like the best thing in my life was just thrown up at the base of a tree." Millie grumbled and then sighed as she sat up. "Hand me the burrito, please."

"Are you sure? You just upchucked by the tree." Josh asked skeptically.

"Give. Me. My. Burrito." Millie said slowly. Josh handed it to her quickly. "Thank you." Millie smiled.

She ate slowly, savoring every bite. She thought the chicken quesadilla was amazing, but this carne asada burrito was complete heaven. Millie sighed when she took her last bite.

"Feeling better, Millie?" Aiden asked and she looked at him. He was smiling at her.

"Mmhmm." Millie hummed as she patted her full belly. "Feels good to have food in me."'

Millie's phone started to ring, and she looked at it. Seeing Beth's name on the screen, she answered it quickly. "Hey."

"Where the heck are you?" Beth said without preamble.

Millie pulled the phone from her ear and looked at the time. "Oh, no." Millie put the phone back to her ear. "I'm on my way. I'll be there in about twenty minutes."

She hung up the phone and got to her feet. Millie started to gather up the trash quickly. Josh and Aiden helped her get everything cleaned up. As they walked back to the cars, Josh grabbed her arm, stopping her before she climbed in.

"Where are you going in such a rush?" Josh asked curiously.

"I forgot about date night." Millie gave him a quick hug. "Thank you so much for this afternoon, but I am so late." Millie turned to Aiden and embraced him. "You guys are seriously the best."

Millie jumped in her car and started it. Beth was going to kill her. Millie promised to babysit so that Beth and Derek could go out on a date. She glanced in her rearview mirror and saw Josh and Aiden watching her as she drove away. How would she have gotten through her appointment without them?

Beth and Derek were relieved to see Millie when she arrived. Millie was just over an hour late getting to their house and she felt terrible. She apologized profusely and they left with barely enough time to catch their movie.

Millie sat on the couch, exhausted. Today had been mentally and emotionally exhausting. She made the decision to keep the baby, which took a load off her shoulders, but also added some stress. How was she going to raise a baby on her own?

"Can we read a story?" Bentley asked.

"Of course we can. Go grab a book and we will read it here." Bentley ran up the stairs squealing.

Millie couldn't help laughing at the little boy's delight. She picked up the baby while she waited for Bentley to return. Melody cooed in Millie's arms, content just to be held. He returned quickly and Millie had the boy giggling within minutes.

They spent the rest of the evening reading books and playing games. She fed the kids and put Bentley to bed. The house was quiet, and Millie sat in a rocking chair rocking Melody. The sweet baby girl was sound asleep, but Millie couldn't bring herself to put her down.

She studied every detail about the infant. Millie felt peace fill her. She knew her decision to keep the baby was the right one. She didn't know how things would work out, but she knew they would.

Chapter 7

Millie was so busy over the past three weeks with homework, group projects, lectures, and work, that she hadn't been able to finish moving her stuff to her new place. The good thing about her apartment was all the big furnishings would stay with the unit. The bad thing about that was she now needed to go shopping.

Money wasn't an issue for her. Her grandmother had a ton of money and an amazing life insurance policy. Everything was given to Millie when she passed. One thing she learned from her grandmother was to live a simple life, even though they had more than enough money.

Millie invested most of the funds and only pulled from the earned interest to pay for school. She had also taken out money to purchase her home. And she would need to again to furnish the place. Baby items and new clothes for herself were on the list to purchase as well. It was getting hard to find pants she could wear in her current wardrobe. Millie was snapped out of her thoughts when she heard someone call her name.

She glanced around the large grassy lawn that had a building on all four sides of it, without slowing her steps. The students referred to this part of campus as The Quad. She didn't see anyone she recognized so she continued walking.

Millie was nearly inside the library when her arm was grabbed. She gasped in surprise as she turned to see who it was. She fully expected to see Lawrence, but it was Aiden.

Millie sighed in relief as she pressed a hand to her stomach. "You scared me." She breathed out.

"Sorry. I did try to get your attention, but you didn't seem to hear me." Aiden smiled down at her.

"Can you two, like, move out of the way." an irritated girl said.

"Sorry." Aiden told her as he put an arm around Millie's waist and pulled her off to the side.

"What are you doing here?" Millie asked, leaning against the wall.

"I just got done with a group meeting for English. What about you?" Aiden was standing so close that Millie could smell his aftershave. He shifted closer to her as a group of boys walked by, nearly bumping into them.

"I have a group meeting in two hours so I'm avoiding going back to my apartment until then." Millie shrugged.

"Why are you avoiding your apartment? Did something happen?" Aiden asked, concern lacing his voice.

Millie unconsciously put her hand on his chest. "It's just Cindy. She has been a giant pain for the two years I have lived there. Thankfully, it won't be an issue much longer."

"Oh?" Aiden raised a brow.

Someone bumped into Aiden's back, and he stumbled into her. "Maybe we could go somewhere else if you want to talk." Millie suggested in a whisper.

Aiden grabbed her hand and led her up the stairs and down a few hallways until they reached a secluded lounge area. Not many people were around, and Millie collapsed onto a couch, out of breath. Aiden took the seat next to her.

"Next time can we take the elevator?" Millie asked, turning her head to look at Aiden. "I get so winded lately."

"Oh, sorry." Aiden said softly. "I didn't realize..." his voice trailed off and Millie shrugged. "You were saying Cindy wasn't going to be an issue for much longer?"

Millie nodded. "Yeah,"

"Hey, Aiden." A man approached them with a big grin on his face. "Man, I haven't seen you all semester."

Aiden stood and shook the man's hand before sitting back down. "How's it going, Cory?"

"Same old, same old. School, work, sleep." Cory's eyes shifted to Millie, and she felt her cheeks heat at his admiring gaze. "Are you going to introduce me to your lovely companion?"

"This is Millie. Millie, this is Cory. We had a few classes together last semester." Aiden didn't sound thrilled to be making the introductions.

Millie gave a small wave before grabbing Aiden's arm. She hated it when the attention was on her, and Cory was definitely focused on her.

"So, how did you two meet?" Cory asked.

"My car had issues. Aiden and Josh helped me out." Millie said quietly.

"They are some of the nicest guys." Cory nodded. "Are you two dating?"

Millie tensed. Why did this keep happening? Her grip on Aiden's arm tightened. She could see out of the corner of her eye that Aiden looked down at her. "What do you think?" She asked Cory.

"I think Aiden would be a fool not to date such a beautiful woman. And it would surprise me if you were single." Cory scratched his jaw as if pondering something. His eyes narrowed as he studied her. "Wait. Millie, as in Lawrence's Millie?"

Millie's face paled. How did Cory know her and Lawrence? "I never belonged to anyone. That would be slavery. As for Lawrence, he has been out of my life for four months now." Millie's grip on Aiden's arm had to be painful for him, but she couldn't let go.

"That's weird. He's been asking about you." Cory looked confused. Millie's stomach clenched at the thought of Lawrence asking about her.

Aiden's hand covered hers and her hand relaxed enough that he pulled his arm away and draped it around her shoulders. "So, what brings you to the library?" Aiden asked Cory.

Millie laid her head on Aiden's left shoulder. His right hand grabbed her hand that she placed on his chest, lacing their fingers. Millie tuned out Cory and Aiden as they talked about classes and sports. Her eyes began to droop, and her body started to relax.

"I think your girl is asleep." Cory said quietly. Millie didn't move. Maybe he would leave if he thought she was sleeping.

"Hmm?" Aiden shifted slightly as if he was trying to see her face. "Millie isn't my girl; she is just a friend." Aiden softly said.

"If I were you, I would rethink being in the 'friend zone'. I have known you for a while now Aiden, and not once have I seen you hold hands let alone cuddle with a woman before. Even if you don't realize it yet, my friend, you have feelings for her." Cory commented seriously.

Aiden ran his fingers over her arm slowly. "She is something else. Smart, beautiful, funny, playful, brave. I have never met anyone like her before." Aiden's already quiet voice got quieter.

Millie's heart skittered to a stop before double timing it to make up for the skipped beat. Cory laughed and Millie jumped. She made a show of looking around as if she were disoriented. She didn't want either of them knowing she had heard them.

"I'm so sorry. I didn't mean to fall asleep." Her eyes met Aiden's and she felt herself blush. Millie prayed that he would think her blush was from falling asleep on him, and not that she had overheard what he had said.

"It's okay, I don't think Aiden minded." Cory smirked at them. "Remember what I said about zones, Aiden." Cory winked at her before walking away.

They sat quietly for several minutes. Millie's mind turned back to her massive list of what she needed to buy for the house. Millie sat up and turned to face Aiden. He moved his arm to the back of the couch as he angled more towards her.

"Can I borrow your truck this weekend?" Millie asked.

"That shouldn't be a problem, but can I ask why?" Aiden asked softly.

"I need to purchase some furniture."

"Furniture? Like a crib or something?" His hand moved a little and Millie became aware that he was still holding her hand.

Millie smiled. "Like a bed, dresser, dining room table and chairs, a couch or two, end tables, TV, and a few other things."

"Sounds like you are furnishing an entire house." Aiden commented with a confused expression.

"I am." Aiden only looked more confused, so Millie continued. "I can't handle living next to Cindy anymore, Aiden. It's been nonstop Lawrence this and Lawrence that. Why have you been staying out late? Who are those two guys? You can't be dating both at the same time. You should try to patch things up with Lawrence. Why haven't you been at church?" Millie mimicked Cindy's voice.

"Why is she so up in your business?" Aiden asked as his lips twitched. He looked like he was trying to hold back a laugh.

"She says she is my ministering sister, so she is supposed to know what's going on in my life." Millie let out a frustrated huff. "I kind of yelled at her and told her my personal relationships have nothing to do with her before slamming the door in her face." Aiden's smile broke free and he chuckled. "Within a week, I was purchasing a house."

"You purchased a house?" Aiden sounded surprised.

"Yeah. I have been slowly moving my stuff over to it for several weeks now. And I have been going to church with Beth and Derek to avoid Cindy." Millie sighed. "I am a terrible person."

Aiden tucked her hair behind her ear before stopping at her neck. His thumb brushed her jaw lightly. "You are not a terrible person, Millie. You are a saint for putting up with Cindy for so long." The smile he gave her made her insides melt. "Now, about this weekend..."

"Can we trade vehicles Friday night and then trade back Sunday at Beth and Derek's?" Millie found she couldn't pull her eyes away from Aiden's.

After her appointment three weeks ago, she had hung out with Aiden and Josh several times. They watched movies and played board games. She found that she really enjoyed hanging out with them. She was comfortable with them, and they were turning out to be great friends. However, she often had to remind herself that Aiden was only a friend, nothing more.

He was staring at her with an intensity that was making it hard for Millie to concentrate. Lawrence had never looked at her this way, and she definitely had never felt like this with him either.

"I don't think that is going to work." Aiden's smile became crooked as his eyes brightened with humor.

"You just said I could borrow it." Millie pouted. Aiden's thumb lightly brushed her jaw again which was crazy distracting.

"I did. But how are you going to get all this furniture into the house by yourself?" Aiden asked and Millie's brow furrowed. She hadn't thought about that. "I will pick you up at eight on Saturday morning and we can go together. Unfortunately, Josh has a huge project he will be working on this weekend, but I am sure Derek and Beth would come help unload stuff."

"Aiden, I am sure you have better things to do then help me buy furniture." Millie said. As much as she would like to spend the day with him, she couldn't ask him to change his plans for her.

"I might be overstepping here, but I don't like the idea of you lifting heavy things in your current condition." He whispered as he glanced down towards her stomach.

Millie tried to fight the smile that wanted to break free but lost. "You do realize that I am pregnant, not an invalid, right?"

Aiden scowled at her. "I never said you were an invalid. But I still don't like the thought of you lifting furniture by yourself. There is no need for you to risk yourself or the baby getting hurt when I am here to help."

Millie studied Aiden's face and sudden tense posture. He seemed to really be upset. Did he really feel this protective of her? They were sitting so close on the couch that their faces were almost touching. Millie leaned forward and pressed a quick kiss to Aiden's cheek.

"Thank you, Aiden, for looking out for us." She stood and grabbed her backpack off the floor. "See you at eight on Saturday." Millie resisted the urge to turn back around to see his reaction as she walked away.

She couldn't believe she had kissed him. It was only on the cheek but still, they were friends. Memories from the conversation she wasn't meant to hear between Aiden and Cory came back to her. He said he had never met anyone like her before, but that didn't mean he liked her romantically. And who would want to tie themselves to a woman who was pregnant with another man's baby?

Chapter 8

Millie exited the doctor's office and got into her car. Dr. Spaulding was glad that Millie was starting to finally gain a little weight. She had lost nearly twenty pounds in her first trimester. Now that she was sixteen weeks, Millie knew that she wasn't going to last much longer without buying clothes that fit. These days, she either wore sweatpants or yoga pants.

Millie arrived at the bank just before closing and was able to pull money from her savings account so she could purchase furniture and clothes the next day. Beth had reached out to Millie the other day to get the address of her new place so they could meet her there to unload the truck.

By the time Millie got home, it was late. She parked and headed up the stairs, ready for some food and to go to bed. Millie unlocked her door and headed straight for the kitchen. A noise in the front room startled her and she spun around. Sitting on the couch was Lawrence. Millie gasped in surprise.

"Hey, baby." Lawrence stood as he smiled at her.

"How did you get in here?" Millie asked as she inched towards the hallway.

"You are my wife, Millie. It didn't take long to convince the apartment manager to let me in." Lawrence smirked at her.

"We are not married, Lawrence. You made sure of that. Now leave." Millie demanded.

"I'm not going anywhere. I plan on spending the night with my wife." Lawrence eyed her up a down.

Millie felt sick. She turned and bolted for the bathroom. She slammed and locked the door. With shaking hands, she pulled her phone out of her pocket.

"Come on out, Millie. We need to talk about what happened so we can go to bed." Lawrence said from the other side of the door.

Millie: Are either of you busy?"

Josh: I am still at the school trying to finish an assignment.
Aiden: I'm free.
Millie: Can you come pick me up?
Aiden: Right now?
Millie: Please.
Aiden: Be there in five.
Millie: Just send a text when you get here.

Lawrence knocked again. Millie took several deep breaths and opened the door. She shoved past him and went to her room and locked herself inside. She grabbed a week's worth of clothing, her brush, and her laptop and shoved them into a duffle bag while Lawrence begged her to open the door. His voice was becoming more and more irritated while his words remained apologetic. A bad feeling settled over her, and the need to get out of the apartment grew.

Millie's phone dinged and when she saw it was a text from Aiden, she opened her bedroom door and pushed past Lawrence again. She wanted out of this apartment and away from him as fast as possible. She didn't care where she went.

"I get that you are mad, Millie. Just talk to me." Lawrence followed her to the door.

She opened it and he tried to grab her. Millie twisted away from him and ran down the stairs. Tears began to fall when she saw Aiden's truck idling at the curb.

Lawrence grabbed her arm and spun her around to face him. "Where do you think you are going? You belong with me."

"Let go of me, Lawrence." Millie once again twisted and broke his hold.

She immediately started running for the truck again. Aiden was getting out of the truck, and she ran right to him. She dropped her bag on the ground as he wrapped his arms around her. She clung to him, feeling a little safer now that Aiden was there.

"You have no right to be touching her!" Lawrence yelled.

"Aiden, please can we go?" Millie begged.

"Climb in and slide over. I will grab your bag." Aiden whispered as he pushed her gently towards the truck, shielding her from Lawrence.

"You take one more step and I will call the police." Aiden warned. "Millie obviously doesn't want to be around you right now, so I suggest you back off."

Millie glanced through the open driver's side door and watched as Aiden slowly reached down and grabbed her bag. Lawrence was glaring at her; his face was red and his hands were fisted at his sides. He looked ticked. Aiden hopped up into the truck and drove away.

Millie turned to look out her window as her shaking grew worse. She could not believe Lawrence had been in her apartment. The tone in his voice and the way he had just looked at her scared her. She had never seen him like that.

Why would her apartment manager let him in? Especially after she had her apartment re-keyed. Millie didn't understand Lawrence's motives for trying to get back together. It had been nearly four months since their botched wedding. She had told him to leave her alone several weeks ago and then changed her number. Why couldn't he take a hint?

"Millie?" Aiden's soothing voice was quiet.

Millie glanced around her. They were parked along a street in a neighborhood. Her door was open, and Aiden was standing there. He watched her with concern as she trembled from her encounter with Lawrence.

Aiden took a step back to allow her room to get out, but she threw her arms around his neck as she slid out of the truck. His arms held her tightly to him. He didn't say anything as she cried. Her tears were a mix of frustration, fear, and relief that Aiden had been willing to come, no questions asked, in the middle of the night.

Aiden's hand cradled the back of her head as she buried her face in his chest. "Did he hurt you?" Aiden asked softly.

Millie squeezed her eyes shut. Would Lawrence have hurt her if she had stayed in the apartment? A shutter ran through her.

"Millie, did he hurt you?" Aiden asked more firmly, his body tensing slightly.

Millie slowly shook her head. "No." she tilted her head back to look up into Aiden's face. "But Aiden, Lawrence was in my apartment when I got home."

Aiden rested his forehead against hers as he closed his eyes briefly. "I don't think you should go back to the apartment alone and I think we should get you moved out as soon as possible."

Millie nodded before laying her head against Aiden's chest. She closed her eyes and listened to the rhythmic sound of his heart beating. After several minutes, her shaking stopped, and she started to relax. She felt safe and protected with Aiden.

"Do you know that car?" Aiden whispered close to her ear.

Millie turned slightly to see what car Aiden was referring to. She recognized Lawrence's yellow sports car immediately. It was driving slowly down the road. Millie's hands on Aiden's chest clenched, causing her to grab fistfuls of his shirt as her whole body tensed.

"Aiden." Millie whimpered softly.

Millie's eyes were glued to the car as it reached the end of the road and turned around. Aiden cupped her cheek, forcing her to look at him. He pushed her up against the side of the truck and pressed his body close.

"I think he recognized my truck, but I don't think he saw us." Aiden whispered. "Hopefully, he doesn't see us and drives past again."

Millie held as still as she could, not daring to even breathe. Aiden's body tensed and she knew that Lawrence was driving past them. Millie silently prayed that he would just drive by, that she and Aiden would be protected.

"Okay, he continued going, but it looks like he is going to turn back around." Aiden whispered. "We are going to head to the house."

Aiden moved away from her and grabbed her hand, but Millie didn't move. Lawrence was going to see them. He had followed them all the way here; for crying out loud. What did he want? "Aiden," Millie started to protest.

Aiden pressed a kiss to her forehead and her protest died on her lips. "We can make it inside before he drives back this way, but we need to go now."

Millie allowed Aiden to lead them through the shadows as they moved down the next street. Millie immediately recognized Beth's home three houses down. Aiden had brought her to Beth's. Gratitude for this man swelled in her. She hadn't even thought of where she was going to stay for the night, but Aiden had.

Tears burned Millie's eyes as her emotions began to surface. Lawrence's sudden appearance, then Aiden's protection and thoughtfulness, had Millie feeling like a time bomb that was ready to explode.

All the windows were dark as they approached the house. Instead of going to the front, Aiden pulled her around to the back. Just as he closed the gate behind them, the sound of a car driving slowly on the road reached Millie's ears. Aiden moved to the sliding door. He tried to open it, but it was locked.

Aiden pulled out his cell phone, hit a few buttons, and placed it to his ear. Millie could hear it ring before it went to voicemail. Millie used her free hand to wipe away the tears that had managed to escape. Aiden glanced at her before wrapping his arms around her. He held her close as he made another call. Millie pressed herself closer to Aiden as she bit the inside of her cheek to keep herself from crying again.

"Aiden, what's going on?" Derek's sleepy voice whispered through the phone.

"I am so sorry for waking you, but I didn't know where else to go." Aiden said, keeping his voice low.

There was a brief pause before Derek spoke again. "What's going on?"

"I would love to know all the details, too, but I think we should get Millie inside before we go into explanations." Aiden answered. "We are on your back porch."

The phone call ended and two minutes later the kitchen light turned on. Derek yanked open the sliding door and Aiden ushered Millie in. Beth came running into the kitchen wearing a robe over her pajamas. When she saw Millie clinging to Aiden, she rushed to her side.

Beth touched Millie's shoulder as she studied her. "What on earth is going on?" Millie's chin began to tremble again. Beth turned her attention to Aiden when Millie couldn't seem to answer.

"Millie texted asking if Josh or I could pick her up. When I got to her apartment, she was running towards my truck. A man grabbed her, and she broke from his hold. I got her in the truck and drove off. She wouldn't respond to any of my questions." Aiden explained. "I didn't know where else to take her. So, I drove here and parked around the corner."

Millie hadn't heard him during the drive. She had no idea that she was unresponsive. Lawrence's sudden presence had really messed with her.

"I noticed a car driving slowly and Millie recognized it. We came to the back door so he wouldn't know which house we went to." Aiden's arms around her relaxed a little as he spoke.

"Did he hurt you?" Derek asked as his jaw clenched.

Millie shook her head. "No." Millie sighed tiredly. Now that she was safe, she felt exhausted.

"Come on, Millie. Let's get you sitting down. You look dead on your feet." Beth said and grabbed Millie's hand.

Millie grudgingly followed Beth into the living room. Only a small lamp was on, giving enough light for them to see, but not bright enough to see through the blackout curtains. Beth led Millie to a couch and pulled her down next to her.

"Tell me what happened." Beth's said softly.

Millie laid her head on her friend's shoulder. "It was late when I got done with a project and I went home. I unlocked my door and walked into my kitchen. I heard something behind me. When I turned around, Lawrence was getting off the couch."

"What? We re-keyed your lock. He shouldn't have been able to get in." Derek interrupted.

"He said the apartment manager let him in after he told him he was my husband." Millie swiped a tear away. "I told him we weren't married and that he needed to leave, but he refused. He kept saying we needed to talk about things so we could go to bed. I locked myself in the bathroom and texted Aiden and Josh. When Aiden agreed to come pick me up, I went to my room and packed some clothes."

"Where was Lawrence while you were packing?" Beth asked.

"Knocking on the door, begging me to talk to him." Millie scoffed. "As soon as Aiden texted saying he was out front, I ran outside. Lawrence was so insistent. I have never seen him like that. It scared me." Millie looked at Aiden. "Thank you for coming in the middle of the night to get me."

"You aren't going back to your apartment." Derek stated firmly. "If you need something from there, one of us will get it for you."

"I don't have much left. Most of my stuff is at the house." Millie yawned.

"Josh is going to be so angry that he was working on a project tonight." Beth commented.

"We need to figure out what to do about Millie's apartment and Lawrence driving around the neighborhood. Millie's bags are still in the truck, and I don't want him coming here." Aiden said.

"Let him come." Derek said menacingly. "Let him try to get to her."

Millie's eyes began to droop as her friends continued to talk. She was so exhausted. Beth started to run her hands through Millie's hair, lulling her closer to sleep. Millie's body grew heavy, and her eyes fully closed.

"Aiden, you can stay here tonight." Beth whispered. "You can sleep in Derek's mancave above the garage and Millie can take the guest room upstairs."

"I can sleep on the couch." Millie mumbled.

"Not a chance. I am sleeping on the couch to make sure that guy doesn't come here. Aiden, get her upstairs while Beth gets your bedding and I get my gun out of the safe." Derek said.

Millie opened her eyes as Aiden scooped her up into his arms. She laid her head on his shoulder. "I can walk." Millie whispered.

Aiden chuckled. "You are already falling back asleep, Millie."

"Thank you, Aiden." Millie sighed as Aiden started climbing the stairs.

"Anytime." Aiden whispered. Millie's eyes were closed but opened them when Aiden laid her on a bed. He brushed her hair back from her face. "Are you sure he didn't hurt you, Millie?" He studied her with concern evident in his eyes.

"He didn't hurt me. I was more scared and freaked out than anything. I was so tired when I got home, then he was there, and I panicked. I thought telling him to leave me alone and then changing my number would have driven home that point." Millie closed her eyes and took a deep breath.

"Try to get some sleep." Aiden whispered.

"Aiden." Millie's eyes flew open, and she bolted upright. He had only taken a few steps away. He was back at her side in seconds when he saw the panicked look on her face.

"What is it?" he asked.

Millie bit her lip and looked down at her hands. Aiden couldn't stay with her, she knew that. She didn't know why she had panicked when he started to leave. Aiden was a great friend and went out of his way to help her more than once. But they weren't dating, and she never thought he would ask her out.

"Never mind." Millie whispered.

"I will be just above the garage and Derek is downstairs." Aiden hooked his finger under her chin, and she looked up at him. "You are safe, Millie."

Millie let out a tense breath and nodded. "Good night, Aiden."

There was a moment of hesitation before Aiden left the room. Millie took off her sweatshirt and tossed it aside. She crawled under the covers and closed her eyes again.

Chapter 9

Millie stretched and opened her eyes. She was in an unfamiliar room and a moment of panic took the air from her lungs. A child's laughter floated into the room moments before Bentley came running in.

"Mil!" Bentley yelled. "Mom said you were sleeping."

Millie smiled when she caught Bentley as he jumped on her. "Good morning to you too, young man." Millie blew a raspberry on the little boy's tummy before setting him back on the floor. "Where is your mommy?"

"The kitchen." Bentley said as he grabbed her hand, pulling her from the room.

Millie walked into the kitchen with Bentley. Beth was setting bowls of cereal on the table for the kids. When she saw Millie, she smiled.

"I was beginning to wonder when you would wake up." Beth pointed to the table and Bentley took his seat and she gave him a bowl.

"What time is it?" Millie asked, taking a seat next to Bentley.

"Almost nine. Derek and Aiden left a little bit ago to pick up your car and Josh." Beth said as she rinsed a dish off in the sink.

"When do they get back?" Millie was a little hurt that Aiden didn't tell her he was leaving. Why hadn't they woken her up?

"I'm not sure. Derek said he would call when they were headed back."

Millie bit her lip as she thought. She needed to talk with Mrs. White about Lawrence's behavior last night and she still needed to go shopping. "Can I borrow your car today?" Millie walked over to Beth. "I have so much I need to do."

Beth looked unsure. "The guys seemed really worried about you. Do you think you should go alone?"

"I won't let Lawrence dictate my life. If I let what he did last night keep me from living my life, I am catering to him." Millie leaned against the counter.

"I doubt he will be at any of the places I am going to anyway. I don't see him going to a maternity store."

Beth looked down at Millie's growing stomach. Without her sweatshirt, you could now start to see a baby bump. Millie tugged the hem of her shirt down to fully cover her stomach.

Beth laughed as she retrieved her keys. "Okay but be careful. Call if you need anything."

"Thank you, Beth." Millie hugged her before running back upstairs to get her sweatshirt.

Beth gave Millie store suggestions for maternity clothes before she left. As Millie drove, she pulled out her phone and called her lawyer. She prayed the older woman would answer the phone, even though it was the weekend.

"Good morning, Ms. Larson. What can I do for you?" Mrs. White said.

"I'm sorry to bother you on a weekend, but Lawrence showed up at my apartment last night." Millie said quickly.

"What do you mean, he showed up at your apartment?" Mrs. White sounded concerned.

Millie filled her in on the previous night's events. Mrs. White assured her that she would start the paperwork to file for a restraining order immediately. Millie felt marginally relieved after the phone call. Even though Mrs. White was starting the process to get the restraining order, she wasn't sure if she would be able to get it in place before the weekend was over.

Spotting the first store Beth had suggested, Millie pulled into the parking lot. Millie could not believe how expensive maternity clothes were. She only needed a few pairs of pants and a few shirts right now. She was just big enough that her normal clothes didn't fit, but small enough that she didn't fit into most of the maternity clothes.

After several hundred dollars, Millie walked out of the store with a new wardrobe. It was hard for her to spend so much money all at once, but it couldn't be helped. Millie loaded the clothes into the trunk just as her phone began to ring.

"Hey, Beth." Millie answered as she sat behind the wheel.

"Okay, so I am in trouble." Beth said dramatically.

"Why is that?" Millie laughed as she started the car.

"Because I let you take the car." Beth sighed. "Apparently the world is now going to come to an end. Hey!"

"Where are you, Millie?" Derek's voice came on the line.

"Good to talk to you too." Millie pulled onto the street and started to drive to a furniture store where she was hoping to find a few things.

"Where are you?" Derek asked again.

"Running errands. Why?" Millie didn't understand why he was so upset.

"Your ex lied and wormed his way into your apartment to ambush you in the middle of the night. Aiden had to rescue you. Then your ex drove around the neighborhood until I called the cops." Derek fumed.

"You called the cops?" Millie asked in disbelief.

"You better believe I did." Derek said.

Millie needed to let Mrs. White know that the police were called. "I have to go." Millie hung up the phone and dialed Mrs. White. She told her about Derek calling the police.

Mrs. White told Millie to be careful and to stay away from the apartment. Millie agreed and hung up the phone as she pulled into a parking spot. Before getting out of the car, she sent a quick text to Beth letting her know that she was fine, that she had to take an important phone call, and to apologize to Derek for hanging up on him.

The store was everything she had hoped for. The furniture was made of solid wood and had a farmhouse feel to it. She found a table she liked that had a white weathered base and legs with a dark wood top. She got matching chairs to seat eight and a matching buffet table.

While looking at the couches, Millie found a coffee table and side tables that were miniature versions of the dining room table. She chose a light grey living room set that had a couch, loveseat, and two armchairs.

Millie was inside the store for nearly four hours by the time she found everything she wanted. She got a queen-sized bed, a desk and computer chair, bookcases, bedside tables, couches, tables and chairs, barstools, a dresser, coat and shoe rack, and a porch swing. She felt immensely proud of herself for only having to go to two stores to get everything she needed.

Millie had spent a few minutes looking at the baby furniture and vowed to come back when she was preparing the nursery. They had the cutest cribs and baby furniture at the back of the store. Millie climbed into Beth's car and reached for her phone. She had realized she had left it in the car when she was making her purchase.

Millie sighed when she had multiple missed calls and texts from Derek, Beth, Aiden and Josh. Deciding Beth would be the less volatile person among them, she called her.

"You are in so much trouble, missy." Beth whisper-yelled. "You are lucky that I am upstairs feeding Melody right now. The guys are having a freaking cow."

"I'm sorry. I accidentally left my phone in the car while I was inside the store." Millie apologized as she headed to the grocery store.

"Where are you, now?"

"I am heading to pick up groceries. Could you and the guys meet me at my new house at three?" Millie asked. "And bring your swimsuits."

"Sure thing, but I'm not telling them until it is time to go." Beth laughed. "You would think that they care about you or something."

"I care about them, too. It's been nice having brother-like protectors." Millie laughed.

"I'm not sure Aiden has brother-like feelings for you." Beth said with a smile in her voice.

"What are you talking about? We are just friends." Millie's stomach did a somersault and her cheeks heated.

"I am saying we need to have a girls' night because there is definitely something going on between you two." Beth teased.

"A girls' night sounds amazing." Millie sighed. "I will meet you at my house soon. Is there anything you want me to pick up for dinner?"

"Whatever you decide will be fine." Beth answered as she lowered her voice. "Oh shoot, Derek is coming up the stairs. See you soon."

Millie laughed as the phone call ended. She stopped by a drive-thru on her way to the grocery store, since she hadn't eaten much all day. She walked around the store stocking up on all the essentials and staples she would need: toilet paper, plates, silverware, towels, shampoo and conditioner, food and seasonings, pool toys, hangers, trash can and liner, and cleaners. By the end, she had two overflowing grocery carts.

The cashier was amazing and called for a cart boy to help her out to her car. He even helped load everything. Millie was exhausted by the time she pulled onto her driveway, but a smile spread across her face as she drove down the long tree line lane.

The house came into view and Millie's breath caught. She loved this house. The house was a two-story white paneled farmhouse style home with a grey stone foundation and white pillars. The porch wrapped around to each side. There were two large doors at the top of wide steps with a chandelier that hung over the entry.

She parked the car in the garage and went inside with an armful of grocery bags. She set them on the counter. It took Millie thirty minutes to unload the car and put the groceries away. She was glad she had purchased a fridge and standing freezer several weeks ago.

Millie was placing her last few bags of clothes in the master bedroom closet when a notification went off on her phone. Beth texted saying they were five minutes away. Millie smiled as she went out onto the front porch and sat down. She wished she could see Beth's face when she first saw the house.

The sound of multiple vehicles on the gravel driveway reached her moments before three cars came into view. Derek's car was in the lead, followed by her car and then Aiden's truck. Millie got to her feet as Derek stopped the car in front of the house.

Beth slowly got out of the car with her mouth wide open. Her gaze finally landed on Millie. "*This* is the house you bought?"

"Do you like it?" Millie asked, turning to admire her home.

Millie laughed when Beth smacked her shoulder. "You told me you bought a cute house. This is not cute, Millie. This place is gorgeous."

"You haven't even seen the inside yet." Millie slung her arm over Beth's shoulders. "How mad are they? I'm afraid to turn around." She whispered.

Beth laughed as she turned them both around before stepping away from Millie. All three men were gaping at the house. Josh was the first to recover. He stepped up to her and gave her a hug.

"Why didn't you say something like 'crazy ex. Need help asap.'? I would have done my homework later." Josh squeezed her tighter. "Did he hurt you? Is the baby okay? Where have you been?" Josh asked rapid fire questions.

Millie put her hands on his shoulders and gave him a little shake. "I am going to need you to breathe, Josh. I am fine. Lawrence didn't touch me. And I had some stuff to do today."

"He grabbed you." Aiden stepped up to her side.

"I am fine." Millie stated firmly.

She let out a squeak of surprise when Derek pulled her into a hug. She hadn't seen him come up on her other side. "You can't scare me like that." he said softly. "You are more than my wife's best friend, Millie. You are family, a sister."

Millie hugged him back, hiding her face as tears welled up in her eyes. She had never imagined she would have such great friends or that they would become family. She blinked back her tears before stepping back and smiling at him.

"Mill!" Bentley hugged her legs. She picked him up and put him on her hip "Your belly's getting big." He patted her stomach.

"Makes it hard to hold on, huh?" Millie turned towards the house and headed inside to hide her blush. She wore sweatshirts on purpose. They hide her growing belly. "I have a surprise for my favorite little man, would you like to see it?"

Bentley squealed as he squirmed to get down. Millie set him on his feet before opening the front door. Millie heard Beth gasp as they entered behind her.

They stood in a large foyer that was open to the living room straight ahead, with the den on the left and the dining room on the right. Millie walked into the living room holding Bentley's hand. The far wall was glass doors that opened up onto the back porch and pool deck.

"A pool!" Bentley pulled free of Millie's hand and pressed his face to the glass as he stared out at the pool.

"If your mom remembered to bring your swimming suits, we can go swimming while the big boys help unload the truck." Millie crouched down to Bentley's level. "I also have popsicles." She whispered, and he cheered.

"Millie, this place is incredible." Beth breathed out as she walked through the kitchen that was separated from the living room by an island.

"Would you like the grand tour?" Millie asked, walking over to Beth.

Beth nodded excitedly. The guys remained silent as she took them through the house. There was a small hallway that had a bathroom and the entrance to the garage off the kitchen. A huge walk-in pantry and laundry room/ mudroom were also off the kitchen. An office opened off the dining room.

On the other side of the house, by the den, was the master suite. Glass doors opened onto the back porch from the bedroom. There was also a large walk-in closet and huge bathroom. The second floor had three bedrooms, two bathrooms, loft, and media space. The last thing she showed them was the three-car garage.

"We should probably move some of the cars in here before the delivery truck gets here." Millie said thoughtfully. "They should be here in the next thirty minutes."

"Okay, I lied." Beth shook her head as the group headed back inside. "This place isn't beautiful, its breath taking. How did you ever get this place?" Beth asked, turning to Millie.

Millie felt a blush heating her cheeks. "Oh," Millie rubbed the back of her neck. "I had some money in savings."

"What does the mortgage on a place like this cost? Maybe Aiden and I should try getting something like this." Josh was looking around the space, taking in all the details.

"I don't know." Millie shrugged.

Everyone's heads snapped in her direction. "How do you not know what the mortgage is?" Derek asked in disbelief.

Millie cleared her throat as her cheeks heated more. She was sure she was as red as a tomato. "I don't know because I don't have one." She whispered.

Everyone's eyes went wide. "What?" Beth asked in surprise.

"I purchased this house with cash." Millie swallowed hard. She didn't like telling people she had a couple million in the bank. Lawrence hadn't even known. He signed the prenup without really reading it.

"Uh, clearly I'm missing something." Josh scratched his head. "This house has to be worth half a mil easy. And you paid cash?"

"Well, with the twenty acres and six-stall horse barn, it was a bit more." Millie corrected. "Anyway, we should move the cars."

Millie turned for the front door, but Aiden grabbed her arm. She thought he was going to ask her more questions about money, but he surprised her. "You, Beth, and the kids stay here. Derek, Josh, and I can move the vehicles." Millie gave him a grateful smile before he and the guys walked out the front door.

"Okay girl, start talking." Beth had her hand on one of her hips while she held Melody in the other arm.

"My grandma was filthy rich, but we lived very simply. When she died, she had a crazy life insurance plan. She left everything to me because mom was never around. I haven't seen my mom since I was five and she came for a weekend visit. It had always been just me and Grandma." Millie shrugged. "I live off what I make working at the kids center and only pull from the funds to pay for school."

"So, you have like several hundred grand?" Beth asked.

"More like several million." Millie corrected with a shy smile. "I wanted to move away from Cindy, but there weren't any apartments available until next semester, so I started looking at houses. I found this place by chance and fell in love with it. It had a couple other offers, so I offered cash. It didn't even make a dent in my bank account."

"Are you serious?" Josh asked. Millie spun around. She hadn't heard the guys enter through the garage. "Did you say several million?"

"I-I" Millie stuttered. The doorbell rang and she quickly opened it, grateful for the interruption.

"Are you Millie Larson?" A man asked. He had the logo of the furniture shop and a clipboard.

"I am." Millie nodded.

"We have...wow." The man looked at her in surprise.

"It might be easier if I just look at the list and confirm you have everything." Millie extended her hand, and the man gave her the clipboard. She scanned down it and paused at the last item. "I didn't purchase this." Millie pointed at the item and the man glanced at it before looking at a page underneath.

"Mr. Garcia saw you looking at it, and since you purchased so much, he threw it in for free." The man said reading off his notes. "And he told me to tell you congratulations. Where would you like everything?

Millie stared at the man for a long moment before giving herself a mental shake. She told the delivery guy what rooms to place each item in, while he wrote it down. Derek, Josh, and Aiden followed her so that they could help direct the delivery team.

She followed the guys onto the front porch to sign the delivery papers. "And you said that once everything is in, I need to sign a second form, saying there was no damages?" Millie asked.

"Yes, ma'am, or your husband can sign it." The man nodded towards Aiden.

Millie bit her cheek to stop the blush from coloring her cheeks. Before she could find her voice, all the men were at the back of the delivery truck, and she was standing alone. Millie went back inside and changed into her swimsuit before pulling a large t-shirt over it.

When she rejoined Beth in the living room, several of the dining room chairs had been moved in. She helped Beth get the kids outside and into the fenced pool area. She had the fence installed three weeks ago. She wanted to make sure Bentley and Melody wouldn't have any accidents.

"I got floaties." Millie pointed to the baby floatie and the life jacket on a deck chair.

"You are the best." Beth laughed as she grabbed the baby floatie and headed for the pool stairs with Melody.

Bentley clung to Millie as she entered the pool. "You know this is like a giant bathtub, there isn't anything to be scared of." She told the boy. "And maybe later tonight after dinner, we can come back out and swim with the lights on. They make the water turn whatever color you want."

"Are you serious?" Beth asked as she laughed. Melody was sitting in her baby floatie with a smile on her face.

"It's pretty cool. I also have a pack 'n play if she needs to go down for a nap." Millie smiled at Beth. "I thought about ordering pizza for dinner."

"I want cheese pizza!" Bentley yelled.

"Pizza it is." Millie and Beth laughed.

They played with the kids for an hour before Aiden stepped out onto the back porch. "Hey, Millie." Millie looked at him. "They are ready for you to come examine the furniture and sign off on everything." He opened the pool gate, holding a stack of towels.

"Alright, Bentley, time to get out for a little bit. Aunt Millie needs to order the pizza." Beth said as she made her way to the stairs.

Millie followed her, and Aiden handed them towels while he dried off Bentley. Millie noticed Aiden glancing over at her several times after she pulled her t-shirt off and hung it over the fence. Her tankini shirt wasn't long enough to cover her stomach anymore. She had a feeling he was noticing that her slightly rounded tummy was sticking out. Embarrassed, she wrapped a towel around herself, and they headed inside.

Chapter 10

It took forty-five minutes to go over every piece of furniture, but it all looked fine. The pieces complimented the house nicely and she was super excited. As soon as she signed the paper and the delivery guys left, Millie ordered the pizzas. When she was done, she noticed everyone was outside by the pool.

She stepped outside and they looked at her. "Pizza will be here in thirty minutes." She informed them as she stepped into the pool area.

"Good, cause I'm starving." Josh said before jumping into the pool, splashing everyone.

"Where is Melody?" Millie asked looking around.

"I set up the pack 'n play in the master bedroom and cracked the door open." Beth told Millie as she leaned into Derek as they lounged on a deck chair.

Aiden was already in the pool. He watched her as she moved back to where she had hung her shirt and pulled it on quickly. The fabric was cold, and she gasped. She tossed her towel on a chair and started for the stairs.

"Millie, you can't just walk into the pool." Derek called to her. "The rule is you have to jump."

Millie narrowed her eyes at her friend as all activity in the pool ceased. "It's my pool. Shouldn't I get to set the rules?"

Beth lifted a brow in challenge. Millie sighed. "Okay fine." She could play their game. Before she got pregnant, she swam and danced multiple times a week. She could do several different flips. It shouldn't be too hard to incorporate a flip into a dive.

Millie stood at the edge of the pool and took several deep breaths. She pulled her shirt off as she walked to the diving board. She shook her hands before doing a handstand. It was tougher to balance with her growing belly, but she managed to walk to the middle of the diving board on her hands. Her back was to the pool so she couldn't see anyone's faces.

She took a deep breath before pushing off her hands and landing on her feet, facing the pool. As soon as her feet hit the board, she sprang into a front flip. She rotated one and a half times and dove into the water. When she surfaced, it was quiet.

She wiped the water from her face and smiled at Derek. "That good enough for you?"

"I was honestly expecting just a cannon ball or something." Derek shrugged, even though his eyes were still wide.

"Come on Bentley, it's your turn to jump in." Millie extended her arms to him.

Bentley ran and jumped to her as Aiden moved closer to them. "You are full of surprises today." He smiled at her.

"How so?" Millie asked as she tossed Bentley into the air. "You never expected me to catch Bentley as he jumps into a pool?" Millie glanced over at Aiden and smirked.

"I was thinking more about you taking off this morning, this amazing house, and your ability to dive." Aiden chuckled.

"As for this morning, I refuse to let Lawrence have any control over my life and I desperately needed furniture so I would have a place to sleep. This house," Millie paused and looked back at it and smiled. "Is what I have always pictured myself having. And the diving, I have never done before. I have several things I do weekly to keep myself busy."

"Like diving?" Josh laughed.

"No." Millie kissed Bentley's cheek. "Swimming, boxing..."

"Boxing?" Aiden said in surprise.

Millie laughed. "Twice a week for the last five years. Well, until I became pregnant." Millie blew a raspberry on Bentley's cheek, causing him to laugh and squirm in her arms.

"A baby? Like Melody?" Bentley asked, patting Millie's cheeks. "Are you a mommy like my mommy?" Millie swallowed hard.

"Come on, Bentley, I think your dad just left to get the pizza." Josh lifted Bently out of Millie's arms and she blinked hard.

Millie watched as Josh put Bentley on the pool deck. The little boy ran to his mom, and she wrapped a towel around him. She was going to be a mom. She knew she was having a baby and was slowly getting used to the idea, but Millie never thought of herself as a mom.

A hand touched her back softly and she looked at Aiden. "Are you feeling okay? You went a little pale."

"Yeah, just realized something." Millie turned away from watching Beth and her son, to Aiden. "We should probably get out too." Millie said before she was grabbed from behind.

Josh's laughter rang in her ear as he dragged her to the deep end. She was fighting to get out of his hold while trying not to laugh. He was no doubt going to dunk her. Aiden was laughing as he slowly followed them.

"You know, Millie, squirting my best friend in the face with a hose wasn't very nice." Josh laughed.

"That was weeks ago, Josh. I think your revenge is coming rather late." Millie turned to face him.

"Revenge doesn't have an expiration date." Aiden chuckled.

Millie stopped struggling and allowed Josh to pull her to deeper water. Once they were treading water, she grabbed her stomach and doubled over, gasping as if she were in pain, while her arm went over Josh's shoulders to keep herself above water. Josh instantly loosened his hold on her and Aiden got a panicked look on his face as he swam towards them.

Millie placed her hands on Josh's shoulders and her feet on his chest and pushed off hard, angling her body down. She managed to dive beneath Aiden before she swam along the bottom of the pool, only coming up once she reached the stairs.

She was laughing as she climbed out of the pool. Josh and Aiden were only halfway across when they looked up and saw her with a towel wrapped around herself. As she closed the pool gate, she blew them a kiss.

"I'll try to save a piece of pizza for you both." She called over her shoulder as she hurried inside.

"What's the rush?" Beth asked just as Millie heard the door behind her open.

Arms grabbed her again and she squealed. She was lifted off her feet as Aiden and Josh carried her outside, while Derek opened the door and gate. She continued to try to break free, but before she could, Josh and Aiden jumped in the pool with her. She screamed just before she hit the water.

Millie came up coughing while Aiden and Josh laughed. "That was a dirty trick." Josh scolded her with a grin on his face.

"Says the guy that was trying to dunk me." Millie shot back. She ducked under the water and came up a few feet away, smoothing her hair from her face.

"You made us think that Josh hurt you." Aiden followed her.

"You can't out do me, Aiden. I thought you learned that lesson watching Kevin." Millie smiled at him as she once again climbed out of the pool. She dried herself off with another towel before tossing it to Aiden.

"I'm no quitter." Aiden caught the towel she tossed at him while he held her soaking wet one in the other hand.

Millie felt a stab of irritation. Learning doesn't mean you quit. She glanced over at him, only to find Josh looking between the two of them with narrowed eyes as if trying to decipher something.

"Learning a lesson isn't quitting. If it were, then I am the biggest quitter of all, because I have learned some pretty hard lessons the past several months. Ones I will never repeat again." Millie opened the gate. "I'm going to change."

"Millie, wait." Aiden called after her, but she slipped into her room, closed the patio door and locked it.

Millie took a deep breath to try to calm herself. She had no idea why she was getting so upset. Aiden had been teasing and she knew it. Millie walked into her closet and pulled out pajama pants, a new shirt, and a sweatshirt. Before dressing, she took a quick shower to rinse off the chlorine.

When she walked out of the bathroom, Melody was cooing. She smiled as she picked up the baby girl. Millie took a few minutes to snuggle Melody before heading for the kitchen.

"Look who woke up." Millie kissed Melody's cheek.

"Did you want me to take her?" Beth asked as she took a bite of pizza.

"I've got her. You enjoy eating without a child in your arms." Millie sat in one of the chairs in the living room.

It felt so good to sit down. She had been on her feet all day. After a minute, Beth sat in the chair next to her. "You never did tell me how your appointment went."

"Well, I gained two pounds since my last appointment. But considering I lost more than twenty pounds since I got pregnant, I'm not sure if only a few pounds is good or not."

"Any gained pound is a win for you right now. I only lost like five pounds during my first trimester. I can't imagine losing twenty." Beth shook her head. "What else did the doctor say?"

"She told me I could get back to exercising as long as there is no cramping, and I don't lose weight. The baby's heartbeat is strong, and my blood tests look good." Millie shrugged. "They are planning on doing an anatomy ultrasound at my next appointment."

"Are you planning on finding out if you are having a boy or girl?" Beth asked excitedly.

The guys joined them in the front room. Bentley climbed up on her lap and she shifted Melody to the side to make room for him. Her belly was making it harder to have Bentley on her lap. At least with her hoodie, no one could tell she was getting bigger.

"I'm not sure. I haven't given it much thought."

"You should find out. That way I can buy him or her clothes. And we can know if Melody is going to have a best friend." Beth smiled.

"You should wait." Derek suggested. "That way you could drive Beth crazy."

Millie laughed as she shook her head. "I'll probably flip a coin before going in."

"If it's a boy, you should name him Josh. It's a very strong name." Josh reclined back on the couch as he smiled.

"I haven't even thought about names. It's still hard to believe that I am having a baby. I haven't really planned very far ahead." Millie ran her hand through Bentley's hair as he rested against her.

"We usually picked names that had meaning for us. Family members we wanted to honor." Beth commented.

"I don't even think my mother knew who my father was, and mom dumped me on my grandma within a few days of me being born. I haven't seen or heard from her since I was five. So, I don't know if that method of finding a name is going to work for me." Millie gave Beth a half smile. "We could always throw darts or something."

"You can't name a baby by throwing darts." Derek looked horrified.

"You know what we should do?" Beth sat up in her chair excited energy rolling off her. "We should do a gender reveal party."

"What for?" Millie asked. "You four are the only ones that would be there."

"We can invite people from the ward that you have met, and it can be here. I know for a fact that some of the single men in the ward think you are cute. We could invite them too. I will come help decorate and everything." Beth carried on, oblivious to Millie's sudden anxiety.

"Beth." Millie finally cut her friend off from her ramblings. "I can't have a party." Millie said firmly.

"Why not?" Beth asked, confused.

"My first experience with a group bigger than ten was when I came to college. I have severe social anxiety. I have had private tutors instead of going to school. I can't do a party." Millie's hands grew sweaty just thinking about it.

"Okay." Beth said softly with a kind smile. "We won't do a party." Millie let out a tense breath and closed her eyes.

Conversation turned away from her and the baby and Millie found herself relaxing. Beth and Derek stayed for only another hour before taking the kids home to put them to bed. Josh and Aiden stayed a while longer. After Millie yawned for the fourth time, Josh stood and stretched.

"I think we should head home, Aiden. I have to make sure I have all my assignments done before tomorrow." Josh pulled Millie to her feet and gave her a hug. "If you need us, just call or text."

"Thanks, Josh. I will." Millie said as she yawned.

Aiden tossed Josh his keys. "I will be out in a minute. I am going to help clean up dinner."

Josh nodded before going to the garage. Millie heard the truck start and saw it pull around to the front of the house. Millie started putting the extra pizza into plastic bags. Aiden moved to her side as he began helping.

"I need to apologize. What I said by the pool..." Aiden said quickly.

"Aiden, don't." Millie cut him off. "You do not need to apologize."

"I do though. I did not intend to hurt you, but I did and I'm sorry."

Millie turned to him and put her hand on his chest. "You were messing around, and I got upset. I still don't even know why I did. I knew you were joking." Millie shook her head and grabbed the bagged pizza before putting it in the fridge.

Aiden was stacking the empty pizza boxes when Millie turned back around. She watched him for a moment before he met her gaze. A crooked grin spread on his lips.

"What is that look for?" Millie asked suspiciously.

"What look?" Aiden's innocent tone didn't fool her.

"Aiden, I'm too tired for games right now, so whatever you are planning, just stop." Aiden walked over to her, and she leaned back against the counter by the sink as he approached. "You know," Millie said, eyeing him. "On second thought, I might be up for a game."

"Is that so?" Aiden's crooked grin appeared.

Millie put her arms around his neck and gave him a hug. "Goodnight, Aiden."

She pulled back, slipping a handful of ice cubes from the sink into the collar of his shirt. It took a second, but then he was dancing around trying to get the ice cubes out. It was better than normal because his shirt was tucked in. Millie was laughing so hard she stumbled as she ran for the front door.

Aiden caught her easily, dropping an ice cube down the back of her shirt. Millie only smiled more as she stood still. Aiden still had an arm around her, which stopped the ice cube from dropping out the bottom.

"Why are you not trying to get the ice out?" Aiden asked in frustration.

Millie laughed as she wrapped her arms back around him. "Nice try, but I don't mind a little ice." Millie stepped away still grinning. "But I am going to kick you out so I can go to bed."

Aiden shook his head at her. "Goodnight, Millie." Aiden kissed her cheek before walking out the door, leaving her standing stunned in the entryway.

Chapter 11

Millie's life had fallen back into a routine. School kept her busy, as did working three days a week. Both Aiden and Josh were at her house most evenings to play games or just hang out while they all did their homework. She had grown really close with them.

She sometimes caught Aiden watching her with a small smile on his lips, but when their eyes met, he would quickly look away. Josh had made a few comments about feeling like a third wheel throughout the weeks, but Millie knew he was teasing. She would never admit that she had only grown more attracted to Aiden, and there seemed to be a tension between them that she couldn't explain.

She often reminded herself that she and Aiden were just friends. They texted each other often throughout the day, even though they spent most evenings together. He always asked how she was doing and if she had taken her medications.

Millie was trying to understand what was happening between her and Aiden. He was her best friend, but he had kissed her cheek the night she moved in and was acting like nothing happened. That night she had texted Beth, agreeing they desperately needed a girls' night.

They had been waiting four weeks now. Either Millie had homework and work, or Beth had in-laws staying with them for a visit or the kids got sick. Derek had the day off and Beth was meeting Millie at the doctor's office. Today was Millie's ultrasound and she was nervous.

Beth, holding Melody, was waiting just outside the office door when Millie pulled up. She got out and hurried to her friend. "I'm so glad you could be here." Millie told her.

"Me too. I'm so excited." Beth beamed. "I'm also excited we get to spend the rest of the day together."

Millie opened her mouth to say something but was cut off. "Hey, ladies." Josh walked up to them with Aiden at his side. "I didn't know you had an appointment today, Millie?"

"That's probably because I didn't mention it." Millie shrugged.

"So, why is Beth here?" Aiden asked looking between them.

"Millie is a little nervous about the ultrasound, so I'm here for moral support." Beth patted Melody's back as she grinned proudly.

"That's today?" Josh rubbed his hands together in excitement. "Can we come?"

Millie and Beth glanced at each other. Beth looked like she was holding back a laugh. They had talked about how Josh and Aiden were more excited about Millie's baby than she was at the moment. Beth had even joked about them sneaking into her appointment.

"I guess." Millie barely got the words out before Josh opened the office door and ushered everyone inside. They stepped up to the reception desk and Edna was sitting there. Millie had known her all her life.

"Good to see you, Millie." The older woman said with a smile.

"Good to see you too, Edna."

"I saw your name on the schedule and insisted on greeting you when you got here." Millie smiled at her and waited. Edna looked at Millie's companions and her smile turned into a look that reminded her of her grandmother before Millie got a scolding. "You are only allowed one person back for the ultrasound."

"Beth will be coming with me." Millie said. Beth quietly cheered and Millie smothered her laugh.

"Not your fiancé or mentally challenged brother this time?" Edna raised a brow in challenge.

"Since I am special needs, I don't think I should count towards the number of people in the room. My dear sister has to keep an eye on me." Josh put an arm around Millie's shoulder.

"Young man, I helped deliver Millie when I worked as a nurse at the hospital, and her grandmother and I were friends. I helped change her diapers. I know for a fact that you are not her brother." Edna glared at Josh.

Millie was having a hard time not laughing at Josh's wide-eyed, stunned expression. "Edna is my godmother." Millie laughed. "I thought you were in Florida." Millie turned to the old woman.

"I came back. Too many young people and the heat was not for me." Edna stood and handed Millie a specimen cup as she eyed Aiden. "But I am not sure about you."

"Me?" Aiden asked in surprise.

"That boy tried to pass as her brother and failed. The question is, are you really her fiancé or is that a lie as well?" Edna studied him closely.

"I, uh," Aiden rubbed the back of his neck and his cheeks turned pink.

"Josh told the staff that Aiden was my fiancé." Millie leaned on the desk. "Edna?" Millie said slowly. "If you are back from Florida...?" A smile slowly spread across the old lady's face before she laughed.

"You haven't changed a bit, young lady." Edna wagged a finger at her. "And the answer is yes. But you have to wait for a few days."

"That's hardly fair." Millie pouted.

"Suck that lip back in." Edna put her hands on her hips. "You have a lot of explaining to do, young lady."

Millie's shoulders slumped. Of course, Edna would want answers. She was the one that introduced her to the missionaries and had sat with her through every discussion.

"Is this the father?" Edna glared at Aiden.

"No." Millie said quickly. "Edna, can we discuss this later? You can come over to my house in the morning and I will make you waffles."

Edna hummed in thought. "Fine. But Mildred Louise Larson, you better tell me everything."

"Yes, ma'am." Millie sighed.

"Have a seat, it will be a few minutes."

Millie went to the far side of the waiting room, out of sight of the reception desk, and sat down with a huff. She folded her arms and scowled at the floor. She hated being in trouble, and judging by Edna's reaction, Millie was definitely in trouble.

"She seems nice." Beth sat next to her and whispered.

Millie laughed. "Edna was like a second mother to me."

"She is a bit scary." Josh shivered as he smiled.

"You should have seen it when both my grandmother and Edna were together when I was caught doing something I probably shouldn't have been doing. Now, that was scary." Millie smiled at the memory of the time she painted the neighbor's horses' hooves with nail polish.

"Millie Larson." A nurse called.

Millie and Beth left the guys in the waiting room. Before they fully disappeared into the back, Beth stuck her tongue out at them. Millie laughed at their scowls. When they got to the exam room, Beth sat in a chair and began feeding Melody.

"I told you that Josh and Aiden would try to sneak into your appointment." Beth laughed. "I haven't seen Josh get scolded like that in years."

"Edna never did put up with lies." Millie chuckled.

They talked more about Edna while they waited. Melody finished eating and Beth was burping her. Suddenly Beth gasped and held Melody a little away from her. Millie watched in horror as the baby girl blew out of her diaper. Poop was up her back and down her legs.

"I left the diaper bag in the car." Beth sighed. "I'm sorry, Millie, I will be back as soon as I get her changed."

"Don't worry about it, Beth." Millie smiled at her friend, even though her anxiety about doing this alone started to come back. "Get Melody and yourself cleaned up. I can tell you all about it when we get back to my house." Millie pointed to Beth's shirt.

Beth groaned when she saw that Melody had leaked all over her too. "I will send one of the guys in, so you aren't alone." Beth said before closing the door.

Millie leaned back on the bed and stared at the ceiling. A few minutes later the door opened, and she glanced over. Aiden stepped in and gave her a small smile.

"Glad I'm in here with you instead of changing that diaper." Aiden said as he sat.

Millie laughed as she sat up. "Is Josh out there pouting now that you are in here?"

"He probably would be, but he got a phone call and had to go help a member of his group with something. He left a few minutes ago."

There was a light knock and then a nurse entered. Her name tag said her name was Lauren. "How are you feeling today, Millie?"

"A little nervous." Millie admitted.

"There is nothing to worry about. The ultrasound will take thirty minutes to an hour. We take a bunch of measurements to make sure the baby is growing and developing how it should. Are you wanting to know if the baby is a boy or girl?" Lauren asked.

"Um. I'm not sure." Millie rubbed her arm nervously.

"I'll tell you what, I will turn the screen so you can't see anything when we get to that part of the ultrasound. I will write the gender down and put it in an envelope so you can look whenever you decide to."

"Okay." Millie whispered.

"Lie back on the bed and lift your shirt." Lauren instructed as she turned on a computer screen next to the exam table. "And you may want to scoot closer if you are wanting to see anything." She told Aiden.

Aiden looked at Millie for permission, and she gave him a small nod. He scooted his chair close to the bed and gave her a big smile. Millie turned her attention back to the monitor as Lauren put the ultrasound wand to her stomach.

Millie gasped when the image of a face filled the screen. Aiden's hand grabbed hers and gave it a squeeze. Lauren began pointing things out as she took measurements. Millie felt tears on her cheeks as she watched the baby lift its tiny hand up to its face.

"I think your baby is going to be a thumb sucker." Lauren laughed.

The door to the exam room opened, and Beth slipped in holding a clean Melody. "I think I just traumatized some poor guy." She laughed as she walked over to the other chair. She saw the screen and gave an apologetic smile. "Sorry." Beth whispered.

"Pull up a chair." Lauren invited. "Okay. I am going to turn the screen for a few minutes."

Millie blinked her eyes to clear the tears and looked over at her friends. Aiden was smiling at her, and Beth was studying Aiden. Lauren turned the monitor around and Millie turned to watch it.

Lauren finished the ultrasound and helped Millie wipe the jelly off her stomach. "You are still small, but this is your first pregnancy, and you are very fit. Those abdominal muscles of yours are holding in the baby. But that won't last for much longer. The baby will start growing faster now. Have you felt the baby move yet?"

"I'm not sure." Millie shrugged.

"At first it may feel like butterflies or flutters. But as the baby gets stronger, they will become more noticeable." Lauren smiled. "Dr. Spaulding will be in in a few minutes."

The nurse left and Millie leaned her head back on the bed. She turned to her friends. Aiden was smiling at her while Beth was studying Aiden. "What did you do to traumatize the guy?" Millie asked.

"He saw me and Melody leave the office." Beth laughed. "His eyes were practically bugging out of his head."

A knock on the door proceeded Dr. Spaulding walking in with a smile. "How are you feeling?" She sat on the wheely chair.

"Still nauseous all the time." Millie sighed.

"You have gained a little weight since the last time you were in. Which is good." They spent the next several minutes discussing how the baby was doing and what Millie could expect in the coming weeks. Dr. Spaulding patted her leg before getting up. "I will see you in four weeks." She handed Millie a sealed envelope and several images from the ultrasound.

"Thank you." Millie said as she looked down at them.

The three of them exited the office and Beth handed Melody to Aiden before grabbing the images from Millie's hands. "Oh my gosh! Is the baby sucking its thumb?" Beth gushed. "That is so cute." Beth pulled out her phone. "Can I take a picture to send to Derek? He is so jealous that he couldn't be here."

"Sure." Millie laughed and watched as Beth pulled out her phone and started taking pictures of all the ultrasound images.

Aiden stepped closer to her, putting a hand on her lower back. He leaned close and whispered in her ear. "I think that Beth and Derek are more excited about your baby then they were with their own."

Millie laughed and looked up at him. He was smiling down at her, and her heart skipped a beat. His brown eyes shone with amusement. Beth gasped and gushed about one of the pictures and Aiden winked at Millie.

Millie turned to Beth. "Are you ready? We have plans, remember?"

Beth put her phone away with a grin on her face. "How could I forget? I have been looking forward to this day for weeks." She reached for Melody, but Aiden moved her out of reach.

"Where are you two going in such a hurry?" Aiden asked.

"We are going back to Millie's for some girl time. You boys are always around and stealing Millie's attention from me." Beth scowled playfully. "Now give me back my baby."

"A girls' night, huh?" Aiden smirked at them.

"Yes, and we would love to get to it." Millie bumped his shoulder. "Hand Melody back to her mom so we can get going."

Aiden laughed and passed Melody over. Then his smile faded into a serious expression as he surveyed the parking lot. He sighed and rubbed his face.

"What's wrong?" Millie asked.

"Josh has the car. We didn't think about it when he left."

"That's okay. I will go grab the food and Millie can take you home." Beth said as she began walking to her car.

Millie stood there for a minute before giving herself a mental shake. "Come on, let's get you home." She smiled at Aiden before heading for her car. "We are getting Mexican, and I don't want to miss it."

Aiden chuckled as he got in the car. "You are still craving Mexican food?"

Millie sighed as she started the engine. "I can't get enough of it. I can't tell you how much money I have spent on carne asada burritos and nachos. This morning, I ate chips and salsa for breakfast." Millie shook her head. "The stuff is addicting."

Aiden was full on laughing now. "At least you aren't throwing up anymore."

"Well," Millie shrugged. "It's not as bad, but then again, I am on two different medications."

Millie glanced over at Aiden when he didn't say anything. He was watching her. She looked back at the road and bit her lip as she tried to think of something to say. Aiden cleared his throat and looked out the window. Millie turned on the radio to fill the quiet.

She pulled into the parking lot in front of Aiden's apartment. She got out to thank Aiden for being there with her at the appointment but froze when she saw Lawrence stomping towards her.

Chapter 12

"Millie, what the heck are you doing?" Lawrence growled as he grabbed her arm and pulled her close to him.

"Let go of me." Millie said as she tried to move away from him.

"You got a restraining order? I am your husband, yet you are shacking up with some other guy?" Lawrence's grip tightened.

"Let her go, Lawrence." Aiden was at her side suddenly.

Lawrence's grip loosened for a moment and Millie took advantage of it, pulling free of him. Aiden stepped between her and Lawrence with a hard expression on his face. Millie pulled out her phone and texted Beth to call the cops and send them to Aiden's apartment.

Her heart was racing as she watched the two men face off. "How does it feel to be hooking up with a married woman?" Lawrence sneered.

"I am not married to you, Lawrence." Millie said angrily. "You can't be here; I need you to leave."

"I promise I will be a better husband than I was before. I messed up, but I've changed." Lawrence looked at her.

Millie stepped around Aiden as her anger flared. "A husband? You are ready to be a husband? Are you serious, right now?" Millie fisted her hands. "You may be saying you are ready to be a husband, but I doubt you are ready to be a father."

Lawrence blinked in surprise as his brows drew down in confusion. "A father? What does that have to do with us?"

Millie's jaw tightened. "Because I'm pregnant, Lawrence."

"You got her pregnant?" Lawrence yelled at Aiden as he pulled his fist back and started to swing.

Millie's punch connected first, causing Lawrence to stumble back and he missed Aiden. "You did!" She yelled.

"Why the heck didn't you get an abortion? We took steps to make sure you wouldn't get pregnant." Lawrence ran a hand over his jaw where Millie had punched him. "It's not too late. Let's go get this over with." He tried to grab her again, but Aiden blocked him.

"That's not your decision to make." Millie said.

"Like hell it isn't!" Lawrence yelled. "Neither one of us wants a baby, and I am not going to pay for or raise a kid I don't want."

"I never asked you to." Millie snapped back. "The only thing I want from you is for you to leave me and *my* baby alone."

"You think this guy is going to stick around? As soon as he gets what he wants from you, he will leave, just like I did." Lawrence smiled at her. "No one is going to want a woman who has been used and tossed aside. Not even that precious cult of yours will want you; the scarlet letter among the pure."

"That's enough." Aiden warned as Millie blinked back tears.

"We can take care of this little hiccup and start our life together like we planned." Lawrence took a step toward her.

"Excuse me, is there a problem here?" A police officer came jogging up to them. Two other squad cars were pulling into the parking lot as well.

"No problem, officer. My wife and I were just leaving." Lawrence extended his hand to her, and she took a step back.

"I have a restraining order against this man." Millie pointed to Lawrence.

Lawrence lunged for her. Aiden and the officer grabbed him, preventing him from reaching her. Millie was backed up against her car. She closed her eyes as Lawrence screamed at her.

"You owe me, Millie! I want my half! I'm not paying a cent for that thing!" Suddenly his shouts were muffled.

Millie opened her eyes and saw that Lawrence was now sitting in the back of a patrol car. The other two officers had joined Aiden and the first officer. One of them hung back by the patrol car while the others walked in her direction. Aiden touched her arm, and she blinked back her tears. She refused to let Lawrence know he had affected her.

"Ma'am, we need you to tell us what happened." A male officer said.

"First," The female cop elbowed the male officer. "Are you okay?" Millie swallowed the lump of emotion lodged in her throat and nodded. "Your arm looks a little red. What happened?" she said kindly.

Millie looked down and gently rubbed her forearm. "Um, Lawrence grabbed me." She whispered.

The female officer pulled her off to the side and asked her more questions about Lawrence, the nature of their relationship, and everything that had happened. When they were done, Aiden pulled her into a hug. She burrowed more into him, and he tightened his arms around her as he cradled the back of her head.

"Don't listen to a word he told you." Aiden whispered in her ear. "He was just trying to hurt you." Millie nodded, keeping her face buried in his chest. She took a calming breath.

"Millie!" Josh's worried voice called out. "What do you mean I can't go see her?" he asked angrily.

Millie looked up to see one of the officers blocking Josh's path. "Aiden, we should tell them Josh is okay to come over." Millie said quietly but made no move to step away from him.

"Officer Norton," Aiden called. "He's fine. Josh is like a brother to Millie."

Josh ran over and touched Millie's shoulder. "What happened? They made me park down the road, and when I got here, I noticed that everyone was gathering outside. People were saying something about a crazy ex, and then I saw Aiden."

"Millie was dropping me off after her appointment. Lawrence came out of nowhere and grabbed her. He said some pretty harsh and untrue things." Aiden explained.

"I'm sorry for interrupting." The female officer came back over. "Mr. Hansen said you assaulted him, Ms. Larson."

"What?" Aiden asked angrily. "He violated his restraining order and now he is claiming Millie assaulted him?"

"I did punch him in the face, Aiden." Millie pointed out. She turned in Aiden's arms to face the officer. She grabbed his hands tightly in hers, keeping his arms around her. "Lawrence was angry and tried to punch Aiden. I just happened to be faster, and my punch landed first."

The officer smiled at her. "I saw a video of it. One of the guys recorded the whole thing. Do you box?"

"I do. Well, did. I'm currently taking a break because of this." Millie rubbed her stomach.

The officer nodded. "We will be clearing out in the next few minutes. If you need anything, don't hesitate to give us a call."

"Thank you." Millie said shaking hands with the officer.

Ten minutes later, she was sitting in Aiden and Josh's apartment. Josh had found the guy with the video and watched the whole thing. He was currently pacing the small living room with clenched fists.

Millie was much calmer now and felt like she could drive. "I should get going. Beth is waiting for me, and we only have a few hours left before she has to go home."

"You can't go alone." Josh stated.

"Josh, I really appreciate your level of protectiveness, but Lawrence is currently at the police station." Millie gave him a hug before heading for the door.

"I'll walk you out." Aiden followed her.

"Be careful, Millie." Josh called after them.

Aiden opened Millie's car door and waited. Millie turned to face him. She wanted to thank him for protecting her today, but he spoke first.

"Lawrence was wrong." He stepped closer to her, lightly putting his hands on her waist. "I will be here for you and this baby, no matter what. You aren't ruined or tarnished. You are smart and beautiful and brave. This baby is only going to add to your long list of attractive qualities." Aiden's voice was soft and warm as he moved closer.

Millie's breath caught in her lungs as his head began to lower towards hers. He paused just before their lips touched, giving her time to push him away. Millie placed her hands on his chest. After another heartbeat, Aiden's lips pressed to hers softly.

Closing her eyes, Millie returned the kiss. Warmth spread through her, and her stomach did a summersault. Aiden pulled back, but Millie rose on her toes and pressed her lips back to his. Aiden's hand tangled in her hair, keeping her close. Millie could have sworn she saw fireworks exploding behind her eyelids.

Someone cat-called, pulling them out of their bubble and they broke apart. Aiden looked as dazed as Millie felt. The realization of what they had just done hit her. Had she really just kissed Aiden? Did he mean what he had said?

Aiden took a step back. "I'm so sorry, Millie." The look of regret on Aiden's face was like a punch to the gut.

"Sorry for what, Aiden?" Millie said evenly. "Sorry for telling me you disagree with Lawrence's assessment of me? Sorry for kissing me?" When he didn't say anything immediately, Millie crossed her arms over her chest. "Sorry for what?" She repeated.

"I shouldn't have kissed you. I don't want to ruin our friendship." Aiden rubbed the back of his neck as he stared at the ground.

Millie nodded slowly. "Don't worry, Aiden. I've got the message loud and clear." She got into her car and drove away, refusing to look back.

*   *   *

Millie stormed into her house. Beth was sitting on the couch with Melody playing on the floor. "I can't believe him." Millie fumed. Who kisses someone like that only to immediately say it was a mistake? Aiden, apparently.

"Was it really a surprise? Lawrence is kind of a piece of work." Beth said patting the seat next to her. Millie plopped down on the couch and grabbed a licorice, ripping off a bite. "What happened?"

Millie sighed and told her everything that had happened with Lawrence. "And then Aiden walked me to my car."

"Okay so, why are you so upset? Lawrence was arrested."

"I am irritated with Lawrence, but I'm mad at Aiden. Who kisses someone and immediately says sorry for doing it?"

"Aiden kissed you?" Beth gasped. "I knew it! I knew he liked you. I mean look at the way he is looking at you." Beth pulled out her phone and opened her picture app. She passed it over to Millie.

The picture was of her and Aiden. He was holding Melody as they stood outside after her appointment today. He was looking down at her while she looked up at him. They both had smiles on their faces. Beth captured the moment after Aiden had made the joke about Beth and Derek.

Millie passed the phone back. "Beth, he kissed me and then said he shouldn't have, that he was sorry, and he didn't want to ruin our friendship. You should have seen the regret on his face." Millie took another bite of her licorice. "Maybe Lawrence was right, no one would ever want me. He even said Aiden would stick around long enough to get what he wanted and then leave. Well, he kissed me and immediately started backing away."

"You don't really believe Aiden is that kind of guy, Millie. I know you don't." Beth touched Millie's arm. "You said it yourself. He didn't want to ruin your friendship. Maybe he thought that you didn't feel the same way and didn't want to ruin what you two had."

"I don't even know what we had before." Millie turned to face Beth. "Since the day I met him, he has always been sweet and nice. He has gone out of his way to help me. When I needed comfort, he's been there. He has held me, I don't even know how many times, and told me everything would be okay."

"Sounds like a friend to me." Beth commented as she pulled her feet up under her.

"We have hung out a lot and I honestly feel like he is one of my best friends. But then he kissed my forehead the night he brought me to your house when Lawrence was at my apartment. And kissed my cheek before he left the night I moved in."

"Okay, not what a friend would do." Beth smiled.

"I'm so confused." Millie groaned as she threw her hands over her face. "He acts like none of that has happened."

"How do you feel about him?" Beth asked.

"I think I like him. Like a lot." Millie sighed and dropped her hands in her lap. "I love joking around with him and just hanging out. I'm comfortable with him. I feel safe and protected with him."

"What did you think of the kiss?" Beth smiled.

"Like fireworks." Millie smiled as well at the memory of their kiss, then she frowned. "But the regret in his eyes and his apology was enough to make me realize that Aiden doesn't feel the same."

"I'm sorry, Millie. Aiden really shouldn't have kissed you if he didn't mean it." Beth gave her a hug.

"What am I going to do about it?" Millie asked. "I don't want to lose him, but I don't think I can pretend it didn't happen."

"You are not going to answer his phone calls or texts, you are not going to hang out with him, and you are going to binge watch chick flicks while eating junk food with me." Beth stated. "Aiden can be in time out for a bit."

Millie laughed and hugged her friend. They spent the rest of the night cuddling Melody and watching movies. It was a little after eleven and Beth was getting ready to go home when Millie's phone rang. She didn't recognize the number, but something told her to answer it.

"Hello?"

"Hello. Sorry for calling so late, but is this Mildred Larson?" A male voice asked.

"It is." Millie met Beth's curious stare.

"I am calling on behalf of Monica Larson." The air left Millie's lungs in a whoosh and she sank down on the couch.

"What about Monica?" She whispered.

"She was in a terrible accident. She is currently in the hospital, but the doctors aren't sure if she is going to live much longer."

Millie covered her mouth with a shaking hand. She hadn't seen or heard from her mother in sixteen years. Now she was at death's door, who knows where, and some stranger was calling to let her know.

"Where?" Millie asked.

"Anchorage, Alaska." The man said.

Millie closed her eyes and shook her head. "Okay. I will fly out as soon as I can."

"I can meet you at the airport if you send me your flight plan." The man offered.

"I'm sorry, who are you?" Millie asked. Beth sat on the couch next to her, concern written all over her face.

"I am Monica's husband, Franklin Moore." Franklin said. "I'm sorry for not introducing myself at the beginning. It's been a rough couple of days." Millie was speechless. Her mother was married? "I can send you money for your flight out here." He offered.

"That won't be necessary. I will also get a rental car, so you don't have to leave Mom." Millie told him in a quiet voice. "I will need to go so I can book a flight and pack. I will let you know when my flight is." Millie took a deep breath. "Thank you for calling me, Franklin."

When she hung up, Beth immediately asked what was going on. "My mom was in an accident and the doctors don't know if she is going to make it."

Millie reassured Beth that she was fine and that she would let her know when she was leaving. Millie promised to keep her updated while she was gone. Appeased, Beth went home, and Millie went to the study.

She sent all her instructors an email about her mother's critical condition and her need to leave town immediately. Next, she booked a flight that left around ten in the morning and reserved a rental car. She sent a text to Beth and Franklin with her itinerary.

Millie went to her room and packed two large suitcases. She had no idea how long she was going to be gone. When she was done packing, Millie took a quick shower. She set her alarm and collapsed into her bed, completely exhausted.

Chapter 13

The alarm going off woke Millie from a deep sleep. It was six in the morning, and she had only gotten four hours of sleep. She dressed in comfortable clothes for traveling and made herself something to eat. Millie checked her emails during breakfast. She was surprised to see that all of her instructors had emailed back, wishing her the best and told her they would make sure she was able to take her finals, even if it were remotely.

Millie was packing last-minute items when her phone rang. Josh. Millie hesitated but decided to answer it. "Hey, Josh, a bit early to be calling, isn't it?"

"It's seven, not even in the too early category. I wanted to talk to you about something."

"Okay, but I don't have much time." Millie added a few snacks into her carry-on, along with her medications and her laptop.

"I'm going to get straight to the point then…I saw you." Josh said and Millie stopped what she was doing.

"Saw me what?"

"Well, more accurately, I saw you and Aiden last night."

Millie shook her head. "I see."

"I don't think you do. You are like a sister to me, Millie."

"Whatever happened between Aiden and I won't affect our relationship, Josh." Millie tried to reassure him but wasn't sure if it was true. She wouldn't make him choose between her and Aiden.

"Okay, so what is happening with you two?" Josh asked.

"What did your best friend tell you?" Millie checked the time and went around the house, making sure everything was locked up. She activated her security system on her way out to her car.

"I haven't told him that I saw you two yet. He went straight to his room last night and then left early this morning." Josh sighed.

"You pretty much saw everything. Aiden kissed me. End of story." Millie said as she pulled out of her garage.

"That can't be the end. Aiden looked upset and you don't sound normal."

Millie wished Josh was with her so she could glare at him. "Emotions were high after Lawrence and mistakes were made."

Aiden's name flashed across her screen, and she ignored it. "I don't know if that is fully true. I had a feeling there was something happening between the two of you. But you two never hung out alone, so I didn't think you were dating."

Her phone beeped with a missed call. "Aiden and I aren't dating."

"That's not the feeling I got from the two of you yesterday." Josh scoffed. "Aiden and I grew up together. I have seen him date before, and he has never acted the way he acts around you." Josh paused. "And why are you not answering your front door?"

"Are you at my house?" Millie asked with a laugh.

"No, but apparently Aiden is. He just texted asking if I could call you and see where you were, because you aren't responding to his calls or texts." Josh sounded like he was reading something.

"Well, I am currently on the phone with you, so that would explain why I am not responding to him, and I'm not home right now." Millie could hear the protest starting to form on the other end of the phone. "Josh, I appreciate whatever it is you are trying to do, but Aiden apologized for the kiss, and I went home. We are friends, nothing more, nothing less. I have to go. I will talk to you later."

Millie didn't wait for a response before she hung up. She turned on her Sunday playlist and turned up the music. The drive to the airport wasn't crazy long, and she got there with two and a half hours to spare before her flight.

She was sitting at the gate reading the scriptures on her phone and accidentally answered the call. She hadn't even seen who was calling when she hit the button that popped up on the screen. Aiden's voice came through the line, and she slowly brought the phone to her ear.

"Millie?"

"Hey, Aiden."

"We need to talk." he said quickly.

"About what?" Millie had a feeling she knew but didn't want to hear his rejection again.

"About what happened last night. Can we meet up somewhere?" Aiden asked.

"I can't right now." Millie rubbed her stomach absentmindedly. "Plus, you already made it clear that we are friends, and what happened last night shouldn't have."

"Millie," Aiden started to say, and she cut him off.

"I have to go, Franklin is calling." Millie hung up and answered the other call. "Hi."

"I got your itinerary." Franklin sounded tired. "Are you sure you don't want me to pick you up?"

"I'm sure. How is mom doing?" Millie asked.

"The same." Franklin sighed. "I'm glad you are coming." They talked for a few more minutes before Franklin had to go and Millie put her phone away.

She had an hour to kill before her flight, so she decided to walk around a little. There was a gift shop that drew her attention, and she made her way there. Millie looked through the store slowly, taking her time. She spotted a bookshelf and moved over to it.

A baby name book caught her eye, and she picked it up. She chewed her lip in indecision. She needed to start thinking about names and everything else the baby would need. She had brought the envelope with the gender, just in case she decided to look at it. Millie purchased the book and started a group chat with Derek, Beth, Aiden, and Josh. She sent them a picture of the book with a message: Looking towards my future.

Beth: About time, girl. How does it feel accepting the fact that you are actually having a baby?

Millie: Uh... I'll let you know when I'm not hyperventilating.

Derek: Deep breaths, Mils. I don't want to have to find an unconscious pregnant woman.

Millie made it back to her gate and found a seat. People were beginning to fill the area as the departure time drew closer. Millie's anxiety started to grow. Beth sent her a private message.

Beth: How are things going? Are you at the airport yet?

Millie: I made it. But I'm kind of freaking out, Beth. There are a lot of people.

Beth: Breathe slowly. Everything is going to be just fine.

A group of guys sat down around her, and Millie squeezed her eyes shut for a moment before getting up and walking to a corner. She dialed the first person she thought of.

"Aiden?" She whispered. Relief at hearing his voice had her leaning against the wall.

"Millie, where are you? It sounds busy." Aiden asked. There was a note of confusion in his voice.

"I'm sorry for bothering you, I know you are probably at church right now."

"Taking your phone calls is never a bother, Millie." Aiden said. "What's going on?"

"Nothing." Her voice squeaked with anxiety.

"Millie, you are anxious about something. I can tell just by your voice."

Millie let out a tense breath. "Am I that easy to read?"

"Not all the time, but I'm learning." She could hear the smile in Aiden's voice. "So, are you going to tell me where you are?"

"Are you going to tell me something that will distract me?" Millie asked in return.

Aiden chuckled. "What do you want me to say?"

"Anything." Millie breathed out and rubbed her forehead. "Aiden, there are so many people here now and I feel like I can't draw in a good breath."

"Millie, I don't like this." Aiden's anxious voice wasn't helping her own anxiety.

"Please help me through this." Millie begged quietly. "I can't leave and I'm not doing so good."

Millie slid down so she was sitting on the floor. There had to be over a hundred people at this gate alone, and she still had a few more minutes before they were boarding. She tried to take a deep breath, but she couldn't seem to draw in air.

"Have you thought of any names yet?" Aiden asked after a minute.

"I don't even know what I'm having."

"You haven't looked in the envelope yet?"

"I have been a bit busy, Aiden."

"We should do that sometime, so you know what kind of clothes to start getting."

"What if I decide I don't want to know?" Millie felt some of her tension going away.

"You would torture me like that?" Aiden asked.

"Torture?" Millie smiled. "I didn't think you were as invested in this baby as Beth and Derek are."

"Oh, I am. They just happen to know what to expect, I don't." Aiden said seriously. "I meant what I said last night, Millie. I am always going to be here for you and the baby."

Millie closed her eyes. "Aiden, don't make promises you don't intend to keep." They started calling for people to board.

"Are you at an airport?" Aiden asked in surprise.

"I need to go." Millie said quickly.

"Millie, wait. Where are you going?"

"I'm sorry, but I have to go. Something happened last night, and I can't miss this plane." Millie got to her feet. "I'll talk to you later, okay?"

Millie hung up the phone and got in line. She had purchased first class so she wouldn't have to deal with as many people. She boarded quickly and pulled out her phone to turn it off for the flight. There was a text message.

Aiden: Please be safe. I don't know what I would do without you.
Millie: I'll text you when I land. Thank you for talking with me.
Aiden: For the record, I don't make promises I don't intend to keep.
Millie: Then promise me something.
Aiden: Anything
Millie: I need you and Josh to raid the food at my house. I didn't have time to get rid of the stuff that might go bad.
Aiden: How long are you going to be gone?
Millie: I don't know yet. It depends on what I find when I get there.
Aiden: What are you hoping to find?
Millie: Family

"Ma'am, I need you to put the phone away." A flight attendant told Millie in a bored tone.

Millie turned her phone on airplane mode and buckled her seatbelt. She opened her photo app and looked at the picture that Beth had sent her of her and Aiden. She sighed and put her phone away.

*   *   *

Millie was in an airplane restaurant eating a burrito while waiting for her next flight. Now that she had food in her stomach, she was feeling better. The flight was rough on her. She had never flown before, and she had been sick the whole time.

Glancing at her phone, she had two hours left of a three-hour layover. Everyone should be at Beth and Derek's by now. Taking a deep breath, she called Beth's phone, knowing she would probably have to tell everyone about her mom.

"Did you make it?" Beth asked without preamble.

"No." Millie groaned. "I have never flown before and it freaking sucks."

"Oh no, what happened?" Beth sounded worried.

"I threw up four times." Millie admitted. "My stomach is still in knots, and I have an even longer flight in two hours."

"I thought you had pills to help with the whole throwing up thing." Josh asked.

Millie groaned. "Beth, why am I on speaker?"

"Because I stole the phone and put it on speaker." Derek sounded proud of himself.

"Well, thank you, Derek. That was so kind of you." Millie stirred her drink with her straw.

A man took the seat across from her and Millie sat up startled. "Hey, beautiful. Where are you heading?" he asked.

"Look, buddy, I'm twenty weeks pregnant, emotionally unavailable, and I am on a phone call, so if I were you, I would buzz off." Millie snapped at him.

The man's eyes widened in surprise, but he stood and walked away. "Are you feeling that bad, Millie?" Beth asked with a laugh.

"Worse." Millie sighed.

"I know you are queasy but try to eat something. An empty stomach will make it worse." Beth said sympathetically.

"I found a Mexican place in the airport, and so far its staying down." Millie took a sip of her water. "Does it ever go away? I'm so tired of feeling sick and tired."

"Hey, Millie, you should try a ginger energy drink. Ginger to help your stomach and the energy drink to give you an extra boost." Josh suggested.

"Yeah. Don't do that." Beth said, and Millie could hear Beth smack Josh. "The energy drink and caffeine, in general, is really bad for the baby."

"Hey, Angel." Another man came up to her. The guy from earlier was standing behind him. "I heard you weren't really nice to my friend here."

"For the love." Millie muttered. "Let's get a few things straight." Millie turned to the two men. "First off, I am no angel. Secondly, your friend sat at my table without an introduction or invitation and started talking to me while I was on the phone. And lastly, I am not in the mood to deal with two over inflated egos who think they are God's gift to women."

"Amen!" Someone shouted from a nearby table, while others clapped.

The two men looked around the restaurant and noticed several tables watching them. They were smarter than she thought they would be, and they left without saying another word. A table of women raised their glasses and smiled at her.

"Dang, Millie." Josh laughed.

Millie turned back to her beverage. "It's the hormones." Beth whispered and Millie laughed.

"I just want to lay down and sleep." Millie whined.

"Did you get any sleep last night?" Beth asked.

"I got to bed after two and woke up at six."

"Honey, you need sleep." Beth scolded. "After your encounter with Lawrence, the phone call, and the baby, you've been through a lot. And if you don't get some rest, you can get sick, or it will affect the baby."

Millie covered her face with her free hand. "I don't know when I can. I don't even get there until two in the morning, and then I need to get to the hospital first thing. You heard what Franklin said."

"Who is Franklin?" Aiden asked.

"He is apparently married to my mother." Millie sighed. "He called me last night and let me know that my mom was in an accident, and they don't think she is going to last much longer."

"Millie, where are you going?" Aiden asked.

Millie wiped a tear off her cheek. "I haven't seen her in sixteen years. I wasn't even sure she was alive. But now that she is at the hospital and she might die before I see her again," Millie swallowed. "I don't know."

"Listen to me, Millie." Aiden said firmly. "Josh and I can fly out there as soon as we can arrange it."

"Yeah, Millie. You shouldn't be going through this alone." Josh stated.

"No, you won't." Millie laughed. "You both have finals, work and other things you have to do. There is no reason for you both to fly out here. Plus, you are always telling me I'm not alone, a few thousand miles doesn't change that."

"Hey, Mils, before your next flight, see if you can find a shop that has motion sickness pills. Beth would get car sick on the straightest roads when she was pregnant with Bentley. It might help you on the plane." Derek suggested.

"Thanks, Derek, I will take all the help I can get." Millie stood and left the restaurant and started down the walkway where she saw a shop. "Any other helpful tips?"

Millie continued to talk with everyone until her flight was called. She promised to keep them all updated and hung up. Right after she boarded, she took some of the pregnancy approved motion sickness medicine she had found. She prayed it would help.

Sitting and waiting for the plane to take off, Millie once again looked at the picture of Aiden and her. She had done a lot of thinking on the flight, when she wasn't throwing up. She had come to know a few things. One was that Aiden and Josh were both important people in her life, and she didn't want to lose either one. And the other was that she would need to bury her growing feelings for Aiden in order to keep their friendship, because she needed him.

No one was able to calm her like he could when she was feeling overwhelmed. No one could make her laugh when she was falling apart like he could. She needed him in her life, even if that was only as her friend.

Chapter 14

Millie looked up from her laptop. She was trying to study but couldn't concentrate. Glancing across the hospital room, she found Franklin watching her again. He was the complete opposite of her mother in appearance. Monica was short with blonde hair and hazel eyes. Franklin was of medium height with salt and pepper throughout his dark brown hair. His eyes were a rich blue.

"Those pills really did a number on you, didn't they?" He asked with a small lift at the corner of his lips.

Millie had woken up to her phone ringing. Franklin had called to make sure she got in safely. She barely remembered the flight attendant waking her and finding a taxi to take her to the hotel. Her mind still felt like it was in a deep fog.

"My friend suggested the motion sickness medicine to help with my nausea on the flight." Millie yawned. "I have a feeling he knew it would put me to sleep. They were worried I wasn't getting enough rest."

Franklin chuckled. "They sound like they care about you."

"They are the only family I have." Millie rubbed her eyes, then froze. She looked at her mom. Tubes and bandages were everywhere, making it hard to even see her face. One of her legs was in traction and her arm was in a cast. She was hooked up to multiple machines. Monica Larson looked completely broken. "I didn't even know if she was alive or dead, until you called."

"Monica talked about you all the time." Franklin said softly. He cleared his throat and stood. "I think I am going to go find some food. Do you want anything?"

"A sandwich would be fine." Millie said as she watched her mom's sleeping form. Franklin nodded his head and left.

If her mom talked about her all the time, why didn't she at least call or send a letter or something? Sixteen years is a long time to just disappear. And it hadn't even been her mom that reached out to her, but Franklin.

Millie pulled her phone from her pocket and called Derek. He answered on the third ring. "How was your flight?"

"That was a dirty trick." Millie accused.

"So, I take it, the flight was uneventful?" Derek sounded pleased with himself.

"Your little deception worked so well that I fell asleep on the flight, had to get a taxi because I couldn't drive, slept in the taxi, don't remember checking into my hotel, and I still can't stay awake." Millie huffed.

"How many did you take?" Derek asked alarmed. "Beth just got a little sleepy, but it never knocked her out cold."

"I took the normal dose. But you should have warned me about the drowsiness. I can't even take half a pill of Benadryl without sleeping the whole day." Millie rubbed her face. "I feel like my whole body is packed with sand."

"I'm sorry, Millie. I had no idea you were such a light weight." Derek sighed. "How are things going there?"

"Mom is hooked up to so many machines and tubes, I don't know what goes to what. Franklin seems nice. He picked me up from the hotel, since I'm in no condition to drive."

"I'm sorry about the sleepiness, okay?" Derek said. "What did the doctors say?"

Franklin walked back in with a plastic bag in his hand. "I didn't know what you liked so I got several different options."

"Thank you, Franklin." Millie gave him a thankful smile.

"Finish your phone call. No rush." Franklin whispered.

"I'm not completely sure of the whole situation here yet." Millie said as she stepped out into the hallway. "She has a shattered leg, broken ribs, broken arm and collar bone. Franklin said she had some internal bleeding at the beginning, but they managed to get it stopped quickly. Her skull was also fractured."

"I'm so sorry, Mils. What can we do to help?" Derek's voice was soft and worried.

"Just keep her in your prayers." Millie felt her emotions rising to the surface.

"Already on it. And how are you doing, other than the sleepiness?" Derek asked.

"I'm not sure. I'm still trying to process everything. Can you let everyone know that I made it safely and that I miss you all." Millie began walking back to her mother's room.

"You just did." Beth said with a laugh. "We miss you, too. How long are you staying?"

"Until either the funeral or Mom gets stable." Millie yawned and shook her head. "I should go, Franklin brought food and I need to eat before I fall back asleep."

"Keep us updated, okay?" Beth said quickly.

"I will. Bye guys." Millie hung up and reentered the hospital room. She was feeling a little lightheaded from the medication and needed to sit down.

Franklin was holding her mom's hand with tears rolling down his cheeks. He was looking at her mom's face as he whispered to her. He hadn't seemed to notice that Millie had returned.

"Millie looks so much like you. She even has some of your stubbornness." He pressed a kiss to her hand. "Sweetheart, please wake up. You need to see how grown up our girl is. Please."

Their girl? What did Franklin mean by that? Millie's lungs ceased working. The world around her started to spin and she stumbled forward a step. Was Franklin her father?

"Millie?" Franklin's voice sounded far away. Millie's phone slipped from her hand, and it clattered to the floor. Her vision began to fade. The last thing she remembered was the feeling of falling.

* * *

Millie groaned as she rubbed her head. What had happened? "Millie?" she turned her head in the direction of the voice.

Franklin was standing next to her with a worried look on his face. Millie looked around to get her bearings. She was lying in a hospital bed with a thick cloth band around her stomach. The band was connected to a monitor that was tracking what looked to be a heartbeat.

"What happened?" Millie asked as she sat up.

"You passed out." Franklin told her. "You stumbled and looked pale. Then you collapsed."

The memory of overhearing Franklin speaking with her mother came back to her. She stared at Franklin, not saying anything. Millie's eyes were the same shade as his. Both her grandmother's and mother's eyes were hazel-green. They also had blonde hair while hers was a rich brown.

Franklin's expression became guarded as he watched her. "How long were you in the room?"

"Long enough to find out that you are probably my father." Millie crossed her arms over her chest. "Why didn't you tell me?"

Franklin sighed as he took a seat in a chair near the bed. "That is a long story. One that we can talk about after we get back to Monica's room." He studied her for a moment. "How is your head? You hit it when you fell."

"It hurts a little." Millie reached up and touched the side of her head and winced. There was a goose egg near her temple.

"The doctor said you have a concussion from hitting the edge of the counter. He also said your baby is doing well." Franklin watched her closely.

Millie moved her hand to her stomach. Thank goodness her baby was fine. She closed her eyes and thanked the heavens that nothing happened to her child. She looked back at Franklin, giving him a small smile.

"Thank you." She said as she looked down at her belly. "I'm sorry to have caused you to have to leave mom's side."

"Don't apologize, Millie. I have been bouncing between you two. It has given me a reason to get some exercise. Your mother is doing just as well as she has been, and you seemed to be resting peacefully." He paused, scratching his jaw. "You were calling out for someone while you slept. Aiden must be important to you."

Millie's cheeks instantly began burning. She looked out the window as she tried to cool her blush. Aiden was important to her. He was her best friend.

"Is he the father?" Franklin asked slowly.

"No. Aiden is not the father. I was already pregnant when I met Aiden." Millie turned back to Franklin. His brows were pinched in confusion. She explained about Lawrence and then finding out about her pregnancy, Aiden and Josh's rescue and about Beth and Derek, and about her friendships with them. She left out her growing feelings for Aiden and how he kissed her.

"So, this Aiden is just a friend?" Franklin asked skeptically.

"Yes." Millie stated firmly. "Other than Beth, he is my best friend. Nothing more."

"Hmm."

A knock pulled their attention to the door. A man with a white coat walked in. He was an older gentleman that was mostly bald and the hair he did have was white. He smiled when he saw her sitting up.

"Good evening. I am Dr. Wilson." The man extended his hand.

"Millie Larson." Millie said as she shook his hand.

"How are you feeling Ms. Larson? Any dizziness or nausea?" Dr. Willson asked as he looked at the monitors.

"No dizziness and no more nausea then normal."

Dr. Wilson smiled at her. "Morning sickness?" Millie nodded. "How far along are you?"

"I am twenty weeks."

"Are you currently on any medications?"

Millie nodded. She told him about the two anti-nausea medications she was on and the motion sickness medication she took on the plane. Dr. Wilson took out a small flashlight. He checked her eyes and looked at the bump on her head.

"You need to rest for the next couple of days. No driving until you have seen your primary care doctor, and you are cleared to do so. You may have a headache for a few days. You can take Tylenol to help with the pain." Dr. Wilson patted her hand. "Your baby is completely fine. No signs of distress and its heart rate has stayed consistent. Now, do you have any questions for me?"

"Can I leave?" Millie asked, causing the doctor to laugh.

"I don't want you left alone for a day or two, but yes, I am releasing you. It can take a few days to a few weeks for you to fully heal from this concussion, so take things slow. If your symptoms worsen or if you notice a difference in the baby's movements, come back to the hospital immediately."

"Yes, sir." Millie smiled as the doctor unhooked her from the monitoring machines.

She wobbled a little, but Franklin caught her elbow. They walked slowly down the hallway until they reached Monica's room. Millie sat down on the couch and rubbed her forehead. Her headache had gotten worse just from the short walk back to the room.

"Franklin. Do you know where my phone went?" Millie asked after she reached into her hoodie but didn't find it.

"I'm sorry, Millie. It broke when you dropped it." Franklin said apologetically. "But you can use mine if you need to call anyone until we can get you a new one."

"Can I call Beth really quick? I should let her know that my phone is broken, and she won't be able to reach me for a few days."

Franklin handed her his phone and excused himself to get snacks and drinks. The only number Millie knew by heart was Beth's, so she quickly dialed it.

"Hello?" Beth's voice sounded distracted, and Millie smiled.

"Hey, stranger."

"Millie? Oh my gosh!" Beth shouted.

"Wow, no need to be so dramatic and loud." Millie closed her eyes and leaned back. "Am I just talking to you or are the guys around?"

"Josh and Aiden are taking finals and Derek is at work. Where have you been? I have been trying to call you for two days." Beth asked in concern.

"Two days?" Millie asked in surprise. "I must have been out longer than I thought."

"What are you talking about? You better start explaining." Beth snapped.

"Okay, but can you just keep the volume down please. I have a splitting headache." Millie explained what she overheard Franklin saying and then about passing out. "So yeah, I can't be left alone for a few days, and I can't drive until I see a doctor and they clear me."

"Oh man, the guys are going to freak when they learn that you fell and have a concussion. Aiden has not been himself since you left and haven't been answering his calls. Then when he found out that you weren't responding to any of us, he has been so worried."

"They aren't going to freak out because you aren't going to tell them. Both me and the baby are fine, I just need to rest for a few days. I have finals on Thursday and Friday and then I won't have to worry about anything. All you need to tell them is that I dropped my phone, and it broke. I will get a new one as soon as possible and will message everyone then."

"Millie, a concussion isn't something to mess around with. Are you sure you don't want one of us to come out there?"

"I'm sure, Beth. Franklin is here and I will follow the doctor's orders to the letter. This is Franklin's phone, so if you need anything, you can call me on this phone. But I will call you once a day to keep you updated." Millie smiled at Franklin when he walked back in. He held up a bottle of Tylenol and bottled water. "I need to go, Franklin just got back with something for my headache."

"Be careful, Millie. Talk to you tomorrow." Beth said before hanging up.

Millie gratefully accepted the medicine and water. After taking it, she laid down and faced the back of the couch. She didn't want to talk or think, she just wanted her head to stop pounding. The constant beeping of the machines needled at her brain until sleep finally claimed her.

Chapter 15

Millie's recovery was slow. It had been three weeks and she still suffered from headaches. Her mother's condition hadn't improved any, but it hadn't gotten worse either. Millie prayed every day that her mother would open her eyes. There was so much she wanted to ask her, so much she wanted to know.

She had had several conversations with Franklin over the weeks. Long hours in a quiet hospital room seemed to bring out his confession. Millie had stayed silent the whole time Franklin explained to her what had happened.

Franklin and Monica had been together for several years. They got in a big fight that led to them breaking up. Monica had gone back home, and he went traveling.

Monica reached out to him six months later, crying, saying she had a baby girl and didn't know what to do. She couldn't be a mom, that the baby deserved better than her. Monica had been into drugs and didn't want the baby to be exposed any more to them.

Franklin had suggested having Monica's mom take the baby until they could get clean. He hopped on a plane and was at Monica's side when they asked her mom to take Millie until they could raise their baby in a drug-free environment.

They had their ups and downs. At Millie's fifth birthday party, Monica's mom caught her in the bathroom using. She kicked them out, telling them not to come back or contact Millie until they were clean for at least five years.

By the time Monica and Franklin were clean, they were living in Alaska and Millie was twelve years old. So much time had passed, they were scared that Millie wouldn't accept them. They had tried so many times over the years to make contact, but each time they chickened out.

Franklin had cried while telling Millie his and Monica's story. He apologized for being a terrible father and a coward. He asked for her forgiveness and asked if they could try to have a relationship.

Millie had asked for time to think about the matter. He nodded and gave her space. As soon as she could be alone, Franklin took her back to her hotel. He had let her borrow his phone for the time being. When she got to her hotel room, Millie called Beth and Derek and told them everything she had just learned. She had so many mixed emotions.

On one hand, Millie was ecstatic that she found her mother and father, but on the other, they had stayed away from her all this time because of their fear. Beth told her to pray and if she needed to, find a ward in the area, and see if she could get a blessing.

Millie was currently getting dressed for church. Her maxi dress was no longer hiding her round belly. No one could mistake the fact that she was pregnant. Millie slowly ran her hand over her stomach. Just this last week, the baby's kicks had become much more noticeable. Nighttime seemed to be the baby's favorite time to be active.

She had just finished putting on lip gloss when the phone rang. "Hey, I'm almost ready to go. Can you give me ten minutes?"

"Ready to go where?" Aiden asked.

"Aiden?" Millie gasped in surprise before a smile spread on her face. She was so happy to hear his voice. It had been weeks since she had talked to him.

"Yeah, Millie, it's me." He chuckled. "Beth gave me this number. So, where are you going?"

"Hey, I'm going to put you on speaker so I can finish getting ready." Millie clicked the screen and put the phone down before she started curling her hair. "So, what have you been up to?"

Aiden cleared his throat. "Nothing much. Just helping my parents with the ranch for a few weeks."

"I didn't know your parents had a ranch." Millie commented as she curled another section.

"Yeah, we raise cattle and a few other things."

Millie smiled. "If you are at the ranch, then who is feeding my cat?"

Aiden laughed. "You don't have a cat."

"I did when I left, and I asked you to feed her."

"I can totally see that smile of yours, Millie. You aren't fooling me." Aiden laughed:

Millie looked down at her phone to see Aiden's face on the screen. Millie's smile widened. "I guess you can." She sprayed hairspray on her hair to hold the curls before putting a necklace on. She picked up her phone and walked over to the couch. "If you are a ranch hand, does that mean you have a horse?"

"I have three." Aiden said with a chuckle. "You look beautiful by the way."

"Thank you, but stay on topic, Aiden. Why haven't you taken me to see your horses yet?" Millie glared at him.

"The ranch is five hours away, Millie. It's not a quick trip kind of thing." Aiden looked like he was walking outside.

Millie sat up as she stared at the phone. "Oh, please tell me you are taking me to see the horses."

Aiden winked at her as he stepped into a building. He stopped by a stall and a horse stuck its head over the gate and nuzzled his shoulder. The horse had the unmistakable face of an Arabian.

"This is Aladdin, he is a five-year-old..."

"Arabian." Millie finished Aiden's sentence. Aiden raised a brow in surprise. "I may or may not be totally crazy about horses." Aiden laughed as he continued to show her the various horses he owned.

A text came in from Franklin telling her he would be there in fifteen minutes. "Aiden, I only have a few more minutes. Franklin is on his way to drop me off at the church."

"Why is Franklin dropping you off? Don't you have the rental car?" Aiden's brows drew down in confusion.

"I can't drive yet." Millie said without thinking. She was used to talking with Beth, who knew about her fall, and she hadn't thought to censor her answer.

"Why can't you drive?" Aiden's smile was no longer on his face. In its place, was concern.

"Oh, um. Well, you see..." Millie tucked her hair behind her ears as she looked away from the phone. Looking into Aiden's eyes made it hard to not tell him everything.

"Millie, look at me." Aiden's voice was soft but filled with worry.

Millie looked back at the phone. She scowled at him. "It's not fair, I can't lie to you when I'm looking at you."

"Good. Now, tell me why you can't drive." Aiden smirked at her, but the worry in his eyes didn't fade.

She huffed in frustration. "Okay, fine. After our phone call with everyone the day I got here, I went back to mom's room. I was feeling a little lightheaded from the motion sickness pills and was going to go sit down. Franklin was talking to mom and didn't see me. He mentioned something and I had a panic attack and ended up passing out. My phone broke when I dropped it. When I fell, I hit my head on the counter and got a concussion."

"Millie." Aiden breathed out as he closed his eyes as if calming himself.

"The baby is completely fine. I'm just getting periodic headaches. The doctors are just being cautious and told me not to drive for a while." Millie rushed on.

Aiden looked at her with even more concern. "Why didn't you tell us?" Hurt crossed his features.

"I made Beth promise to keep it to herself. You guys are so protective, and I didn't want you to worry. There isn't anything you can do. Time is the only thing that will help. There was no reason to bother you with it."

"Millie, your well-being, along with the baby's, are not a bother." Aiden looked deadly serious. "Please don't hide something like this again. I don't care if you think I will be worried."

"Aiden, I..."

"Promise me, Millie. Promise me you will tell me everything that affects you and the baby." Aiden's face softened as he looked at her.

"I really am sorry, Aiden. You are right, I should have told you." Millie gave him a small smile. "You seriously want me to tell you everything that happens with the baby?"

"I am."

"The baby is now strong enough that I can feel it moving."

"Seriously?" Aiden's smile was back on his face.

"Seriously." Millie laughed. "Nighttime seems to be its more active time. Last night, I could feel the baby kicking my hand."

"I'm missing everything." Aiden whined, even though the smile was still on his face. "When will you come home? How is your mom?"

"She is the same. She isn't getting worse, but she isn't getting better either." Millie shrugged. "I feel like I need to be here with her. Franklin says that my butt is going to be on a plane no later than twenty-eight weeks, regardless of mom's condition. He doesn't want to hear about me giving birth on a plane." Millie rolled her eyes.

"I am on board with that. I won the coin toss." Aiden smiled.

"What coin toss?" Millie asked suspiciously.

"At least between me and Josh, I get to hold the baby first." Aiden said smugly.

Millie laughed so hard she dabbed at her eyes. "Stop making me laugh, my makeup is going to start getting messed up."

"You still look beautiful, Millie." Aiden's smiled at her, and she felt her cheeks flush. "How come you never dressed up for church while you were here?"

Millie smirked. "I dress up for church most weeks, Aiden. You just have never gone to church with me before."

"You don't look like this when we see you in the evenings." Aiden lifted an eyebrow in challenge.

"Ah, that is because this," Millie gestured to her face. "Gets wiped off as soon as I get home. I only wear makeup when I feel the need to impress someone."

"Who are you trying to impress at church?" Aiden asked with a frown. He almost looked jealous and Millie bit her lip to keep from laughing.

"Well, back home there is a boy that likes to play with my hair when it's down and he always plays with my necklace. Today, it's just out of habit, I guess." Millie shrugged.

"I didn't know you were seeing anyone. You never mention him." Aiden ran his hand through his hair.

"I talk about him all the time, Aiden." Millie gave him a flirtatious smile. "You and I have had several conversations about him."

"I think I would remember you talking about a boyfriend, Millie." Aiden shook his head.

"I never said anything about having a boyfriend because I don't have one." Millie laughed, causing Aiden to scowl.

"Then who are we talking about?" Aiden growled.

"Bentley." Millie wiped tears from her eyes as she continued to laugh. "And I want to look my best for my Savior."

Aiden shook his head, but his smile was returning. Millie wiped another tear from her eye as she reigned in her laughter. She stood and moved back to the mirror and sighed. Her eye liner was smearing. She put the phone on the counter and started fixing her makeup.

"Thanks a lot, Aiden, now I have to fix it." She grumbled.

Aiden chuckled. "It's not my fault you were laughing so hard."

"Is that Millie?" Josh yelled. Moments later he was next to Aiden. "Dang, Millie! You look hot."

Millie rolled her eyes as she put her makeup away. "You don't look too bad yourself." He was in a button-down shirt with his hair all a mess.

"Are you going on a date?" Josh asked.

A knock sounded at her door. "Hold on a sec." Millie glanced through the peephole to see Franklin standing there in a dress shirt and tie. She opened the door and invited Franklin in.

"You ready to go, Honey?" Franklin asked.

"Who the heck is calling you 'Honey'?" Josh called.

Millie gave Franklin a smile before picking the phone up from the counter. She moved to stand next to Franklin. Neither Aiden nor Josh knew that Franklin was her father. "Guys, this is Franklin."

Josh glared at Franklin. "Franklin? As in the dude that is married to your mom?"

"The very one." Franklin smiled. "So, you've been talking about me?" Franklin winked at Millie, and she smiled.

After the initial shock wore off, Millie and Franklin had been getting to know each other and Millie realized she got her playful nature from him. He was always joking around. The nurses always left the room with a smile on their faces.

"Isn't Millie a little young for you, not to mention the fact that you are married to her mom?" Josh's face was turning red as his anger grew.

"Josh, let me try this again." Millie cleared her throat. "Aiden, Josh. Let me introduce you to Franklin, my father." The shock on Aiden and Josh's faces caused her to laugh. "Okay, I miss you guys and wish I could chat longer, but I need to go. I don't want to be late for church."

"I'll meet you in the hall." Franklin said before he stepped back out the door.

"Have fun, Millie. And get your phone fixed so you aren't such a stranger." Josh said before walking away from Aiden.

Aiden watched Josh for a few seconds before he looked back at Millie. "I miss you too, Millie. Josh doesn't keep me on my toes like you do." He gave her a crooked grin. Millie's stomach did a summersault as her heart sped up.

"I will call you later." Millie wished she was there with him. All she wanted was for Aiden to hold her. Tears suddenly pricked her eyes as she blinked rapidly to keep them from falling. She missed Aiden so much. Video calling only seemed to make it worse.

"Hey," Aiden said softly. "Where's that smile of yours?"

Millie squeezed her eyes closed. She refused to allow the tears to fall. Why was saying good-bye so hard? "I need to go." She whispered as she slowly opened her eyes. Aiden was looking at her in concern. She forced a smile on her face. "I'll talk to you later, Cowboy."

"You can count on it, ma'am." Aiden winked, but Millie wrinkled her nose.

"Ma'am makes me sound old."

"What do you want me to call you then?"

Millie's smiled at the teasing tone in Aiden's voice. "I'm not supposed to come up with my own nicknames. That's your job."

"Alright, sweetheart, I'll think of something." Aiden was grinning ear to ear. "Now that you are smiling and no longer close to tears, it's time for you to go to church. We can talk later."

"Alright." Millie sighed. "I love you. Bye."

Millie hung up the phone and then froze. Did she just tell Aiden she loved him? Her phone started to ring again. Millie's heart began to pound in her chest as she recognized the number as Aiden's.

Millie silenced the call and put the phone on vibrate as she stepped out into the hall. Franklin was waiting for her. They didn't talk much as they headed for the church. To her surprise, Franklin stayed with her for the full two hours.

Franklin had asked her why she seemed so distracted. She blamed it on a headache and being tired. He didn't seem to believe her but stopped asking. He took her back to her hotel room to rest.

She spent the rest of the day trying to read her scriptures, but thoughts of Aiden just kept resurfacing. Millie hadn't known she had fallen in love with Aiden until the words slipped out without her thinking about it. It had seemed so natural to say them. While at church, Millie thought about what had happened and realized that what she said was true. She was in love with Aiden Coleman.

Chapter 16

Millie was sitting on the couch in her mother's hospital room. She had finally convinced Franklin to go to her hotel room to rest. For the six weeks Millie had been there, he had refused to leave Monica's side; unless he was driving Millie somewhere.

Monica's condition hadn't improved much. Her right arm was no longer in a cast and her leg was out of traction, even though it was still in a cast. Not once had Monica woken up. Millie was starting to get anxious to be home. She was twenty-six weeks pregnant and needed to start getting things ready for the baby.

Her cell phone rang, and she answered it quickly. She knew it would be Beth. They talked at this time every week. Everyone would be there. It was the only time she talked with Derek, Josh, or Aiden.

Millie had avoided talking to Aiden alone for the last two weeks. She hoped he thought that her saying she loved him was a friend kind of love, and not the romantic love she felt for him. If he didn't, he would just tell her that they would be better off as friends. Millie didn't think she could handle seeing the regret on Aiden's face a second time.

Bentley's smiling face filled the screen. "Hey, handsome. How are you doing?"

"I miss you." Bentley pouted and Millie had to bite the inside of her cheek to keep from laughing at the look on his face.

"I know, honey. I miss you all, too. How was church? Did you learn anything new?"

"No. I don't like church anymore." Bentley scowled.

"Why?" Millie was completely surprised to hear the little boy say such a thing.

"You aren't there anymore. Mom doesn't have necklaces like yours."

Millie laughed as she rubbed her belly. The baby was currently kicking up a storm. "Well, young man, if you promise to keep going to church and listening to your mommy and daddy, I will bring back a few new necklaces for you to play with."

"Really?" Bentley squealed in delight.

"Really, really. Now where is your mommy?"

"I'm here." Beth took the phone from her son. "How are things going, Millie? How's your mom?"

Millie glanced over at her mother on the other side of the room. Monica was the same as she had been for weeks. Millie stood and slowly walked over to her mom's side. "She is the same as she has been." Millie turned so that Beth could see both her and her mother.

"You look like her." Beth said softly.

Millie's chin trembled. "That's what Franklin says, too. I just wish she would have reached out; you know? Why did it have to come to this before I got to see her again?"

Someone grabbed Millie's hand and she screamed. The phone slipped from her hand and fell to the floor as she spun around. Monica's eyes were blinking slowly, her hand clasped onto Millie's.

Millie stood frozen for a second before she burst into tears and hugged her mom. Her mother stroked the back of her head. Someone touched Millie's shoulder and she turned to see three nurses there. The one that touched Millie's shoulder gently pulled her out of the way while the other two hit the call button and started taking vitals.

The nurse led her to the couch and told her to take a seat. Millie couldn't take her eyes off her mother as her tears continued to flow. The nurse handed her back her phone.

Beth was yelling at someone, others were yelling back, and Melody was screaming in the background. "I have to go." Millie said quickly and hung up. She immediately dialed Franklin. As soon as he picked up, Millie started crying again. "She...she..."

"Millie, honey, what's happened?" Franklin's panicked voice was enough to snap Millie out of her shock enough to talk.

"Mom's awake." Millie sniffled.

Franklin hung up the phone immediately. Millie dropped the phone onto the couch next to her and watched as more nurses and Dr. Wilson rushed into the room. It was complete chaos for the next twenty minutes. Franklin came running into the hospital room.

There were so many people around her mother that he moved to Millie's side and wrapped his arms around her. He kissed her forehead as they watched the doctor and nurses continue to evaluate Monica. Five minutes later, only the doctor and one nurse remained.

Franklin and Millie moved to Monica's side. He released Millie and grabbed hold of Monica's hand as he began to cry. Millie watched the loving interaction between her parents. Several minutes went by before her mother turned tear filled eyes to her.

"Millie?" Monica whispered.

"Hi, mom." Millie wiped her cheeks. "I've missed you." Monica extended a hand to her, and Millie went to her.

"Baby girl." Monica's whisper was thick with emotion. "I'm so sorry."

Millie shook her head before she laid her head on her mom's shoulder as she cried. Monica kept a hand on Millie's head as she whispered apologies. Franklin rubbed Millie's back until her tears stopped.

Dr. Wilson finally told Millie and Franklin to allow Monica time to rest. Millie lay on the couch, emotionally drained, while Franklin pulled a chair close to Monica's bed and held her hand. Millie closed her eyes. A few minutes later, a blanket was draped over her, and someone kissed her head. She cracked her eyes open to see Franklin returning to his chair.

"She is beautiful." Monica said quietly. "She has your eyes."

"And your stubbornness." Franklin kissed Monica's hand again.

"You called her?"

"Sweetheart, I thought you were going to die. Millie deserved to see her mother one last time. She has been here for the past month and a half."

"Her husband let her come all this way while pregnant?" Monica sounded surprised.

"That is a long story, my love. But the short of it is, Millie isn't married." Millie closed her eyes and pulled the blanket more around her. "We can talk about that scumbag later, right now both you and Millie need rest."

"I've been resting for weeks, Frank. I don't want to miss another moment with Millie." Monica sniffled.

"We are not going to lose Millie, Monica. I am sure that even when she goes back home, she will keep in touch."

"How do you know? So many years have gone by, we have missed so much." Monica's voice cracked.

"Because while you were recovering, Millie and I have been getting to know each other a bit. She knows I am her father and about the reasons we stayed away." Franklin chuckled. "She has some really good friends and protecters in her corner." Millie listened to her parents talk for a while before sleep finally claimed her.

*   *   *

Millie sat in the passenger seat of Franklin's car as they drove to his house in Big Lake. Monica had been improving every day over the last week. Dr. Wilson wanted to keep her a little longer to run a few more tests before releasing her. Monica insisted that Millie stay at their house for a few days, since she was expected to go home at the end of the week anyway.

Franklin volunteered to drive her. Millie shifted in her seat trying to alleviate some of the pain in her lower back. The size of her stomach was making her so uncomfortable. She rubbed her belly absentmindedly as the baby kicked. She didn't know how she was going to get any bigger than she already was, but she still had twelve weeks left.

Millie had texted Beth about her mom waking up and that things were crazy. She hadn't been able to talk to any of her friends in nearly two weeks, and she missed them terribly. She planned to call them as soon as she got to her parents' house.

"Is the baby moving around a lot?" Franklin asked as he glanced at her.

"Mmhmm." Millie gave him a half smile before looking back out the window.

"I think you are going to like the house. We have five additional cabins on the property that we rent out for short term visits." Franklin told her. "Two of the cabins are currently being rented out for the week."

"That's cool. Do they get booked out often?"

"During certain seasons. I just wanted to let you know in case you see anyone on the property."

"Oh, okay. Thank you." Millie kept her attention on the passing scenery. Alaska was beautiful and wild. She could see why her parents stayed here.

A few minutes later, Franklin turned down a side road and Millie sat up. She watched as Franklin stopped in front of a large log cabin. She climbed out, grateful to be able to stretch. Millie turned to go to the trunk to help get her bags when she heard the front door slam.

"Millie Louise Larson!"

Millie's head snapped in the direction of Beth's voice. Standing on the front porch of the cabin was Beth, Derek and Melody, Bentley, Josh, and

Aiden. Tears sprang to her eyes as she started towards them. Beth closed the distance at a run, slowing her steps before colliding with Millie, and pulled her into a tight hug.

"Holy cow, you look pregnant now." Beth laughed, pulling back and rubbing Millie's belly.

"You think?" Millie laughed as she wiped her cheeks. Bentley slammed into her legs, causing her to take a step back. She lifted him onto her hip, placing a kiss on each of his cheeks. "How are you doing, buddy?"

"We got to ride on a plane." Bentley said excitedly.

Josh was at her side next, and he took Bentley from her with one arm and hugged her with the other. "You are a sight for sore eyes."

"I missed you too, Josh." Millie laughed as Derek gave her a hug next.

Millie smoothed Melody's hair back, causing it to stand on end. Derek stepped away from her and she saw Aiden. His smile was soft as he watched her. She wrapped her arms around his waist and buried her face in his chest as he held her tight against him. Millie had to stand at an angle because her belly was so big.

"I have missed you." Aiden whispered in her ear before stepping back from her.

"What are you guys doing here? How are you guys here?" Millie looked from one person to another.

"That would be my fault." Franklin put an arm around her shoulders. "After your mom woke up and you crashed, I noticed my phone on the floor. You had eight missed calls. When I called back, this young lady started to chew me out for screaming, hanging up the phone, and then not answering when she called back."

"You didn't hear the scream. She was freaked out. Then she was crying, and pale, then hung up on us." Beth crossed her arms over her chest.

"I offered them all tickets to come out here to see you." Franklin kissed her head before releasing her. "But you should probably go sit down, Millie."

Aiden grabbed her hand as they followed everyone inside. Millie found herself sitting between Josh and Aiden on a long sofa. Beth was sitting next to Derek and Melody. Bentley fought against Josh until he finally relented and let the little boy slide onto Millie's lap.

Millie shifted to get more comfortable, and Bentley pushed on her belly. The baby kicked back, and Millie smiled at Bentley's wide eyes. "Did you feel that?" Millie asked. Bentley nodded. "I think the baby just gave you a high five."

"I want to feel." Beth stood and came over. "I can't believe how big you are now. Last time I saw you, you couldn't tell unless you were wearing something more form fitting."

Beth laid her hand against Millie's belly and laughed when the baby started kicking again. "Are you calling me fat?" Millie asked, placing a hand over her heart.

"In your condition, fat is a compliment." Beth smirked at her.

Millie stuck her tongue out before sighing and leaning her head back against the couch. "When did you guys get here?"

"Last night." Aiden said as he put his arm along the back of the couch.

"Millie, if you are okay here, I am going to head back to the hospital." Franklin set her bags on the floor. "Your room is at the top of the stairs, first door on the left. The fridge and pantry should be stocked."

Beth lifted Bentley off Millie's lap and scooted back to give Millie room to stand. She managed to get up relatively easily, compared to the low couch at the hospital. "Thank you, Franklin." Millie gave her father a hug before he left.

She returned to her seat and Josh put his arm around her shoulders, pulling her closer. "I can't tell you how much we missed you. Aiden and Beth have been so grouchy."

Millie laughed and pulled away. She stood back up with a groan. She couldn't seem to get comfortable sitting, and when she stood, her back ached. Beth smiled sympathetically before coming to Millie's side.

"That uncomfortable?" she whispered.

"I can't seem to get a break. My back aches and my stomach muscles feel like they are being ripped apart and I still have twelve weeks left." Millie whispered back.

"Is everything okay?" Aiden asked as he watched her with concern.

"When a woman gets that big, everything hurts." Derek said as he placed Melody on the floor. "The baby's weight is straining the muscles in the back to support the baby and the abdominal muscles are being stretched beyond what they should. Not to mention the swelling and the mood swings and the restlessness at night trying to get comfortable, only to have to pee once they finally do."

"Thanks, Derek. I think we all get that pregnancy is uncomfortable." Josh shook his head.

"Want to know how bad it gets during labor?" Derek asked innocently.

"No!" Josh and Beth shouted at the same time, causing Derek to laugh.

"Alright guys, what do you want to eat?" Millie asked, heading into the kitchen.

"The guys have babysitting and dinner covered. You and I get to go sit on the swing and catch up." Beth grabbed Millie's arm and pulled her out the front door, down the front steps, and across the yard to a porch swing that was hanging from a tree.

"So, tell me what is happening between you and Aiden."

Chapter 17

Millie sat down next to Beth on the swing with a sigh. She laid her head on her friend's shoulder and started the swing gently rocking. "I don't know what you are talking about."

"Oh, come on Millie. You and Aiden used to be really close. Whenever we were all together, you two would be inseparable. You were always texting each other. Then there was that kiss,"

"Okay, point taken." Millie sat up and rotated to face Beth. "I have been trying to do what you suggested after me and Aiden kissed. I thought it was going well. I was focusing on building a relationship with my father and on my future."

"You don't even look at him, and he watches you like there is something he wants to tell you." Beth raised her brow.

Millie covered her face with her hands and groaned. "Aiden called me a few weeks ago." She lowered her hands and looked at Beth. "I ended up hitting the video call button instead of speaker. Seeing Aiden, I realized just how much I missed you guys, but it was nice to talk with him."

"I don't see where the problem is. You had a good conversation so why all the emotional distance?"

"I was saying good-bye because I was heading to church and may have told him I loved him." Millie whispered.

"Wait, what?" Beth gasped.

"It just slipped out. I said I had to go and then 'I love you. Bye.' Then hung up before I even realized what I had said." Millie said in a rush.

"Do you? Love him that is." Beth asked quietly.

Millie closed her eyes briefly as she took a stuttering breath. "I do. But the regret on his face when he kissed me was enough. I don't want to see it again."

"So, you are just going to ignore him?"

"No. Other than you, he is my best friend, and I don't want to lose him. That is why I am going to pretend that it was a friendly 'love you', like I say to you and Derek." Millie rubbed her forehead. "I just don't know how to act around him anymore."

"Oh, Millie." Beth gave Millie a hug. "You can't avoid him forever. Best to rip the band aid off. If you want him to think you only like him as a friend, tell him that. But if you want a possible future with him, you should tell him the truth."

"I'm pregnant with another man's baby, Beth. Aiden is a great guy, but I wouldn't blame him for not wanting to be a part of this." Millie gestured to her belly. "It would be asking a lot of him to raise someone else's child."

"I don't think you are giving Aiden enough credit. You didn't see the awe on his face as he watched the ultrasound." Beth rubbed Millie's arm. "You have my advice and that is all I'm going to say on the matter. Even though you two are so cute together."

Millie shook her head as she smiled. "When are you guys planning on heading back home?"

"We go home when you do. Franklin doesn't want you travelling alone."

"Franklin is exaggerating." Millie sighed in exasperation. Beth raised an eyebrow in challenge. "I have been getting lightheaded, the doctor said the baby is sitting really low and pressing on blood vessels or something like that. Which is making the normal pregnancy lightheadedness worse."

"Millie, I can't believe you haven't said anything." Beth got to her feet. "Come on, let's get you inside so you can lay down."

When they walked into the living room, Aiden looked up from playing with Melody on the floor. He smiled at her, and butterflies took flight in her stomach. Beth pushed her towards the couch and forced her to sit down.

"Beth, it's not that bad." Millie protested.

"What's not?" Aiden asked.

"Millie has been having dizzy spells because the baby is sitting too low." Beth told him. "That's why Franklin has been keeping a close eye on her and doesn't want her traveling alone."

"Is there anything we can do to get the baby up higher?" Aiden asked, getting to his feet and walking over to them.

Millie laughed as she shook her head. "You are all making a bigger deal out of this than you should. I am completely fine. The doctor said that if I feel faint, sit or lay down and to stand up slowly. He didn't seem concerned, so neither should you."

"I'm going to check on dinner and let the others know to keep an eye on you." Beth stood and walked from the room. Millie stared after her in disbelief.

Aiden sat down next to her, and she met his gaze. "We need to talk." He kept his voice low so that the others wouldn't overhear. Millie swallowed to clear her suddenly dry throat. "Why didn't you answer my calls right after the video call?"

"I put my phone on silent because I was going to church."

"And you didn't return the calls?" Aiden studied her face.

"Things got busy."

"Did you mean what you said?" Aiden pressed as he turned his body more towards her and laid his arm along the back of the couch.

"Of course I love horses." Millie stood and walked towards the window to get some distance from him, but Aiden followed her.

"That's not the part I was talking about."

"Aiden, I'm not in the mood for games." Millie tried to walk past him, but he grabbed her arm, spinning her to face him.

"Good. Neither am I." Aiden said before pressing his lips to hers.

Millie was momentarily stunned and stood frozen. After a moment, she relaxed and returned his kiss. He kept one arm around her waist while the other tangled in her hair. Warmth spread through her. Millie's hand touched Aiden's jaw lightly.

Aiden pulled away just enough to speak, his lips brushing against hers as he did so. "Millie, I need you to understand something." He gave her another quick kiss. "I am in love with you."

Millie pulled back farther to see his face. "You said we could only be friends."

"Don't remind me of my stupidity." Aiden shook his head. "I regret those words and letting you leave. These past seven weeks have been complete torture. You became so distant, not just physically, and it was killing me not being able to beg your forgiveness."

Millie studied Aiden's face. Pain filled his eyes as he met her gaze. Millie's heart was beating so fast it was making her lightheaded. She closed her eyes and grabbed onto Aiden's shirt. "Aiden, I think I need to sit down." She opened her eyes and the world tilted.

Aiden's hold on her tightened, and before she knew it, she was sitting on the couch with Aiden's arms around her. "Millie, are you okay?" Aiden sounded near to panicking.

She nestled herself against Aiden and closed her eyes again. "I'm okay." Aiden tucked her hair behind her ear and kissed her forehead. "What does this mean for us?" she asked quietly.

"That depends entirely on you." Aiden paused and Millie looked up at him. "I love you, Millie, and would love nothing more than to make you my wife. But if you don't feel the same, I will respect that, and we can be friends."

"Aiden, I'm pregnant." Millie started to say but stopped when Aiden chuckled.

"I am well aware of that fact." His eyes shifted down to her belly before returning to her face.

"It's not just me you would be getting. You would be,"

"Raising the baby as my own. I understand that, Millie. You and this baby are the center of my world." Aiden kissed her again before resting his forehead against hers.

Millie felt tears wetting her cheeks and she tried to look down so Aiden wouldn't see them, but he cupped her face. His brows furrowed in worry as he used his thumb to brush her tears away. "Please don't cry, Millie." He whispered.

"Are you sure about this, Aiden? I wouldn't..."

Aiden pressed his lips to hers, cutting off her protest. "I have never been more certain about anything in my life." He gently stroked her cheek. "Will you marry me, Millie?"

More tears rolled down Millie's face. "Yes." She breathed out. "I love you, Aiden."

Aiden's smile spread from ear to ear and Millie giggled as he rubbed the tip of his nose against hers. He kissed her tenderly and Millie wrapped her arms around his neck. Aiden's hand moved down her back before settling on the side of her stomach.

They had been kissing for several minutes before the baby kicked where Aiden's hand rested. He jerked back in surprise, causing Millie to laugh. She grabbed his hand and replaced it on her belly as the baby continued to kick. Aiden let out a little laugh as he stared at her belly in awe.

He lifted his eyes to her face with a big grin. "What's going on in here?" Josh came into the room holding onto Bentley's hand.

"The baby is moving." Aiden said excitedly. "You should feel this. It's crazy."

Josh walked over and sat on the floor. He put his hand on Millie's belly where Aiden's hand had just been. His eyes widened in surprise. "What does it feel like for you?" he asked Millie.

"It's kind of hard to explain."

"I think you are far enough along that the baby will move away from a flashlight if you shine it on your belly." Derek said as he walked into the room.

"Do we know where a flashlight is?" Josh asked enthusiastically. Josh and Derek went back into the kitchen to see if they could find a flashlight, once again leaving Aiden and Millie alone.

Aiden grabbed her left hand and kissed it before sliding something onto Millie's ring finger. Millie gasped when she saw the ring. It was just a simple white gold ring with three small diamonds inlaid into the band on either side of a larger diamond. "Aiden, its beautiful." She whispered as she studied it.

"I was hoping you would agree to marry me." Aiden grinned at her.

Millie put her arms back around his neck. "I love you." She whispered against his lips before Aiden deepened the kiss.

"Yuck." Bentley said causing them to pull away from each other again. His nose was scrunched in disgust as he looked at them. "Mommy said it's dinner."

"Alright, buddy, we are coming." Aiden chuckled and Bentley ran from the room. "When are we going to tell the others?"

Millie shrugged. "Why don't we tell them tonight after the kids are in bed?"

"Sounds like a great idea." Aiden stood and helped Millie to her feet. She wobbled slightly but found her balance quickly. Aiden released her to pick Melody up off the floor.

Millie told him to go ahead, that she just needed to grab something before dinner. He gave her a hard look before moving to the door that led to the kitchen and waited. Millie unzipped the front pocket of her suitcase and slipped the envelope and pen into her pocket without Aiden seeing.

There were two seats next to each other and Millie took the one at the end while Aiden put Melody in her highchair next to Beth. Aiden took his seat and Derek offered the prayer. Millie rested her left hand in her lap as she took a drink of water.

"So, what took you two so long after we sent Bentley in to get you." Derek asked as he dished some potatoes onto Bentley's plate.

"I needed to get something from my bag." Millie shrugged.

"They were kissing." Bentley added, causing Aiden to choke on the bite he just took.

All the adults at the table froze as they stared at Bently. Derek turned his head slowly towards Millie and Aiden. "Kissing?" Josh asked. Aiden's face had gone red, and Millie was trying her best to act normal but when Beth started laughing, she couldn't help but laugh as well.

"I want a ring, too." Bentley called from the other side of the room. "Please."

"What did you get from your bag, Millie?" Aiden asked, turning to her.

"We are not changing the topic yet." Derek said before she could answer. "We all knew that Aiden was smitten with you from the beginning, but what ring?"

Millie looked at Aiden, who winked at her. She smiled as she lifted her left hand to show everyone the ring. Aiden put his arm along the back of Millie's chair as everyone started talking all at once.

"Are we to assume that since the ring is on your finger and Aiden is smiling again, that you said 'yes'?" Josh sat back in his chair with a big smile on his face.

"After trying to convince me that I didn't know what I was getting into." Aiden smirked at her.

"If that is how you are going to be, I won't be sharing this with you." Millie pulled the envelope out of her pocket and held it up.

"Is that?" Aiden's eyes widened in excitement.

"That's *the* envelope." Beth clapped and Millie laughed. "It's about freaking time. Have you looked at it yet?"

Millie shook her head. "It hasn't been opened since the card was put inside." Aiden reached for the envelope, but Millie moved it out of his reach. "Not so fast, Aiden." Aiden reached for it again and she shoved it down her shirt and smirked at him. His eyes narrowed as he glared at her.

"Come on, Millie. We have all been dying to know what the baby is." Aiden whined.

"Everyone looks pretty alive to me." Millie took another bite of her food.

"You know, Aiden may not be willing to go there yet, but I sure will." Beth warned.

Millie laughed at how red Aiden's face got. Beth stood and Millie pulled out the envelope. "I am starving and want to eat before we open it."

"Forget that." Beth said as she pulled the envelope from Millie's hand.

Just before Beth could open it, Aiden took it from her and shoved it in his back pocket. He retook his seat with a triumphant smile. "Millie is right. Eat now, then we can find out what is inside the envelope."

Chapter 18

A fire was crackling in the fireplace, giving the room a cozy feel. Aiden sat holding Millie's hand while they waited for Beth and Derek to finish putting the kids to bed, and for Josh to finish cleaning up dinner.

Aiden pulled his hand from hers before putting his arm around Millie, drawing her closer. Millie looked up at Aiden and he kissed her. They sat like that for a while before someone cleared their throat and they turned to see Beth and Derek sitting on the other couch.

"I knew you two were going to work things out." Beth smiled and Aiden chuckled.

"I am so ready for this." Josh said as he walked into the room, drying his hands on a dish towel. "I think we should have the mom and dad find out first."

"Mom and dad?" Millie asked, confused. Did he mean Monica and Franklin or Beth and Derek?

Josh gave her a funny look. "Yeah, you and Aiden. You are the baby's mom and Aiden is going to be its dad, right?""

Millie nodded slowly and gave Aiden the go ahead to open the envelope. Aiden kissed her forehead before pulling it out of his pocket. The room became quiet as Aiden broke the seal. It was almost like everyone was holding their breath.

Millie bit the inside of her cheek to keep from smiling. She knew what he was going to find. This wasn't exactly what everyone was thinking it was. Millie hadn't told anyone this, and she was excited to finally share the news with them.

Aiden pulled out the piece of paper and stared at it with a confused expression. "What does it say?" Beth practically yelled.

Aiden turned the card over, but the other side was just as blank as the first side. "It's blank." Aiden said in confusion. Millie laid her head on his shoulder as he passed it to Josh.

"Millie, did you take out the card from the doctor?" Beth asked as she looked at the blank card when it was passed to her.

"No." Millie laughed. "Here, let me see." The card was given to her. She slipped a blacklight out of her pocket before passing it back to Aiden.

"You knew that the card was going to be blank." Derek accused her with a scowl.

"It's not blank. The ink is just invisible." Millie sat up to allow Aiden to use both hands.

He clicked the light on and aimed it at the card. A date was illuminated. Aiden cocked his head to the side as if trying to figure out what it meant. "It's a date and time." He told the others. "That's what...two weeks away?"

Millie's excitement grew and she grinned. "Yes."

"What does it mean? Do we have to wait until then to find out the baby's gender?" Josh asked.

"This has nothing to do with the baby's gender." Millie stood and moved to stand in front of the fireplace.

"I'm confused. Isn't that the envelope from the doctor's office?" Beth asked.

"No. I put this one together a few days ago." Millie shifted her weight from one foot to the other. She was so excited about this that she could hardly contain herself.

"What is happening on this date?" Aiden asked as he watched her.

"We are going on a day trip. I have a sitter already set up to go with us so she can watch the kids while we are inside." Millie couldn't contain her excitement.

"Inside where?" Derek asked.

"The temple. I just went through the temple prep classes and talked with the bishop here and back home. That is the day and time I get my endowment."

Beth squealed while Aiden jumped to his feet and pulled Millie into his arms. His grin was almost as big as hers. He gave her a quick kiss as everyone gathered around them. Everyone was excited for her.

Once they all retook their seats, Josh's mischievous grin made an appearance. "So, you successfully turned the topic away from you two, but

I'm bringing it back." He crossed his arms over his chest. "When is the wedding?"

Aiden chuckled. "I just barely convinced Millie to marry me. We haven't talked about the particulars yet."

"Why wait? Get hitched now and we can party later." Josh laughed.

Millie's heart began to speed up as thoughts of Lawrence saying almost the exact same things filled her head. Memories of them eloping and then her waking up alone flooded her mind. Aiden pressed a kiss to her temple, pulling her out of her spiraling thoughts.

"Sweetheart, I'm not going anywhere. We will get married when you are ready, and not a moment sooner." He whispered in her ear so no one else could hear. Millie turned to look into Aiden's eyes, needing to see his sincerity. "I promise." he said, brushing his lips against hers lightly.

"Millie, have you decided who you want in the delivery room?" Beth asked, breaking the bubble Millie and Aiden had been in.

"Not really. Hopefully I make it there and it would probably be good to have Dr. Spaulding present as well." Millie shrugged as she turned, leaning her back against Aiden with her feet up on the arm of the couch.

Beth scoffed and rolled her eyes. "I was talking about your support team."

"I was kind of hoping you would be willing to be there." Millie told Beth. "Since you have gone through it a few times."

"Yes!" Beth pumped her fist in the air. "I am so there. What about Aiden?"

Millie felt her cheeks flush. "I hadn't really thought about the guys being there since, you know."

"That makes sense. I guess it would depend on if you two were married or not before you have the baby." Beth nodded in understanding.

"Why can't we be there?" Josh asked offended.

"Because a woman in labor is in nothing but a hospital gown and when it comes time to push, let's just say she is quite exposed. No offense, but I am not willing to be there for anyone but my wife." Derek kissed Beth on the cheek.

Josh's eyes widened. "I didn't think about it that way. No wonder you haven't invited me into the delivery room, Beth."

Millie laughed at the embarrassed look on Josh's face. The group continued talking. The topics changed to sites they could see before they headed home. Millie's body began to grow heavy, and she started to doze. She was just about to fall asleep when her phone rang.

"Hello?" Millie said as she sat up.

"I'm sorry for calling at such an hour, but I have some news for you." Mrs. White said in her business tone.

"Okay, I'm listening." Millie stood and walked outside.

"How soon can you get back home?"

"As soon as I can book a flight. Why?"

"Mr. Hansen has filed for paternity rights." Millie felt the blood drain from her face. She sat down on the steps and covered her mouth in shock.

"Why would he do that? He wanted me to get an abortion. He tried to drag me to a clinic himself."

"I reached out to him, like we talked about, to see if he would voluntarily give up parental rights, but he refused. When I got his paperwork, trying to establish paternity, I immediately filed to get his rights involuntarily removed. I even submitted the police report and restraining order. The court issued a hearing date for Monday."

"I will be there." Millie wiped tears of frustration from her cheeks. Why couldn't Lawrence just leave her alone? "Thank you, Mrs. White. I am going to see when I can get a flight home."

Millie hung up and went back inside. She went immediately to her bags and pulled out her laptop. While it booted up, she sat on the floor and pulled out her wallet. Thank goodness Franklin didn't have a password on his Wi-Fi and she connected easily.

"Millie, what is going on?" Aiden asked as he sat next to her.

"I have to go." She sniffled. "Lawrence is filing for paternity, and I have to be in court on Monday morning. I need to be there as soon as I can to make sure Mrs. White has everything she needs." Millie scrolled through flights as she explained the situation. "Why is he fighting for this?" she growled in frustration.

Aiden took the computer from her and clicked on a flight that was leaving in three hours. He grabbed her wallet and removed her Drivers' License so he could fill out the information. Next, he put in his.

"You aren't going to do this alone, Millie." Aiden told her when she started to ask what he was doing. In less than ten minutes, Aiden had booked them first class tickets home. Millie watched him turn the laptop off and put it back in her bag.

"We will be flying home on Saturday, so we will be there too." Beth said firmly.

"Aiden, go get your stuff packed." Josh grabbed Aiden's hand and pulled him to his feet. "We will make sure Millie's stuff gets in the car and that you guys have some food to eat."

Aiden kissed Millie before running out the door. Beth hugged her as they watched the guys pack snacks into her carryon and load the car. Aiden was only gone for twenty minutes before he shoved his bag in the trunk next to hers. Derek, Josh, and Beth hugged them goodbye, and they were on their way.

* * *

Millie sat with Aiden in the waiting room of Mrs. White's office. They had arrived in at four that morning and Millie was exhausted. She leaned on Aiden and closed her eyes.

"Sweetheart, they are ready for us." Aiden whispered in her ear, and Millie opened her eyes.

Mrs. White was standing there with a sympathetic smile on her face. "You look exhausted, Millie, but I am glad you were able to get here so soon."

They followed Mrs. White into her office. Once the door was closed and the older woman was sitting behind her desk, she studied Aiden carefully. "I'm sorry. I don't think we have met before. I am Mrs. Susan White, Millie's lawyer."

"Aiden Coleman. It's a pleasure to meet you, ma'am." He shook hands with Mrs. White before sitting back in his chair.

"Aiden is my fiancé." Millie clarified when Mrs. White continued to eye Aiden.

Mrs. White's eyes snapped to Millie's as she leaned back in her chair and tapped her fingers on the desk. "When are you getting married?" she finally asked.

"We haven't decided yet." Aiden answered.

"Hmm." Mrs. White straightened up and pulled out a folder. "Is the reason you wanted Mr. Hansen to give up parental rights so that Mr. Coleman could adopt the baby?"

"Aiden and I weren't engaged when I asked you to reach out to Lawrence about relinquishing his rights to the baby. I was afraid of what he would do since I got the restraining order and refused to get the abortion." Millie clarified.

"Mr. Coleman are you wanting to adopt the baby once you and Ms. Larson are married?"

"If Millie is okay with it, I would love nothing more." Aiden grabbed hold of Millie's hand.

"When did you learn of Ms. Larson's pregnancy?"

"A few days after she did, I believe." Aiden looked to her for confirmation.

"I found out about my pregnancy and then three days later, Aiden knew." Millie confirmed.

"Have you been involved in the pregnancy?" Mrs. White took down a few notes.

"I was at the twelve-week appointment when we heard the heartbeat for the first time and the twenty-week appointment, when they did the ultrasound." Aiden answered.

"Just the appointments? You haven't been assisting with anything else?" Mrs. White looked up from her paper.

"He helped move furniture into the house. He has also made sure I have been eating, even when I didn't feel like it, and he texted me constantly to make sure I was taking my medications. Aiden was at the house at least three nights a week until I flew to Alaska. He also helped with dishes and other chores." Millie said, and Aiden squeezed her hand.

Mrs. White continued to write a few things down. When she was done, she looked up at them and threaded her fingers together as she rested her hands on her desk. She seemed to be weighing her words.

"How long have you two been together?"

Millie glanced over at Aiden. "We met the day she found out about her pregnancy and have been friends ever since. I realized quickly that I had stronger feelings for her, but I didn't act on them until yesterday."

Mrs. White raised her eyebrows in surprise. "From what you have told me, with Mr. Coleman going to your prenatal appointments, helping you move, taking care of you, you sound like you have been in a romantic relationship much longer than twenty-four hours. Those aren't things a guy friend would do."

Millie thought about it. Josh went to some of the appointments and hung out with them, but he never pushed her to eat or reminded her to take her medication. Josh acted more like a brother to her and an excited uncle when it came to the baby. Mrs. White was right; Aiden had been stepping up above the role of a friend.

"This might work in our favor. If Mr. Coleman does want to adopt the baby and has already established the fact that he has been present while Mr. Hansen has not, it might sway the judge." Mrs. White put her papers back into a neat stack. "Too bad you two weren't already married." She muttered under her breath before looking back at them. "I will reach out to your doctor's office to see if I can get witnesses of Mr. Coleman being present at your appointments."

Mrs. White talked to them a little more about how the proceedings were going to go on Monday and how Lawrence was suing her for keeping the pregnancy from him for so long. When she was done, she told Millie to go home and get some rest. Aiden held Millie's hand as they exited the office building.

Millie sighed as they descended the steps slowly. "Sounds like you have been taking on the role of husband already, just without the official title." Millie smiled as Aiden winked at her.

"I did tell you that you and this baby had quickly become my world." Aiden pulled her closer before kissing her. "I didn't want to miss anything."

"I have an appointment tomorrow." Millie told him.

"Are you saying I get to be there?" Aiden asked.

"Only if you want to." Millie laughed at the scowl he gave her.

They were walking hand-in-hand through the parking lot, when Millie saw the courthouse down the street. Mrs. White's muttered comment came back to her. Millie, too, wished that she and Aiden were already married. That way he didn't have to leave her side. It had been hard to say goodnight for the few short hours between the time he dropped her off at her house and when he picked her up this morning.

Millie stopped walking and Aiden gave her a questioning look. "Aiden," Millie said slowly. "What if we…" That idea was crazy. They couldn't get married today. "Never mind." She shook her head and started walking again, but Aiden pulled her to a stop.

"What were you going to say?" he asked. "That look was an 'I'm thinking of something' kind of look."

Millie shook her head. "It was just a crazy thought, Aiden. I don't know why it even popped into my head."

"Humor me." Aiden said, grabbing her other hand.

"I hated saying good night this morning." Millie shrugged. "I saw the courthouse and thought, what if?"

"What if we got married? Today?" Aiden looked down the road with a thoughtful expression on his face. When he turned back to her, he had a twinkle in his eyes. "I'm willing. Once the baby is born and the adoption is finalized, we can get sealed. We can have a luncheon afterwards for everyone and celebrate then."

Millie's eyes widened in surprise. "Aiden, this is crazy."

Aiden gently took her face in his hands. "I hated saying goodnight to you as well, Millie. I love you and if you want to wait, I will wait. But I will be more than happy to make you my wife before the day is done. My only question is, do you want to see if your bishop can marry us, or do you want to see if we can find someone else?"

Millie just stared at Aiden for a long moment. "This is crazy." she breathed out as excitement began to spread through her.

Aiden smiled. "It is totally crazy, and we will have to deal with some upset people when they fly back in a few days."

"If we do this, I need you to promise me something." Millie said.

"Whatever you want, sweetheart." Aiden kissed the tip of her nose.

"You have to sign the marriage certificate first." Millie said seriously.

Understanding shone in Aiden's eyes. "You better believe I will be signing first, and I want you to watch me do it. I will be watching as you sign as well. I am going to make you my wife, Millie. I will make sure everything is done right because I do not plan on giving you up."

He kissed her then and she melted against him. Once he finally ended the kiss, Millie nodded. "Okay. I will call Bishop Taylor."

"Yeah!" Aiden exclaimed before he kissed her again, causing her to laugh.

Chapter 19

Millie shifted trying to get more comfortable. Sleeping was so hard nowadays. An arm around her waist tightened slightly and she froze in fear. Then she remembered what had happened the previous evening. Millie slowly looked over her shoulder. Aiden was asleep and holding her.

Tears sprang to her eyes. She had been terrified to go to sleep last night, so afraid that Aiden wouldn't be there when she woke up. Lawrence had left an emotional scar that she didn't even know she had, until last night. Aiden hadn't pushed anything. He told her they had nothing but time and held her until she fell asleep.

Millie rolled over as carefully as she could manage, which was not at all graceful, and snuggled as close as she was able to. Aiden's hand rose to her head and brushed the hair from her face before pressing a kiss to her forehead.

"Good morning." Aiden's voice was gravelly with sleep. Millie buried her face in his chest as she continued to fight her emotions. She was so relieved he was still here. "Please tell me those are happy tears." He whispered as he held her close.

"I'm sorry." Millie sniffled and wiped her cheeks. "I guess I didn't realize how much Lawrence had affected me."

"Millie, I don't blame you for having these fears, but I want you to understand something." Millie looked up when Aiden paused. He pressed his lips to hers gently. "I will never leave without letting you know first."

Millie nodded before she kissed him again. When they finally broke apart, she was smiling. "The appointment is at eleven." She whispered against his lips.

"What time is it now?" Aiden asked as he rolled onto his back and grabbed his phone off the side table. "We have two hours. We should probably get up and get some food in you."

Millie rolled and sat up on Aiden, straddling his waist. His hands moved to her hips as she smiled down at him. "I need to jump in a shower first." Millie smiled down at him. Aiden swallowed hard but didn't say anything.

Aiden closed his eyes and took several deep breaths. Millie patted his chest before getting up. As she walked to the bathroom, she slowly started removing her clothes. She was smiling as she turned the water on.

"Are you inviting me to join you?" Aiden asked from the doorway.

Millie glanced over her shoulder at him. His eyes were glued to her, but he stayed just outside the bathroom threshold. "The decision is yours, Aiden. I'm not going to ask you to do anything you don't want to do." Aiden kept his eyes on her as he took a step into the room, closing the door behind him.

*   *   *

Aiden stood next to Millie as she laid back on the exam room bed. Even though they had two hours to get ready, they still ended up being nearly ten minutes late. She hadn't fully expected the morning to go exactly like it had. After Lawrence, she had felt somewhat empty. This morning had left her feeling giddy and cherished.

Millie smiled up at Aiden, causing him to chuckle as he leaned down. "What is that look for?" he asked.

"I was just thinking." Millie shrugged as she bit her lip to try to stop smiling.

Aiden's smile grew. "About what?"

"About what needs to happen today."

"And what would that be?"

"We need to go shopping. The house needs food, and we should probably start getting things for the baby's room. We literally only have a crib."

"You haven't started setting up the baby's room yet?" Dr. Spaulding's voice caused both Aiden and Millie to jump in surprise. Millie hadn't heard her enter.

"Not yet. We just got back from Alaska yesterday." Millie looked at the doctor.

"Have you at least started thinking about names?" Dr. Spaulding asked as she scanned through Millie's chart.

"I have read through some names, but I haven't really thought about it since I don't know if the baby is a boy or girl yet." Millie confessed.

Dr. Spaulding looked up from the file. "Are you not wanting to find out? If that is the case, I will make a note in your file, so I don't accidentally slip."

"No, I want to find out. I just didn't want to while I was in Alaska, and everyone else was here." Millie said quickly.

Dr. Spaulding looked between Millie and Aiden for a long moment. "Well, I think the most important person is here. Did you want to find out right now?"

Millie turned to look at Aiden. "It's up to you, Millie." Aiden said as he grabbed her hand and gave it a squeeze.

She could tell by the look in his eyes that he desperately wanted to know. "That would be great, Dr. Spaulding." Millie said and Aiden's smile grew even bigger.

"I believe congratulations are in order. How long have you been married?" The doctor asked with a smile.

"Since yesterday." Aiden was beaming and Millie couldn't help her own smile as he kissed her hand.

"In that case," Dr. Spaulding began turning on the ultrasound machine and dimming the lights as she spoke. "Count this as my wedding gift." She gestured for Millie to lay down.

Millie laid down and Dr. Spaulding lifted Millie's shirt up before squirting the warm jelly on her belly. Aiden's grip tightened when the image of the baby filled the screen. Dr. Spaulding pointed out the hair that was now on the baby's head, the baby's hiccups, and fingers.

"And that right there," Dr. Spaulding pointed at the screen again. "Tells us that the baby is a boy."

Millie stared at the baby on the screen in shock, while Aiden let out a little laugh. He kissed her hand again in excitement. Dr. Spaulding was smiling as she turned on the lights and wiped the jelly off Millie's stomach.

Millie was still trying to process that the baby was a boy. Everything suddenly felt so real. She was having a baby boy. "A boy." She breathed out.

Aiden kissed her forehead before looking into her eyes. Excitement shone in his eyes. He touched Millie's cheek, gently wiping a stray tear away. Millie hadn't even known she had been crying. She looked up at him and smiled. More warm tears spilled out of her eyes. Aiden wiped them away as well with a soft smile.

The rest of the appointment went well. Millie had gained back the weight she had lost in the first trimester. Dr. Spaulding told them about preterm labor and what to look out for. They scheduled their next appointment for two weeks and left.

"Can we go get something to eat?" Millie asked as they walked toward the car. "I think I worked up an appetite."

Aiden opened her door for her as a sly smile spread on his lips. "Good to know that's a good way to get you to eat." Millie rolled her eyes as her cheeks burned. "You up for Mexican food?"

"Always." Millie laughed. She was surprised when Aiden pulled into the parking lot of the Mexican restaurant down the street. "Do we have to come here?" she asked as he opened her door.

"They had the best tacos. Plus, if that guy hits on you again, I can tell him you are taken now." Aiden gave her a brief kiss before grabbing her hand and leading her inside. "Table for two please." Aiden told the hostess.

They were led to the same table they had been sitting at the last time they were there. Millie groaned when she saw the same guy walking towards them. When he saw them, a cocky smile spread on his face.

"What can I get you to drink?" he asked.

"Two waters." Aiden said while he looked at his menu.

"Anything else?" the waiter winked at her.

"Please stop winking at my wife." Aiden didn't even look up.

The waiter blinked in surprise before he hurried off. Millie couldn't help the laugh that bubbled up. Aiden turned and winked at her. "Do you know what you want?" he asked.

Millie leaned forward and kissed him. Aiden slid his hand around the back of her neck as he deepened the kiss. The sound of a glass being placed on the table caused Millie to finally pull away from Aiden.

"Do you know what you want?" the waiter asked, his voice more subdued than a few minutes ago.

Millie gave Aiden a playful smile. "I think I do."

Aiden's eyes twinkled as he returned her smile with a wolfish one. "She would like a carne asada burrito and I will have the fish tacos." Millie's eyes widened in horror. "Actually, make the tacos shredded chicken instead."

The waiter left and Millie smacked Aiden's chest. "I can't believe you were going to get fish right now. Just the thought of fish is making me queasy."

Millie laid her head against Aiden's chest. "I didn't know the f-word affected you. I thought it was just the smell, and I wouldn't have actually gotten it." Aiden kissed her head as he wrapped his arms around her.

Millie took several slow deep breaths to try to calm her suddenly churning stomach. "I think we should go get your truck after lunch."

"What all do we need to get?" Aiden asked. "I've never shopped for a baby before."

"Car seat, clothes, diapers, wipes, stroller, dresser, blankets, and diaper bag, those are just some of the basics. Beth gave me a list of must-haves before the baby is born." Millie took a sip of her water.

"We will go switch your car for my truck when we are done here. Are you going to feel up to all that shopping? You haven't gotten much rest over the last two nights."

"We don't have to get everything today, but I feel that we need to get at least the necessities. Then I want to go home and take a nap."

Aiden chuckled. "I could go for a nap too. If I am feeling this tired, I can't even imagine how tired you are feeling."

Their lunch was brought out and Millie's earlier appetite came back as soon as she smelled the deliciousness in front of her. She moaned as she took a bite of her burrito. No words could describe how much she had missed Mexican food while in Alaska. They finished lunch quickly and left, hand-in-hand.

* * *

Millie was putting away groceries while Aiden moved the baby stuff upstairs into the baby's room. Her back was hurting so badly today, and she just wanted to find relief. Millie put the last of the food in the fridge and leaned back against the counter.

Her eyes moved to the glass patio doors and the pool beyond. It was cooler outside now that the sun had set, but the pool was heated. Millie walked into the backyard, tossing her phone onto the patio table as she passed it. The water would help take the weight of the baby off her back.

Millie took off her clothes and walked into the pool, sighing as the pressure on her lower back lessened. She swam to the deep end and to the low seat on the far side. She closed her eyes and leaned her head back as she stared at the stars.

"Millie, you out here?" Aiden's voice called from the living room doors.

"Yeah." She called back. "I'm in the pool."

The gate squeaked as it swung open, followed by the click as it locked closed. Millie took a deep breath of the evening air. She smiled when Aiden stood over her. It was so dark that she couldn't see his face, and she was sure he couldn't really see her either.

"I thought you wanted to relax the rest of the evening." Aiden said as he crouched next to her.

Millie rotated, resting her arms on the edge of the pool. "I am relaxing. You know that weightlessness being in a pool gives you?" Aiden nodded. "This baby is killing my back. I figured a little time in the pool would help take the weight off."

"Mind if I join you?" Aiden asked as he stood.

"Sure." Aiden headed for the pool gate and Millie had to bite her cheek to keep from laughing. "Aiden." She called after him, causing him to stop just before he got to the gate.

"Yeah?"

"No one is around and its completely dark." Millie told him.

He remained standing there for several minutes. "Are you...?"

"Skinny dipping? Yes, I am." Millie laughed. "I did most nights you guys weren't here."

Millie could only see Aiden's silhouette against the living room lights as he pulled his shirt off. In less than two minutes he was in the pool and swimming towards her. She wrapped her arms around his neck when he got to her.

"I'm sorry your back is hurting. What can I do to help?" Aiden asked softly.

"I don't think you can do anything." Millie ran her hand through Aiden's hair. "And I still have twelve weeks left, which means, it's only going to get worse."

"I don't mind coming out here every night if it helps you." Aiden said before kissing her.

"I'm sure you don't." Millie laughed and allowed Aiden to hold her as he slowly moved around the pool. After a few minutes, Millie couldn't stop herself from kissing Aiden again. "Aiden, we're having a boy."

He smiled against her lips. "I take it the shock is wearing off."

Millie giggled. "A little." Aiden pulled her closer. "When are we going to tell the others? About us being married and about the baby being a boy." Millie asked as she rubbed the tip of her nose against his.

"They fly in late tonight. I am sure they will be at church tomorrow." Aiden shrugged.

"Won't Josh wonder why you aren't at the apartment?"

"By the time he gets home, he will most likely assume I am asleep. I don't think he will realize I am gone until morning."

"What are we going to tell them? They are going to be so mad at us for not waiting for them." Millie chewed her lip nervously as she pictured Beth's face tomorrow.

Aiden moved them to the low seat in the deep end and sat down with her straddling him. "They are definitely going to be mad, but when we explain about the timing with court on Monday, the courthouse closed on the weekends and us feeling the need to get married, I think they will understand. And if they stay mad, we can hold the fact that we know the baby's gender over their heads."

"That is terrible." Millie scolded him, but she was grinning. "They will probably be even more mad that we didn't immediately call them to let them know about the baby, then about us getting married." Aiden pressed his lips to hers and Millie's hands moved to cup his face.

Chapter 20

Aiden wrapped his arms around her and kissed her cheek while she flipped a pancake. "Beth called." Millie glanced over her shoulder at Aiden.

"Already? That was quick. I would have thought she would be sleeping in." Aiden released her to grab two plates out of the cupboard.

"Melody had a rough night, so Beth hasn't been able to sleep." Millie loaded one plate with five pancakes and the other with only two. "She wanted to know if we were going to be at church. Josh stayed the night with them, and she was thinking Josh could ride back home with you."

"That would work out really well. He can help me bring your car back." Aiden set the plates on the table and Millie sat in front of the one with five. "What are you doing?" Aiden laughed.

"Sitting down to eat. What does it look like I am doing? And why can't I just drive my car back?" Millie narrowed her eyes at Aiden.

"Sweetheart, there is no way you are eating that many pancakes." Aiden grabbed two off her plate and added it to his. "And about the car…Millie, I don't want anything to happen to you or that little guy. You nearly passed out this morning standing in the closet picking out clothes for today."

"Aiden, everything is fine." Millie started to protest, but the look on Aiden's face stopped her. His whole body was tense.

"Please, don't fight me on this. I can't lose you." Aiden's eyes took on a desperate look.

Millie slowly nodded. "Okay."

Aiden closed his eyes as the relief he felt instantly caused his tense muscles to relax. He pulled her to him and kissed her. The tenderness in his kiss made Millie sigh.

"Now that you aren't going to give me a heart attack, you should eat something before we need to get ready for church." Aiden said softly as he tucked her hair behind her ear.

They ate quickly and Aiden volunteered to clean up the kitchen since she cooked. Millie locked herself in the bathroom and started on her hair and makeup. She decided to switch her maxi dress for a blue maternity blouse that hugged her belly and a knee-length skirt.

Aiden knocked on the door just as she was putting on her necklace. The pendant was a T-Rex, and she knew Bentley would love it. "Millie, we need to go, or we are going to be late."

"I'll meet you in the truck. I just need to get my shoes on." She called back.

Millie slid her feet into a pair of strappy heels and hurried to the garage. Aiden was waiting by the passenger door for her. When he saw her, his eyes lit up. He took his time admiring her, which caused Millie to laugh.

"I thought you said we are going to be late." Millie raised her eyebrow in challenge as she waited for Aiden to open the car door, since his hand was on it.

"Were we going somewhere?" He asked.

"Aiden, come on." Millie pushed his hand off the door and opened it. Before she could climb in, Aiden pulled her to him.

"I can't believe I never thought to go to church with Derek before now."

"I dress to impress." Millie shrugged and climbed into her seat.

Aiden climbed behind the wheel and started to drive. "Who are you impressing today?" Aiden asked after several minutes of silence.

"My husband wouldn't like it if I said anything."

Aiden scowled at her as he took her hand in his. "Dang right he wouldn't like it if the answer is anyone but him."

Millie laughed but didn't say anything more. She could tell it was driving Aiden crazy. He parked in the back of the parking lot and turned to her. She could tell he was going to say something, so she kissed him. When he tried to pull away, Millie deepened the kiss. Aiden lost the will to fight and pulled her across the bench seat.

Millie's phone dinged with a notification after several minutes, and she broke the kiss. Beth texted to ask where they were. "Time to go, Cowboy." Millie checked her makeup in the mirror before looking back at Aiden. "I do have a question though," she asked as he quirked his brow before opening the door. "Was he impressed?"

"What am I going to do with you?" Aiden muttered as he climbed out of the truck. Millie slid out the same door. "It's a good thing you told me to meet you by the truck or we wouldn't have left the house for a couple of hours."

They made it to the chapel as the bishop stood to begin the meeting. He looked amused as Aiden quickened his step, and they slid onto the bench next to Josh. Bentley immediately pushed past everyone to get to her. She helped him onto her lap.

"Dinosaur!" He yelled as he grabbed her necklace.

"Shh." Millie laughed. "Remember you only get to play with my necklaces if you are quiet." Bentley nodded quickly and made a show of sealing his lips.

Josh got up and said the opening prayer. He sat on the end by Millie when he returned to his seat. He leaned close to her ear so no one would be able to hear. "We saw the truck when we got here and assumed you were already inside. Were you two just making out in the truck?"

"What would give you that idea?" Millie asked back.

"Maybe because Aiden looks like he is wearing lip gloss." Josh smirked at her.

Millie looked at Aiden and bit her lip to keep from laughing. She sent Bentley to get the wipes from the diaper bag. When he returned, Millie handed one to a confused Aiden. Josh was snickering while covering his mouth to keep from laughing too loud.

"You are wearing my lip gloss." Millie whispered in his ear. He ducked his head and wiped his mouth. She had worn a light pink lip gloss today, and it was totally noticeable on his lips. Josh snorted before getting up and making a quick exit. "Still like it when I wear makeup?" Millie asked when Aiden sat up straight again.

"I will just make sure to check before we come inside next time." Aiden winked at her.

The rest of church went by quickly. They went back to Beth and Derek's house for dinner. Josh teased Aiden about the whole lip gloss thing. In response to the teasing, he had kissed Millie in front of everyone, causing everyone to laugh and Millie to smack his chest.

Now that dinner was done, Millie was feeling exhausted. She snuck away from clean up duty and curled up on the couch. Josh found her there a few minutes later.

"Found her!" Josh called before looking back down at her. "You know, you could have told us you needed to lay down instead of just disappearing."

"Mmm, where would the fun be in that?" Millie sat up and Josh helped her to her feet. "I swear this kid gets bigger every day."

"That's because it does." Beth laughed as she walked into the room. "Are you guys headed out?" Beth asked as Derek and Aiden walked into the room.

"Tired?" Aiden asked as he put an arm around her, and she leaned against him. Millie noticed that he kept his left hand in his pocket. They had talked about not making their marriage known until after court on Monday.

"She was pretty much asleep on the couch." Josh told him.

"I think you should get her home." Derek said. "Millie needs to be there early tomorrow."

They said their goodbyes and headed for the truck. The reminder of court in the morning had Millie feeling uneasy. Aiden helped Millie into the shotgun seat while Josh climbed into the back. The guys talked the whole way and Millie stared out the window.

"So, why am I driving Millie's car back to her house? Shouldn't she just drive it?" Josh asked as they pulled into the apartment complex.

"Millie has been getting her dizzy spells again and I don't want her driving." Aiden said as he pulled into the parking spot next to her car. "After we drop Millie and her car off at the house, I will bring you back here."

"Uh, that didn't sound right." Josh shook his head. "Do you mean that after dropping Millie and the car off, *we* will be coming back here?"

"Aiden, just tell him." Millie looked over at Aiden.

"Have you been staying with Millie?" Josh looked completely shocked at the idea. "Guys, there is so much wrong with that."

"Not as wrong as you think." Aiden muttered.

Josh practically growled in frustration. "The only thing that would make staying together okay would be if you two were…" his voice trailed off. "No. You guys wouldn't have…not without us." Josh's voice became softer as he studied them.

"Josh, hear us out before you blow up, okay?" Millie said as she turned in her seat. Josh's eyes widened in surprise. "Court is on Monday, the courthouse would be closed on the weekends, and Aiden and I felt like we needed to get married before the court hearing."

Josh fell back against the seat. "Are you serious?"

Aiden told Josh about their visit with Mrs. White and how she had made the comment about how things would be easier if Millie and Aiden were already married. Both Millie and Aiden had felt like they should get married before Monday. However, they didn't want a big fuss about it until everything with Lawrence was settled.

Josh blew out a long breath. "Beth is going to be so ticked."

"We know." Millie sighed.

"Wow, this has been a busy weekend for you guys."

"Between meeting with the lawyer, getting married, Millie's doctor appointment, shopping, and moving some of my stuff over to the house, yeah it's been busy." Aiden smiled over at her.

"Okay, so no talking about you guys being married. Anything else?" Josh asked.

"If you want you can stay the night with us in the guest room and go with us to the courthouse." Millie offered as she leaned her head against the window.

"Aiden, take your wife home...man that sounds weird...and I will drive her car over once I grab a suit for tomorrow." Josh shook his head as he opened his door.

Millie didn't remember the drive home. She was startled awake when Aiden opened her door. "Come on, sweetheart. Let's get you in bed."

Aiden helped her change into her pajamas before she collapsed in bed. She barely registered him giving her a kiss on the head before she was out.

Millie bolted upright breathing hard. She was covered in sweat. A moment later, the bedroom door burst open, and Aiden came running over to her. Josh was right on his heels. "Millie, sweetheart, what's wrong?" Aiden wrapped her up in his arms, holding her tight.

Millie buried her face in his chest, taking a shuddering breath. She had been in labor and Aiden was on his way from classes. Lawrence walked into her hospital room, telling the nurses he was her husband. No matter what she said, he wouldn't leave. The baby came and she barely got a glimpse of him before Lawrence walked away with him.

Millie sat back and looked up into Aiden's face as the terror of that moment came rushing back to her. "He took the baby." Millie choked out with a sob.

Aiden pulled her head back to his chest as he kissed her forehead. "He won't get the baby, Millie. I promise you; Lawrence won't touch our son." Millie continued to cry. "Josh, can you get a glass of water?"

Millie's tears dried up as she listened to the steady beat of Aiden's heart. She took a sip of the water Josh offered her before falling back against Aiden. Josh excused himself and closed the door as he left.

Aiden laid down with her in his arms. He continued to stroke her hair slowly. Millie clung to him as if he could keep the nightmares away. Aiden's presence helped Millie feel safe enough that sleep reclaimed her.

Chapter 21

Millie woke up exhausted. She was glad that once Aiden came to bed, she didn't have any more nightmares. Aiden got up early to make breakfast. Millie threw up a few times while she showered and did her hair, but she didn't tell Aiden or Josh about her upset stomach. They seemed worried enough after her nightmare, even though neither of them said anything.

She knew her lack of appetite wasn't lost on Aiden. He watched her closely as they ate. Well, Aiden and Josh ate, Millie nibbled on toast.

Millie went back to her room and got dressed in a pencil skirt, blouse, and blazer. She did a light amount of makeup to hide her pale skin and dark circles under her eyes. She pulled on her most comfortable flats and headed back out into the living room.

"Are you guys ready?" Millie asked when she saw them on the couch.

"You look beautiful, Millie." Aiden said as he stood and walked over to her. He put his arms around her waist before kissing her softly. "We are ready when you are."

Millie nodded and the three of them climbed into Millie's car. The ride to the courthouse was silent. She wasn't sure if it was from everyone's nervousness or if they could sense her rising anxiety. Aiden held her hand firmly in his, and she took comfort in knowing she was not in this alone.

Clinging to Aiden's hand, Millie entered the courthouse. Mrs. White was waiting for them at the end of the hallway. "You are right on time, Ms. Larson. Mr. Coleman, it is a pleasure to see you here today."

"I wouldn't be anywhere else." Aiden said, and Mrs. White nodded in approval. "This is our friend, Josh Peterson."

"It is good you have so many supporters. The Benedicts are already sitting in the court room. Gentlemen, Ms. Larson and I will be having a private counsel before the proceedings. You are welcome to join the Benedicts." Mrs. White gestured toward a pair of double doors.

Aiden gave her a quick kiss before he and Josh slipped into the courtroom. Millie entered the room that Mrs. White pointed to, with the lawyer right behind her. They spent a few minutes discussing how the day would go, and Millie tried to keep calm. Last night's nightmare had her nervous. Before they left the room, Millie threw up again.

"Are you okay?" Mrs. White looked concerned.

"Just morning sickness. It's been like this the whole time." Millie waved off her concern as she wiped her mouth.

They entered the court room a few minutes late, thanks to Millie's stomach. Mrs. White approached the judge and whispered something to him. His eyes shifted to Millie before giving a small nod. Millie could only assume that her lawyer explained why they were late.

Millie glanced to her right. Lawrence was ogling her, but the moment his eyes fell on her rounded belly, he scowled. The judge introduced the case. Lawrence was there to establish paternity. He was suing her for emotional trauma that he sustained knowing she was never going to inform him of his impending fatherhood and how he missed out on important milestones of the pregnancy. Millie was there to get Lawrence's parental rights removed.

The judge introduced himself as Judge Stevens before both lawyers gave their opening statements and Mr. Hawkings, Lawrence's lawyer, called his first witness. Hours ticked by as the lawyers took turns questioning the various witnesses, including Dr. Spaulding and the man that had performed their marriage ceremony. He apparently had gotten himself licensed to officiate weddings since Lawrence's and Millie's pretend wedding.

Millie felt extremely hot and a bit out of it. Her hand had a slight tremor to it as she pressed it to her forehead. All she wanted to do was lay down.

Mrs. White stood, and Millie looked up. Lawrence was sitting on the stand. His eyes were glued to her. She hadn't even noticed that he had moved up there. After a few minutes of questioning Lawrence, Mrs. White stopped pacing and faced him directly.

"Mr. Hansen, did you convince Ms. Larson to elope with you?" Mrs. White asked.

"I did. We were in love, and I didn't see a need to wait." Lawrence smirked at Millie. His eyes had not strayed from her the whole time.

"And you were the one who planned the whole thing? You found the officiator, the venue, witnesses?"

"I did. Millie was taking classes at the university, and I wanted to make things as easy as possible." Lawrence shrugged.

"How many times did you ask Ms. Larson to move in together?"

"I don't remember. It's the natural progression of things. Boy meets girl. Girl moves in with boy."

"How many times did you ask to spend the night with Ms. Larson?"

Lawrence finally pulled his eyes away from Millie and turned to Mrs. White. "I don't know. A few."

"According to Ms. Larson's neighbors, it was several times a week, starting from a month after you two started dating."

"A man has needs." Lawrence sat back with a guarded expression.

"Did she ever allow you to stay the night?"

"No. Millie had this thing about getting intimate with a guy before marriage." Lawrence rolled his eyes.

"What thing?" Mrs. White put her hands behind her back.

"She refused to. Something about personal and religious beliefs, or something like that."

"And you dated for nine months and were engaged for three months?"

"That's right." Lawrence crossed his arms over his chest.

"So, you knew that Ms. Larson was not comfortable with sexual intimacy from the start of your relationship, yet you continued to ask her multiple times a week, for almost a year, to be intimate with you?" Lawrence's eyes narrowed slightly as he remained quiet. "Mr. Hansen, please answer the question. Did you or did you not try to get Ms. Larson to become sexually involved with you, even though she expressed to you multiple times that she would not until after marriage?"

"People can change their minds." Lawrence said evenly.

"Thank you. I have no further questions at this time, your honor." Mrs. White said before taking her seat.

Millie dropped her eyes back to the table in front of her. Seeing Lawrence was hard, especially after her nightmare. He was giving her the same condescending smile now as he had in her dream when he walked away with the baby.

"I would like to call Ms. Mildred Larson to the stand." Mr. Hawkings said as he stood.

Millie swallowed and took a deep breath before standing. She paused for a second before continuing to the witness stand. Millie's vision tilted and she stopped walking. The Bailiff grabbed hold of her elbow as he studied her face.

"Are you alright, Ms. Larson?" he asked her quietly.

"I just need to sit down." Millie whispered back as she touched the back of her hand to her head. The Bailiff's hold on Millie tightened when she began to sway.

"We will take a quick one-hour recess." Judge Stevens called. His voice sounded as if it were coming through a long tunnel.

Millie didn't know what happened next. When she opened her eyes, she was lying on a leather couch with Dr. Spaulding taking her blood pressure. "There she is. How are you feeling, Millie?"

"Where's Aiden?" Millie asked, looking around the room. It was a large office with tons of bookshelves. Judge Stevens, Mr. Hawkings, and Mrs. White were standing off to the side watching her.

"He is most likely in the court room." Dr. Spaulding gave her a smile. "When was the last time you ate something?"

"I ate some toast before we came." Millie tried to sit up, but Dr. Spaulding put a hand on her shoulder, keeping her down. "Can I see Aiden?" She looked to the judge.

"Who is Aiden?" the judge said gently.

"Aiden is her husband." Dr. Spaulding said as she handed Millie a cool water.

Judge Stevens opened the door and whispered to someone in the hallway. A few minutes later, Aiden came into the room. His sole focus was on Millie as he quickly crossed the room and knelt on the ground next to her. He pressed a kiss to her forehead while brushing the hair off her face.

"How are you feeling?" Aiden whispered as he studied her. "I don't think that toast was enough this morning."

"It might have been if she hadn't thrown it up before the trial started." Mrs. White commented.

"You threw up again?" Aiden asked as he stroked her cheek.

"A few times this morning." Millie sighed.

Aiden looked concerned at her admission. "We should get you something to eat." He rested his forehead against hers. "I don't think I have been more scared in my life, watching you collapse like that."

"Maybe we should set a new date for the trial." Mrs. White suggested as she moved closer.

Millie shook her head and pushed herself into a sitting position. "I want this over with. I am fine, I have a granola bar in my bag that I can eat."

"Millie, this wasn't one of your dizzy spells, you passed out." Aiden watched her anxiously. When he saw the determination on Millie's face, he sighed and hung his head. "Okay. Where is your bag?"

"I will send someone to retrieve it, so you can stay with your wife." The judge said as he sat in a nearby chair. "I don't think I have ever seen someone lose consciousness in my court room before."

"I am so sorry, your honor." Millie quickly apologized.

"Ms. Larson's baby is sitting low enough to put pressure on the veins in her pelvis, making her more lightheaded than normal. Additionally, she suffered from a mild concussion a few weeks ago that as left her with frequent dizzy spells." Dr. Spaulding quickly explained.

"I am fine. I just need a little water and a snack. I am so sorry for disrupting the trial, your honor. But I would really like to see this through." Aiden moved to sit beside Millie as she spoke to the judge.

Judge Stevens sat quietly for a long time as he observed her. Millie held to Aiden's hand as she tried not to squirm under the judge's gaze. A man came in holding her bag. Aiden accepted it and quickly pulled out a few granola bars.

Aiden opened the wrapper before handing it to her. Millie took a small bite as she leaned her head against Aiden's shoulder. Aiden rested a hand on her belly as he kissed her temple.

"Sir, Mr. Hansen is asking if this is going to take much longer, or if he is free to go." The man whispered to the judge.

Judge Stevens raised a brow in surprise, while Mr. Hawkings pinched the bridge of his nose. Millie scarfed down the rest of her granola bar before standing. Aiden bolted to his feet, wrapping an arm around her back.

"I am ready." Millie said opening another granola bar.

"Millie," Aiden started to protest, but she cut him off.

"I will be sitting the whole time. I will be fine."

"If you are sure, Ms. Larson. No one will begrudge you a few more minutes." Judge Stevens got to his feet as well.

"I appreciate the offer, your honor, but I am feeling much better. I would really like to just get through this as fast as we are able to." Millie leaned into Aiden as she took the last bite of the granola bar.

Judge Stevens nodded slowly. "But if you start feeling the least bit unwell, you will let us know. I do not want another episode like an hour ago."

Millie nodded her head. "Of course, your honor."

"Thank you, sir." Aiden said in relief.

They all started to file out of the room. Aiden was directly behind her, followed by the judge. "You sure have your hands full with that one." Judge Stevens whispered, but Millie still heard him.

"She definitely keeps me on my toes." Aiden muttered, and Millie rolled her eyes.

Chapter 22

Millie sat at the front of the court room. Aiden had retaken his seat with the others and whispered something to them. Whatever he told them, made them all relax a little. Mr. Hawkings spoke quietly to Lawrence before standing up and walking towards Millie.

"Ms. Larson, it is good to see you with color back in your cheeks." Mr. Hawkings gave her a slight nod of his head.

He cleared his throat before asking her questions about her relationship with Lawrence and if she willingly eloped with him. He asked her if she had any intention of informing Lawrence about her pregnancy. Millie told him that she had Mrs. White reach out to Lawrence and ask him to voluntarily give up his parental rights once the baby was born.

"You do realize that if Mr. Hansen gives up paternity rights, he will not be obligated to assist with the child in any capacity, including child support?" Mr. Hawkings told her.

Millie looked him straight in the eye. "The only thing I want from Mr. Hansen is for him to sign over his paternity rights and to stay away from me and my child."

"No further questions." Mr. Hawkings retook his seat as Mrs. White stood.

"Ms. Larson, you dated Mr. Hansen for nine months, is that correct?"

"Yes." Millie kept her eyes away from Lawrence.

"During that time, were you ever sexually involved with Mr. Hansen?"

"No. I am firmly against a man and woman engaging in such behavior before they are married." Millie fought the urge to glance at Aiden.

"So, when Mr. Hansen would ask to spend the night, you would tell him, no?"

"That's correct." Millie nodded.

"When would he ask you?"

"Mr. Hansen always walked me to my door. He would usually ask when he was kissing me goodnight."

"Was Mr. Hansen ever allowed in your apartment?"

"No. I had a firm rule that no boy friends were allowed in my apartment for any reason."

"Mr. Hansen did have a key to your apartment though." Mrs. White pointed out.

"After we got engaged, I gave him a spare key. I had lost my keys a few times over the previous weeks. Mr. Hansen suggested that I give him a key so I wouldn't have to bother the landlord so much."

Mrs. White looked down at her notes for a minute. "When did the wedding plans change to an elopement?"

"We were working on some wedding details when Mr. Hansen suggested eloping. I thought he was joking, but he pointed out that neither of us had any family that we absolutely had to have at the wedding, and we would be saving money. After thinking about it, I agreed that an elopement sounded like the best plan." Millie explained.

"Is that why you and Mr. Hansen came in several weeks early to sign the prenup?" Mrs. White asked.

"Yes." Millie confirmed.

"Can you walk us through the wedding?" Mrs. White asked.

"Mr. Hansen volunteered to get everything in order for the wedding. He found the officiator, venue, asked a few of his friends to be witnesses, and insisted I wear the wedding dress I had purchased the previous month. After the ceremony, Mr. Hansen had me sign the marriage license. His friend, Jaxon, asked me a few questions while Mr. Hansen signed the document. Then we went back to the hotel room we had reserved for the weekend."

"Can we assume that you and Mr. Hansen became intimate that night?" Mrs. White asked.

Millie's face heated. "Yes, ma'am."

"What happened the next morning?"

"I woke up to an empty hotel room. I found a note on the bedside table where I had put my wedding ring. Mr. Hansen left me notes all the time on my car or on my apartment door when we were dating. I picked it up and it said, 'Thank you for the fun night.'. Under the note was the marriage license. My signature and that of the officiator were the only ones on it."

"Your honor, I have both the note and marriage license here." Mrs. White handed the documents over to the Bailiff, who passed it to the judge.

He looked at the papers before looking up. Mrs. White continued. "Ms. Larson, what did you do after you found the note?"

"I tried calling Mr. Hansen, but his number had been disconnected. I then tried to look at his social media accounts, but they had all been deleted. I was confused and hurt. I packed my things and tried to leave. The hotel manager saw me in the lobby and told me that the card on file didn't work and I needed to provide a different card immediately."

"So, you had to pay for the hotel?"

"Yes, ma'am."

"Then what happened?" Mrs. White rested a hand on the table where her notes were.

"I went home. I contacted you and asked you to look into the legality of the marriage, file for divorce if it were legal, and to see if Mr. Hansen could be located. The divorce was not needed since Mr. Hansen never signed the document, and the officiator wasn't certified to perform a marriage."

"Is it safe to say that if you knew that the marriage wasn't legal, you would never have spent the night with Mr. Hansen?" Mrs. White asked.

"That's correct." Millie nodded firmly.

"Ms. Larson, how and when did you find out you were pregnant?"

"I thought I was sick with a flu bug that never went away. I had midterms coming up and went to the doctor to see what could be done to get me through my exams. I asked Dr. Spaulding to test for everything she felt was necessary. She came back in before they took any blood, like we had talked about. She informed me that the pregnancy test they performed came back positive. I was eight weeks pregnant at the time."

"How did you feel about the news?"

"I was shocked and terrified. Mr. Hansen had used protection, and I was on the pill. I had a hard time accepting the fact that I was pregnant. Dr. Spaulding gave me multiple options to think about. It took me weeks to decide what to do about the baby."

"What were the options you were considering?"

"I only had two real options, I could keep the baby and raise it on my own or I could give the baby up for adoption."

"Why not have an abortion? This pregnancy wasn't planned, and the baby's biological father was nowhere to be found."

"I think an unborn child has every right to life as any person living outside the womb. In my mind, abortion is only okay if the mother's health is severely at risk, in cases of incest, and sometimes rape. Me and my child didn't fall in any of those categories." Millie folded her arms across her chest.

"Ms. Larson," Mrs. White said slowly. "If the only reason you willingly became sexually intimate with Mr. Hansen was because he misled you to believe you were legally married, then that is still rape."

The courtroom became so quiet that Millie could hear a pin drop. Her eyes snapped to Lawrence. The smug look that was on his face earlier was gone. Now, he was glaring at Mrs. White. Millie's eyes shifted to Aiden and her friends. Beth had her hand over her mouth while Aiden, Josh, and Derek stared at her in concern.

Lawerence stood suddenly. "She never told me she had millions in the bank!" He roared. "If she had, I would have made sure to make the marriage legal."

Mr. Hawkings pulled on Lawrence's arm as he told him to sit down. Lawrence yanked his arm away as he continued to yell at her. "You had to be so stubborn. You took months from my life without giving me what I wanted. I lost a lot of money because you wouldn't put out for twelve months. You owed me, Millie. Then I find out through a buddy that you are the granddaughter of Samantha Larson."

The Bailiff tried to stop Lawrence as he approached her, but Lawrence shoved him aside as he grabbed her arm. He nearly pulled Millie over the rail in front of her. "You owe me more than a night of pleasure; I want the money."

Millie tried to pull away, but Lawrence yanked on her arm as the Bailiff grabbed him from behind. Millie had had enough. She pulled her fist back and threw as much power as she could into Lawrence's face. Pain exploded through her hand, but Lawrence's grip on her loosened enough for her to pull away.

More officers arrived and quickly dragged Lawrence out of the courtroom. Millie shook out her hand as she stared at the closed door Lawrence had disappeared through. She looked down at her knuckles and knew they were going to bruise. She sighed as she sat back down.

Judge Stevens was on his feet, banging the gavel, and calling for order. Once everyone was seated and things were quiet again. He turned to Millie. "Ms. Larson, are you alright?"

"I am fine, your honor." Millie gave him a small smile before looking at Aiden and the others.

Josh and Derek looked ready to kill someone, their bodies were stiff, faces red, and jaws clenched. Beth was wide-eyed and pale as she stared at Millie. Aiden's jaw was clenched, and he looked ready to run to her. Millie gave him an encouraging smile and he shook his head as he ran a hand down his face.

"Mrs. White, are you finished questioning Ms. Larson?" Judge Stevens asked.

"Yes, your honor." Mrs. White seemed a little unsure. "There is a video I wish to present to the court."

"Ms. Larson, you can take your seat." Judge Steven said. "Then we can take a look at the video.

Millie stood slowly and carefully made her way down the two steps from the stand. She walked carefully to her seat and sat with a sigh. Mrs. White stood as a TV was wheeled to the front of the courtroom. Millie could feel Aiden's gaze on her, but she resisted the urge to turn around.

The video started and Millie watched the fight in the parking lot unfold from an outside perspective. Lawrence looked so intimidating as he yelled at her. His voice carried all the way to the person filming. Millie informed Lawrence of her pregnancy and he yelled at her. He pulled back a fist to punch Aiden. Aiden shifted his stance as if preparing to take the blow. If he had dodged or moved out of the way, Lawrence would have hit Millie.

The image of Millie punching Lawrence caused the corners of her mouth to turn up in a genuine smile. He demanded that she get an abortion. The video ended with Lawrence being put into a police vehicle.

Mr. Hawkings gave his closing statement quickly and without any heart. He didn't seem to care about his client's case anymore. Mrs. White stood and addressed the court.

"My client only wants Mr. Hansen's parental rights removed. She wants to live a life free of the man that tricked her into thinking they were married. Free of the man that abandoned her. Free of the man that tried to force her to get an abortion. She wants to start a life with her child without fear that Mr. Hansen would manipulate her or her child." Mrs. White returned to her seat.

Judge Stevens sat back in his chair as he stared at the wall at the side of the room. Everyone sat in silence as they waited. After twenty minutes, he finally turned back to the room.

"Can we get Mr. Hansen back in here please?" He asked the Bailiff. "I want him escorted." The Bailiff nodded and left through the side door.

A few minutes later, Lawrence walked back in with two guards and the Bailiff. His eye was already showing signs of bruising and there was a little swelling on his cheek. Millie ran her fingers over her tender knuckles.

"Mr. Hansen, attacking a person in my courtroom is unacceptable. You are being held in contempt and will be charged for assault. As for your lawsuit, I am throwing it out. You claim to be upset that Ms. Larson didn't tell you about her pregnancy, but when you did find out, you immediately demanded an abortion. That doesn't sound like someone upset about losing out on fatherhood."

Judge Stevens glared down at Lawrence. "I am issuing a court order to confirm paternity at the time of the baby's birth. As soon as the results are in, we will set another court date. If Mr. Hansen is the father, which I don't doubt he is, I will then order an Involuntary Termination of Parental Rights."

Millie felt a weight lift off her shoulders. Lawrence was escorted back out and then everyone stood as the judge exited. As soon as they were free to leave, Aiden was at Millie's side. He pulled her into his arms, and she rested her head against his chest. His hand cradled the back of her head as he held her protectively.

"My hand hurts." Millie said after a long moment.

Aiden chuckled as he pressed a kiss to her forehead. "I bet it does. Josh had to grab my arm to keep me from jumping over the gate." Aiden took a deep breath and let it out slowly. "Did he hurt you?"

Millie shook her head, and Aiden's body relaxed a little. "Ms. Larson?" Millie turned to see Mr. Hawkings standing a few feet away. "Might I offer a little advice?" Millie nodded and watched as he took a step closer. "If I were you, I would talk with Mrs. White about pressing criminal charges." Mr. Hawkings gave a quick nod and walked away.

Millie pulled back enough to look up into Aiden's face. "Can we go get Mexican food?" She wanted time to talk with Aiden about what happened today after she had time to think. But she could hardly think with how hungry she was.

Aiden rolled his eyes, but his lips twitched as he fought a smile. "You and your Mexican food. Is there anything you love more than a carne asada burrito?"

"I love *you* more than a carne asada burrito." Millie laughed.

"Thank goodness. I was wondering which one of us came first." Aiden grabbed her hand, and they walked out of the courthouse.

Josh, Derek, and Beth were waiting outside when they reached the front steps. They each gave Millie a quick hug. Beth started crying and Derek wrapped his arms around her.

"I didn't even think that what Lawrence did to you was classified like that." Beth sniffled.

Aiden's hold on her hand tightened. Millie gave Beth a forced smile. "Are you guys coming with us to get some food?"

"Aiden said you weren't feeling well." Derek said confused.

"I bet anything Millie wants Mexican." Josh gave her a teasing grin.

"So, what if I do?" Millie stuck her tongue out at him.

"Alright you two," Aiden pushed Josh playfully. "We are heading out. You are all welcome to join us."

"We are going to pick up the kids and meet you there. Just send us the address." Derek gave Millie another hug before pulling a still tearful Beth towards their car.

Aiden dropped Josh off at his apartment on the way to the restaurant. When they finally parked, Millie unbuckled and climbed into Aiden's lap. It wasn't the smoothest transition, but she managed it. Aiden put his arms around her and held her close.

"Today was hard." Millie complained as Aiden ran his fingers through her hair.

"Millie, we should probably discuss what Mrs. White said." Aiden said softly.

"Can we talk about that part of the trial later?" Millie snuggled closer to Aiden. "I don't want to think about it right now. Please."

"Okay, sweetheart." Aiden held her tighter.

Millie sighed as she began to relax. She started to play with the buttons on Aiden's shirt. Aiden gently grabbed Millie's hand and raised it so he could see it better. He ran his thumb across her bruising knuckles before placing a kiss on them.

Millie looked up at Aiden and gave him a flirtatious smile. "Aiden?"

"Hmm?" his eyes dropped to her lips.

Millie's smile grew as Aiden's head began to dip towards hers. "Can we go inside now?"

Aiden froze. "I think you just put carne asada above me."

Millie laughed as she pulled Aiden the rest of the way down to her. "You will always be at the top of my list."

"I better be." Aiden reclaimed her lips.

A knock on Aiden's window caused them both to jump. Aiden groaned when he saw Josh standing there with a smirk on his face. Aiden opened his door and helped Millie out of the car. Josh was chuckling when Millie finally got her feet under her.

"You two are going to have to cool it if you want to keep it a secret for a while." Josh laughed.

Millie stuck her tongue out at Josh again. "Let's just go eat. This lady and this baby are starving." She patted her belly. Josh and Aiden laughed as they followed Millie inside. "Laugh all you want, but you guys will never know what it feels like to want food so much that you are willing to kill for it."

"They really won't." Beth laughed as they walked in behind them. "I thought you guys would have found a table already."

"We would have, but Aiden and Millie got sidetracked." Josh commented.

"Making out in the car again?" Derek asked, causing Josh to laugh. The hostess came out of the back room and the conversation died as they were seated.

Chapter 23

Millie sat on the couch next to Aiden as he and the guys watched a football game. Bentley was playing under the kitchen table and Beth was upstairs feeding Melody. Aiden put his arm around her without taking his eyes off the game.

The trial had been rough, and Millie was so glad it was all over. Beth came down the stairs and settled on the couch next to Derek. Millie picked up the remote and turned the TV off. The guys started to protest, but Millie sent them a glare.

"I have something I wanted to give you guys for putting up with my craziness these past few months." Millie said as she stood and went into the master bedroom. She came out holding three gift bags. Aiden didn't know about these, and he gave her a questioning look.

"Millie, you don't have to give us anything for being your friend." Beth accepted the bag Millie handed her.

"Yeah, Mils. You are family, these weren't necessary." Derek took his bag.

"Well, I will accept them back only after you see what is inside." Millie sat back down next to Aiden.

Millie ignored Aiden's whispered question and watched as Josh, Derek, and Beth pulled shirts out of the bags. Beth's shirt said, 'I'm only here for my nephew'. Josh and Derek's shirts said 'Leveling up to Uncle' in different designs.

Derek and Josh both smiled as they looked at the shirts and turned them around to show everyone. Millie could tell they liked them, but they weren't overly excited. She knew that that was how they would react. She only got them shirts to distract them from Beth's for a few minutes. Beth stared frozen at hers with her mouth slightly open. She hugged it to her chest as she looked at Millie.

"Are you going to show us what shirt you got?" Derek asked Beth.

Beth jumped to her feet and ran over to Millie and sat down next to her. "Are you serious? Like this is one hundred percent legit?"

"What does it say?" Aiden asked.

"You know, don't you?" Beth glared at him.

"Know what? I don't know what the shirt says." Aiden laughed.

"Just show everyone already?" Josh said in exasperation.

Beth turned the shirt around and Aiden started to laugh. "Yeah, I knew. That's probably why I didn't get a shirt."

"A boy? You're having a boy?" Josh laughed. "Man, you guys are full of surprises this week."

Aiden stiffened, but Millie only laughed. "We are. But I wanted to give you your shirts before I kicked you all out. I am super tired and want to call it an early night." Millie yawned. "But we will be hosting dinner tomorrow."

"You do look done in. Not to mention the fact that you passed out in the courtroom, punched Lawrence in the face, and didn't sleep well last night." Josh stood and stretched.

"I'm so excited for you. Boys are so much fun." Beth said as she gave Millie a hug. "But Josh is right, you look ready to fall asleep."

Aiden helped wrangle Bentley out from under the table and walked him to their car. Millie and Aiden stood together as they were saying goodbye to the others.

"Shoot." Josh said suddenly. "I almost forgot my overnight bag upstairs. I'll be right back."

Before he could leave Beth grabbed his arm. "You spent the night here?" She asked in shock.

Josh realized what he had done and turned panicked eyes to Millie. He mouthed 'sorry' while Beth looked between the two of them. "To be fair," Millie finally said. "Aiden was here too."

"You guys can't be staying here overnight." Derek smacked both Josh and Aiden's arms.

"Josh stayed at your house on Saturday, I fail to see how him staying here last night was any different." Millie had to bite the inside of her cheek to keep a straight face. Beth and Derek stared at her like she was insane.

"For starters, me and Derek are married, Millie." Beth said in exasperation. "Josh wasn't staying in the house with an unmarried woman." Aiden coughed and ducked his head to try to hide his smile.

"This isn't funny, man." Derek snapped at Aiden.

"I still don't see the difference." Millie said shrugging.

"Being engaged isn't the same as being married." Beth said.

"I wholeheartedly agree." Millie leaned against Aiden's chest.

He put his arm around her shoulder and Beth's eyes focused on his hand. "Are you wearing a ring?" Beth finally asked.

"Yeah, Millie and I got it on Thursday. Do you like it?" Aiden asked innocently.

Derek and Beth stared at them for a minute before it finally clicked in Beth's mind. "You didn't wait for us! Why didn't you wait for us?"

Millie jumped forward and covered Beth's mouth with both hands. "Before you start lecturing us, let me explain. I won't take my hands off until you agree."

Beth nodded while she glared at her. Millie slowly removed her hands and stepped back. "You, my friend, better have a good explanation."

Millie explained about the visit to the lawyer's office and then her crazy impression in the parking lot. "We will be doing the whole party thing once we go to the temple and get sealed. We want to wait and be sealed after the baby is born."

"And I have legally adopted him." Aiden finished.

Derek nodded his head. "Makes sense to me. I bet the judge wouldn't have let Aiden back to his office if he wasn't her husband."

"Don't encourage this. I wanted to be there." Beth smacked Derek's chest and he wrapped his arms around her as he nuzzled her neck.

"If it makes you feel any better, we were married in the bishop's office and we were in t-shirts and jeans." Millie put her arms around Aiden.

"How long has Josh known?" Beth asked.

"Since last night when Aiden wouldn't go home with me." Josh shook his head. "They listened to this whole talk last night. Millie went to bed and Aiden got another earful."

"Thank you for sparing me." Millie yawned. Aiden told everyone that they could talk more about this tomorrow because he needed to get Millie to bed.

Once everyone was gone and Millie was finally laying down, thoughts of the trial came back to her. She had never thought that because Lawrence had lied to her about the legality of the marriage, he had essentially raped her. The old feelings of being violated came crashing back and Millie struggled to hold back her tears. She didn't want to be alone.

Aiden was still up, since it was only nine, and Millie had gone to bed an hour ago. She got out of bed and walked into the living room. Aiden was reclined on the couch with a laptop on his lap and the TV was muted with the game on. He glanced up and when he saw her, he set his laptop to the side.

"Hey baby, what's the matter?" he asked as Millie sat on his lap and laid her head on his shoulder.

"Aiden, what should we do?" she asked softly. Aiden was quiet for several minutes. Millie wasn't sure if he understood what she was asking, but she couldn't bring herself to say what Lawrence had done to her. "I have talked with therapists and Mrs. White, no one mentioned or even told me it was a possibility that what Lawrence did was…" Millie shook her head.

Aiden pulled her against him, kissing her temple. "It would be a criminal trial with a jury. Are you wanting to go through all this again? Don't get me wrong, I want to see that man behind bars, but I understand and will support you if you don't want to go through this a second time."

"I don't want Lawrence to do this to anyone else. When he left and I learned that the marriage was a sham, I felt violated and struggled with the fact that I gave a part of myself away to someone that had manipulated me. I am still struggling with it." Millie wiped a tear off her cheek. "I didn't think anyone could ever love me because of it."

"Millie, Lawrence lied to you and took advantage of you, but that doesn't make you any less of the wonderful person you are. I was already falling for you before I knew the extent of what Lawrence did." Aiden tilted her chin up so that she was looking at him. "I saw a beautiful woman who had the shock of her life, and was willing to push past it. You were strong and brave. The fact that you were pregnant didn't bother me."

"You found out I was pregnant only hours before I had a break down and told you everything." Millie said.

"But in those hours, I watched you battle morning sickness and play Pictionary with a bunch of people you just met. You were quiet but observant, stunningly beautiful, and I knew that whatever happened, I was going to be a big part of your life and the baby's. I just thought it would be as a friend and uncle figure." Aiden kissed her. "I am kind of liking this alternative though."

"Were you working on something?" Millie gestured to the laptop.

"Not really. Just looking at baby names while procrastinating homework." Aiden's cheeks turned pink as he shifted. "You look so tired, Millie. You should try to get some sleep."

Millie laid her head back on his shoulder. "I don't want to be alone." she admitted. Aiden got to his feet, forcing Millie to hers in the process. "Aiden, what are you doing?" she asked when Aiden turned off the TV and guided her back to bed.

"We are going to bed." Aiden kissed her. "You need rest, and if that means me coming to bed with you, I am more than happy to oblige."

Millie sighed when Aiden scooted up behind her and draped his arm over her. He pressed a kiss to her shoulder as he held her. "Millie, I have a confession to make."

Millie rolled over so she was facing Aiden. He slipped his arm under her neck and tucked some of her loose hair behind her ear. Millie didn't say anything as she watched the outline of his face in the darkness.

"I am sorry you had to go through everything you have with Lawrence. I am sorry that you became pregnant when you weren't planning or ready to. I'm sorry for all the emotional damage that Lawrence has caused you." Aiden breathed out slowly. "I feel so selfish. There is a part of me that is glad that Lawrence did what he did and that you got pregnant."

Millie swallowed hard. She didn't know what to say. Why would Aiden be glad she was taken advantage of and that she is going to have another man's baby? She tried to pull away from him, but he didn't let her. Was this some sick joke?

"Let me finish." Aiden begged. "I'm glad because if none of that happened, I wouldn't have met you. Millie, I am so in love with you. I can't picture my life without you in it. We had been going to the same school for years and went to church in the same building, yet we never met. It took something tragic to bring us together. I wish with all my heart that Lawrence never touched you, but at the same time I..." Aiden touched his forehead against Millie's. "This isn't coming out right." He muttered.

Millie touched Aiden's face gently. She pressed her lips to his in a slow tender kiss. "I am glad we met too. It would have been nice if it were under different circumstances. I really wasn't my best self, but I have you now and that's all that matters." Millie whispered.

"You were a little out of it when Josh and I found you." Aiden chuckled.

"And just so you know, I do know how to change a tire." Millie smiled.

"I never doubted your ability to change the tire, but my mother raised me to be a gentleman and help those in need." Aiden kissed her forehead again.

"Oh no, Aiden." Anxiety rose in Millie, and she covered her face. She didn't even think about calling her parents or his. What would her parents say? She left without saying anything. And what about Aiden's family? What would they say when they learned he got married to some pregnant girl?

"What's wrong?" Aiden rose on his elbow and looked down at her in concern.

"Our parents." Millie groaned. "I didn't even think to contact my parents when we left. And what are your parents going to say when they find out you married me, of all people?"

Aiden cut off her rambling with a kiss. "First off, Franklin called Thursday to see if we made it home safe. Beth let him know why we had to leave immediately." He kissed her again. This time longer before pulling back. "And my parents are going to love you."

"I am pregnant with another man's baby, Aiden." Millie was biting back tears, she felt so ashamed of herself.

"Millie, I want you to listen to me." Aiden said seriously as his hand cupped her face. She could just make out the details of his face in the darkness. "This baby's biological father might be someone else, but I fully intend to be his dad. I will be there for every major event of his life. From the moment I heard his heartbeat, I have thought of him as mine."

"I know that, but your parents,"

"Know that I was planning on asking you to be my wife. When you left and stopped taking my calls after we kissed, I panicked. I went home to try to distract myself, but mom picked up on my depression. She ended up pulling everything out of me. That I had fallen in love with the most amazing girl and that I had been to several of her prenatal appointments. They told me to proceed with caution, but Josh told them that if I didn't snatch you up, I would be making the biggest mistake of my life."

"Even if they aren't going to be totally against me, we eloped. What if they think I tricked you into marrying me?" Millie's anxiety continued to climb.

"Sweetheart, if they are going to be upset with anyone about us eloping, it will be me. I plan on telling them on Wednesday when they get here."

Millie sat up. "They are coming here?"

"I just got off the phone with them before you came out. I needed them to bring a few things." Aiden pulled Millie back down next to him. "Tomorrow, we need to get your phone replaced and I need to get a few things sorted out before my family arrives."

"We need to get more beds for the guest rooms. Is it just your parents coming?" Millie bit her lip, still feeling unsure about all this.

"My parents and Josh's. The apartment isn't big enough for Aunt Sally and Uncle Brett, so I said they could stay here."

"Aunt and uncle? Wait, are you and Josh…cousins?" Millie asked in disbelief.

"I thought you knew." Aiden said in confusion.

"Not once did you guys say that you were cousins." Millie poked Aiden's chest. "Anything else I should know about?" Millie asked.

"Josh is Beth's twin, and I own a share in my family's ranch. I run the horse breeding side of things." Aiden shrugged.

Millie's mouth fell open. "Are you serious?" Millie sat up again.

Aiden sat up as well, turning on the side table lamp. "I pick all the pairings, oversee the selling of the foals, and I manage all the ranch hands that work in that area of the ranch." He shrugged his shoulder. "We aren't doing too bad."

"Oh my gosh." Millie breathed out as she shook her head. "If you already have a job, why are you going to college?"

"I am getting a business degree to help with running the business." Aiden smiled.

"Okay, so you are getting a business degree so you can run your family's horse breeding business. What do you mean by you aren't doing too bad."

"Over the last four years, we have been quite successful. We pay all our workers a good amount. I get a paycheck as well as a portion of the main ranch. Everything else goes right back into the business. I have six figures in my personal account." Millie stared at Aiden in surprise.

"Your parents are going to think that I am a gold digger." Millie covered her face.

"Says the woman with several million in the bank." Aiden laughed. "Now, sweetheart, what can I do to help you relax enough to sleep? You and this little guy need rest."

Aiden turned the light back off and laid down. Millie laid her head on his chest with her leg over his. He slowly ran his fingers through her hair. After several minutes, Millie began to relax. She snuggled as close to Aiden as her belly would allow.

Chapter 24

Millie was laying on the couch enjoying some down time. Aiden took her to get a new phone first thing this morning. Then they picked out furniture for two guest rooms. Millie convinced Aiden she would be fine alone for a few hours. He relented only after she reminded him that she had a phone and that someone needed to be home when the furniture was delivered.

Aiden took Josh with him to finish some of his other errands with a promise to be home in time to help with dinner. Millie wasn't worried. She put a ham in the oven and the rolls were rising. With nothing else to do, Millie decided to lay down. She picked up the book she got at the airport and started reading through baby names.

A knock at the front door had Millie sighing. She felt like she had just laid down. She slowly got to her feet and walked to the front door. She opened the door expecting to see the delivery guys, but two women stood there.

"Oh, you must be Millie." The woman with long brown hair and brown eyes said, with a forced polite smile.

"Yes," Millie nodded. "I'm sorry, do I know you?"

"I am Ava Coleman, Aiden's mother, and this is my sister, Hazel Peterson." Ava gestured to the other woman.

"Oh, it's so nice to meet you. Why don't you come in?" Millie offered, stepping back to give them room. She was so confused. Aiden had said his family wasn't coming until tomorrow. She had hoped to have Aiden there with her when she met them.

"I didn't expect to see you here?" Ava commented as she looked around the living room. "Is Aiden around?"

"Uh, Aiden is out with Josh getting a few things. We weren't expecting anyone until tomorrow or I'm sure he would have been here." Millie moved towards the couches. "Please, have a seat." She invited.

"This is a lovely home." Hazel said as she sat in one of the chairs.

"Thank you." Millie gave her a smile. "When I saw it, I just knew I couldn't pass up the opportunity."

"I'm sure you couldn't." Ava said dryly.

Millie eyed the woman carefully. She wore a mask of politeness, but she was definitely frosty in her demeanor. Millie knew that Aiden's parents wouldn't be happy with her, but she didn't expect this level of hostility. Then again, Aiden wasn't there, so Ava didn't need to hide her disapproval.

"I'm sorry, but there seems to be a misunderstanding here." Millie said as she crossed her arms over her chest. "I am too tired to play games, so I am just going to be bluntly honest with you. This is *my* house. I purchased this home for me and my baby before Aiden and I got together."

"Then why would he tell us we would be staying here." Ava folded her arms over her chest too.

"That would probably be because I have three extra bedrooms upstairs and Josh's apartment is too small to host four additional adults. Look, I understand that I am probably the last person you would ever want your son involved with. I get it. I would feel the same way if I were in your shoes." Millie shrugged and got to her feet. "Did either of you want something to drink?"

Millie walked into the kitchen just as her phone rang. She answered it as she began pulling a few bottles of water out of the fridge. "Hey."

"Just calling to check up on you." Aiden said and she could hear Josh laughing in the background.

"I am fine. Stop worrying. I'm a big girl and can take care of myself."

"Did you take your pills?"

"Aiden, you are getting ridiculous. I promise, both me and the baby are just fine. And yes, I will eat something. No, I won't go swimming without you here and yes, I am taking my medications." Millie smiled as she grabbed her antinausea medicine.

Aiden chuckled. "Just know that I love you. If you feel the least bit dizzy or lightheaded…"

"I will call you, Beth, or EMS. Stop worrying. And I love you too." Millie turned around and leaned back against the counter. Ava and Hazel were watching her. Millie made eye contact with Ava and held it. "Oh, your mother and aunt are here."

There was a pause before Aiden groaned. "Josh and I are an hour away. Are you okay?"

"Of course I'm okay. They just arrived, and we were getting to know each other."

"Do we need to bring you some carne asada? Please don't kill my mom." Josh yelled.

"Oh my gosh, Josh, seriously? You two just finish up whatever you are doing. We are fine and there will be three people alive here when you get back." Millie rolled her eyes and she saw Hazel's lips twitch.

"Seriously, Millie, if they give you trouble, just text us and we will come home."

"Aiden take a deep breath. I honestly don't know if you are more concerned about me or your mom, but we are adults and will be just fine." Millie couldn't help the smile that spread on her face. "You almost sound like you are nervous."

"I am nervous. My mom and aunt can be..." Aiden trailed off as if trying to find the right word.

"Scary and intimidating when they get overprotective." Josh finished.

"You two need to take a chill pill. I am just a hormonal pregnant woman, and they are a protective mother and aunt. What could go wrong?" Millie fiddled with the pill bottle in her hand.

"That's what I am afraid of." Aiden muttered.

"Finish your errand and then when you and Josh get home, I will put you two to work setting up the guest rooms. Be safe out there, Cowboy, and I will see you when you get home." Millie said goodbye, took her pills, and grabbed the bottles of water before heading back to the couches.

Millie handed each woman a bottle before retaking her seat. "I'm sorry, where were we?" Millie asked, taking a sip of her water.

"You were being bluntly honest with us." Ava lifted her brow.

"That's right. Here are the facts. I was engaged to a man that convinced me to elope with him. We got married, but when I woke up the next morning, he was gone. He left the unsigned marriage license on the nightstand. When I got home, I contacted my lawyer and found out that the marriage wasn't legal for two reasons. The officiator was a fake and without all the signatures, the marriage was void."

Hazel gasped and looked horrified. "What did you do?"

"I tried to find him, but he changed his number and deleted his social media accounts. I could do nothing but move on. Then I found out I was pregnant, which was terrifying. Two guys I didn't know saw me sitting on the ground next to my car with two flat tires, and I was a complete mess with the shock of it all. They offered me a ride home.

"Long story short, Aiden and Josh became great friends. When my ex showed back up, Aiden dropped everything to help me get away and drove me to Beth and Derek's." Millie turned to look at Ava. "You raised an amazing man. I honestly don't know where I would be without him. He not only looks after me physically, but he is always there when I need a listening ear. He makes me laugh when I am emotionally burned out. He is my best friend."

"So, where is this ex of yours now? I am sure that he will be part of the baby's life." Ava asked.

"I think he is in prison at the moment." Millie scrunched her brows as she tried to remember what happened to Lawrence after the trial. "He attacked me in court yesterday and the judge is charging him with contempt and assault."

"Why were you in court?" Hazel asked.

"My ex wanted to establish paternity rights and was trying to sue me for the emotional trauma of not telling him I was pregnant." Millie shifted to a more comfortable position. "I asked him to sign his parental rights over. After everything was said and done, the judge ruled for a paternity test right after the baby is born and we will have another court date to get the results."

"Why is a paternity test needed if you know he is the father?" Ava eyed Millie suspiciously.

"Contrary to what you may think of me, Mrs. Coleman, I am not someone who sleeps around. The only reason I slept with Lawrence was because I thought we were married. In fact, I am going to pursue criminal charges against Lawrence for rape by deception, since he led me to believe we were married." Millie's hands were beginning to shake as she said the word out loud for the first time.

The timer going off in the kitchen saved Millie from having to continue. She stood and began putting the rolls into the second oven. When she turned around, Ava and Hazel were standing in the kitchen too. Ava stepped up to Millie and wrapped her arms around her. Millie's composure crumpled and she began to cry.

What happened with Lawrence was still hard for her to deal with. Finding out she was having a baby boy drove home the fact that she was carrying his child. Then the whole court thing yesterday, Millie was at the end of her rope emotionally. Having Aiden's mother judging her for something she thought she was doing right, but ended up being a lie, was the final straw.

Millie finally pulled herself back together. "I'm sorry." She whispered as she stepped back and wiped her cheeks.

Both Ava and Hazel had tears in their eyes too. "No, we are sorry." Ava said, grabbing Millie's hand. "I judged you without knowing your whole story. All we knew was that Aiden was head over heels for a girl who was pregnant. He mentioned something to his father about a civil ceremony and I assumed you..."

"I understand." Millie gave her a small smile. "If it makes you feel better, I am getting my endowment on Saturday."

They moved back to the living room and continued talking. Ava asked Millie about growing up and what she did now. Millie told them about going to school and working. As Ava began to learn more about Millie, she seemed to relax. She even told Millie some stories about Aiden when he was younger, that had everyone laughing. Millie just finished telling Ava and Hazel about the time she had sprayed Aiden in the face with the hose when he and Josh walked in.

They froze when they saw the three of them laughing. "This isn't exactly what I had expected to come home to." Aiden admitted as he walked into the living room.

Aiden tried to sit down next to Millie, but she shoved him away. "Don't you dare sit down on the couch like that. What have you been doing, rolling around in the field?"

"Can't I just sit down for a minute?" Aiden asked, looking at her with puppy dog eyes.

"Go take a shower and change into something clean. Give Josh something to wear too. Then you can sit."

"Fine." He grumbled before he bent down and gave her a quick kiss. Josh was laughing as he followed Aiden to the bedroom. Josh went upstairs with a towel and stack of clothes. Five minutes later, both men were showered and clean. "Can I sit now?" Aiden asked sarcastically.

"Not with that attitude." Millie said with a straight face.

"Careful, sweetheart, you might end up in the pool again." Aiden chuckled as he put his arms around her. Millie leaned into him and sighed. "How have things been going here?"

"I seriously thought someone was going to have a black eye when we got back." Josh smiled at Millie as he sat in the chair next to his mom.

"What are you doing here, mom? I thought you weren't going to be here until tomorrow?" Aiden asked.

"Hazel and I wanted to come check on things here." Ava shrugged innocently.

"You wanted to meet Millie when I wasn't around." Aiden said evenly.

"Aunt Ava, Millie is seriously the sweetest person you will ever meet as long as you don't threaten her, then she puts her boxing hobby to good use." Josh said.

"You didn't tell me you boxed." Ava turned to Millie.

"I didn't really have time." Millie shrugged.

"Why did you feel the need to come check out Millie when I wasn't here?" Aiden asked a little worried.

"Because you came home depressed and anxious, talking about some girl. You and Josh were always talking about her and her baby, and if she was seeing a doctor. Then you tell me and your father that you plan on marrying her." Ava threw her hands in the air in frustration. "Can you blame a mother for being worried that her son wanted to marry a pregnant woman? And why are your clothes here?"

Aiden stilled and Millie knew he was trying to figure out what to do. "Blunt honesty?" Millie asked and Ava narrowed her eyes on Millie. The earlier hostility returned.

"Mom, stop looking at Millie like that and get Dad on the phone." Aiden said firmly as he tightened his arms around her protectively. Ava paused for a moment before she pulled out her phone. "Hey, Dad." Aiden greeted. "You should have given me a heads up that Mom was coming."

"Son, we wanted to make sure you weren't making a mistake." A deep voice came through the phone speaker for everyone to hear.

"Dallas, I think they are living together." Ava snapped out.

Aiden sighed and kissed Millie on the temple. "Of course I am living with Millie, she is my wife." There was no hesitation, no regret in Aiden's voice.

There was silence on the other end of the phone while Ava and Hazel stared at them in shock. "I thought..." Ava couldn't seem to shake the surprise.

"We were married last week by her bishop. We wanted to get married before we had to appear in court yesterday. We will have a wedding celebration after the baby is born and the three of us are sealed." Aiden told them. "I don't expect you to fully understand our decision, but I do expect you to respect it. Millie is my wife and will be treated with the respect she deserves."

"Aiden, calm down." Millie whispered. His whole body was tense, and he looked irritated. "You have to think about it from their perspective. What if our son grew up and did what you did? How would you feel?" Aiden looked at her with a clenched jaw. "You would want to make sure he wasn't making a huge mistake."

Aiden sighed before kissing her. "You're right. I would want answers and to meet the lady." Aiden put his hand on her belly.

"But we didn't give them that chance. They have every right to be upset with us."

Aiden rested his forehead against hers. "This little guy won't be putting you through any sort of worry."

Millie laughed. "You better believe he will. After all, he has you, Josh, and Derek for role models."

"Nauseating, aren't they?" Josh stage whispered. "And if that baby is at all trouble, you have no one to blame but yourself and Aiden. You two are ridiculous with all the pranks you pull on each other."

Millie sat back from Aiden as her cheeks heated. She had forgotten they weren't alone. Ava had tears in her eyes again and Hazel was smiling at them. Millie resisted the urge to bury her face in Aiden's chest and hide from those around them.

A chuckle from the phone caused Aiden to start laughing too. A knock on the door proceeded it bursting open. Bentley ran directly to Millie. "Hey, handsome." Millie kissed his cheek.

"Bentley, look who's here." Josh pointed to Hazel.

"Hi, Grandma." Bentley smiled but made no move to get down. "This is my Millie."

"Mom?" Beth asked. "What are you doing here? I didn't think you were coming until tomorrow?"

"We wanted to meet Millie." Hazel got to her feet and hugged Beth and Derek.

"They didn't scare you, did they?" Derek asked as he came over and patted Millie on the head.

"You all seem rather fond of Millie." Ava observed.

"Why wouldn't we, Aunt Ava." Beth sounded offended. "Aiden is lucky that Millie even gave him a chance. I don't know if I would have been ready to open my heart again after everything she has gone through. Not to mention that Millie is way out of Aiden's league."

"She really is." Derek chuckled as he pulled out Millie's ponytail.

"Seriously, Derek?" Millie swatted his hand away. "Remember who is making your food." Derek chuckled as he lifted Bentley off her lap. Millie sat up and re-tied her ponytail as she glared at Derek. "Why do you insist on doing this every time I put my hair up?"

"Because Aiden asked me too." Derek shrugged.

Millie turned to Aiden, but before she could say anything, he covered her mouth with his. Aiden pulled her ponytail out again while he kissed her.

Millie pulled away and glared at him. "You sir, need to stop. I put it up for a reason."

"What reason is that?" Aiden asked.

Millie stayed quiet as she put her hair up into a bun. She made eye contact with Beth and Beth pursed her lips. "When was the last time you ate and held it down?"

Millie rolled her eyes. "I am staying on top of things."

"Millie," Aiden nuzzled her neck as he pulled her closer. "Do you need to eat a snack to tide you over until dinner?"

"I ate something before your mom arrived. I will be fine." Millie told him.

"Are you sure you are okay?" Aiden whispered so only she could hear. "I need you and our son to be well enough for tomorrow."

A knock on the door drew everyone's attention and Millie stood. Aiden started to protest, but she shot him a look and he stopped. Millie answered the door. It was the delivery guys. Aiden showed them where to take the furniture. It took thirty minutes to get everything upstairs and another hour before everything was set up.

Chapter 25

"Aiden, I will be just fine. I can babysit for a few hours. I am not as fragile as you seem to think I am." Millie was starting to get irritated with Aiden's smothering. They had been arguing since they woke up. Aiden didn't want to leave Millie alone, especially if she was babysitting.

"Millie, I watched you collapse a few days ago. Then I had to watch as the Bailiff carried you out of the court room with the judge and Dr. Spaulding hot on his heels. Not to mention the fact that you passed out while in Alaska and ended up with a concussion." Aiden said in exasperation as he followed Millie out of their room and into the kitchen.

"Alaska was a combination of the motion sickness pills and learning that I had a father, not because I was pregnant. Aiden, I know that you are trying to keep me and the baby safe, but you are going a little overboard." Millie touched his arm. He was tense, and she could feel his frustration.

"Fine. If that is how you feel." Aiden started to head for the door.

Millie blinked in surprise. Aiden reached the garage door before Millie found her voice again. "Aiden Coleman, don't you dare walk out that door." Millie growled out. "You won't like the results."

Aiden turned to look at her in surprise. "Is that so?" He pulled the door open.

"Don't test me on this, Aiden." Millie warned. Her hands were fisted into tight balls. "We are not done with this conversation."

"You don't want me to worry about you anymore." Aiden stared at her with a guarded expression.

"That is not what I said. I said you are taking it overboard. There is a difference." Millie snapped. "I just feel like you are treating me like a baby."

Aiden closed the door and walked over to her. Millie wrapped her arms around herself as she turned away from him. Aiden put his arms around

Millie from behind. He kissed her neck before he rested his chin on her shoulder.

"I love you, Millie. I just don't want to see you or the baby hurt." Aiden whispered.

Millie turned in Aiden's arms. "I love you, too, but Aiden, I can't live in a bubble." She gently touched the side of his face. "I don't need a babysitter. I have my phone and if anything goes wrong, I will call you."

Aiden tucked the hair behind Millie's ear. "Did we just have our first fight?"

"I think so."

"Does that mean we need to make up for it tonight?"

Millie giggled as she shook her head. "Your family is here."

Aiden kissed her. Millie's lips molded to his as he held her close. His head tilted to the side, deepening the kiss. Millie's knees grew weak, and she melted against Aiden. A throat cleared behind them and Millie jumped. Aiden chuckled and gave her a quick kiss before looking over her head.

"Good morning, mother." Aiden continued to hold Millie snugly in his arms. She laid her head on his chest, not wanting to break contact with him. She didn't like that they had argued.

"I heard you two arguing." Ava said, sitting down at the bar. "Millie is right, you are coddling her. Your father would get that way every time I got pregnant. But at the same time, I can see why Aiden is so worried if you have passed out a few times."

Aiden kissed Millie's forehead. "How did you and Dad find a balance?"

Ava laughed. "I told your father that if he didn't take a deep breath and relax, I was going to spend the next few months at my parents."

"I don't like that idea." Aiden grumbled, causing Millie to laugh.

"Neither did your father. That is why he took a step back, so he wasn't suffocating me."

"What do you mean by taking a step back?" Aiden asked.

"He stopped micro-managing my every move. Millie seems completely capable of babysitting for a few hours." Ava gave Millie a wink.

Aiden's phone dinged with a text message. He kept his arms around Millie as he replied. Millie tried to pull away from him to get some toast and take her medicine, but he kept his arms around her. Millie gave Ava an exasperated look, which only seemed to amuse her.

"Aiden, can I get myself something to eat?" Millie asked, looking up at him.

"Of course you can." he said distractedly as he continued to look at his phone.

"Then can you let me go so I can?" Millie laughed.

Aiden smiled down at her. "If I must." He pressed a quick kiss to her lips before taking a step back. "Don't forget your meds."

Millie shook her head as she reached for the bread, but Aiden pulled her back to him before she could grab the loaf. "Aiden." Millie whined.

His eyes twinkled as he stared down at her. He maneuvered them closer to the fridge. "There are a few carne asada burritos in the fridge, if you want that instead."

"You better not be joking." Millie narrowed her eyes before pulling the fridge open. Aiden released her before leaning back against the counter behind them.

"I would never joke about carne asada." Aiden put a hand over his heart as if Millie's words wounded him.

Millie pulled a foil wrapped burrito out of the fridge with a big smile. She grabbed a plate out of the cabinet and stuck her unwrapped burrito in the microwave. She turned around and Aiden watched her with a smug smile on his face.

"Don't eat them all at once." Aiden kissed the tip of her nose when she pulled back from giving him a hug.

"What is up with the burritos and the medications?" Hazel asked as she took a seat at the bar next to Ava.

"Those burritos are the only things that Millie can hold down when she is sick. And the meds are for her nausea. Without them she would most likely be in the bathroom all day." Aiden explained.

"You poor thing." Hazel gave her a sympathetic look. "I was so sick when I was pregnant with Josh and Beth, but it went away after the first trimester. I can't imagine being that sick the whole time."

"Yeah, it's not exactly my favorite." Millie took out the burrito and sighed as she took a bite.

Aiden shook his head and chuckled before looking back down at his phone. "I need to get going. Josh is outside and we have things we need to get done before my dad gets here." He kissed Millie's cheek. "Mom, Aunt Hazel, are you coming with us?"

"Yes, we are." Ava said getting up from the stool.

Millie swallowed the bite and grabbed Aiden's arm before he walked away. "Can I talk to you for a moment?" He gave her a concerned look but nodded. Ava and Hazel walked out the front door and Aiden gave Millie his full attention. She ran her hands up his chest as she dropped her gaze to his shirt. "I want to press charges." Her voice was quiet, but she knew Aiden heard her when he stiffened.

Aiden tilted Millie's chin up so he could see her face. "You are the bravest woman I have ever met, and I will be by your side every step of the way. Have you already contacted Mrs. White?"

Millie nodded as she bit her lip. "I sent her a text last night. But, Aiden, I'm scared. I don't want to face him again."

Aiden wrapped his arms around her and held her close. She felt so secure and protected. Millie pressed herself closer, needing the comfort Aiden provided her.

"Millie, Lawrence will never hurt you again. I promise you that." Aiden held her tighter. "I love you." Millie closed her eyes and took a deep breath. "Sweetheart, look at me." Aiden said gently. Millie raised her head, and he gave her a crooked smile. "I need you to take it easy today, okay? I will be bringing something home for you and I need you to be able to see it." He pressed a long kiss to her forehead.

"Better than carne asada burritos?" Millie asked, causing Aiden to laugh.

"I honestly don't know, but I am curious to find out." A horn honked out front and Aiden kissed Millie again. "I love you, Millie. I will call you in a little while."

"I love you, too." Millie followed Aiden out on the porch and watched him climb behind the wheel of the truck. She waved as they drove away.

Millie went back inside and finished eating her burrito. She went into the den and turned on the surround sound. She didn't think Aiden even knew about this. Millie had splurged on rigging a sound system around the whole house. She turned on every section except the one for the pool area. Aiden told her to relax, music helped her relax.

The music was blasting, and Millie was in the kitchen baking some cookies for Bentley to decorate when he got there. She was swaying her hips and dancing as she sang. She didn't hear the front door open or Beth walking in with the kids. Millie screamed when Bentley wrapped his arms around her legs. She nearly fell when she jumped.

Millie grabbed the remote off the counter and paused the music. "You gave me a heart attack." Millie put a hand to her racing heart.

"We did knock." Beth laughed as she looked around the kitchen. "Looks like you are planning a fun day."

"I have a few things planned." Millie smiled. "So, do you know what is going on?"

"Aiden is my cousin, if he wanted Derek to help out, then he had to spill the beans." Beth handed Melody over to Millie. "And no, I will not be telling you. I need to go so I can be there when Uncle Dallas and my dad get there. You sure you are okay to watch the kids?"

"Go and have fun. Me and the kids are going to be having a party all our own." Millie kissed Melody's chubby cheek.

"I didn't realize you danced too." Beth leaned against the counter with a huge grin on her face.

"I told you my grandma had me in dance classes." Millie pointed out. "Now go. I've got things covered here."

Millie ushered Beth out the front door. She locked the door this time. She put Melody in a highchair with some snacks while she helped Bentley decorate sugar cookies that were in the shape of dinosaurs, footballs, and cars. Millie turned the music on softly in the background. The kids were loving the fun, upbeat songs that were playing.

They had just finished cleaning up the kitchen and dining room when 'The More Boys I Meet' by Carrie Underwood came on. She made faces whenever she got to the part about kissing a frog. Bentley was laughing so hard he almost fell out of his chair.

"Would you guys like to have a dance party upstairs in the music corner?" Millie asked, and Bentley nodded enthusiastically.

She lifted Melody out of the highchair and followed Bentley upstairs. She turned the music up and danced with the kids for a few songs. Her stomach grew hard and uncomfortable as a wave of nausea hit her. Millie told Bentley that she needed to sit down for a little while. She pulled Melody into her lap as she watched Bentley continue to dance. They played upstairs until it was lunch time.

Millie put Melody in the crib, but she was not happy and screamed. Millie turned the music off, causing Bentley to complain. "Why don't we sing Melody a lullaby?" Millie asked as she sat at the piano.

"Can I help?" Bentley climbed up on the bench.

"Of course you can. What song should I play?" Millie asked, but Bentley only shrugged. "Why don't I play the guitar instead of the piano?"

Millie grabbed her guitar and quickly tuned it. Melody was still screaming in the next room. Millie only knew two lullabies from what she remembered her mom singing. It wasn't even a lullaby, but Millie had loved it. She began to play 'Wild Things' by Lo Spirit. Bentley watched in fascination as Millie sang and played.

Millie immediately switched to 'Mama's Boy' by Ryan Griffin. She changed the lyrics a little. She sang it in third person instead of first. Bentley's smile grew as he listened. When she was done, Bentley hopped off the piano bench and started jumping up and down.

"That song is about me and daddy." His enthusiasm and pure delight caused Millie to laugh.

"Shh. I think your sister is asleep." Millie whispered. Can you watch my guitar while I check on her?"

Bentley eagerly nodded. Millie snuck into the room and smiled when she saw the baby girl fast asleep. She quietly left the room, leaving the door cracked so that she could hear when Melody woke up. Millie put the guitar away and invited Bentley to sit with her again at the piano. She began to play, and Bentley clapped.

It had been so long since she had played. It felt good to be playing again. She played everything she could think of, from 'A Thousand Years' to hymns. After a few songs, Bentley climbed down and laid on the pile of blankets that they had set up for Millie and Melody to lay on while Bentley danced. Three songs later Bentley was asleep, but Millie continued to play.

Millie glanced up as someone sat next to her on the bench. Aiden was looking at her as if he was trying to figure something out. "I didn't know you could play?"

"Why would I have a piano if I didn't play?" Millie smiled at him.

"You're good." He commented.

"I better be. Grandma had me taking piano lessons since I was three." Millie leaned her head on Aiden's shoulder when she finished the song she had been playing.

"Does that mean you play the cello, guitar, and violin?" Aiden asked as he looked around the loft.

"Yes." Millie said slowly. "You are back earlier than I thought you would be. The kids are down for naps."

Aiden stood and extended his hand to her. "Dad got here sooner than I thought he would. Everyone is downstairs."

Millie pulled Aiden to a stop. "How long have you been here?"

"Long enough to realize that you weren't playing piano music through a speaker, because there wasn't a long enough pause between songs." Aiden pressed a kiss to her lips. "Don't look so scared, sweetheart. You sounded fantastic."

"I don't play for people. I don't...I can't go down there." Millie started to hyperventilate. The thought that people heard her play was causing her anxiety to skyrocket.

"Hey." Aiden said softly as he pulled her into his arms. "It's okay, Millie. Everything is okay." Aiden stroked her cheek with his thumb. "Slow breaths, sweetheart."

Millie squeezed her eyes shut as she clung to Aiden. She took a deep breath and caught the scent of fresh straw, dirt, and Aiden's aftershave. She pressed her face into Aiden's chest as she tried to calm herself down. Aiden was right; everything was okay. She didn't need to freak out. So what if people heard her playing the piano? She had been fine with the kids and Aiden hearing. What were a few more people?

Slowly Millie relaxed as she listened to Aiden's comforting voice whispering that everything was going to be okay. When she tilted her face up to see Aiden, he kissed her gently. The kiss was slow, and Millie could feel the love Aiden was no doubt trying to convey. Aiden didn't seem to be in a hurry to go back downstairs.

Millie sighed as she pulled back. "Thank you." Millie whispered as she blinked slowly.

Aiden's crooked grin slowly spread across his face. "For what exactly?"

"For stopping my panic attack." Millie said slowly as she tried to shake the fog the kiss seemed to have put on her mind.

"Here I thought you were thanking me for kissing you senseless." Aiden looked quite proud of himself.

"Mmm, that too." Millie leaned into him, and he chuckled.

"Ready to go downstairs?" Aiden asked.

"If I say 'no', will you kiss me like that again?" Aiden's laugh caused Bentley to wake up. "Come on, bud. Your mom and dad are downstairs." Millie told him when he looked around disoriented.

Millie followed Bentley and Aiden down the stairs as she clung to Aiden's hand. When they stepped into the living room, it was like all conversation stopped and everyone's attention zeroed in on Millie. Josh got to his feet and threw his arm around Millie's shoulders, pulling her away from Aiden.

"You box like a cage fighter, are as tough as nails, and play the piano like a concert pianist, is there anything else you are holding out on us?" Josh asked.

"You should see her dance. I'm betting before the whole big belly thing she could be on dancing with the stars as the professional." Beth commented.

Josh stopped walking with her and looked at her with his mouth open. "A dancer too?"

"I told you guys that my grandma had me in tons of classes." Millie shrugged. "Dance, piano, cello, guitar, voice, martial arts, swimming, boxing. If my grandma found a class for it, I was in it."

"Silly song!" Bentley tugged on her hand. "Can you sing the silly song again? The one with the frogs."

"Uh," Millie swallowed, glancing around the room. Aiden looked like he was torn between coming to her rescue and wanting to hear the 'silly song'. Millie crouched down to Bentley's level. "I don't know if now is the right time for the song, buddy."

"Please." Bentley stuck his bottom lip out in the biggest pout she had ever seen. "Silly song and then my song."

Millie pinched the bridge of her nose. She was tempted to give in to his adorable face. "The silly song requires the stereo, and the other song requires my guitar. We can sing them next time I babysit you."

"I will go get the guitar." Josh ran up the stairs, returning moments later. "I can't wait to hear this." He was practically bouncing with excitement.

"Thanks." Millie said as she glared at him, which only made him smile bigger.

"And the stereo can be controlled by that controller in your back pocket." Beth pointed out.

"Okay, fine. But you guys owe me big time." Millie pulled the remote out of her pocket.

She sat on the ground with her back to the room and Bentley sat across from her as if she was going to tell him a story. "Bentley, if you keep spilling my secrets, you aren't going to get a cookie for snack time." she muttered.

Several people laughed, but she refused to look behind her. Bentley reminded Millie to sing the silly song first. Sighing, Millie turned on the living room speaker. She switched to her phone and turned on 'The More Boys I Meet' by Carrie Underwood. She took a deep breath to steel her nerves.

Millie started playing the guitar with the music as she sang. She made sure to make the faces she did last time in case Bentley made her sing it again. Playing helped calm her as she sang. The song ended and Millie tapped her phone to pause the music as she began playing 'Mama's Boy' by Ryan Griffin. She changed the lyrics, just like she had before.

Bentley had the biggest grin on his face by the time she was done. Millie set the guitar off to the side and touched the tip of Bentley's nose with her index finger. "Can I be done now?" She asked.

"You're the best." Bentley threw his arms around her neck in a quick hug, before running to his mom.

Millie rotated around and scooted back against the fireplace. Josh and Aiden were staring at her with mouths slightly open and the others were just looking at her, stunned. Millie's anxiety began to come back, and she reached for her guitar. She strummed without really thinking about what she was playing. She just needed an outlet so she didn't have an anxiety attack, and music had always been one.

Chapter 26

"So, is everyone going to just stare at me, or can we move on to something else?" Millie finally asked.

"How did we not know you could sing like that?" Aiden asked in amazement.

"Probably because I only sing when I am alone or working with kids." Millie shrugged.

"Now you need to dance for us." Beth stated.

"That is a hard pass." Millie shook her head. "I only dance for fun and having you all watching me doesn't sound fun." Not to mention the fact that she still was feeling weird.

"What kind of dancing do you do?" A man asked. Millie hadn't met him yet. He was sitting next to Ava, so she assumed he was Dallas.

"Ballet, hip-hop, salsa, ballroom, line-dancing." Millie continued to play the guitar quietly. "A little country swing, but I only took a class about a year ago."

"Dang. How did you have time to do all this?" Derek asked.

"You are forgetting I was homeschooled and hated being around people. I was in extra classes from six in the morning to two in the afternoon. At which point, I did schoolwork until five at night. I was never given the opportunity to get into trouble." Millie shrugged.

"I doubt that." Josh laughed. "You are full of trouble. I am curious about something though; did you have a dog growing up?"

Millie smirked at him. "I may or may not have still found ways to get into trouble. As for the dog, I would have traded my kidney for my grandma to let me have one."

The two older men laughed. "I'm sorry, I don't think we have met. I'm Millie." Millie gave them a smile.

"Oh sorry. Millie, this is my dad, Dallas and my Uncle Brett." Aiden said quickly, pointing to each man in turn.

Aiden stood and reached down to help Millie up. She gratefully accepted his help. There was no way she was going to try to get up without assistance at the moment. Once she was back on her feet, Aiden put an arm around her.

"I think it would be good to go show Millie what you brought from the ranch before it gets dark." Aiden said, and the group all got up. Aiden retrieved Millie's shoes from their room and Millie slipped them on. "Are you okay to go for a little walk?"

"Lead the way, Cowboy." Millie smiled at him, and he pressed a quick kiss to her lips before walking out the side door.

The rest of the group walked in front of them, and Millie was glad to not be the focus anymore. She walked slowly with Aiden's hand in hers. She furrowed her brow when she realized they were heading to the barn. Millie didn't say anything, but her curiosity grew.

Millie stopped walking when she noticed a dark brown horse in the field. "Uh, Aiden? Why is there a mare and foal in the field?" She walked to the fence and put her arms over the top rail.

Aiden let out a whistle and the mare's head snapped up before she trotted in their direction. Millie was practically buzzing with excitement. The foal ran after its mother. The mare hung her head over the fence when she reached them. Millie stroked the mare's wide blaze in wonder.

"This is Mojo and her colt." Aiden said with a big grin on his face. "She was the first foal born after I took over the breeding program. I have raised and trained her. What do you think?"

Millie pulled her eyes from the horse and beamed up at Aiden. "She is beautiful." She turned back to the horse. "How is she with people around her baby?"

"Mojo is pretty chill. Are you saying you want to play with the colt?" Aiden laughed.

"That is exactly what I am saying." Millie said as she climbed the fence and dropped on the other side.

"Millie, we have gates." Aiden said irritably. "What if you had fallen?"

Millie smiled as the colt came up to investigate the newcomer to the field. Millie was so absorbed with how soft the colt's coat was, she hadn't noticed that Aiden had joined her.

"What is the plan for this guy?" Millie asked as Aiden stroked Mojo's neck and watched Millie.

"We are keeping him. By the time our son is old enough to ride, I will have had at least two years of training with him."

Millie turned wide eyes on Aiden. "Our son isn't even born yet, and you got him a horse?"

Aiden became slightly nervous. "Uh, is that a problem?" he asked with uncertainty.

"Yeah, that is a huge problem, Aiden." Millie put her hands on her hips as she glared at him. She watched as he swallowed hard. Josh, Derek, and the others came out of the barn with various expressions of concern and confusion. "You can't give the baby a horse."

"Why not?" Aiden asked with little volume to his voice.

"Because it isn't fair. I have wanted a horse for eighteen years and my son is going to get one before I do? Nope, sorry, not happening." Millie crossed her arms over her chest.

Aiden ran a hand down his face and the relief she saw there had her heart racing. "Sweetheart, I didn't just bring Mojo and the colt." Aiden grabbed her hand and pulled her along the fence to a red gate. He led her inside the barn with the others following her. Millie gasped when she saw five horses inside the barn. Aiden stopped at a buckskin, turning Millie to face it. "This is Fish Sticks."

"Her name is not Fish Sticks." Millie scrunched her nose. Her already upset stomach rolled uncomfortably. "So help me, Aiden. If you cause me to throw up, I am going to be so mad at you." Millie closed her eyes and put a hand to her mouth, fighting the urge to vomit.

"Shoot." Aiden muttered as he rubbed her back slowly. "I forgot. I'm sorry, Millie."

Millie nodded and took a slow deep breath. "What is her real name?" she whispered, trying to distract herself.

"Uh, Mayflower, but we usually just call her May." Millie opened her eyes to see Aiden watching her closely. "Dad, do you have any water in your truck? Do you need to sit? You lost all your color."

Millie shook her head and gave him a small smile. "I'll be fine. Just a bit queasy."

"I'm so sorry." Aiden had a pained expression on his face.

"Even the word has you up chucking?" Josh asked as he stepped up to Millie, passing her a water. "What did the scaley creatures ever do to you to make you hate them so much?" Josh was smiling.

That did it. Millie sprinted to the door, not caring what anyone thought. She managed to make it outside and to the side of the barn before hurling. Someone helped gather her hair and held it out of the way. When she looked up, Ava stood there.

"I'm so sorry, dear. Why don't we get you sitting down?" Ava led her to a grassy spot in the shade. "How are you feeling? Your lips don't even have color."

"I'm okay. Just the mention of fish makes me sick." Millie sighed as she took the water bottle Ava offered her. "Where is Aiden?"

"Aiden, Derek, Dallas, and Brett are giving Josh an earful about pushing you over the edge." Ava laughed.

"Josh didn't even say the word, Aiden did. Josh just mentioned scales." Millie took a sip of the water to hopefully settle her stomach. "Thank you for helping Aiden with this."

"He was beyond excited when Dallas told him Mojo had a colt. He can't wait to start teaching you and the baby to ride." Ava smiled at Millie.

"Should I pretend I don't know how to ride then?" Millie asked with a sly grin, causing Ava to laugh. "Do I need to wait to ride until after the baby is born? I am only twenty-nine weeks."

"Honey, I was riding until thirty-five weeks when I was pregnant with Aiden. The real question you should be asking is, will Aiden let you?"

"Good point. Thank you for coming out with me, but I think I am ready to go back in." Millie said as she got to her feet.

They walked back in the barn to find Aiden looking daggers at a sheepish Josh. Millie walked up to Aiden and punched him in the gut. It wasn't very hard, just enough to cause him to grunt. Next, she turned to Josh. He raised his hands as if he was trying to fight her off.

"You two know better." Millie smacked the back of Josh's head. "Can you two please refrain from talking about those things for the next eleven weeks?" Both of them nodded quickly. "Now, is Mayflower going to foal soon or are you planning on breeding her?"

"Millie, I am so sorry. I wasn't thinking. Are you doing okay? You are still pale." Aiden put his arm around her, and she rested her head on his shoulder.

"I am as good as I am going to be at the moment." Millie said quietly.

Aiden kissed the top of her head. "Mayflower isn't currently pregnant. The decision to breed her is up to you. She has produced some pretty good foals in the past."

"Me? Why would that decision be mine? You are the one with all the knowledge on horse breeding." Millie asked, confused.

"You get to make the decision, because May is your horse. Three of the other horses are in various stages of pregnancy, and the other one is mine." Aiden's earlier large grin was back on his face. Millie stared at him with her mouth open in surprise. "Oh, and Dad brought Pepper. I hope you are okay if we keep her here. I guess she has been tormenting the other dogs and driving Dad crazy wanting in the house."

"Just so we are clear. You are talking about a dog?" Millie asked. She didn't think she could get any more excited than she had when she saw the horses, but she was wrong.

"Less of a dog and more of a puppy." Aiden said, rubbing the back of his neck.

"Aiden found the little thing on the side of the road on the way to the ranch. The vet said he thinks she is around four months old. But he let her sleep with him while he was there. Now she thinks she is a house dog and not the ranch dog she should be." Dallas told Millie.

"Pepper was scared and lonely." Aiden defended himself. "She was crying in the barn the whole first night."

"Millie, tell Aiden, no." Josh said with a serious expression even though his voice had a teasing edge to it.

"You can't say, no, until you see her." Aiden pulled Millie down the row of stalls to the far end, stopping at the last one.

He opened the stall door, and a black and white border collie puppy came running out. Millie crouched and scooped the puppy up. She buried her face in the puppy's fur. Pepper began to whine as she licked Millie furiously with a tail that was wagging so fast that it was just a blur. Millie was beyond sold.

"So, what do you think?" Aiden asked with his eyes glued to her. "Can I keep her?"

"The answer is, no. You cannot keep the puppy." Millie said with a straight face before turning and walking away. She still held the puppy as she walked out of the barn.

"No?" Aiden asked. "Where are you taking her? Why can't I keep her?" Aiden followed closely behind Millie.

Millie glanced over her shoulder and noticed that Aiden wasn't the only one that followed her. Everyone was watching their exchange. Millie put Pepper down and she immediately started jumping up on Millie's legs. "Aiden, you can't keep the puppy, and that is final."

"But..."

"You can't have her because she is mine." Millie smirked at him.

Aiden narrowed his eyes. "But I rescued her from the side of the road."

"You may have rescued her, but she is now mine." Millie rose on her toes and gave a stunned Aiden a kiss. "And thank you, she is the cutest."

Millie continued walking down the path to the house. She wouldn't fully admit it to Aiden, but after throwing up, she felt like she needed to lay down for a while. Pepper followed on Millie's heels the whole way.

She entered the house to find Beth sitting on the couch watching cartoons with the kids. Millie went immediately to her room, grateful that no one saw her or the puppy. She quietly closed her door and went straight to the bathroom. She splashed cool water on her face before patting her face dry and picking up Pepper.

Millie climbed into bed allowing Pepper to settle on the mattress next to her. The puppy curled against her belly and Millie ran her hand through Pepper's thick coat. It didn't take long before Millie fell asleep.

"Millie, sweetheart. Can you wake up for me?" Aiden said gently as he combed his fingers through Millie's hair.

"What time is it?" Millie mumbled as she blinked her eyes open.

"It's dinner time. You have been in here for two hours." Aiden sat down on the edge of the bed. "How are you feeling?"

"I needed to lay down for a few minutes." Millie said as she sat up. Pepper climbed onto her lap. "I'm sorry for neglecting everyone."

"Don't even worry about that. I'm concerned about you. You are still pale. Would you like me to bring you anything? A Gatorade or a burrito?" Aiden asked as he studied her face.

"Yeah, that sounds great." Millie rubbed her forehead. "Aiden, I don't feel so good."

"You don't look like you feel very good. Is the baby moving a lot?" Millie could hear the worry in Aiden's voice.

"He is moving around normally. I just feel so tired. I can't seem to keep my eyes open." Millie leaned her head back and closed her eyes. "Maybe I just need to eat something."

"I am going to have Josh get you something to eat while I call Dr. Spaulding. I will be right back." Aiden kissed Millie's forehead and hurried out the door.

Millie looked down at the puppy in her lap and smiled. The poor thing probably needed to use the bathroom. Millie climbed out of bed and carried Pepper to the patio door. She slipped outside and put the puppy down, after she sat on a chair.

Her belly felt completely hard and her back began to hurt. Millie closed her eyes. The uncomfortable sensation of being squeezed didn't last long, and she relaxed back into the chair.

"Millie?" Aiden's voice came from inside their room.

"I'm out here." Millie called and when Aiden crouched next to her, she gave him a small smile. "I figured Pepper needed a potty break."

Aiden looked down at the puppy who was attempting to jump up on Millie's lap. "Did she go?"

Millie shook her head. "She just wants me to hold her."

"After I get you back in bed, I will take her back out and see if she will go without you around." Aiden patted the dog's head. "Dr. Spaulding asked if you had been having any contractions. I told her I didn't know. She told me to make sure you stayed in bed until the appointment tomorrow."

"Okay." Millie stood slowly and Aiden put an arm around her.

"No arguing?" Aiden asked teasingly, but there was a hint of worry behind his words.

Millie climbed into bed and Aiden laid down facing her. He placed his hand on her belly as he studied her face. Millie stroked Aiden's cheek and gave him a soft smile.

"I love you." Millie's words drew a genuine smile to Aiden's lips. "Thank you for today. I can't wait to go riding with you."

Aiden pressed a kiss to Millie's lips. "Not until we know you and the baby are doing okay. My dad and uncle think you are the greatest. They thought you teasing me about the whole puppy thing was a riot."

"I wasn't teasing. Pepper is so not yours." Millie's smile grew as she spoke. Her stomach grew hard again, and Aiden looked down at his hand as he gently rubbed her belly.

"Is that the baby?" he asked, confused. "I have never felt him like that before."

"I don't think that is the baby." Millie said. The tightness went away, and the baby began kicking up a storm. "I think that was a contraction."

Aiden froze and looked at Millie's face. "It's too early, right?"

"Braxton Hicks contractions are normal Aiden. At least that is what Dr. Spaulding said. As long as they aren't regular and don't grow closer together." Millie tried to soothe Aiden's worry while hiding her own. "Where's that burrito you promised me?"

"Right here." Josh stepped into the room with a plate and a Gatorade bottle. "Man, Mils. You don't look like you are feeling very well. I'm sorry for earlier. I wasn't thinking."

"It's okay, Josh. I am fine. It's been a long week, and it is probably just catching up to me." Millie accepted the plate after sitting up.

"I'd say so. Your mom waking up from a two month coma, getting married, going to court, having to face the man that raped you, meeting the in-laws, getting horses, and a puppy all in a week or two is insane."

Millie flinched at the word 'rape'. "Way to be tactful, Josh." Aiden muttered.

Josh winced. "Sorry, Millie. How are you feeling, truly?"

"Tired mostly." Millie took a small bite and chewed slowly.

"Aiden, I think we need to get Millie to the hospital. She isn't inhaling her burrito." Josh joked.

"Millie?" Bentley came into the room.

"Hey, buddy." Millie smiled as Bentley climbed up on the bed. "Why such a sad face?"

"Mommy said we have to go home." Bentley snuggled up to Millie's side.

"We had fun today, didn't we?" Millie combed Bentley's hair from his forehead as he nodded. "Why don't I play you one more song before you go?" Bentley smiled up at her and Millie's heart melted. "Why don't you have someone go get my guitar?" she whispered to him, and he jumped off the bed and ran from the room.

"You don't have to, Millie. You can play with Bentley another time." Aiden put his arm around her. "I don't want you pushing yourself too much tonight."

"Music is relaxing to me." Millie leaned heavily back against Aiden. "I haven't played since before Alaska and it's been nice to get back to it."

The sound of her guitar smacking against something hard had her wincing. Josh ran from the room when the sound came a second time. Bentley came running into the room with a huge smile on his face. Josh followed holding the guitar.

"It might have been knocked out of tune." He apologized. "Do you want me to see if Derek can tune it for you?"

"No need, just give it here." Millie extended her hands, and Josh handed her the guitar. "Bentley, next time only an adult can carry the instruments, okay?" Bentley nodded as Millie began tuning the guitar. She closed her eyes as she concentrated on the notes. It took her a few moments before she felt she had it right.

Millie began to play, but after a minute Bentley stopped her. "Sing too." He demanded.

"You all better get in here; I know you are out in the hall." Millie continued to strum the guitar as Beth and Derek, holding Melody, entered the room, followed by Dallas and Ava.

Millie turned her attention back to Bentley. She began to play 'Blackbird' by the Beatles at a slower tempo like her mom did when she sang her to sleep. As soon as she started to sing, Dallas did as well. Even though she was surprised, Millie kept going. Their voices blended together flawlessly. Ava wiped a tear from her cheek when they finished the song.

"Another." Bentley clapped.

"I agree we need another song. Millie, your voice is phenomenal." Derek said as he wrapped his arm around Beth.

"Do you know 'Titanium'?" Beth asked.

"I do." Millie said slowly. "I usually play that on the piano though."

"I know you are supposed to be resting, but will you play that one for us?" Beth begged.

Millie set the guitar on the bed and stood up. "Okay. But then I am going to bed."

"Deal." Beth looped her arm through Millie's as they walked from the room.

Millie sat at the piano and Aiden sat next to her. "You should be in bed." He said quietly.

"And I will be, after this song." Millie gave him a smile.

Millie began to play, and Aiden started to sing the first verse. Millie's smile grew as she listened to him. She came in on the chorus, their voices complimenting each other. She stared into Aiden's eyes as she sang. How did she not know that he could sing? Aiden watched as she sang the second verse before joining her on the chorus.

When the final notes faded, everything was still for several seconds before Beth began to clap. "Okay, Aiden. When did you learn to sing?" Beth asked in amazement.

"That is a talent he picked up from his father, but he rarely uses it." Ava laughed.

"You never told me you sang." Millie poked Aiden in the chest.

He grabbed her hand as he smiled at her. "Says the woman who kept her own musical talents a secret." He stood and pulled her up before wrapping his arms around her. "We may have to start singing together more often though." He whispered in her ear.

"We might just have to." Millie whispered back before Aiden kissed her.

"I am going to take Millie back downstairs. The doctor said she wanted Millie resting until her appointment tomorrow." Aiden said to the group.

Millie said goodnight to the others and headed downstairs with Aiden. She changed into her pajamas, finished her burrito, and laid down in bed. Aiden kissed her forehead as Millie moved her head to his chest. Her contractions seemed to have gone away, which lessened Millie's worries. She felt like she could breathe again.

Chapter 27

Millie couldn't believe that she was thirty-six weeks pregnant. She felt huge. Beth had invited Aiden and Millie to go trick-or-treating with them, but Millie turned her down. Not only did she not like dressing up and being with tons of strangers on the street, she also was having more contractions lately.

"Millie, is Pepper with you?" Aiden called from the door that led to the garage.

Millie looked down at the puppy in her lap. Pepper was getting much bigger, but she was still a cuddle bug. She followed Millie everywhere. Millie looked over the back of the couch as Aiden stepped more into the house.

"Would it surprise you if I said she has been in here since you came in for lunch?" Millie asked with a smile.

"I was hoping she would be more of a ranch dog once she settled in. Yet every time I take her to the barn with me, she is back here within an hour." Aiden shook his head as he leaned over the back of the couch to pet the dog.

Millie kissed Aiden's cheek. "If I came out to the barn with you, Pepper would stay there longer."

"Probably. But you are on bed rest until this baby comes." Aiden kissed her forehead. "I'm going to shower really quick and then we can figure out dinner."

Millie watched as Aiden went down the hall. She was so tired of being on bed rest. Dr. Spaulding was worried about Millie going into preterm labor and put her on bed rest for the last seven weeks. To help take care of her, Aiden was taking all of his classes online for this semester.

Millie's phone rang and she answered it when she saw that it was Mrs. White. Aiden was still in the shower, so Mrs. White asked Millie to share the news with him. He had been cleared to adopt the baby as soon as Lawrence had his parental rights removed. Millie thanked the lawyer and hung up. She couldn't wait to tell Aiden. He had been stressing with all the hoops he had to go through on top of school and Millie being on bed rest.

"What do you want to eat?" Aiden asked, coming back into the living room.

"No, what do you want to eat?" Millie couldn't contain her grin. If she could, she would be jumping up and down in excitement.

"Am I missing something?" Aiden eyed her. "You seem…enthusiastic all of a sudden."

"I am always enthusiastic to see you." Millie shrugged, but her grin remained.

"Uh-huh. And that look on your face is making me suspicious." Aiden sat on the couch and put his arm around Millie. "You are the worst at keeping secrets."

"This isn't a secret; it is just something I know that you do not." Millie got to her feet, unable to sit anymore.

"Millie, you should be sitting down." Aiden protested as he tried to grab her hand, but she was just out of his reach.

"Aiden, you've been approved." Millie said excitedly.

"Approved for what?" Aiden asked, confused.

"To adopt the baby as soon as Lawrence's parental rights are signed over." Millie watched as Aiden froze as he processed what she had just said.

His eyes misted as he jumped to his feet and pulled her into his arms. Aiden held Millie tightly for several minutes before pulling back enough to press his lips to hers. Millie wrapped her arms around his neck as she smiled against his lips.

"So, my love, what would you like to eat? Tonight, we celebrate." Millie slid her hands down Aiden's chest.

"I can't believe it. I mean I knew it was just a matter of time, but I was expecting things to take longer." Aiden laughed in amazement.

"Food, Aiden. Your wife and son need food." Millie playfully tugged on Aiden's shirt.

"I want to stay in tonight. I would be happy with a bowl of soup and some rolls, as long as I get to sit on the couch and watch something with you."

"Sounds perfect." Millie rose on her toes and kissed Aiden.

Millie was instructed to sit on the couch again while Aiden heated up the leftover soup. They had to put Pepper in her play area in the corner once the food was ready. She was a quick learner. It only took a few days for Millie to potty train Pepper, but she went crazy when food was out.

The movie started and Millie groaned. "You want to watch The Lord of the Rings to celebrate fatherhood?"

Aiden kissed her temple. "No, I want to watch the trilogy to celebrate."

"That is like nine hours." Millie complained. "I don't know if I can stay up that long."

"I will make sure you get to bed when the movies are over." Aiden took a bite of his roll as he smiled at her. "Now eat your food so we can cuddle."

Millie laughed as she settled back and sipped her soup. She had been having contractions off and on all day and didn't have much of an appetite. The movie was half over by the time she gave up on eating and took her stuff to the kitchen. She had a contraction as she was walking back to the couch and stopped walking. It was much stronger than the ones she had earlier.

When she got back to the couch, Aiden was laying down on his back. Millie gratefully laid down next to him, using his shoulder as a pillow. His arms came around her with one hand resting on her belly. Aiden kissed the top of Millie's head before turning back to the movie.

By the second movie, Millie was trying to relax and enjoy it, but the contractions were making it nearly impossible. Another one hit and Millie concentrated on breathing normally. She finally got up and Aiden paused the movie.

"Is everything okay?" Aiden asked as he watched her. "You didn't seem to be able to find a comfortable position."

Millie put her hand to her forehead. Sweat beaded on her skin and Millie brushed it away. "I think I just need to sit up for a little while."

"Come here." Aiden put his arms around her and kissed her gently. "We can take a break from the movies for a little while if you want."

Millie smiled. "I like that plan."

She barely got the words out before Aiden's lips were back on hers. Millie sighed as Aiden cupped the back of her head, drawing her closer. They sat like that for a few minutes before another contraction hit. Millie pulled away and groaned as she put her hand on her belly.

"Millie?" Aiden asked anxiously. His hand was still on her face, and she leaned into it. "Sweetheart, what's wrong?"

The contraction finally ended, and Millie fought her rising panic. The contractions were stronger and coming more frequently. "Where's my phone." Millie asked, sitting back from Aiden, and looking around. She found it on the side table and quickly grabbed it.

"Millie, what is going on?" Aiden asked, he looked worried as he watched as she brought the phone to her ear.

"I think," Millie started to explain but stopped when the call was answered. "Hi, it's Millie. I'm sorry for calling so late."

"That's okay. How are you doing?" Dr. Spaulding asked.

Millie held Aiden's gaze. "Um, I have been having a lot of contractions over the past couple of hours."

"Are they coming regularly and getting stronger?" Dr. Spaulding was all business suddenly.

"Not at first, but they are now coming more frequently, and they are getting stronger." Millie saw the worry intensify in Aiden's eyes as she spoke.

"I want you to head to the hospital immediately." Dr. Spaulding said firmly. "And be prepared for a long stay."

"Okay." Millie said before hanging up. "She said we need to go to the hospital and to prepare for a long stay."

"It's going to be okay." Aiden said. Millie wasn't sure if he was trying to reassure her or himself.

Aiden spent the next ten minutes throwing clothes into a couple of bags and calling Josh to come house sit. Millie climbed into her car while Aiden threw the bags in the back seat. She had to remind him to drive the speed limit several times.

Millie had Aiden grab the hospital bag she had stored in the car weeks ago but told him to leave the others until they knew what was going on. As they were walking inside the ER, another contraction hit, and Millie stopped walking. She breathed through it. A nurse saw them just outside the entrance and came running out.

Before Millie knew what was happening, she was in a wheelchair and being wheeled into an elevator. They made it to the maternity ward in less than ten minutes of arriving at the hospital. Dr. Spaulding had called ahead, and the nurses immediately hooked Millie up to monitors.

Aiden stood back and watched with an anxious expression. A few minutes later, the nurses left, and Aiden stepped up to her side. His eyes were fixed on the monitor that tracked her contractions.

"It seems Waylon doesn't like Lord of the Rings either." Millie smiled up at Aiden but grimaced as another contraction hit.

"Waylon, huh?" Aiden gave her a crooked grin before kissing her brow. "So, you settled on a name then?"

Millie grabbed Aiden's hand. Waylon had been one that Aiden had suggested. She hadn't told him then that she had loved the name. Millie had been calling the baby Waylon for weeks now. "Didn't I tell you?" she teased.

"No, I think I would have remembered if you had." Aiden squeezed her hand.

"You do seem to love keeping us all on our toes." Dr. Spaulding said as she walked into the room. She moved over to the monitors as she spoke. "How are you feeling?"

"A little nauseous and uncomfortable." Millie said as she shifted, another contraction tightened her belly.

"You have had several contractions just in the last half hour. Is it okay if I check you?" Dr. Spaulding asked as a nurse came into the room with a cart. Millie nodded and Aiden kissed her hand.

Millie breathed through another contraction while Dr. Spaulding and the nurse conversed quietly. Aiden's whole body was tense as they waited. Dr. Spaulding came back to Millie's side as the nurse slipped out.

"Millie, I am going to be honest with you." Aiden's hand tightened on Millie's. "You are in labor. We could try to stop it, but I don't think it will help. Your body and baby seem to be saying they are done."

"But she is only thirty-six weeks." Aiden said.

Dr. Spaulding gave him a reassuring smile. "I know that this seems scary, but Millie and the baby are in good hands. Try to relax and get some rest. This will be a long night." She patted Millie's shoulder before leaving.

A nurse came back in and started an I.V. line. Another brought in a pillow and blanket for Aiden. Millie waited until the nurses left before looking at Aiden. He looked like he might throw up.

"How are you doing?" Millie asked.

"Uh," Aiden ran a hand down his face as he sat in a chair next to her bed. "I thought I had a few more weeks to get prepared."

"You and me both." Millie closed her eyes and tried not to let her anxiety take control. She didn't feel ready for this. When she looked back at Aiden, he looked completely panicked. "Are you having second thoughts? I don't blame you if you are."

Aiden's worried expression immediately changed into confusion. "Second thoughts about what?"

"The baby." Millie whispered as she looked down at her belly.

"Look at me, Millie Larson." Aiden said firmly. "You and Waylon are my family. I may be completely freaking out at the moment. But that has nothing to do with me wanting to be Waylon's father and everything to do with the fact that he is coming four weeks ahead of schedule."

"Oh, that is another thing I forgot to tell you." Millie bit her lip. "My last name is officially Coleman now. I got my social security card and driver's license all changed over."

Aiden smiled before pressing a kiss to her lips. "You are just full of surprises today."

"A lot more than I had planned for. I originally was going to tell you about the name change being official, then Mrs. White called about your adoption paperwork being ready to file as soon as Lawrence was fully out of the picture. I hadn't even thought we would be here tonight." Millie tensed with the contraction.

"Sweetheart, you need to relax. Don't fight it." Aiden brushed her hair off her forehead. His eyes looked to the monitor as he watched the progression of the contraction. "Have you thought of any middle names? Or if you are going with Larson or Coleman as his last name?" Aiden asked when the contraction ended.

"What do you think we should do?" Millie asked. She didn't want Aiden to feel like she was pushing this baby on him.

"I had hoped that you would agree to Coleman. Now that your last name is officially changed to match mine, I am even more in favor of it." Aiden gave her a teasing smile. "After all, a child should have the same last name as it's mother."

"Would you have given that line if my last name was still Larson?" Millie asked, cocking her head to the side.

"Definitely, not. I'm being selfish on this. I am voting on Waylon Coleman." Aiden laughed.

"I was thinking Waylon Beckett Coleman, actually." Millie leaned back into the pillows.

"Where did you get Beckett from?" Aiden asked curiously. His smile was no longer on his face as he watched her.

"When we went to the temple last week." Millie said feeling nervous. "As I was waiting for you, it was like someone whispered the name in my ear, but no one was near me. Do you not like it?"

Aiden pressed his lips to hers. "No, I love it. Beckett was my grandfather's name. He and I were really close, but he passed away a few years ago. Waylon Beckett Coleman." Aiden said the name slowly as his smile grew. "Sounds perfect to me."

"Aiden, can you sit with me?" Millie asked softly after a few minutes.

Aiden sat on the bed next to her and she laid her head on his shoulder. Millie let out a tense breath. She was so nervous and clung to Aiden's hand as if it were her lifeline. She read the various text messages he sent out.

He told Josh that Millie was in labor and that he had stuck Pepper out in the barn. He sent a message to his parents, Beth and Derek, and Millie's parents saying that Millie went in labor, and all was going well at the moment. Aiden's phone buzzed nonstop for the next ten minutes. Beth was mad that she was at the ranch and wouldn't be there. Josh told them not to worry about anything, he had it covered. Millie's mom wished her good luck.

Over the next few hours, Millie's anxiety began to grow as the contractions grew stronger. Dr. Spaulding and several of the nurses had checked on her periodically. Millie was now throwing up with the pain and she didn't think she could keep going.

Aiden held her between contractions. She was so glad he was there with her. She couldn't even imagine being able to get through this if she had been alone. Aiden whispered encouragements as she breathed through the contractions. A contraction hit and Millie cried out in pain while Aiden held to her hand as he stood beside her. Dr. Spaulding walked in and put on a pair of gloves.

After checking Millie, she gave her an encouraging smile. "How are you feeling, Millie?"

"I can't seem to get a break." Millie panted out. Her body began to tense again, and she whimpered. "I can't do this!" She cried out.

"You can, because you are doing it." Dr. Spaulding said. A few nurses came into the room with several different carts and tools. "Are you ready to meet your baby boy?"

Chapter 28

Millie was so exhausted as she leaned back on the bed. Seconds later a baby's cry filled the room. Dr. Spaulding put the baby on Millie's chest. Aiden leaned down and kissed Millie's forehead as he smiled at her and the baby. Millie cried as she stared at her son.

He had long thick dark brown hair. He was small, but he had a good pair of lungs on him. A nurse used a clean towel to wipe his tiny body as Millie held him to her chest. Millie closed her eyes as she kissed his head. She felt Aiden's hand next to hers on the baby's back. Millie looked up at Aiden. He was grinning proudly as he stared at the baby.

Aiden kissed her temple. "He is beautiful." He whispered.

"We are going to take him over here to do his measurements." A nurse told her gently with a smile.

Millie didn't want to leave the baby alone with anyone right now. She felt like she was being paranoid, but her nightmare about Lawrence taking the baby away came flooding back and she just couldn't take the chance.

"I will go with him." Aiden kissed her again and Millie nodded her head.

"Have you decided on a name yet?" Dr. Spaulding asked.

"Waylon." Millie said softly while she watched Aiden as he stood near the group of nurses that were tending to Waylon.

Ten minutes later, Waylon was placed back in Millie's arms. He was swaddled in a blanket with a pink and blue striped beanie on his little head. He wasn't even six pounds, but he was completely healthy. Things began to calm down and a lactation specialist came to the room to help Millie learn how to feed the baby.

Aiden stayed at Millie's side the entire time. He had pulled the beanie off the baby's head and gently stroked Waylon's hair while he nursed. Aiden's hand looked so big compared to how small Waylon was.

Waylon ate for thirty minutes. "Aiden?" Millie said tiredly. "Would you like to burp Waylon?"

Aiden's eyes lit up as he reached for the baby. He had much more experience with babies than Millie did. He was a natural. He cradled Waylon's head as he lifted the baby to his shoulder. Millie teared up again as she watched Aiden look at Waylon with nothing but love and pride in his eyes. He kissed the baby's cheek as he closed his eyes. He looked to be savoring the moment.

"Millie, he is perfect." Aiden whispered as he looked at her with a big smile on his face. "Thank you."

"Thank you? For what?" Millie asked, confused.

"For being amazing. For agreeing to marry me. For letting me be Waylon's father." Aiden stood and leaned down to kiss her, but he stopped just shy of their lips touching. "For loving me." He pressed his lips to hers and Waylon let out a cry. "Chill, little man. Your mom and I are allowed to kiss." Aiden straightened as he patted the baby's back.

"I love you too." Millie smiled up at Aiden.

"Why don't you try to get some rest while you can? I will hold this little guy while you do." Aiden settled back in his chair.

"What about you? You have been up just as long as I have." Millie pointed out. She didn't want to leave Aiden to take care of the baby if he was tired too.

"Sweetheart, I didn't just give birth. I can sleep after you get some rest. Plus, I need to let everyone know that you and Waylon are okay." Aiden paused before a mischievous smile spread on his lips. "Actually, I'm only going to tell them that the baby was born and that both of you are doing okay. No details."

"Beth is not going to be happy with you." Millie laughed.

"Her fault for going on a weekend trip to the ranch. She could have been here." Aiden shrugged. "Even though I am glad I don't have to share you or Waylon with anyone else. Now, try to sleep. Your body went through a lot to get this guy here."

Millie nodded tiredly and dimmed the lights in the room using the bed remote. Aiden began to rock the baby. Millie closed her eyes and listened as Aiden began to hum softly.

It felt like no time had passed when a nurse came to check on Millie and Waylon. Millie couldn't get back to sleep. Her body was sore, and she couldn't get comfortable. Aiden watched her for several minutes before he stood and walked over to her.

"Mildred Louise Coleman, you need to rest." Aiden said as he laid Waylon in the bassinet next to the bed before he sat down next to her. "Come here, Love." He wrapped his arms around her, and Millie sighed as she cuddled up to him.

"You know, it's easier to cuddle without a giant belly in the way." Millie commented and Aiden laughed.

"Go to sleep, sweetheart, before Waylon or a nurse needs you again." Aiden whispered, then pressed a kiss to the top of Millie's head.

"I can't believe he is here. It still doesn't seem real." Millie said as she watched her son sleeping. She yawned and snuggled closer to Aiden. He started running his fingers through her hair, and within minutes, her eyes were drooping.

*   *   *

The cry of a baby caused Millie to jerk awake. "Aiden!" She called as she looked frantically around. She found him standing next to the window with Waylon in his arms.

"It's okay, Millie. Waylon is fine." Aiden said, walking towards her. Millie fell back against her pillow and closed her eyes briefly. Her heart was racing as adrenaline surged through her. "Did you have another nightmare?" Aiden asked softly as he sat down next to her and placed Waylon in her arms.

Millie pressed a kiss to Waylon's head before leaning against Aiden. "Yeah." She breathed out. "And then I heard a baby cry."

"Waylon wasn't crying, it was a baby down the hall. Though I don't think Waylon is far from joining the other baby. I think he might be getting hungry." Aiden brushed his lips against Millie's forehead.

"Are you hungry?" Millie cooed as she ran her finger gently down Waylon's cheek. He turned his head toward her finger with his mouth open. Millie smiled before repositioning Waylon so he could nurse. "Did you get any sleep?" She asked Aiden.

"A little, then the nurses came back in. I swear they were in here every thirty minutes. They are all amazed that Waylon isn't having any issues." Aiden sighed as he relaxed more against the raised back of the bed. "Did you get any rest?"

"I feel like I slept for a long time, but at the same time I feel like I barely went to sleep." Millie ran her hand softly over Waylon's head. "I can't believe how much hair he has."

"It was all those burritos you ate." Aiden teased.

Millie looked at him with a smile. "You should see my baby pictures. I think I had more than this. By the time I was one, my grandma was braiding my hair to keep it out of my face."

Aiden kissed her. "His eyes are definitely yours."

"Why do you say that?" Millie looked down at Waylon. His eyes were closed as he continued to nurse.

"Because Waylon's eyes are blue, like yours. If I remember right, Lawrence's eyes are brown." Aiden touched Waylon's hand with a finger. "Not that I would mind if he had brown eyes. I just love your blue ones."

"Everyone would probably think he got his brown eyes from you if they were." Millie kissed Aiden's cheek. "Do you think our other kids will have your eyes or mine?"

"We haven't really talked about kids, have we? I was so focused on you and Waylon, I never really thought about having anymore. But now that you brought it up, I have always wanted two or three." Aiden nuzzled Millie's neck.

"Two or three?" Millie looked at Aiden in surprise.

"Well, how many do you want? Given the fact that you just gave birth, I wouldn't be surprised if you said you were happy with just Waylon."

"Oh no, my love. I have always wanted four or five kids." Millie raised Waylon to her shoulder and started to burp him. The look of shock on Aiden's face caused Millie to laugh.

Aiden shook his head and smiled. "You are a wonder. I remember Beth telling Derek that she was done having kids after Bentley was born."

"I didn't say I wanted to have another baby immediately. I am good for a while." Millie laughed. "Let's get our bearings with Waylon before we think about adding another one to the mix."

Aiden laughed as he kissed her temple. "Agreed. I am ready for you to be healthy and not be throwing up all the time."

A knock on the door drew their attention. Dr. Spaulding walked in with a smile on her face. "How are you and the baby doing?"

"Waylon just finished eating. I am starting to hurt a little." Millie continued to pat Waylon's back.

"It is about time for your next dose of pain medicine. We can also remove your I.V. line now that this bag is finished." Dr. Spaulding said as she examined Millie. "We were prepared for a NICU visit for Waylon, but I don't think he is going to need it. He is small, but that is to be expected since he was born four weeks early."

A nurse came in and gave Millie a few pills. Millie passed Waylon over to Aiden before taking them. Before the nurse left, she removed the I.V. from Millie's left wrist and typed a few things into the computer at the side of the bed.

"When can we go home?" Millie asked Dr. Spaulding as the doctor was examining Waylon.

"Because Waylon was preterm, I want you to stay here for a few days so we can make sure no complications arise." Dr. Spaulding wrapped Waylon in the blanket before handing him back to Millie. "He is looking completely healthy. We just want to be cautious. I hope you two planned for a few days here." She turned to leave but stopped a few steps from the door and turned back to them. "I had the nurses get the DNA swab while they were taking his measurements last night, so you don't have to worry about that. I would also recommend getting some preemie diapers and clothes. That little guy isn't going to fit into newborn sizes for a few weeks."

"Thank you." Aiden nodded and the doctor left. "If you are okay for a few minutes, I am going to run down to the car and grab our bags." Millie reassured Aiden that she and Waylon would be fine while he ran to the car.

While Aiden was gone, Millie changed into sweatpants, a loose t-shirt and pulled her hair up into a ponytail. She felt more human in her own clothes instead of the hospital gown. Waylon started to whimper, and Millie picked him up, patting his back trying to sooth him.

"Oh, my little one, what is the matter? I promise daddy will be back soon." Millie kissed Waylon's cheek. He continued to fuss, and Millie began to hum. He immediately calmed down and stared up at her. "You like the sound of mommy's voice, do you?" Millie smiled. She started to sing 'All The Pretty Little Ponies' by Kenny Loggins, the lullaby that her mom used to sing to her.

"Hushabye, don't you cry. Go to sleep, my little baby. When you wake, you shall have, All the pretty little ponies." Millie loved this song and it felt fitting for her soon-to-be little cowboy. She stood and started to sway as she sang.

She was startled when she finished singing the song and soft clapping sounded behind her. Millie spun around to see her door open with a crowd of people standing there. Two men with a rolling cart of food, and Millie could see at least five nurses there. Aiden suddenly appeared followed by Josh.

"What is going on?" Aiden asked a nurse in a worried tone.

"They were delivering lunches and Mrs. Coleman was singing. It sounded amazing." A young nurse said.

Aiden looked at Millie's panicked expression and shooed everyone away. "Are you okay?" He asked once everyone, except for Josh, was gone.

Millie held Waylon close as she leaned into Aiden, and he wrapped his arms around her. "I was just startled. I didn't know anyone was listening except for Waylon."

"That is a cool name, by the way." Josh said from the couch. Millie smiled over at him. "You are looking really good for someone who just had a baby."

"Thank you." Millie sat next to him on the couch. "It's amazing how less nauseous I feel now. I feel like I have been fasting for a year."

Aiden and Josh both laughed. "Are you still craving burritos?" Josh asked.

"Absolutely." Millie's stomach growled as if to emphasize her point.

"Well, you are in luck because I brought you one." Josh pulled a foil wrapped burrito out of his backpack.

"Okay, you are officially my favorite Peterson." Millie gave him a side hug. "I guess you can hold Waylon now." Millie exchanged Waylon for the burrito.

Aiden put his arm around her, and she curled into his side. Millie sighed as she took a bite. It was so much more comfortable to cuddle with Aiden now that her belly wasn't in the way.

"I am the only Peterson you know, other than my parents." Josh pointed out with a laugh as he looked down at the baby in his arms. "He looks a lot like you, Millie." He said quietly. "What were you singing to him?"

"Oh, it was just the lullaby my mom sang to me when I was really young." Millie glanced over at him. "How are the horses and Pepper?"

"You have spoiled that dog, Millie." Josh glared at her. "She was howling all night, so I brought her into my bed. The little stinker kept running to your room. I don't think I got any sleep because of her."

"Yeah, I gave up on trying to train her to sleep in her kennel. Millie keeps sneaking Pepper into our room." Aiden kissed the top of Millie's head.

"I keep telling you that I don't let her out of her kennel at night, you do. She stays at the bottom of the bed anyway." Millie defended herself. "You haven't once said you didn't want her to sleep with us."

"Aiden wouldn't. He was always sneaking the ranch dogs into his room. Drove his parents crazy." Josh laughed.

Waylon started to cry again. Josh tried to soothe him, but he only cried harder. He passed the baby back to Millie and she snuggled Waylon close, placing a kiss on his head. "Is Uncle Josh not as cool as mommy?" He immediately calmed hearing Millie's voice.

"I am definitely as cool as mommy." Josh protested. "Does he cry with Aiden?"

"Let me see." Aiden lifted Waylon out of Millie's arms. He cradled the baby in his left arm before putting his other around Millie. Waylon started to whimper. "Hey, buddy, no need to get all fussy." Aiden said as he gently bounced him, and Waylon settled down. The baby slowly closed his eyes and fell back asleep.

Josh chuckled as he pulled out his phone. "I think Waylon just knows who his mommy and daddy are." He aimed his phone at them and took a picture. He turned it around to show them.

Millie smiled when she saw it. "Send that to us, please."

"Sure thing." Josh began typing on his phone. "So, last night was crazy."

"Tell me about it." Aiden said. "We were watching the Lord of the Rings trilogy and Millie couldn't seem to get comfortable. Part way through the second movie, she finally called the doctor who told us to get to the hospital."

"Four weeks is kind of early for a baby to be born, right?" Josh asked.

"It is. Waylon is considered a premature baby. Dr. Spaulding is keeping us for a few days to make sure no complications arise." Aiden told him.

"He looks half the size of Bentley when he was born. How much does he weigh?"

"A whopping four pounds eleven ounces." Millie laughed. Aiden pulled her ponytail out and began combing his fingers through her hair. "I just put my hair up." Millie complained.

"Just close your eyes and try to sleep, sweetheart." Aiden kissed her forehead as he continued to run his fingers through her hair.

Millie shook her head before laying it back on Aiden's shoulder with a smile. She reached out and stroked Waylon's cheek softly. Millie smiled as she closed her eyes, enjoying the feeling of having Aiden and Waylon close by. Aiden and Josh quietly talked about school and the horses. She felt her body growing heavy. Her hand slipped from Waylon's cheek and rested on his little chest.

"That didn't take long." Josh said quietly.

"Millie has been through a lot over the last twelve hours. She deserves to get a little rest."

"And how are you doing?" Josh asked. "I don't think I have ever heard you sound so freaked out as you did last night when you called."

"Dr. Spaulding had warned us so many times about the dangers to the baby if he was born early. Millie was tense and restless, and I could see how scared she was when she made the call to the doctor. She was on bedrest since Mom and Dad came. What if something happened to Waylon or Millie?" Aiden let out a tense breath.

"But nothing bad happened to either of them. Millie seems to be in better spirits now than she has been in weeks. Well, really since we met her. And Waylon seems to be doing fine. He is quite the handsome little guy." Josh pointed out.

"I have never prayed so hard in my life than when Millie was in labor. She was in so much pain, and by the time Dr. Spaulding came to check on her to see if Millie could get an epidural, she was too close to delivering to get it."

"So, Millie delivered Waylon with no pain meds at all?"

"No, they gave her some through her I.V., but it didn't seem to be helping." Aiden pressed a kiss to her head. "I have never felt more helpless."

"You were what got me through. I don't know what I would have done without you." Millie said sleepily.

There was a pause before Josh chuckled. "You are supposed to be sleeping." Aiden whispered in her ear.

"If you didn't want me to hear you, then you should have made sure I was actually asleep and not just dozing. This is the second time you have done this."

"Second? When was the first?" Aiden asked.

"In the library when you were talking with Cory." Millie turned her face to look up at Aiden. "And Josh is correct Aiden, Waylon and I are just fine."

Aiden smoothed the hair back from her face. He opened his mouth to say something just as a nurse walked in. The nurse gave them a smile. "Good afternoon. I am here to take Baby Coleman to get his newborn screenings."

"Can you do it here?" Aiden asked as Millie sat up.

"I'm afraid our machine is not mobile." The nurse gave an apologetic smile. Millie grabbed Aiden's arm as her anxiety flared up again.

"Then I will be going with you." Aiden gave Millie a quick kiss before he stood.

The nurse blinked in surprise. "We will just be down the hall, sir. It should only take thirty minutes or so."

"I am coming with you." Aiden repeated firmly.

"Oh, um. Okay. But you will need to place the baby in the bassinet. For safety reasons, babies are to be transported in their bassinets when in the hallways." The nurse glanced at Millie and Josh as she spoke.

Aiden walked to the bassinet and laid Waylon inside. He followed the nurse out, leaving Josh and Millie alone. "What was that about?" Josh asked, turning towards Millie.

"I have been having nightmares." Millie whispered.

"I see." Josh gave her a small smile. "Anything I can do to help?"

"Thanks, but I don't think so." Millie yawned. "I know nothing will happen to Waylon, but the dreams have been so vivid. Lawrence coming in and taking him. I just can't take the chance."

"Oh, Millie." Josh said quietly. He gave her a side hug as his phone alarm went off. "We won't let anything happen to Waylon. Aiden, especially, wouldn't let anything bad happen to him. I hate to just run, but I have to go to class. Tell Aiden I said congratulations to the both of you and I will call you later."

Millie stood and hugged Josh before he left. Millie sat in the quiet room, not knowing what she should do. Her body ached and she was so tired. Millie climbed back onto the bed and laid down. She would only rest for a little bit, until Aiden and Waylon came back.

Chapter 29

Millie was packing her clothes back into her bag while Aiden ran out to the car to get the car seat for Waylon. After a long five days, they were going home. Waylon was finally regulating his own body temperature.

During his newborn screening, Waylon's temperature dropped. It kept fluctuating and he ended up having to stay in the NICU for a few nights. Millie had cried when Aiden had woken her up to tell her that Waylon was taken to the NICU. It had been a sleepless night, but at least Millie had been able to visit him to feed him. Aiden had been allowed to visit Waylon, too, for short periods of time, but Aiden had struggled with not being with Millie or Waylon during the day.

Millie zipped up her guitar case. Josh had brought it to her. She needed music to help her deal with her stress and worry. At first, she had just played, but after a few hours in the NICU, Millie began to sing. The other mom and nurses loved it.

Millie met a mom there with her little girl. They had talked, and Millie learned that Kennedy had two older sons, ages five and seven, from a previous marriage. Her current husband loved the boys as if they were his own. After hearing Millie sing, Kennedy asked if Millie could play 'My Boy' by Elvie Shane when they came in to visit their daughter. That had been last night.

Millie had never heard the song before but had been practicing it all day. Aiden had been running errands, making sure everything was ready for them to bring Waylon home. Millie felt a little bad that she hadn't exchanged phone numbers with Kennedy. When she had promised to play the song, Millie hadn't known that Waylon would be released the next day.

Guilt sat heavy on her when Aiden walked in with Dr. Spaulding. She had hoped she could help Kennedy's husband, Dominic, feel appreciated.

According to Kennedy, he was struggling with some of the judgements of the other fathers on her oldest son's baseball team.

Dr. Spaulding went over the discharge papers and before Millie knew it, they were free to go. Aiden strapped Waylon in the car seat, slung the diaper bag over his shoulder, and then they were walking down the hall towards the elevator. Millie stared at the floor as they waited for the elevator. The doors slid open, and relief flooded her. Millie grabbed Aiden's arm stopping him from stepping onto the elevator.

"Are you leaving?" Kennedy asked.

"Yeah, we were just heading out." Millie set the guitar down. "But I am so glad I got to see you before I left. I was hoping we could exchange numbers and keep in touch."

"Oh…yeah that sounds great." Kennedy said, disappointment heavy in her voice. She glanced at her husband and Millie gave her a smile.

"If you guys aren't in a hurry, I have something for you." Millie reached for her guitar.

Kennedy gasped. "Already? I thought you didn't know it?"

"Know what?" Aiden asked.

"I asked if Millie knew a song. She said she didn't." Kennedy put a hand over her chest as Millie unzipped the instrument.

"I didn't know it yesterday, but I have an ear for music. If you want, I can do it now before we leave?" Millie offered as she began tuning the guitar.

"Please." Kennedy whispered as her eyes misted with unshed tears.

Millie slipped the shoulder strap over her head. She glanced at Aiden, who was watching her with a curious expression. Millie began to play. Down the hall, she saw several nurses poking their heads around corners. She closed her eyes as she tried to block them out as she remembered the notes and words. Millie poured her whole heart into the song. She wanted her new friend and her husband to feel the truth of the words.

When the song ended, Millie opened her eyes. Dominic had tears rolling down his cheeks. He was a big guy, at least six feet tall, with thick muscles, and tattoos everywhere. He stepped up to Millie and pulled her into a tight hug when she removed the guitar.

"Thank you." Dominic whispered.

"You're welcome. But it was Kennedy's idea. She wanted you to know just how much you are appreciated." Millie smiled as Dominic stepped back and wrapped his arms around his wife.

Millie looked over at Aiden, he too had tears on his cheeks. He set Waylon's car seat down at their feet and kissed her. Millie and Kennedy quickly exchanged numbers. Aiden remained quiet as they walked to the car.

Once all their things were loaded and Waylon was inside the heated car, Aiden pulled Millie back into his arms. "I know that I will be here for Waylon's first steps and for his whole life, but I am still just his stepdad. I felt like you were singing that song to me." Aiden's voice was thick with emotion.

"Aiden, you are Waylon's father. It may not be your blood in his veins, but you have been there every step of the way. You were there the day I found out I was pregnant, the day we first heard his heartbeat, the twenty-week ultrasound, when we found out he was a boy, and the day he was born." Millie held Aiden's face in her hands, forcing him to meet her eyes. "He is *our* son. You are and will be the only father he will ever know."

Aiden rested his forehead against Millie's before pressing his lips to hers. "I love you, Millie." He whispered.

"I love you too." Millie smiled against his lips. "Let's get Waylon home."

Aiden nodded and held Millie's door for her. Once they were on the road, Aiden glanced at her. "Just so you know, your parents flew in late last night."

"What?" Millie's head snapped in Aiden's direction.

"Josh told them that with Waylon being a preemie and the stress of the past five days, you didn't want a lot of people at the house. They are staying at a hotel in town. I believe my parents are staying at the same hotel." Aiden glanced in her direction. "Josh barely told me."

"I was hoping for a few quiet days to settle in. And Dr. Spaulding said to keep Waylon away from people for several weeks. "Beth and Derek haven't even seen him yet."

"I know, sweetheart. They are just excited grandparents. I am planning on calling them tonight and letting them know that I will meet up with them at the hotel to tell them more about the situation."

"I feel bad that both our parents have traveled so far to see their grandson but won't be able to. His health is so fragile right now, I don't know if I want to risk it." Millie covered her face with her hands.

"Millie, they will understand." Aiden started to say more but Millie's phone rang, cutting him off.

"It's Mrs. White." Millie told Aiden as she answered it. "Hello."

"How are you doing? How is the baby?"

"He is doing better. We are on our way home, actually."

"That is good to hear."

"I was calling to let you know that Judge Stevens has set a court date to read the paternity results."

"Already? It's only been five days." Millie said in surprise. She had thought it would take weeks to get the results back.

"Yes, it is in four days. Will that work for you?" Mrs. White asked.

"That should be fine. Does Waylon need to be there?" Millie asked anxiously.

"The baby will need to be there. He will be in a separate room. With the baby being so young, you can appoint someone to stay in the room with him."

"Aiden will stay with him. I don't want anyone else." Millie said firmly.

"That is reasonable. I will keep you updated on any other developments. Have a good evening and enjoy that baby."

"Thank you, Mrs. White." Millie hung up the phone before turning to Aiden. He glanced at her with a guarded expression. "They have the paternity results. The three of us have to be in court in four days. Mrs. White said Waylon will be in a separate room, but one person can be with him."

"And you told her I would." Aiden glanced back at her before turning his attention back to the road. "I wish I could be in the courtroom with you, but I also want to be with Waylon."

"I don't know how many people are going to be there and I don't want to expose Waylon to a lot of people if at all possible." Millie sighed as she looked into the backseat. "I don't want to end up in the NICU again."

"You and me both." Aiden reached over and grabbed Millie's hand. They drove in silence for a few minutes. "We can have our parents come one at a time, wearing masks and washing their hands before holding him. But I want to wait a few days. I need some time with just you and Waylon. It's been a rough week having to come home without you each night."

Millie squeezed Aiden's hand. She hadn't rested much either. She hadn't realized just how much she had gotten used to having Aiden with her at night, until she couldn't seem to get any sleep. She would doze off and on whenever he came to visit Waylon, but he had to go home at night.

Aiden pulled onto their driveway and Millie sat up straighter. She couldn't wait to see Pepper. Aiden seemed to sense her sudden excitement, because he chuckled. He pulled into the garage as the door to the house opened. Josh stood there with a big smile on his face. He was holding a squirming Pepper tightly in his arms.

Millie got out of the car and Pepper rocketed off Josh's chest. Josh let out a surprised yell as Pepper, whining like someone was killing her, landed on the ground and ran to Millie. She was at Millie's side in a flash of black and white. Kneeling on the ground, Millie wrapped her arms around her dog and hugged the wiggly body tightly.

"I don't think she missed you." Josh commented as he laughed. "I mean, I have seen those videos of the owners coming home after several months or years away, but you were gone less than a week."

"Come on, Josh. Help me get the bags and Waylon inside, while Millie calms Pepper down." Aiden chuckled as he lifted the car seat from the car.

Millie placed a kiss on Pepper's head before standing up. "Pepper, place." The collie sprinted for the house and Millie followed. Pepper was laying on her dog bed in the front room by the time Millie sat on the couch. Pepper's whole focus was on Millie. "Come."

Pepper ran to Millie again. She had calmed down now that they were in their familiar setting. Pepper started sniffing Millie with her tail wagging. Josh and Aiden walked in and put the bags down on the kitchen island. Aiden carried Waylon's car seat to the coffee table and began unbuckling him. Pepper stayed fixated on Millie.

"Did you know that Border Collies are the smartest dog breed?" Millie glanced up at Aiden with a smile. "Pepper, go get Waylon's blanket." Pepper ran into the master bedroom and returned with the blanket Aiden's mom made for Waylon.

"You taught the dog to retrieve things for you?" Josh said in amazement.

"I had to do something while stuck on bed rest. She can get me diapers, wipes, Waylon's blankets, water bottles, and several other things." Millie extended her hands out for her son. Aiden passed him to her. "Pepper, Waylon." Millie said softly.

The puppy sniffed the baby in Millie's arms, her tail wagging faster. Pepper jumped onto the couch and laid down with her head resting on Waylon's legs.

"That's how she always laid with you before." Aiden sat next to Millie and patted Pepper's head. "Do you think she realized that Waylon is the same as your belly?"

"Maybe." Millie shrugged. "It won't take long for her to learn who Waylon is. She is crazy smart."

"Speaking about how smart that dog is," Josh commented as he sat down. "I figured something out while you were in the hospital. Neither of you were letting her out of her kennel at night. Pepper is an escape artist. She has figured out how to get her kennel open. I had to use a carabiner to keep her in there."

"I told you I wasn't the one letting her out in the middle of the night." Millie turned to Aiden with a laugh.

"I'm sorry for not believing you." Aiden pressed his lips to hers.

"Aunt Ava called and asked when they would be able to come over." Josh's voice held a warning.

Aiden sighed and ran his hand over his face. "Waylon just got out of the hospital after a five day stay in the NICU. Not to mention Millie and I just walked in the door."

"I get it, man. I was there when the doctor was talking about RSV, whooping cough, and all the other risks Waylon is going to face with being a preemie." Josh gave them a sympathetic look. "I told them that you weren't going to be home until late, so that they would not just show up, but you need to talk with them. Beth and Derek at least understood when I told them that you didn't want people at the house for a few days."

"Thank you for making sure no one was here when we got home, Josh." Millie said gratefully. "I am so exhausted. The NICU only had rocking chairs to sleep in."

"You all three deserve some alone time together. I can't even begin to understand the stress that comes from having a baby and then having them in the NICU for five days." Josh shook his head as he got to his feet. "I am glad that you are all home safe. I am going to leave you to settle back into life. Aiden, call your mom and let her know what is going on before she shows up on your porch."

Josh gave them each a hug before leaving. Millie and Aiden sat back down on the couch. Millie sighed as she leaned against Aiden. She had missed him the past several days. He pulled his phone out and called his parents. Ava didn't sound particularly happy when Aiden told her they needed a few days to settle in with Waylon before they wanted guests.

Next, he called Millie's parents. Monica was very understanding. She expressed how sorry she was that Waylon had been in the NICU. When Millie was born, she too was in the NICU for two weeks, but Monica was only allowed to see Millie for a couple hours each day. Franklin told Aiden that he rented a house, and they would be staying in the area for a while. They were fine to wait as long as Aiden and Millie needed, before meeting Waylon.

They sat in the peace and quiet, Millie holding Waylon, and Aiden with his arms around both of them. "I wish my mom was as understanding as your parents." Aiden whispered.

"I don't think she fully grasps how small and susceptible to illness Waylon is yet. After I was able to go home from the hospital, Mom and grandma said I was constantly sick for the first year. I ended up back in the hospital several times. My mom has been through what we are going through, but your mom hasn't." Millie kissed Aiden's cheek. "When she finally sees how tiny Waylon is, I think she will understand a little more."

"I hope you are right." Aiden buried his face into Millie's neck, kissing the sensitive spot by her ear. Millie giggled and she felt Aiden's lips turn up into a smile. "When did you become ticklish?"

"I have never been kissed there before." Millie turned to face Aiden. He had a mischievous smile on his face.

"Hmm. I might have to start kissing you more to see if you are ticklish anywhere else."

"Not while I am holding Waylon." Millie told him as her smile grew.

Aiden pulled her closer and kissed Waylon's head before kissing Millie. "We have plenty of time to discover everything about each other. But right now, my love, what do you want to do now that we are finally home?"

"You are going to sit on the couch and snuggle Waylon, while I fix dinner. Once dinner is done, how about we finish your Lord of the Rings trilogy?" Millie passed Waylon over to Aiden.

"Are you sure?" Aiden stared down at Waylon. "I can make dinner if you want to just relax."

"I have been sitting around for five weeks, Aiden. I need to be active again." Millie got to her feet.

"You just gave birth, Millie. You deserve a little rest." Aiden looked up at her.

"You deserve to have some time with your son." Millie leaned down and kissed Aiden. "I feel just fine. It actually feels good to be up and moving. Go ahead and start the movie, dinner will be done in a little bit."

Millie moved into the kitchen and began pulling out pots and pans so she could make spaghetti. She smiled when Aiden began talking to Waylon instead of putting on the movie. Millie put on an apron wrapping the strings around her and tying them in the front.

As Millie cooked the pasta, she hummed quietly to herself. She could not believe how good it felt to be back to her normal self. She hadn't felt this good since shortly after she had been baptized.

Dinner was almost done. Millie just needed to finish making the sauce. She was stirring the meat and the sauce together when arms slid around her.

Millie smiled. "I thought you were holding Waylon."

"He is sleeping in his bassinet." Aiden pressed a kiss to Millie's neck. "It's cute that you hum to yourself when you cook."

Millie turned the stove off and turned around in Aiden's arms. She slid her hands up his chest and around his neck. "I was right."

"About what?" Aiden asked, rubbing the tip of his nose against hers.

"That this is so much easier without a big belly." Millie rose on her toes and pressed her lips to Aiden's.

Aiden pulled her closer as he deepened the kiss. He turned and gently pushed Millie up against the opposite counter. Millie laughed as Aiden lifted her up and set her on the countertop. One of Aiden's hands rested on her hip while the other tangled in her hair. Millie moaned as Aiden slid her closer.

Waylon began to cry, and Aiden groaned as he pulled back. Millie laughed before giving Aiden a quick kiss. Aiden dropped his head on Millie's shoulder. "I really hope he doesn't cry every time."

Millie kissed Aiden's neck. "Go settle him down while I dish up our plates." She whispered and Aiden straightened. "It's probably for the best anyway. We can't do anything for six weeks."

"These are going to be the longest six weeks of my life." Aiden mumbled as he stepped back enough for Millie to hop off the counter.

"I think you will survive." Millie laughed as she watched Aiden walk back into the living room. Millie quickly dished up the spaghetti and moved to the couch. "I'll swap you." She held up his plate.

Waylon was not a happy camper. Millie kissed his cheek before getting comfortable to nurse him. He immediately calmed down. "Millie?" Aiden asked softly. Millie turned to him with a brow raised in question. "You would tell me if you weren't comfortable with anything I do, right?"

"Of course I would. Where is this coming from?" Millie asked, studying his face.

"We have only been married for two months and we didn't really date before. I just don't ever want you to think you have to do anything you are uncomfortable with or don't want to do."

"Aiden, I love you. I can't tell you how nice it is to know that you would never force yourself on me. I promise I will let you know if I am uncomfortable with anything you do." Millie paused before a smile curved her lips. "For the record, I have been completely comfortable with everything you have done so far."

Aiden leaned over and kissed her. "I love you, Millie."

Millie laid her head on Aiden's shoulder as he started the movie. Waylon fell asleep while eating, and Aiden took him from Millie so that she could eat. She rinsed off their plates when they were both done. When she returned to the living room, Waylon was back in the bassinet. Millie sat in Aiden's lap, causing Aiden to chuckle as he wrapped his arms around her.

Chapter 30

Millie dressed in her pencil skirt and a button up blue shirt. She fit in her pre-pregnancy clothes and this outfit had always made her feel more confident. She had purchased it for her job interview along with the heels she was wearing. Millie had spent extra time on her makeup and hair this morning. She wanted to look her best when she faced Lawrence today.

Millie stared at her reflection in the mirror. She was so nervous, but she didn't know why. Lawrence was Waylon's biological father and the judge had already said his parental rights would be signed over as soon as paternity was confirmed. Millie closed her eyes and took a deep breath.

The bathroom door opened, and arms slid around her. Millie opened her eyes and met Aiden's in the mirror. "You look beautiful." He kissed her neck. "How are you doing?"

"I am freaking out a bit." Millie whispered. "Knowing that Lawrence will be there is completely messing with me." she admitted.

Aiden tightened his hold on her, as he slowly kissed her neck. "How can I help you relax, my love?" Aiden nibbled on her ear.

Millie giggled as she turned around to face Aiden. He pressed his lips to hers in a soft kiss. He pulled her body flush against his. "I'm still nervous to face Lawrence." Millie buried her face in Aiden's neck.

"I know, sweetheart. I wish I could be there with you, but Waylon and I will be waiting for you when you are done. Both our parents, Josh, Derek, and Beth will all be there with you." Aiden whispered, holding her close. "We should head out, though, so that you have plenty of time to feed Waylon before you need to go in."

Millie tightened her arms around Aiden for a brief second before letting him go. "Okay, let's go."

Waylon was fussy and not wanting to eat. Millie sat alone in the room with her crying baby, trying to soothe him. Aiden was with their families in the hall, waiting for her. Millie sang quietly trying to calm Waylon down, but nothing worked. He had been like this for the past several days. Dr. Spaulding said it was colic.

Millie stood and gently bounced Waylon, holding him snuggly against her. After ten more minutes, he finally fell asleep. Aiden slipped into the room. Millie shook her head and he sighed.

"I talked with Mrs. White. She knows that Waylon is colicky and may need you at some point. She said she would let the judge know."

Millie nodded and passed Waylon to Aiden. Aiden held him the same way Millie had been, but he started to squirm and wake up. "Aiden, he didn't eat. He will be starving when he wakes up."

"I will let them know when he wakes up and they will get you." Aiden reassured her. "You need to go though, or you are going to be late."

Aiden gave Millie a quick kiss before she left. Mrs. White was waiting for her in the hallway. She gave Millie a reassuring smile. Millie squared her shoulders and raised her head high as they walked into the courtroom.

Lawrence's gaze slid over her, causing her to shiver in disgust. Millie's eyes moved to the judge. He watched them approach, showing no emotion. Millie and Mrs. White moved to their spots behind their table and waited.

Judge Stevens began the proceedings. "We are here to review the paternity results that will establish if Lawrence Judd Hansen is the biological father of Waylon Beckett Coleman." Ava gasped behind Millie. They hadn't told their families Waylon's full name yet. "Ms. Larson, I must confess that I was surprised that you and your son do not share the same last name."

"Your honor, my client has changed her name to her married name. I submitted the change over a week ago." Mrs. White stated.

Judge Stevens glanced through the papers again before nodding. "My apologies, Mrs. Coleman. I missed that note." Millie gave him a nod. "Is there anything you wish to say before we read the results, Mr. Hansen?"

Lawrence stood and smirked over at Millie. "I still don't think I am the father. I wasn't the only one that night, Millie."

Millie's stomach clenched and she felt her face going pale. "What are you talking about?" she asked as dread began to fill her.

Before anyone could say anything, someone entered the courtroom. The brief moment that the doors were open, Millie could hear Waylon screaming. Millie turned anxious eyes to Mrs. White, who stood.

"Your honor, might we have a brief recess? Mrs. Coleman's baby needs her." Mrs. White said firmly.

"Mrs. Coleman, would you feel comfortable if the baby was brought to you. I am quite curious to see what Mr. Nelson has to say."

Millie nodded and the judge gestured to someone. The room was quiet while they waited. Waylon's crying grew louder until Aiden walked into the room with him. Waylon's face was bright red, and he had a bravado to his cry. Aiden walked quickly to the gate and Millie met him there.

She held Waylon close and whispered to him. His crying began to calm, and Millie kissed his tiny head. She moved back to her seat, and she heard Josh whispering to Aiden even though she couldn't hear the words he said.

"Now that the baby is happy, Mr. Hansen, please continue. What do you mean you were not the only one that night? Wasn't it your supposed wedding night?"

"That's right, your honor." Lawrence said smugly. "We were married that evening, but I had a friend that wanted his turn with Millie."

Millie squeezed her eyes closed. Lawrence's friend had asked her if she wanted to do a group thing that night while Lawrence was supposed to be signing the marriage license. She had flat out refused him. The very thought disgusted her.

"You are telling the court that you were not the only man to have sexual relations with Mrs. Coleman that night?" Judge Stevens asked with a stoney expression.

"That is correct." Lawrence's smile was sickening.

Millie rotated in her chair and passed Waylon back to Aiden. She grabbed the trashcan that was at the side of the table and vomited. She could hear Lawrence's chuckle, which only made it worse. After several long moments, Millie accepted the tissue that Mrs. White handed her. Waylon was thankfully still asleep. She didn't think she could hold him right now.

"Mrs. Coleman, are you alright?" Judge Stevens asked in concern.

Millie fought tears as she looked at the judge. "I honestly don't know." Her voice was small, and she knew Lawrence was loving this.

"Is the other man here today?" Judge Stevens asked Lawrence.

"I am, your honor." A man stood up and Millie couldn't breathe. He was the friend that had been at the wedding.

"Why don't you come sit next to Mr. Nelson and state your name for the record." Judge Stevens invited.

The man had shoulder length black hair and blue eyes. He had an olive complexion and was very similar to Lawrence's build. "My name is Jaxon Simon Smith."

"Mr. Smith, what is your relationship with Mr. Nelson and Mrs. Coleman?" Judge Stevens asked.

"Mr. Nelson and I have been buddies since high school. We share everything, typically. As for Mrs. Coleman, she was business mixed with pleasure." Jaxon smiled wickedly.

"Explain what you mean by business mixed with pleasure."

"Like I said, Mr. Hansen and I shared everything, including girls. The problem with Mrs. Coleman was she didn't go for it. I asked after the wedding, and she shot me down. Mr. Hansen said he could make it happen for a price. Best five grand I had spent in a long while."

"Easiest five grand I have made." Lawrence smirked.

Millie's hand flew over her mouth as realization dawned. Lawrence had insisted the lights remained off all night. He left the room once, saying he needed to get more condoms and when he returned, he hadn't spoken a single word. Millie hadn't felt suspicious though. Most of the night was pretty hazy.

"Mrs. Coleman?" The judge asked, pulling Millie from her memories. By the tone of his voice and Mrs. White's worried expression, Millie guessed it hadn't been the first time the judge had called her name.

"I'm sorry your honor, what did you ask?" Millie refocused on Judge Stevens.

"Do you know Mr. Smith?"

"He was the witness at the wedding ceremony. He also asked if I would be interested in a group evening with him and Lawrence. I told him 'Not in a million years'." Millie's voice lacked emotion. "I had never met him before or seen him since."

"You sure felt me though, baby." Mr. Smith commented. The judge smacked his gavel down and told Mr. Smith to remain quiet.

"How is it possible that you didn't know you were with two different men?" Judge Stevens asked.

"The poor thing doesn't handle champagne very well." Lawrence chuckled.

"Mr. Hansen had given me a glass of non-alcoholic champagne; I gave the bottle to Mrs. White when I first returned home."

"Your honor, I had the bottle tested after our last court hearing. I have the toxicology report right here." Mrs. White held up a piece of paper. The bailiff retrieved it and handed it over to the judge. "The champagne was alcoholic despite what the label says and there were traces of Valium inside the bottle."

"After the drinks, what happened?" Judge Stevens asked as he scanned the report in his hand.

"After that, he turned all the lights off. He said it would add to the experience. I couldn't even see my hand in front of my face. The rest of the night is blurry. I don't remember much." Millie shook her head. "Oh gosh, I feel so sick." She whispered.

"Mr. Smith, I want you to submit a sample so we can run a DNA test if Mr. Hansen isn't the father." Judge Stevens stated firmly.

"Lawrence told me what was going on and I submitted a sample at the same time he did, your honor." Mr. Smith smiled.

"I thought this was Mr. Coleman's results." Judge Stevens held up two packets. "Alright, we will start with Mr. Hansen's results." Judge Stevens opened the envelope, his expression did not change. "Mr. Lawrence Judd Hansen, you are *not* the father of Waylon Beckett Coleman." Millie's stomach rolled again, and she threw up for the second time. Millie felt cold all over. This could not be happening. The judge waited for her to finish before he opened the second envelope and began to read. "Mr. Jaxon Simon Smith, you *are* the father of Waylon Beckett Coleman."

"Great!" Jaxon laughed. "Can I see my kid?"

"No. Mr. Smith, your parental rights to Waylon Becket Coleman are being terminated." Silent tears rolled down Millie's face, as she listened to the judge. "Mrs. Coleman, in light of Mr. Smith's confession in regard to raping you and paying money to Mr. Hansen in order to do so, do you wish to press charges?"

"Hold on a sec." Mr. Smith protested as he stood.

Millie nodded. "Yes, I do, your honor." She said through her tears.

Judge Stevens ordered for Lawrence and Jaxon to be arrested for rape. Waylon began to cry when both Lawrence and Jaxon started yelling as they were put in handcuffs and hauled from the room. Millie sat in numb silence as she stared at the table in front of her, tears still coursing down her cheeks. She felt completely frozen.

Aiden crouched in front of her, and she blinked at his sudden appearance. "Millie?" Aiden's soft voice caused her to start sobbing. He pulled her into his arms, sitting on the floor holding her tightly to him.

Millie buried her face into the crook of his neck as she clung to him. "I didn't know. I'm so sorry." Millie cried.

"I know you didn't, sweetheart." Aiden pressed a kiss to the top of her head. "None of this changes how I see you or Waylon." Millie sat up so she could see Aiden's face. He gently wiped her tears away. "You are *my* wife and Waylon is *my* son. I love you both no matter what." Aiden kept his voice quiet since Mrs. White and Judge Stevens stood several yards away talking quietly.

The lack of Waylon's cries finally registered in Millie's brain. "Waylon. Where is he?" Millie frantically looked around.

Aiden gently cupped her face and forced her to face him. "Our son is with my parents in the room where we had him before. He is safe, probably not the happiest, but he is fine."

Millie closed her eyes and took a deep breath. "I need to feed him." She whispered.

Aiden kissed her forehead. They stood up and Aiden grabbed her hand. Millie clung to his arm with her other hand. He kept her close as they walked down the crowded hall. Millie saw her parents standing next to Josh, Beth, and Derek, and she pulled Aiden to a stop before they reached them.

"Aiden, I don't think I can talk to anyone right now. I need a few more minutes before facing everyone." Millie whispered desperately.

Aiden glanced at her and then to where she was looking. He tugged her forward, and without stopping, opened the door to where Waylon was. His screams filled the air. Dallas was pacing the small room with him while patting his back gently. A range of emotions played on Dallas's face when he saw Millie and Aiden.

He walked over to Millie and passed Waylon to her. Millie immediately walked to the couch as she whispered to her baby. Aiden spoke quietly for a minute with Dallas, before Dallas left. Waylon began nursing and the room instantly became quiet. Aiden sat beside Millie, putting his arms around her. Millie leaned against him and closed her eyes.

"I love you, Millie." Aiden said softly as he laid his head on hers.

"What are we going to do?" Millie asked as tears began to fall again.

"You are going to finish feeding Waylon and then we are going home." Aiden's hand moved to Waylon's head as he spoke.

"I was talking about what happened today." Millie turned her head so she could see Aiden.

His expression was serious as he glared at the wall across the room. "We are going to make sure those two..." A muscle ticked as Aiden clenched his jaw. He looked like he was trying to control his anger. She had never seen him be more than irritated before. "Are held accountable for what they did to you."

"I understand if you don't want..."

"Millie, I want you as my wife and I want to adopt Waylon as my son. Nothing has changed that." Aiden's eyes softened as he looked at her. "You are still the center of my world. I'm not giving up the best thing that has ever happened to me. You, me, Waylon; we are a family, Millie."

"What about our families? They are supposed to come over to the house for dinner." Millie didn't feel emotionally ready to face anyone right now. She just wanted to curl into a ball and forget the world existed for a while.

"I've already taken care of it. I told Dad that we were going to have to take a raincheck on celebrating that Waylon's biological father's rights were terminated. Tonight, it is just you, me, and Waylon." Aiden kissed her temple.

Millie laid her head back on Aiden's shoulder and his arms tightened around her. She closed her eyes and focused on how protected and loved she felt with Aiden in that moment. Waylon nursed for another twenty minutes. She raised him to her shoulder to burp him.

"Mrs. White texted to see if we had a moment to speak with her." Aiden said as he looked down at his phone. Millie gave him a tired nod and a few minutes later, Mrs. White walked into the room.

"Mr. and Mrs. Coleman, I am so glad that you are still here. I wanted to talk to you both about Mr. Hansen and Mr. Smith." Millie stiffened and Aiden pulled her closer to him. "Judge Steven's said there is no need for a trial."

"What do you mean there is no need for a trial?" Aiden asked angrily.

"Mr. Smith admitted, in court, that he and Mr. Hansen tricked you into sleeping with them through lies and manipulation. Not only that, but they also drugged you and there was an exchange of money." Mrs. White looked pleased. "They admitted to the crime, so no trial is needed to determine if the crime happened. Judge Stevens wanted you to know that neither Mr. Hansen nor Mr. Smith will get a plea bargain, because they voluntarily admitted to the crimes."

Millie closed her eyes trying to keep her tears from falling. She was relieved that she wouldn't have to testify about that night. She felt even more violated than she had before. She could not believe that Lawrence had done that to her. He even sold her to his friend. Millie leaned more into Aiden.

"Thank you, Mrs. White." Aiden said. "What else do we need to do?"

"There is nothing more you have to do. Mr. Hansen and Mr. Smith will be behind bars for a very long time. You two need to take that beautiful baby home and enjoy your family." Mrs. White patted Millie's knee before walking out of the room, closing the door behind her.

Millie stood and faced Aiden. "Can we go home now?"

Aiden tucked her hair behind her ear. "I will go get Waylon's car seat and be right back. Then we can go home." He kissed her forehead before kissing Waylon. "I will be right back."

Aiden walked to the door but paused before turning back to Millie. Millie stood frozen holding Waylon close. She didn't want to be alone. Aiden studied her for a moment before he walked back to her. Millie snuggled into his chest as he held her close.

"Why don't we go together?" Aiden said softly and Millie nodded against his chest. "Here, let me carry Waylon." Aiden lifted the baby out of her arms before putting an arm back around her. "Let's go home."

Chapter 31

Millie walked into the kitchen from the garage with Waylon. She was returning from her appointments. She saw her therapist, had her six-week postpartum appointment, and Mrs. White called to see if Millie could stop by her office. With therapy, Millie was finally starting to come to terms with what Lawrence and Jaxon had done to her. Aiden had gone with her a few times and had been so supportive.

Millie smiled as Pepper came running up to greet her. "Hey, girl." Millie stroked the dog's head. "Where is Aiden?"

Waylon was in a total milk coma and didn't even stir as Millie got him out of his car seat. He was finally big enough to fit in newborn clothes. She heard the shower running when she walked into the master bedroom to put Waylon in his crib. She laid Waylon down carefully before entering the bathroom.

She undressed and opened the shower door. Aiden jumped and Millie laughed. "Mind if I join you?"

"Not at all." Aiden pulled her into the shower and kissed her. "How did your appointments go?" he asked.

Millie put her arms around his neck. "Good. Just the normal."

"How did yours and Waylon's appointment go? I'm sorry I couldn't be there with you." Aiden pulled her closer.

"We were both given a clean bill of health. How are the horses?" Millie smiled up at Aiden.

"The vet said the mare should be fine. We need to keep her in her stall for a few days, but she should be good to go by next month." Millie pressed her lips to Aiden's in a slow kiss. "When you say clean bill of health…?" Aiden asked against her lips. Millie smiled before kissing him again. Aiden's arms tightened around her as he deepened the kiss.

* * *

Aiden walked out of the bedroom holding Waylon. "Look who woke up?"

"Hey, little man, will you let your Uncle Derek hold you?" Derek stood from the table and took Waylon from Aiden.

Aiden took his seat next to Millie and kissed her cheek. This was the first time they had people over since the trial. Kennedy, Dominic, Josh, Derek, Beth, and all the kids were there. It was two weeks until Christmas and there was a good two feet of snow outside. They had spent the day together. The guys took the kids outside to build snowmen while Beth, Kennedy and Millie cuddled with Waylon, Melody, and Charlotte by the fire.

Lunch was done and the kids were watching a movie while the adults were setting up a card game. Millie's meeting with Mrs. White was the other day and she had been trying to figure out a good time to tell Aiden. Millie stood from the table and headed for the pantry where she had stashed the papers.

"Where are you going, Millie?" Aiden asked as he turned to watch her.

"I have something for you." She called over her shoulder. She retrieved the wrapped box she had put the papers in. Everyone was looking at her when she returned. "An early Christmas gift."

"Sweetheart, you didn't have to do this. You could have waited for Christmas." Aiden took the box from her. He turned the box over with curiosity.

"I could have, but I didn't want to wait." Millie shrugged as she kept her expression neutral. "If you want to wait until Christmas to open it, that is your choice, or you could open it now."

"Open it, Aiden." Josh said excitedly. "Maybe it's a new card game we can play."

Aiden slowly began to unwrap the paper. He lifted the lid off the box and froze. His brow furrowed in confusion for a minute as he read. Millie knew the moment he realized that the document inside was the adoption approval letter. He picked up the letter but stopped when he saw Waylon's birth certificate with Aiden listed as the father.

He dropped the papers back into the box before standing and pulling Millie up out of her chair. He buried his face in her neck as he hugged her close. She felt his tears on her neck as he took slow measured breaths.

"What is it?" Josh grabbed the box. Millie held Aiden tight as his own arms tightened around her. "Waylon's birth certificate?"

"Let me see." Derek said impatiently. He gave a short laugh of surprise after a few seconds. "Congratulations, Aiden!" he exclaimed.

Aiden finally pulled back enough for his lips to find Millie's. Millie wiped Aiden's cheeks as she smiled. Aiden looked a little embarrassed about the show of emotion and ducked his head. "I cried the day Waylon was born; it's only fitting you cry the day you officially become his father." She teased, even though she had tears in her own eyes.

"Derek, give me my son." Aiden smiled as he reached for Waylon.

Derek laughed and handed the baby back. Aiden closed his eyes as he kissed Waylon's head, causing Waylon to smile. Millie quickly pulled out her phone and took several pictures of Aiden holding Waylon for the first time as his legal father.

"Millie, get over there so we can get a few pictures of the three of you." Beth ordered.

Millie kissed Aiden's cheek as he put his arm around her. "How long have you had the papers?" he asked, grinning down at her.

"Since yesterday. Mrs. White asked me to stop by her office while I was out."

"And you didn't tell me yesterday?" Aiden playfully scowled at her.

"I didn't think ambushing you in the shower with the papers was the best idea." Millie smirked at him. "And I felt like this deserved a little bit more of a celebration."

"So, this is a 'Welcome to Fatherhood' party?" Josh asked.

"Something like that." Millie glanced over at Kennedy and Dominic. Dominic was looking down at the table and Kennedy was fighting her smile.

Millie had texted Kennedy and Beth last night about the adoption letter. Kennedy told Millie that she had Dominic's adoption letters for her two sons. She wanted to do something special for Dominic but didn't know what. Beth had told them both that she was pregnant, and didn't know how to tell Derek, especially with Melody being only nine months old. So, they planned this get together.

Aiden leaned close to her ear. "You did ambush me in the shower, though." He whispered so no one could hear him.

Millie looked up at him. "But not with the papers." Aiden laughed and gave her a quick kiss.

"I got you this." Kennedy handed Dominic a gift bag.

"I thought we were celebrating Aiden becoming a father?" he asked as he slowly pulled the tissue out of the bag. He pulled out a stack of papers, a second later he was in tears.

"Boys, come here please." Kennedy grinned at her husband.

"What's wrong with Dom?" Their oldest son, Theodore, asked as he came running into the dining room.

"You know how your first dad passed away?" Kennedy asked. Both boys nodded. "Dom is your father now."

"I don't need a paper to know that Dominic is the best dad in the world." Theodore hugged Dominic. "I love you, Dad."

William, Theodore's brother, joined the hug. "I love you, daddy. Don't cry." Kennedy joined the hug and Millie snapped several pictures.

Once things started to calm down a little, Beth slid a small box over to Derek. The confusion on his face was priceless. "We aren't adopting anyone." He said, glancing around the table. Beth pushed the box closer to him and he slowly opened it. Inside was a folded piece of paper. He unfolded it and read it. "Are you...is this...?" He looked back at Beth. "We haven't been able to without..."

"I know." She whispered as tears coursed down her cheeks. Derek pulled her onto his lap and kissed her.

"I am thoroughly confused." Josh stage whispered.

"Beth is pregnant." Derek said with a laugh.

"But I thought the doctors said you couldn't without IVF." Josh said to his sister.

"That is what we thought too, but according to the blood report, I am." Beth laughed as she wiped her cheeks.

"Now I just feel left out." Josh folded his arms. "This is a party for fatherhood."

"Oh, Josh, don't worry. I didn't forget you." Millie smiled. She started to walk toward the garage.

"Millie, what did you do?" Josh asked warily.

Millie didn't answer. Once in the garage she went to Pepper's old kennel and opened the door. A ten-week-old red merle Australian Shepherd ran out. She picked up the puppy and put him in a gift box before loosely putting the lid on. She quickly went back inside with the biggest grin on her face.

She had discreetly asked around to all of Josh's family and friends over the past several months. He has always wanted an Australian Shepherd, but never had the space for one and he wasn't at the family ranch enough to keep it there. Josh practically lived over at Millie and Aiden's house. He was at their house four or five days a week, helping with the horses and property, or just to do homework. Millie figured he could keep the puppy here if he wanted.

Josh watched her suspiciously as she walked over to him and placed the box on the table. She rested her hand on the lid so the little guy couldn't pop the lid off. She handed Josh an envelope.

"Open this first." she instructed.

Josh warily opened the letter and read it silently. Millie had typed up the letter herself. It congratulated Josh Peterson on his adoption of Jasper. Josh put his hands over his face. "Please, tell me you didn't adopt a baby in my name."

"Fatherhood comes in all shapes and sizes, Josh." Millie laughed.

Josh looked at her with a horrified expression. "It's illegal to forge someone's signature, especially when adopting a child. I can't be a single dad." Josh looked ready to pass out. "Aiden, did you know about this?"

"I have no idea what is going on." Aiden said quickly.

Millie's smile only grew as she glanced at everyone. They all wore confused and worried expressions. "Did you want to open the box now?" She asked Josh.

"No. I really don't." Josh glared at her.

"If you won't, I will." Millie lifted the lid and Jasper's head poked up out of the box. Josh's mouth dropped open as he stared at the puppy. "Josh, meet your 'baby', Jasper. He is ten weeks old. He is a smarty pants and is already house broken." Millie stroked Jasper's head.

"How did you?" Josh asked, coming out of his shock. "I mean, when did you?"

"I have been talking with everyone for months about it. They just thought they were telling me stories about you." Millie laughed. "I got Jasper two weeks ago."

"How did you get a puppy and I not know about it?" Aiden asked in disbelief.

"You have been busy with the horses, taking me to my appointments, school, and Waylon. I worked with Jasper while you and Josh were out at the barn and kept him in Pepper's old kennel in the garage." Millie shrugged.

"Millie, as much as I want to keep him, I can't." Josh gave her a sad look. "My apartment doesn't allow dogs."

"You can keep him here. You are here most days anyway." Millie pointed out, as Josh lifted the puppy out of the box.

"Millie and I have also talked about building a few guest houses on the property. You could rent one of those when we get it built." Aiden offered.

Josh held up Jasper to get a better look at him and a slow smile spread on his face. "Thank you, Millie."

"You are welcome. I was going to wait until Christmas, but then this all happened," Millie waved around the table with a smile. "And I figured, why not?" Everyone laughed. "I can't believe you thought I adopted a human child for you."

"You are so much more devious now that you aren't pregnant. I wouldn't put anything past you." Josh smirked at her.

Millie winked at him as she moved to Aiden's side. Aiden put an arm around her waist and kissed her temple. "You are quite devious now. Any more secrets I should know about?"

"Umm, oh! I meant to tell you this weeks ago. Before you came up to Alaska and we were like, a thing, I purchased another property."

Aiden pulled back. "Another property?"

"I just figured since I was planning on getting horses at some point, it would be nice to have someplace to ride them." Millie shrugged.

"You wanted to ride horses somewhere other than your twenty acres, so you purchased land?" Beth asked.

"I also like camping and wanted the freedom to ride out to a good camping spot." Millie took a seat at the table. "And I didn't want to worry about horse trailers and all that with a baby. I was planning on being a single mom and wanted to make things easier for me and the baby."

"Wait a minute. You purchased another property on a camping and horse-riding whim?" Kennedy blinked in surprise.

"Millie is kind of loaded, but she doesn't like to flaunt it or use her money very often." Josh glanced at Kennedy and Dominic quickly before turning his attention back to Millie. "Where is this other property?"

"The three hundred and fifty acres that surrounds this property." Millie took a sip of water as she watched Aiden's shocked expression turn to amusement.

"You purchased three hundred acres so you could go camping and ride horses?" Aiden shook his head as he smiled.

"That, and it was also a business venture."

"How so?" Derek asked.

"I love kids. I love working with them, especially those who need a little extra help. I planned on getting degrees in Early Childhood Development, Psychology, and Equine Therapy. My goal was to open a therapy center for kids with disabilities ranging from ADHD to physical limitations. Horses and dogs are great tools in helping kids overcome and cope with various issues."

Aiden stared at her for a long moment before shaking his head again. "You are amazing. Did you know that?"

"Enough about me, this is a party to celebrate you gentlemen." Millie smiled at those around the table.

"I want to know how you planned on getting three degrees while raising a family." Dominic said.

"I wasn't planning on having a family for a while. Waylon was unplanned." Millie smiled over at Waylon. "The semester I found out I was pregnant was my last semester for my bachelor's in childhood development. I am taking a semester off and then I have two years left until I get my master's in psychology."

"You are barely twenty-one. How do you already have a bachelor's degree?" Josh asked.

"I told you I was home schooled. I ended up graduating at sixteen. I started taking college classes online immediately. I wanted to open my therapy center by the time I turned twenty-five. All my time and energy has gone into making that timeline. But now that I have Waylon, I need to re-evaluate my plan and see what I can feasibly do."

"Let me get this straight." Aiden stared at her with wide eyes. "You got your bachelor's degree a few months ago, but didn't say anything to us? Why?"

"It's my second bachelor's degree. I had to fly to Alaska for my mom, remember? Plus, you and I weren't exactly on good terms at the time, and I didn't want a big deal made out of it. I did not walk for any of my other graduations and didn't see a reason to do so for this one or any of my future ones."

"Why weren't you on good terms?" Kennedy asked.

"Because Aiden kissed her, then immediately said it was a mistake." Beth laughed. "She was so mad when she got home. I think the pregnancy hormones just made it worse. Then she got a call that her mom was in a bad accident and Millie booked a flight for the next morning. I told her to not talk to him for a while and that the distance would do them good."

"You were the reason Millie wasn't talking to me?" Aiden glared at Beth. "You have no idea how hard it was not talking with her."

"Maybe you should have kept your lips to yourself until you were serious about her." Beth shot back.

"Hold on a second." Dominic held up his hand with a confused look on his face. "Were you two dating? I thought you two were together for a while."

Josh laughed. "We met Millie nine months ago. Aiden and I found her crying next to her car in a parking lot. We could tell she was going through something, on top of the two flat tires on her car. We gave her a ride home and helped get her car fixed. Millie and Beth met while they were camping, and we all just became friends."

"Aiden liked her a lot. We could all tell, even though he didn't seem to realize it." Derek laughed.

"I cared for Millie and didn't want to ruin our friendship." Aiden patted Waylon's back. "I don't know what happened, but we ended up kissing, and I panicked, thinking I had just screwed things up between us." Aiden smiled at Millie.

"And you did. Just not in the way you thought you had screwed up." Millie shrugged as she turned to Kennedy. She had told her a little about Lawrence while at the hospital. "I had just had a run in with Lawrence and my emotions were already all over the place. Essentially, he had said that no one would want me and that I was just used trash. Then Aiden kissed me and immediately regretted it. It just added salt to the wound, and I was pissed."

Aiden groaned. "I hadn't thought about it like that. I'm so sorry."

"Aiden, there is nothing to be sorry for. I was an emotional wreck of a pregnant woman. I knew you didn't mean it that way." Millie laughed. "And I don't mind how things worked out."

Waylon began to cry, and Millie took him to their room to feed him. The rest of the night became lighter. The kids loved playing with Pepper and Jasper. Derek took Waylon for some cuddle time once Millie rejoined everyone in the front room. Millie smiled while Aiden held her close as they watched all of their friends and family playing and laughing with each other.

A year ago, Millie could never have predicted how amazing her life would turn out. She was married to a man that loved and cherished her, had a son they both adored, and friends that were her family and support. She still had to deal with her emotional scars, but with Aiden and the others, Millie knew that she could do anything.

THE END

The Hunter Guardian Series

The Hunted Guardian
The Stone's Keeper
The Stone's Secret

Other books by this author:

Left Broken
Embracing Dove
Hoodwinked

When Worlds Collide Series

When Worlds Collide
Prey of the Corrupted Alpha

Paranormal Books

Enforcer's Mark

Upcoming Books

Two Sides of the Same Coin
Protectors of the Guardians

www.ingramcontent.com/pod-product-compliance
Lightning Source LLC
LaVergne TN
LVHW012013060526
838201LV00061B/4294